THE STRANGE AND TRUE TALE OF
HORACE WELLS
SURGEON DENTIST

THE STRANGE AND TRUE TALE OF

HORACE WELLS
SURGEON DENTIST

a novel

MICHAEL DOWNS

ACRE

CINCINNATI 2018

Acre Books is made possible by the support of the Robert and Adele Schiff Foundation.

Library of Congress Cataloging-in-Publication Data TK.

ISBN-10 (pbk) 1-946724-04-1 | ISBN-13 (pbk) 978-1-946724-04-5
ISBN-10 (e-book) 1-946724-07-6 | ISBN-13 (e-book) 978-1-946724-07-6

Designed by Barbara Neely Bourgoyne
Cover art: Ca. 1850 tooth key made by Hermann Hernstein, New York City. Image courtesy of Alex Peck Medical Antiques.

The press is based at the University of Cincinnati, Department of English and Comparative Literature, McMicken Hall, Room 248, PO Box 210069, Cincinnati, OH, 45221–0069.

Acre Books books may be purchased at a discount for educational use. For information please email business@acre-books.com.

FOR SHERI

. . . and there shall be no more death, neither sorrow, nor crying, neither shall there be any more pain: for the former things are passed away.

—THE REVELATION OF SAINT JOHN THE DIVINE 21:4

BEFORE AND AFTER

BELLOWS FALLS, VERMONT
MARCH 1829

On another of those melancholy nights, a doctor came to the sick man's bedside and with the boy's help turned the man onto his belly. The boy lifted the damp shirt and in the lamplight saw his father's back, skin grayer than the sweat-dark sheets. Boils clustered, livid along the spine. The backbone cast shadows. From the mattress rose a sour smell, an expression of disease.

"Bind the arms and legs to the posts," the doctor said. He held a green-glass bottle by its neck, shaking the liquid inside to a froth.

"He's too weak to kick."

"Do as I say."

The boy cinched cords across the feverish skin of wrists and ankles, used knots his father had taught him. He had never before seen this naked back, a decent fear of God keeping his father always shirted—even behind the ox on the steamiest days. So he studied as he worked the knots, noting the back's swell and sag at each fitful breath, how the shoulder blades looked sharp enough to cut earth, like a plowshare. He stared with a boy's fascination for what's fouled, observed with a son's regard.

"May I be excused?"

The doctor said no and put forward an oak stick. "Lay hold, boy," he said. "If he breaks it, don't let him swallow the shards."

The boy climbed onto the bed. With two hands, he tested the stick, which was seasoned and did not bend. He placed it like a horse's bit between his father's teeth, then turned the head so it faced forward, bristled chin propped up by the pillow, a liquid gauze over the hazel-green eyes.

What the boy saw in them recalled a nightmare from a few days past, a howling fiend come into his sleep with witches from the woods.

"I'm sorry," he whispered.

"We'll be quick," said the doctor, drawing gloves over his hands. On a bedside table he had set glass cups, handfuls of gathered lint, a matchbox, and a scalpel. He took the scalpel and cut quick dainty lines near each boil. Then he struck a match to the lint and dropped bits of it inside each cup. When the filaments glowed white, he pressed the hot mouths of the cups over the wounds. Skin hissed, and the body jerked. The boy twisted, too, away from the wounding as if the pain were his. Seared flesh stank in his nose, on his tongue. His father's bite broke the stick, and at his scream the boy forgot the splinters, jammed a rag into the gaping mouth.

Outside, in the valley, ash-colored clouds had settled for nearly a month, ever-present, low, choking sunlight. Below, a sloppy thaw, mud clinging to wagon wheels and trouser cuffs, and each day a gray-brown dankness. Since the clouds, Horace Wells, aged fourteen years and two months, had each night climbed the stairs to the room where his father lay, and murmured to his mother, "I'm here," because as the oldest child the night watch fell to him. Mother never greeted him when he arrived, but would instruct. She might say, "We should move him closer to the window," and Horace would answer, "The bed's too heavy." But they'd try and fail, and then his mother would say, "We should move . . ." and point elsewhere. After something in the room at last sat or hung in a new place, she left Horace alone to pass the dark and volatile hours. He'd wind the shelf clock, startle when black branches scraped the windowpanes, endure until morning his father retching into a pail, moaning that an icy wire burned through his groin, groaning in fitful sleep. Something awry lurked even in Father's lucid moments. One night, he summoned Horace with a crooked finger, whispered, "Fluff my pillow," but pillow fluffed, of a sudden shouted, "Away! Take the pillow away!"

Years later, what Horace would remember, what he would dream: moonlight on his father's hand as it clenched Horace's wrist, how he seemed not to know what he held, his eyes on some apparition Horace couldn't see, and how that sharp grip swelled Horace's fingers with blood until it felt they might burst, how his skin purpled the next day. Shaking out the clammy sheets; how they never dried. The bloated, smooth-skinned spiders that took their leisure on the headboard, and which Horace smothered in a rag, afterward opening a window to shake out the broken-legged remains. On a night after the doctor's visit, Horace turned from the window toward his father's whimper, saw his face screwed up, a keen light shining from his eyes. Behind Horace, a bat rushed in, chittering and squeaking, flying a crazy path. Horace crouched near the bed and waited for the bat to find its way back out. When the bat did not leave, he harassed it with a fireplace bellows, his father laughing softly, eyes closed. When Father's teeth began to click-clack from the cold, Horace shut the window. The bat remained.

His mother never noticed it, because it slept during the day, and because Horace respected her hysteria, he never said a word. The bat became a fearful secret he and his father shared. When it chattered and flew, and Father crooked his finger—"Horace, please"—Horace became afraid and crouched in a corner with a blanket pulled over his head. His warm breath stifled, and he drew his legs to his chest, pressed his hands to the sides of his face. He wanted to make himself small, but no matter how small he made himself, he never disappeared, not even when he clawed his own cheeks so it hurt. Many a time, Horace heaved open the window and hoped the bat would fly out and waited—though his father shivered from the inrush of winter, eyes tearing. The bat refused each invitation, beat its path across the ceiling, turns too quick to predict. Did its visit span weeks? Two or three nights? It seemed it had always been in the room, like the furniture.

Then, on one of those countless nights, Horace understood why the bat stayed. He watched his father wince and flinch, saw his jerks and twists, how they matched the bat's flight.

Father's pain, he thought.

He closed the window. The bat squeezed behind the wardrobe, its high-pitched peeps and shrieks now more frightening. Soon after, the floorboards ticked with warmth, telling Horace that his mother had awakened and added wood to the kitchen stove below. It was morning, and in a few minutes she would spell him. He dabbed his father's eyes, muttered a hymn of comfort: *Praise ye Him, sun and moon: praise Him, all ye stars of light.* The bat quieted.

The night death at last blew past, it raised the window with its brittle hands and sucked air from the room. Horace gasped in a panic of asphyxiation, doubling over the bed and the withered body that lay there. A hazy

5

purple light jerked from his father's mouth, yanked toward the window as if pulled. But the light resisted that pull. It zigzagged across the ceiling as had the bat, erratic but ever closer to the window, and Horace knew that the light was his father's soul. The bat flew, too, chasing the light as death reached for his father—and it seemed to Horace that death wanted him, too. His chest ached for air, his eyes dried and stung. He prayed please God please that the bat would chase the light right out that window. Please God please he prayed, and with the meat of his fist he rattled the headboard please God stop it as the bat shrieked, the light pulsed. His father only breathed, a rasp with each draw of life. Over and again, the prayers and the gusts toward the window, the frantic pursuit overhead—but at last an answer came to Horace. Or rather, an answer overcame him, changed him, silenced him.

Of the change he had no awareness, and explaining to him would have been akin to explaining to the ice how it once had been water, to the charcoal how it once had been wood. If you had asked him his name, he would have answered rightly. Asked about the night the doctor visited, recommending glass cups and a bleeding, he would have recalled the foamy river where he rinsed away the blood. Yet he felt nothing of the boy choked by sobs at that river's edge, who loved his father for teaching him how to tie knots. Of the sensations born from the soul, he felt nothing at all.

At bedside, Horace stared at his father's slack mouth, at his dilated and unseeing eyes. Pain is what's left, he noted. Pain and breath. He studied the bat, the purple light.

The feather pillow was flimsy in Horace's hands, old and thin and cold with the sick man's sweat. He leaned over his father's face and with fists gripped the pillow at each end seam. A tiny quill punctured the fabric and pricked a finger. No matter. He gave all his weight and strength to the task, stretching the pillow so tightly across the face that the nose and chin stood out in relief. Though enfeebled, his father tried to jerk his head side to side. Horace felt the struggle in his trembling shoulders, in the clenched muscles of his legs. But these were not things to disturb him. He was ice, he was coal. He felt a peculiar, durable tranquility.

The light did flash out the window; the bat followed. Air rushed into Horace's lungs, a chill hammer that knocked him to his knees at the bedside, wracked by a cough, where his mother found him hours later, a pillow clutched against his body, a low and lasting noise issuing from his mouth that drew her to the floor beside him.

"Was it peaceful?" she whispered, crushing him to her, and to Horace's nod replied, "Lord be praised."

On the funeral morning, she gave him his father's razor kit and told him to shave. "You're old enough," she said. "We must appear presentable before the grave." He had watched his father use the blade but even so was clumsy with it, and standing before a cracked mirror at the wash basin, he nicked his chin so that the soap lather smeared pink.

PHILADELPHIA, 1894

Dentists had always shown him kindness—as they did now, more than two hundred strong, with their polite applause. Charles Thomas Wells had only stepped to the lectern, a glance toward then away from the blinding lights. Behind him, a heavy curtain smelled of dust. His host shook his hand, then departed, stage left. Charles Wells smiled and bowed, waited for his welcome to subside and for his eyes to adjust. He hoped his nausea might not worsen and cause an incident. Nerves. His host had offered laudanum as a suppressant, but Charles had declined. Family history gave him reason to avoid narcotic remedies. Instead, he sipped from a glass of cool water and imagined a cup of tea with honey and the hot bath that awaited him later in his hotel room.

Crowded into the hall, those members of the American Dental Association had before them a stocky fellow of undistinguished height, five-and-a-half decades old, a minor executive with the Aetna Insurance Company, unassuming except for one extraordinary feature that quickly set some dentists to whisper. This feature was Charles Wells's side whiskers, groomed so as to sweep away from the cheeks and grown so long that they followed the collarbone nearly to the shoulder. "An oriole might nest in those," quipped a Baltimore dentist, seated in row M, to his fellow from Grand Rapids.

The applause settled into a respectful and anticipatory silence. With lips pursed, Charles Wells belched quietly—a relief to the pressure in his belly. He removed a pince-nez from his vest pocket, and then a dentist's tooth key, which he set on the lectern beside his scribbled pages. His talk, as titled in the association's meeting program, was "The Courage to Face Pain: A Recollection of Horace Wells, by His Son, Charles." Charles had written this speech mostly on the train ride from Hartford. He'd never before been asked to speak publicly of his father and his father's work, and there'd been a time when the ambivalence he'd felt most of his life would have made such a task impossible. Time softens, though, and when Charles received the invitation to address this assembly, he saw an opportunity to redeem the uneasy love he felt for his father. Therefore, his nervous stomach.

"Mr. President and gentlemen," he began. "My heart is made grateful by the honor you do my father this week, which marks the fiftieth anniversary of his discovery. There is something of his spirit in this chamber, alive in the noble profession of dentistry and in all of you—its practitioners—so that I, an only child, feel your presence as brothers. Yet in addressing you I am at a disadvantage. Because my life's occupation involves actuarial tables rather than tooth science, I have not any knowledge of exhilarating gases or the annulment of pain which might be added to your own. Thus I conclude that you have asked me here to speak about my father as a man. Here, too, though, my capacities are limited. I would like to say that I knew him well, but that would be untrue. My age was only five years and some months when he made the discovery you celebrate. His friends have told me stories and shared with me their memories, and I confess that I now and then confuse my own recollections with theirs. Was that me with him in a meadow, studying a nesting pair of *Sylvia coronata*? Or was it perhaps his friend Riggs, and I have simply considered the story so often it has become my own? Such is the power a father has over a son."

Those words: father, son—like an incantation. For a moment he lost his place in his talk, though he stared at the page before him. The words raised an old ache, at once a hunger and a disappointment, familiar to him since the days when grown-ups called him *Charley*. His father had called him Charley. How might it be, he wondered, were this ache like a tooth, easily plucked?

His stomach. Its upset returned him to the present, brought a sheen of sweat to his forehead. He cleared his throat, swallowed, and raised his face to the crowd, straying from his prepared remarks. "My father's favorite bird, by the way, was that same *Sylvia coronata*. The Yellow-Rumped Warbler. Of this I am certain."

And then he whistled a passable imitation of the bird's song. The dentists chuckled, and Charles again found his place.

"Here is a story that may help you understand my father. I heard this from his colleague, the aforementioned Dr. John Riggs, whom you will recall for his pioneering work in periodontal disease. The story takes place on an afternoon in the years before the discovery which accounts for my father's fame. Dr. Riggs visited to ask about a new tool—a tooth key variation or some such; my father was always tinkering to improve his instruments—and he happened to arrive at the office coincidentally with a man named Wadsworth. If you know Hartford, Connecticut, where my father practiced and where I still live, you know that the name Wadsworth has since colonial times carried all the worthiest connotations. The two men chatted as they approached my father's office door, and Mr. Wadsworth explained to Dr. Riggs that my father had recently performed a most difficult filling of his wife's tooth. 'Did something go amiss?' asked Dr. Riggs, to which Mr. Wadsworth answered no, that the operation was performed with grace and all necessary speed to mitigate her suffering. To show his gratitude, he had brought my father a desktop curiosity he'd collected while in Europe—from France, actually—a statuette of St. Apollonia, whom Roman Catholics call the patron saint of dentistry. I myself never saw that sculpture, likely because my mother—a strict Congregationalist—would have been loath to keep a Catholic icon in her house.

"Dr. Riggs and Mr. Wadsworth found my father securing his tools behind cabinet doors and inside iron-banded chests. Mr. Wadsworth presented the reason for his visit, adding that he had the hope of serving my father's practice by proclaiming its excellent qualities to friends and acquaintances. Imagine. The most important man in the city endorsing my father's work. Yet my father declined the honor, announcing that his practice was closed. When Mr. Wadsworth asked why, my father grew pallid. He replied with only one reason: that nowhere contained in his nature was the capacity to inflict pain. 'Mrs. Wadsworth is brave,' he told the gentlemen, 'and likely has not spoken of her anguish, but I was here. I saw what she suffered in my chair. My doing, you understand. For whatever benefit the reason: my responsibility. And I will hurt no one else.'

"Thus, my father locked his office door and gave up his livelihood. But this next fact, gentleman, is what I hope will give you the best sense of Horace Wells. Several weeks later, he returned. He accepted patients into his chair. He restored their mouths to health. With foreknowledge of the precise agony he would inflict, he once more picked up the tooth key."

Here, Charles Wells took in hand that dentist's tool he'd placed on his lectern. He lifted the key and showed it to the assembly.

"What awesome courage," he continued. "I wonder at such courage. I marvel at the fortitude necessary to face again and again the immense and intimate pain that belonged to my father's time and his work, and which his great discovery forever banished. How many of us here could have stomached it?"

Charles Wells returned the key to his pocket, his speech almost finished. Perhaps that's what soothed his nausea, the task nearly done—or maybe it was that story he'd just told. He knew he'd written something truthful that honored his father. Good enough. He needn't tell the whole story of Horace Wells, a tale greater, in any event, than one evening's speech. That whole saga would require uncountable nights—and voices other than his own. It would require his mother to rise from her grave and to answer questions Charles had never asked. It would demand familiarity with melancholy, with hope, with the tragedy of solace. Limited, he had told these dentists a story he could believe, words that created a father he could love as a son ought.

Now a few in the audience clapped, hesitantly, unsure whether this pause meant the talk was finished. Being the day's last event, its end would open the way for supper clubs and taverns and brothels. With a finger, Charles wiped the blurriness from his eyes and returned his attention to his final lines.

"In my life," he said, "I have read fictions about brave men who risk their sanity, their lives, and their very souls for science and humanity. The finest authors—Mr. Hawthorne, for one; Mr. Stevenson for another—have written such books: novels and stories peopled with imaginary characters. But my father was a breathing man, flesh and bone and beating, compassionate heart. Perhaps better than any other, he understood that pain is no fiction, that its tyranny is no hearthside entertainment. Grappling with it, he risked everything. Thank you for the credit you give him this day."

I
HARTFORD

1

The girl whimpered, then stuttered a low, gape-mouthed moan, and had you been among those in the room with her and her festering tooth on that November day in 1844, you would have been cowed by her pain, awed and struck dumb. The month had been unseasonably warm and bright, and earlier that morning a groundskeeper had enjoyed the weather as he wiped the windows clean; now a cracked pane left a bent shadow sharp on the floorboards. In the sun's blue-yellow light, on a table pushed against a bare wall, a dentist's tool kit lay open but not yet used. The girl whimpered again. She slumped in a straight-back chair, hands busy with a frayed ribbon knotted around a finger, eyes unblinking and damp. Her legs were shackled and her jaw distended as if from a tumor. The girl's mother clung to a corner near a wood stove, wells of darkness around her eyes, the hem of her skirt frayed and dirty. She pressed a quivering fist against her lips. Outside the air was still, and through it traveled other howls from other rooms, carried across the grounds of this place for the insane. Beside the girl, a second woman crouched and whispered assurances. Her hem was clean. She had come that morning to comfort the lunatics, an act of charity she performed regularly on Wednesdays. This time she had brought her husband, a surgeon dentist, to fix the girl's mouth. The dentist stood nearer to the window than the chair, backlit by the cold sunlight. He tucked his hands in the pockets of the apron he wore over his coat, said, "That's a pretty ribbon on your finger."

He imagined the girl's mouth a mix of milk teeth and permanent, thought her older than Charley, who had turned five this last August, whose teeth were still his first, perfect and white.

Closer now, the man noticed that the girl's arms looked a parade of scratches as if she'd raked herself through a bramble thicket. When he lifted her lip with an index finger, she flinched, exhaled a treacly, rancid breath. He palpated the tissue around the maxillary anteriors, peered back to the molars cushioned by an inflamed gum, probed until the girl's right leg jerked. There. An ugly softening near the gum line, on the tongue side, second molar from the back. A permanent tooth, too. It could be saved, he knew: drain the gum, bur out the decay with slow turns of a hand drill, stuff the cavity with foil, a drawn-out agony. The tooth key would be quicker— for her and for him. Yank the problem. A flare of pain. But then, an absence forever in the girl's mouth.

When he lay an open hand across her forehead to check for fever, she howled, from pain or insanity he could not tell. Her head lolled. She spoke, words coming thick and garbled, as if through water, tongue pressing where it was not accustomed to going. "I am queen of the ants," she said. "When ants cross the window sill, I tell them what to do."

In the corner, the girl's mother said, "We can't have ants in the bread, can we, Maggie?"

"When they disobey me, I crush them with a bottle," said the girl. A suck of breath, then a groan.

The dentist kneeled before her, whispered her name until her head stopped lolling and she faced him. "There are people in India," he said, "who pray so hard they sleep on beds of nails and feel nothing. No, don't look at me. Close your eyes. Pray your favorite prayer that the hurt goes away."

Her lips worked some silent chant he couldn't read. But she didn't close her eyes.

He rose, his effort to smile at the girl's mother more of a grimace, and he excused himself. His wife followed him out of the room, closed the door behind them. In the dim passageway, he paced, his breathing shallow, gaze unfocused, his mind's eye engrossed by the foulness of the girl's mouth. He scratched at his cheeks, at his muttonchops.

"You didn't tell me it would be a child," he said.

"I didn't know. The matron didn't say. Just to bring you, that's all."

"She'll scream."

She touched her fingertips to his cheeks. "Be swift," she said.

The sound of slippers shuffling across the floor. They turned toward the interruption, a man dressed in a gingham robe, his head canted left, his lower lip distended, hands clasped near his chin, one a fist and the other its shelter. "Mrs. Wells," he said, drawing near. "Mrs. Wells, will God show mercy?"

Mrs. Wells took the man's arm as if to join him for a garden stroll. His robe fell open, his nakedness made plain. She listened as he muttered, aware of his immodesty and careful to look to the far end of the passageway. He said, "On the palm, Mrs. Wells, the center is soft. Cradles the point. I drove the nails."

She turned him back toward her husband. The madman's hair lay parted straight as a carpenter's line at the center of his head. His neck appeared stretched beyond proportion, the muscles thin and ropy. His cheeks, the dentist noted, required lather and a razor. Mrs. Wells called him Simon, asked where he aimed to go.

"The man's disrobed, Elizabeth," said her husband, wanting to regain her attention. He reached for the garment's tie and spoke as he knotted it. "What's awful is that children don't resist. They make themselves so helpless. Their pain changes me. Who I become is not Horace Wells. That man—who has been a husband, a father, a son—he becomes lost, and a fiend remains who is more practiced at causing pain than any man should be. It's happened so many times, Elizabeth. Believe this: after today, I will end my practice."

"You be quiet," Simon barked at him. "You ring like a bell."

"I believe you," Elizabeth said, her tone as gentle as if she were reminding Simon the lunatic about the need to keep one's robe cinched. "Close your practice tomorrow. But today that girl's tooth needs correction. Like any other fault."

She meant for her husband to recall that morning, and he did: how Charley, from his favorite spot under the family table, had refused to leave a picture book and empty the kitchen ashcan. She had summoned Horace, handed him the birch switch. Horace knew what Elizabeth expected, knew what action his own father would have taken. Yet he hesitated. He mentioned the switch in a loud, firm voice so Charley in the other room would hear. He warned of the wages of disobedience. The answer came that Charley wanted to be left alone, please, if you don't mind. Horace tapped the switch against the floor. He scratched at his cheeks. Elizabeth scooped more ash. She scooped and scooped until the bucket brimmed. Her husband's will, she knew, depended on her own. She whispered his name, and Horace at last fled to his son, dragged him by his pant leg from under the table. Charley wailed at the lashing, and Elizabeth in the kitchen stopped her work and told herself not to go to her son, that Charley would be improved by the discipline. As would her husband and his too-tender heart. This was how fathers made sons and how sons made fathers. Later, she brought sweet biscuits and blackberry jam to Horace in his workshop, where she found him weighing powders on a scale, a measuring stick in the back pocket of his trousers. Apothecary's jars lay upset upon shelves, concoctions evaporated into mist from glass bowls above candle flames, and everywhere pervaded the stink of sulfur. Outside on the window ledge, birds bobbed and joggled where he'd left cracked corn. She set her tray on an unbalanced table stacked with newspapers, books, and scribbled notes. Horace thanked her. Redness rimmed his eyes. When she kissed him his lips felt swollen. He asked, was Charley behaving? and upon hearing her answer, said, "Praise God."

In the passageway, Simon admired the knot at his waist as if it were a rose bloom. "In Jerusalem, I was the hammer-and-nail of the Lord," he said. "Look at me now. In Hartford, Connecticut. Unredeemed."

From behind the door where the girl waited, the mother called. Elizabeth now gave her full attention to Horace, her eyes to his. Girlhood friends had called this Elizabeth's Righteous Glare. Her eyes—too large for her face, green and fire-bright—seemed always to see more deeply into you than yours could see into her, as if Elizabeth possessed power beyond normal, something sorcerous, a clear view to your secrets. Only practiced liars and lunatics could deceive her.

"I wonder why you ever chose dentistry," she said.

He had often wondered the same. "Farmer's son," he told her, smiling. "Fond of tools, fixing and making." A simple answer, and true, but he knew another lurked, murkier, having to do with such as this, when God's earth held nothing brighter or blacker than a child's vivid pain. If he could have told that to Elizabeth . . . but a nervous exhaustion clouded his thoughts. "I always assigned Morton to the children," he said.

18

"I'm glad Morton served some purpose in your practice. Now, I must return Simon to his room. Ask Maggie's mother to hold her hands."

Then, as if Horace were already gone to his work, she straightened the collar of Simon's robe and coaxed the madman with her favorite hymn, because she believed he ought to know God's love even as he wandered the gore-smeared corridors in his skull.

In the clean light of his improvised operating room, Dr. Wells wiped the girl's nose with the bib around her neck and watched her blue eyes jitter. "Brave girl," he said, in a voice constricted by the thickening in his throat. His muscles ached, and he wondered whether this would be the surgery when his hand would cramp. Many nights he had dreamed of his hand cramping, the tooth key locked in his grasp, surgery never ending. At the table now, he pulled a stopper from a vial; a miasma of cloves spread, and across the room the girl's mother coughed. Carefully, he touched a cotton swab to the clove oil, then pried open the girl's mouth with his free hand and dabbed her gum. She winced. He nudged the tooth with the butt of a long-shafted iron tool, concealing the screw-point tip with his palm so as not to alarm her; the tooth's root held strong.

The girl's cheeks flushed. She breathed too fast, then not at all, then too fast again.

He said to the mother, "What is your name?"

"Nan," she said.

A decade or so younger than himself, he guessed. She had been a mother too young. An unfortunate. She wore a heavy mane of black hair past her shoulders, only enough ribbon to keep the hair from her face. The same ribbon as tied about her daughter's finger. Her skin looked polished to translucence. Two pinprick moles grew at the corner of her right eye. He saw no ring on her wedding finger. She smiled at him. "You have a kind face."

He said, "You must hold her hands," and he beckoned her to leave the corner near the woodstove.

"Mrs. Wells?" Nan asked.

"She has another concern."

So Nan came near and kneeled where Elizabeth had been, and she held her daughter's hands. Light caught in the mother's damp eyelashes, and Horace felt stabbed by sympathy.

"I can pay in eggs," she said. "I keep laying hens in an alley coop behind my room."

He shook his head, no, no, because his wife, you understand, Christian charity, the both of them, you know, and—heaven above—why should you pay for this? Then he looked for the spittoon. Elizabeth had assured him there would be a spittoon. The girl's bib wouldn't be enough. He untied his own apron, placed it over her. She tried to smile, a grotesque rearrangement of her face.

He said to Nan, "Your face is familiar to me."

"I've seen you," she said. "Sometimes, I'm in the taverns."

"Where you sell eggs."

She gave no answer. He positioned himself as if about to wrestle a calf, with one arm around the girl's head and his hand ready to force open her jaw, while the other hand—as if a blind reach would decide the tooth's fate—found the long-shafted tool with the screw tip. He blinked his vision clear, called once more on the Lord's grace, and then noticed a new cast to the girl's eyes, which seemed to grow smaller, tiny crystals of fading light. She saw what he held in his hand and shuddered as if from fever.

He remembered that her name was Maggie and as quickly forgot.

The girl's mother, as if she could read his thoughts, said, "If you can endure her carrying on, she'll endure whatever you do. She's known worse."

"No," he said. "She hasn't."

He squeezed open the girl's jaw.

The tongue flapped about. He aimed the screw tip at the gum where he believed the tooth root met bone, then drove the point. The girl's torso spasmed, but he clenched her head. Blood gagged her, muffled her sudden cry. He forced the tip deeper, dug and twisted through the softness until it touched bone. Then he pried.

Just like a spade under a garden stone, he had instructed Morton. Unearth it.

Sunlight and blood. Squinting into both, Horace leaned across her brow, the weight of his torso securing her head. The girl's shoulders jumped. Her tongue twitched and pressed against the iron shaft, pressed against his fingers, tongue acting on its own, beyond the girl's control. Everything under God's heaven lay beyond the girl's control.

The screw-tip tool slipped from his fingers to the floor. He wiped his hand on his shirt, reached for the tooth key, its T-shaped handle fitting in his fist, a fast grip for fast work. Shaft into her mouth and the hook end caught, like that spade under a stone. He cocked his elbow—a hard twist, a crunch, and her scream hurried across his fingers, across the sticky bits of hair on his knuckles, kept traveling out of her mouth and into his face.

He recoiled as if bitten.

Blood on her like a necklace. Her face smeared.

The woman, her mother, kneeled upright, staring hard at her daughter's face, their fists clasped as if they meant to wrestle across a table, forearms taut and trembling.

The girl's name returned to him: Maggie.

"Do not let Maggie go," he said. "She may hurt herself."

His legs had lost their strength. He lowered himself against the far wall until he sat. With a swatch of linen from his pocket, he wiped himself from forehead down.

Believe me, Elizabeth, that I change. Believe that, as a dentist, I am done.

The girl sobbed now in the relieved manner of children, all the violence gone from her as it had from him, their misery still locked in the claw of his key, small, helpless, corrupted, never to do harm again.

2

After midnight, outside the front door of his cottage on Lord's Hill, Horace Wells stripped his overclothes and hung them on a peg. Even after riding Newton, the mare, through the clean, cold December night, his clothes reeked of Dutch Point: the smoke from wood-scrap fires lit by vagabonds in alleys; the greasy pig maws he'd eaten; the rude perfumes of certain women who needed only brush a man's sleeve to leave their mark. None of which bothered him, true. Though he had suspended his practice since that business at the retreat for the insane, he was a surgeon dentist, after all, and visiting Dutch Point—where the Hog River emptied into the Connecticut—was like visiting Hartford's mouth. The mouth of the river, the mouth of the city. No place more alive than a mouth. A dark garden. A swamp.

Still, nothing Elizabeth wanted inside the cottage.

So he stayed out of doors as he undressed in that deliberate manner of one who has enjoyed his beer but not too much. A mug early, a mug late. He had his rules.

Though tonight hadn't he drunk a third?

In a tavern near the docks on the southern bank of the Hog River, he'd spent many evenings studying pain and its relief. He'd gathered an inventory of complaints: a throbbing knee, a burn in the gut, erratic explosions behind the eyes. Ailing men took his pennies and in exchange let him poke where they hurt and where they didn't. He proffered tinctures, waved his fingers before their eyes, observed what herb or salve or balm brought relief and what didn't. When he could, he treated them. They made fun of his name, called him Dr. Wails, and tolerated him better, he found, when he had beer on his breath.

It was never pleasant, this work, and tonight had been worse. Monkey-Face Pete brought a boil; relief required a knife. "Like you ripped off a toe," Pete had said, grimacing. Such agonies put sweat on Horace's lip, gave a tremble to his hand, and inwardly he cursed his morbid compulsion toward others' pains. Repulsed and drawn all at once, and inflicting pain to cure it! Horrible. The contradictions confounded—how he could not bear a patient's suffering in his chair yet sought pain in the taverns. Perhaps pain made more sense amidst the rough and vulgar than it did in the rest of his neat and ordered life.

He sat on the bench outside the cottage door to unlace his boots. Wanting a last bit of the clear night before joining Elizabeth in bed, he turned toward the half moon, hanging behind a veil of clouds. Would pain feel different up there? Immersion in water eased some aches, he knew, particularly if the water were excessively cold or hot. How would the moon's atmosphere change a man's sensation of burn or bruise? He reached into a liner pocket of his coat, wrote his thoughts with the charcoal pencil and notebook he kept there. Earlier at the tavern he'd written, "exhilaration" and "Mesmer's hypnosis," and he'd written "pain's purposes," and now he thought about those things and studied the half moon. He'd have to go back. Test new concoctions. Have patience. That moon had shined on human suffering since the first parents fled Eden, and neither laudanum nor Mesmer nor clove oil nor a draft guzzled from a hollowed-out unicorn's horn had vanquished the pain of centuries. It would be reasonable to spend months—years!—in search of his variant of the philosopher's stone. Powder, potion, ointment, vapor. Someday, some alchemy would work. Then they'd call him Dr. No-Wails.

As he jotted those thoughts about the moon, he startled at a noise—rapid and loud. He turned, wary of whatever thrashed about in that shadowy, denuded forsythia. Holding a lamp, he edged near and noticed a small bird. Brown, crested. A female cardinal, not perched but dangling oddly, a leg broken and wedged between twigs. He brought his face close, then snapped back when she fluttered her wings. That was the noise. Wings beating too fast to see. After a short pause, the burst repeated, each random flutter a fury.

Long breaths, he told himself. Identify your response. Yes. It had a familiarity. The same as each time he stuck his fingers into the mouth of a suffering patient. A person in pain behaves irrationally, unpredictably, and it was the unpredictability in the bird that flustered him. He preferred the rational, the described, the anticipated. The mouth, for example, was a predictable place. When new teeth pushed up, old teeth fell away. Without proper care, teeth rotted. When gums were cut, they bled. All of these were the unsurprising responses of the human body. But when drill gouged tooth, the patient's actions could not be foreseen. Many remained docile, understanding that pain must be inflicted to relieve pain. Some strong women kept placid as tonight's half moon but moaned low and looked at him with a child's imploring eyes. Once, a dockworker struck him a blow that somehow bruised both shoulder and neck.

As with people, this bird. He peered closer and noticed that the cardinal's abdomen lay gashed open; its entrails, gray and glistening, hung free. The bird fluttered and chirped, and Horace thought to grab and kill it. What hope did it have of recovery, broken-legged and eviscerated?

But he thought a kindness would be to free it from the tangle, allow it to die in a place of its own choosing. Every suffering creature wants to be home. He calculated, deciding that the bird could do no lasting damage—a scratch or peck perhaps. Thus, he thrust his hand into the heart of the shrub. The cardinal thrashed, its orange beak opening, silently now. Horace snapped the twig where the leg twisted, and the bird fell, righted itself before it struck ground and lifted, dragging its viscera through the air, disappearing into the dark, damp night.

Elizabeth was awake, of course, though huddled under the quilts, a lamp burning softly on the table next to Horace's bedside. He slid in beside her, the quilts and woolens whispering around them, and she kept still even as he nestled close and wrapped an arm around her waist just above her hip. He moved his hand about her ruffled gown until he felt comfortable and thought she might, too.

She said, "It's late."

"I did good work." He rubbed his feet against each other, sucked in a deep breath.

She took his hand, grunted, and returned it to his side. "Your hands smell. Scrub up, will you?"

He pushed himself out of bed, and when he returned kept his back to her, hugged the edge of the mattress, let a clean hand dangle off the side.

"I found an injured bird when I came home. Trapped in the forsythia. I set it loose."

"Charley fussed before bed," she said.

She shifted nearer, pulled his hand up to her face to sniff his fingertips. Then she kissed them. In his ear, she whispered, "I miss how you once smelled of cloves."

"You used to hate that smell."

"I did. Now I miss it."

Clever, his Elizabeth. Each of the several times he had quit dentistry came with his fierce conviction that he would never go back. This time was no different. But he knew his responsibilities, that he could not quit dentistry for life. Elizabeth meant only to coax. "I'll return soon," he said, squeezing her hand. "I know the accounts are low." The sleepy noise she made sounded like assent.

Later, she kicked her legs as if disturbed in a dream, and the kick woke him. A nightmare, he supposed, and when she whimpered he rested a hand on her shoulder and whispered, "Everyone's safe," and she calmed but didn't wake. He lay there a while, and imagined how in the morning he'd explain to her how his Dutch Point work was still dentistry, in a way, even if it didn't pay.

Restless, he left bed, pulled on his coat and boots, and visited Newton in the small barn with its single stall. With a hammer he tapped the wafer of ice that capped the mare's bucket. Brushed her by the dusty yellow light of an oil lamp. His head ached a bit, and he recounted aloud, as if to the mare, how many mugs he'd drunk. Three, wasn't it? When he finished with Newton, he snuffed the lamplight and strolled around the cottage, hoping the cold air might relieve whatever ailed his head. Six years in this simple home, with room enough in the parlor for Elizabeth to Bible study with half a dozen ladies, a guest bed upstairs should his mother ever visit from New Hampshire. A few instruments of ease, such as the coal sifter for the stove—his own invention, which he'd made in secret to surprise Elizabeth, and in which she delighted. He had selected this parcel with care, for its half-mile distance from the city, its oak woods, its vistas. From this yard he often stared across the Connecticut River Valley, enjoying its virgin green in spring and its low fog of winter, listening to railroad clatter and factory bells ringing. On clear days city voices reached Lord's Hill, shouts about who knows what, though it seemed that with each passing week those voices—once infrequent and distant—sounded louder, nearer. The years would prove him right; Hartford's bounds were spreading like nodding thistle in a pasture, and soon the city would follow Asylum Avenue right up to the Wellses' doorstep. Even this night, breathing the cold quiet and studying the dark valley and the darker river, Horace felt an unease in his chest as if his cottage were already surrounded by the office buildings and schoolhouses to come, Yankees living shoulder to elbow. He decided he would sell the cottage before then. Yes, he thrived amid people and their bustle, but a little land was necessary to his evergreen soul. An outskirts man, a man at the edges. Always wanting some of this, some of that. Hartford's mud but also the meadows of Lord's Hill. Doctor of pain, and someday, pray God, His instrument that will wash it all away.

Clouds had passed, the stars and moon shined clear. He noticed his shadow despite the dark, and looked to the moon, which was full and round as hope.

But hadn't it been at half earlier?

He recalled the calendar, and yes, it predicted a full phase with no expectation of eclipse. Why had he seen it earlier as half? He gazed skyward awhile, perplexed, imagining the science that might explain this mystery. Finding none, he felt himself in the presence of magic and decided that for the moment magic would suffice.

Across the river the sun's light had started to color the lowest sky. Soon the printers would put the day's news in their windows, let readers carry it home for a half-dime. A walk to buy a newspaper might relieve that ache in his head. Yes, a walk and a visit to the barber. So he fetched his father's shaving kit, then launched himself down the road with such speed that rocks rolled underfoot, and he nearly stumbled.

3

Coles Barber Shop, near the train station, was a family business begun by the current Mr. Coles's grandfather, who had made a scandal in 1773 when outside the shop door he hung a wooden sign that read No Loyalists. All these decades later the sign remained, though of loyalists in Hartford there could be no more than three—toothless arthritics who expressed their allegiance by eating off Hanover silver behind shuttered windows. Mr. Coles kept the sign posted—and his razors sharp and mirrors clean—because he believed that good habits led to habitual customers. Among his best customers were the dentist, Horace Wells, who in years past had patronized the shop alongside a man who was then his student, William T. G. Morton. Dr. Wells always paid for both their shaves. A year or so ago the pair had left to open a Boston office, sell some new kind of dental plate. Mr. Coles didn't know what acrimony broke that partnership, only that Dr. Wells came back to Hartford and Dr. Morton remained in Boston. Now and again, though, Dr. Morton returned with his wife to visit her kin in nearby Farmington, and he stopped for a shave. These days, neither dentist had a good word for the other. And that's why on this December morning Mr. Coles steeled himself as Horace Wells jingled the doorbell of the shop. The barber had just finished lathering William Morton's chin.

Wells hesitated at the threshold. Mr. Coles wiped his hands, and he caught the eye of the boy he employed, a foot-scuffler now sweeping cut hair into a pile. The boy understood and swept his way to the far side of the shop.

"Horace!" cried Morton. A dollop of lather dropped to his lap. "I was just asking Coles whether he expected you. How are you?"

"Headache at the moment." Wells grimaced, then mumbled as if making a note to himself. "It's mostly a dull gnawing at the back of my neck. Worse when I talk."

"Better to be silent then."

Wells hung his coat.

The men all three shook hands, then Wells found a chair. Mr. Coles worked under Morton's jaw, reminding himself not to rush, and Morton stretched so his chin pointed toward the ceiling. Given that he had something of an underbite, it took little effort.

Wells said, "My Elizabeth would want me to ask."

"I'm not convinced I owe you a penny," Morton replied. "I've a man looking over the papers. He'll figure it out eventually."

"The contract was plain—"

"We don't talk money in Coles Barber Shop," said Mr. Coles.

"An agreeable protocol," said Morton. "What should we argue instead? Methods for soldering dental plates?"

"That sounds right," said Coles. "I'd like to hear that."

He gestured to the foot-scuffler, who put aside his broom to tie a bib around Wells's neck. Wells handed his kit to the boy.

"Still carrying that old razor, Dr. Wells?" said Mr. Coles. "Lost its good edge years ago. You'd better have a new one. I've nice kits for sale. Imported from London."

Wells shook his head. "It was my father's."

"I respect that. Hard to keep an edge on a razor that old, that's all."

The boy took Wells's razor and stropped it.

"Can't afford a new razor kit, can you?" asked Morton. "Scuttlebutt says you've given up dentistry again."

Wells's glance prompted Mr. Coles to shake his head as if to say "not from me." He did not gossip, nor would he about Dr. Wells. He did not think less of the man for closing up shop. He'd hurt customers, too, though an inadvertent razor nick seldom troubled him, and sometimes he did slip his blade into the chin of a rude man because the fellow deserved it. Worst was the time his mind wandered, and he'd snipped a farmer's earlobe nearly clean. You can bet that day Mr. Coles shut his doors. The way his hands trembled as he keyed the lock, he feared he'd never cut hair again.

"A temporary leave," said Wells.

"This is becoming habit with you. Is this the third, fourth time? It's un-American, Horace. We don't take holidays. It's what separates us from the French."

"I'm not on holiday. I work every day."

"It's not work unless you get paid for it. Whatever you're about is a hobby."

"What I'm about matters a good deal more than a hobby, Will, and you know it."

Mr. Coles shook lather from the razor into a sink, cleaned another patch of Morton's cheek. "We don't argue money is what I said." Then he addressed the foot-scuffler. "Give Dr. Wells a neck and shoulder rub. Loosen the muscles back there. Relieve that headache before the shave."

The foot-scuffler began to knead, digging his thumbs in near Wells's shirt collar. Mr. Coles observed the dentist's whole body go slack in reply. What awful work to be a dentist, he thought, and thanked heaven that modern barbers were done with teeth-pulling and bloodletting.

"We're not arguing money," said Morton. "We're defining labor and leisure. Which is which."

Wells yelped. He pitched out of his seat, hand to jaw. The boy looked stricken. "I was just rubbing," he said, "like you showed me."

Wells raised his foot as if to stamp the floor, a grimace tightening his face. He lowered that foot carefully but kept a hand still to his jaw. A groan came from deep within him, and breath puffed through his nose.

Morton wiped his face with the bib tied around his neck, followed Wells about the room until he cornered him. "Lean back," Morton said, reaching for Wells's mouth. "Let me see."

"There was no jaw pain until just now," said Wells. "A headache, that's all."

Morton probed with his fingers. "I've known patients who felt tooth-aches in other parts of the body," he said. "Yes, there's an inflammation, slight. I've got my tools."

Wells pushed past Morton and returned to his chair. "Your generosity impresses me, Will," he said, and Mr. Coles heard a seam of anger in his tone. "Thank you, but John Riggs is my dentist. I'll trust my trouble to him."

Morton dragged the back of his hand across his soapy cheek. He looked at what he'd wiped as if expecting to find something repulsive there, then turned to Mr. Coles. "Am I done? I have a carriage to meet."

"Just a spot," said Mr. Coles. When he finished, the barber wiped the last smears of lather from Morton's temples and chin, squeezed dampness from the shirt collar, then took his fee, and Morton left without a nod toward Wells.

After Mr. Coles began to chik-chik-chik the razor along Wells's cheeks, Wells called to the boy who'd caused him pain. "Please," he said, "forget that earlier hurt I suffered. Don't let it darken your day."

"Why would it?" asked the boy, his expression showing honest curiosity.

4

A GRAND EXHIBITION of the effect produced by inhaling NITROUS OXIDE, EXHILARATING or LAUGHING GAS! will be given at THE HARTFORD UNION HALL, THIS (Tuesday) EVENING, Dec. 10th, 1844.

FORTY GALLONS OF GAS will be prepared and administered to all in the audience who desire to inhale it.

TWELVE YOUNG MEN have volunteered to inhale the Gas to commence the entertainment.

EIGHT STRONG MEN are engaged to occupy the front row, to protect those under the influence of the Gas from injuring themselves or others. This course is adopted that no apprehension of danger may be entertained. Probably no one will attempt to fight.

THE EFFECT OF THE GAS is to make those who inhale it either Laugh, Sing, Dance, Speak, or Fight, etc., etc, according to the leading trait of their character. They seem to regain consciousness enough to not say or do that which they would have occasion to regret.

N.B. The Gas will be administered only to gentlemen of the first respectability. The object is to make the entertainment in every respect a genteel affair.

Mr. COLTON, who offers this entertainment, gave two of the same character last Spring, in the Broadway Tabernacle, New York, which were attended by over four thousand ladies and gentlemen, a full account of which may be found in the New Mirror of April 6th, by N. P. Willis. Being on a visit to Hartford, he offers this entertainment at the earnest solicitation of friends. It is his wish and intention to *deserve* and receive the patronage of the first class. He believes he can make them laugh more than they have for six months previous. The entertainment is *scientific* to those who make it scientific.

Those who inhale the Gas once are always anxious to inhale it the second time. There is not an exception to this rule.

No language can describe the delightful sensation produced. Robert Southey (poet) once said that "the atmosphere of the highest of all possible heavens must be composed of this Gas."

Mr. COLTON will give a private entertainment to those Ladies who desire to inhale the Gas, TUESDAY between 12 and 1 o'clock, FREE. None but Ladies will be admitted. This is *intended* for those who desire to inhale the Gas, although others will be allowed to enter.

Entertainment to commence at 7 o'clock. Tickets 25 cents—for sale at the principal Bookstores and at the Door.

5

Elizabeth Wales Wells was a woman of twenty-six years that December day in 1844 when Mr. Gardner Q. Colton advertised an exhibition in Hartford having to do with the gas nitrous oxide. She was not a handsome woman, as her husband's sister had noted once in a letter to Elizabeth's mother-in-law, but she had grown pretty at least in that way women do who age beyond the glossy sameness of girlhood but have yet to either loosen or harden into matrons. Her cheeks held a febrile blush longer than most, comely on cold days, or when she laughed or wept. She liked to tell people that the feverish quality of her cheeks had first drawn her husband's attention because of his concern with medicine. Some even believed her; she carried that sort of authority. She brought to marriage what she believed was skill in managing a household, and by and large she was capable of baking bread or pickling an egg, of instructing their son, Charley, in hymns and psalms and in basic arithmetic, of polishing pewter and brass, of sewing and mending, and of playing flute to accompany her husband on his accordion—their music made only in private. Though neither shared the belief of their minister, Dr. Hawes, that entertainment is sinful, they did understand glee to be a personal thing, and sharing it was an expression of their love. One spring morning of the sort that appeals to butterflies and budding trees, when even a practicing Calvinist could fool himself into believing that perfection on earth was attainable, Elizabeth and Horace took a basket to a meadow that edged a pond. Pregnant then, she welcomed his attentions, how he chose their picnic spot in a place that was soft but not damp, how he arranged pillows on their blanket just so. They ate bread with apple butter, read verse. Then, made drowsy and comfortable by the breeze and the trill of insects, Elizabeth napped. When she woke, she heard Horace laughing—or perhaps his laughter woke her—but he did not seem to realize she was awake, because she saw him striding about as if in leisurely flight along the pond's edge. His arms he spread like wings, each lengthened by cut stalks of cattails he gripped in his hands, and with them he nudged the air. Sunlight flashed off mayflies that flittered near his shoulders. When at last he noticed her watching, he smiled and turned, a big gentle bird gliding in circles around her and the blanket. A soft whistle passed his lips, and at her applause, he launched up a nearby grassy slope. Turning and rising and rising and turning, he at last crested the hill, then dipped behind its horizon. In that moment she felt a satisfying shift at her center, a fuller love for him and his joy, something round and rich as the life in her belly. She gathered herself up, left behind their basket and blanket, and followed after.

That morning of the laughing-gas entertainment promised by the newspaper advertisement, Elizabeth smudged shoe polish from its jar onto a cloth long blackened by such work. She wore white gloves already ruined, fingertips stiff with dried polish, and she lifted one of her husband's shoes to the light. The work pleased her. Part of her pleasure stemmed from the sharp, acrid, and altogether appealing quality of the polish's vapors. But she also appreciated how she could take a dirty, scuffed shoe and with a few wipes and brushstrokes make it new. Nearby, a stove burned oak, its vents adjusted for a slow burn. Across the kitchen, Horace, his jaw swollen from his bad tooth, read the *Courant* as he drank coffee. Her teacup was empty. She had never learned to sip tea, despite her mother's instructions, especially when the brew was sweetened with honey and cream as hers had been this morning. Let others talk and sip and titter—as proper women ought—and wait for the tea to cool. Elizabeth gulped. But as a guard against gluttony, she limited herself to the one cup at morning and another in the afternoon.

Near the stove, three bowls of dough were set to rise, damp cloths draped over each. Elizabeth sat close enough to smell the yeast, but also at a vantage from which she could see into the dining room. There, an Advent wreath decorated in tinsel sat at the center of the table, and underneath, in his favorite spot, Charley lay counting with numbered ivory blocks. From that same room, canaries in their cages sang, a linnet chirruping at interludes. Outside, dense clouds clogged the sky, and with such little sunlight

Elizabeth worked on her husband's shoes by oil lamp. He read the newspaper by the same.

"These nitrous oxide parties," he said, the words pronounced as if without a tongue. "They're the rage among chemistry students at Yale. In Europe, too. We should go tonight. Riggs and Cooley will be there, I'm sure."

"Will you ask Riggs to look at your tooth?"

"They say that people who inhale the gas begin to forget a bit of who they are."

"That's a horrid thought." Once more, she appraised the shoe, then, deciding the polish was sufficient, set it on brown paper on the floor. She began another. "Charley expects you to take him sledding. I told him he had to wait until you fixed your toothache. He asked me how a dentist can get a toothache. I told him being a minister doesn't stop a man from committing adultery."

"You did not. Charley and I will be sledding by the weekend. I'll not forget him. How did you really answer him about the dentist and the toothache?"

"I told him you aren't a practicing dentist, and your teeth are taking the opportunity to rebel."

Horace folded his newspaper in messy squares and grinned until she spoke again. She knew he loved her best when she presented herself as a gentle, teasing puzzle.

"I told him cobblers' children have no shoes," she said. She flicked a speck of dried mud from the shoe's sole and made note to sweep it later. Mud from the crude streets by the docks. Horace had been off again to Dutch Point the night prior. "Inquiry," he'd told her. She'd chosen to believe him but still felt unsettled.

Horace unfolded the *Courant* and resumed reading. His skin was clear and white, his hair neatly parted and straight until it splashed around his large ears in messy curls. Like a falls, she thought.

"Someday I'd like you to take me to Niagara Falls," she said.

"Happily. Will you settle for the Union Hall tonight?"

"Peg Trumbull has been to Niagara Falls. She reports that she saw God in the water. Got soaked, too."

But he was reading again. She rubbed polish into the shoe's toe, then set it aside to dry. Charley called to her that he'd won his game, so she left her chair to look and clap for him, wondering as she did how she would ever tell this husband too distracted to hear her desires for a sightseeing holiday that she also wanted another child.

Horace drove their carriage too fast for a dark night on a country lane, but just a whit too fast. Nothing breakneck, just at greater speed than propriety suggested. They were not late; he always drove as if driving were a waste of time, because in his mind only the destination mattered. Even as he dressed, he had wanted the night's entertainment to have begun, and if racing to the Union Hall might make the show start faster, then let the mare be wary. Horace had wooed Elizabeth with the same urgency, following all the requirements of courtship but without the customary wait between stages. The kiss came early and not too much later the conversation with her father. And that same night, the public appearance at a Vespers service, Horace joining Elizabeth's family in their pew. Each act in proper order, only a little faster than was seemly, suggesting that Horace broke rules but not too boldly. That combination allowed Elizabeth to feel safe with him and thrilled, too. True then, true now, as Newton hurried the proper-yet-daring dentist and his wife down dark Asylum Hill.

They'd left Charley with a neighbor. With him away, and within the privacy of night, Elizabeth snuggled under her husband's arm. The stars showed just enough light to remind them all of the road's direction. The brittle cold tightened Elizabeth's skin, forced tears from her eyes. She closed them and thought, *He will return to dentistry*. She knew him well enough to know that. In daily prayers she had asked that he recover the sensible part of himself. But at the same time, she did not want him to become a different Horace Wells, one hardened to the pain his practice inflicted on others, one who might not glide with cattail wings alongside a pond. During their courtship, it was just that mix of empathy and prudence that she found endearing. She remembered his letter proposing terms, which she'd read often enough to memorize.

Elizabeth,

Permit me to suggest the propriety of making my visits periodical, for the present. I would therefore propose to make you a one-half-hour call, on each Tuesday evening at 7½ o'clock.

If this time would be inconvenient, I hope you will not fail to inform me. If I mistake not, the right-hand bell belongs to you. If I am mistaken, please inform me; the mistake itself would be a small one, but sometimes little things cast great shadows.

Yours, Horace

The first Tuesday evening he showed early for his appointed time (of course), but she let him wait as her aunt had advised. It was the second week of March, and a chill rain fell as if the sky itself felt bitter about winter's long spell. When she at last came to him, he stood in the parlor waiting with a soldier's attention. Water, she noticed, puddled around his feet on the floor. She gave him the full scrutiny of her eyes, for she had already learned their power to make people speak truly, and she said with all the seriousness she could muster, "Why are your shoes wet?"

"In my haste, I splashed through puddles."

She smiled to let him know she approved of his answer but was not done toying with him, that his hopes were not guaranteed—but nor were they unwarranted. When she held out her hand for him to take, he did not misunderstand. His fingers felt cold in her palm, so she brought him a blanket, and he dried himself. As they made chitchat she found her way to a small couch with two cushions. She moved with care, but also as if he were not there with her (though she knew his eyes focused on her). He coughed twice, then crossed the room to her, wet shoes squeaking.

They talked more, sitting so their shoulders leaned away, but soon she allowed her knee to brush his in a way he could not take to be accidental. Well, that ruffled him. When he smiled, she said, "You have pretty teeth."

Then, because she had prepared, she added, "Particularly your maxillary premolars."

Five months later, they wed.

Outside the Union Hall, oil-burning sconces made an acrid smell and a dull light, and Elizabeth felt a twinge of anticipation for the day when the whole city shined as did Front Street, with its new gas-fired lamps. Gas. Gas was the future! In fact, there was Mr. Eaton saying so in his conversation with Mr. Brandywine, who inhaled a pinch of snuff, then wiped his fingers on his pants. Mrs. Morgan, in passing, complimented Elizabeth's brooch. "A gift from my Aunt Dorothy," said Elizabeth, and she in turn praised Mrs. Morgan's silk tassel. Over there: the abolitionist crowd—and there the Jacksonian Democrats thundering on about Oregon and Texas and Polk's recent victory, and there the Whigs, so restrained, and near them the bankers and factory owners who did not much care for abolition because of the sanctity of property rights. Horace led Elizabeth by the arm past them all to the scientists: Riggs, Horace's first student and now in practice for himself; and Sam Cooley, the young drug clerk and relation of Abial A. Cooley, the apothecary with a shop on gas-lighted Front Street. The pair had already stopped that evening for a mug, and their manner suggested joviality. Cooley's always-clownish grin spread so wide he gave the impression of a man who'd sell rotgut rum by calling it molasses punch. He seemed to be laughing at Riggs's beard, which was cut in some new fashion and resembled a bib of wool taped to the man's chin. By way of hello, Horace reached out and tugged.

"My goodness, Wells," answered Riggs. "Why that swelling at your jaw?"

"I hoped you'd tell me. Do you have space tomorrow in your chair?"

"Come by at ten."

Horace nodded. "Probably a pull. I might have let it go too long."

Elizabeth rose on her toes to kiss her husband's scalp. "Horace has been busy."

"Birds on the brain?" asked Cooley.

"Those. And pain."

"Poet!" Riggs poked Horace's shoulder.

Horace shrugged. "I've been thinking about Descartes, his theory that pain is experienced through the body and transferred to the mind or soul. As if the nervous system acts as a canal or road by which pain finds its way from the nick on your elbow to your brain. How, then, to interrupt that transfer? What dam? What roadblock?"

"Build a toll gate," said Riggs. "Charge pain a road tax it can't afford."

"Isn't Descartes the one who said, 'I suffer, therefore I am?'" asked Cooley.

Riggs chuckled. "If he were a dentist, he might have said, 'I inflict pain and therefore I am.'"

"When I inflict pain, I sometimes feel that I am *not*," said Horace, his voice serious and low, his gaze focused away from the crowd and out into the dark street. "That's always troubled me."

Elizabeth recalled something similar he'd said at the retreat for the insane, on that last day he had practiced dentistry, when he had pulled the mad girl's tooth. She'd been too distracted then by the girl's need and other matters to give it much attention. But now she tilted her head as if a new angle might better reveal her husband. "Feel that you are not Horace Wells," she asked, "or not anyone at all?"

"Just *not*."

"I suppose it is true," said Cooley, pointing at Horace's swollen jaw, "that suffering is evidence for existence."

"Now this is a silly discussion," said Elizabeth. "Existence is self-evident. Pain no more proves it than any sensation. You men of science are poor philosophers."

Then the Union Hall doors opened wide, and a bellowing voice invited ticket holders to take seats. Inside the dimly lit hall, it was difficult to discern shadows from soot stains on the wallpaper. Ushers showed men to the front and ladies to the back. Elizabeth found Peg Trumbull, and together they chose seats near the center of a row so as not to be bothered by others coming and going. Elizabeth asked about Niagara Falls, and Peg began to tell how her littlest, Susannah, aged five, had failed to be impressed. "It's just a bunch of water," the girl had said, which made Elizabeth laugh and wish aloud for such a practical-minded daughter.

"And when might we expect such a blessing?" asked Peg.

The question stopped Elizabeth's breath, and she chided herself for letting the conversation wander where it might. This matter of a daughter was none of Peg's concern. The only answer would invite her into Elizabeth's marriage bed—where a long habit of quiet guaranteed no children, a silence of bodies even Elizabeth did not understand. The thought of Peg prying further left her skin cold, brought the walls of the chamber close, made the air sticky.

But then Gardner Q. Colton arrived onstage, and all attention turned toward this man of some thirty years, with forthright brow, robust mustache, and dark hair that swept back off his head to wave thickly at his collar. His face could have appeared on a dozen sculptures of heroic soldiers. From her distance Elizabeth could not tell for certain, but Colton appeared to have a single eyebrow that crossed the length of his forehead. She whispered to Peg, "Our chemist appears to have a bit of the werewolf in him."

"A bit? Or a bite?"

"To wit."

As promised in the newspaper, eight young men of considerable bulk sat in the front row. None of these stalwarts was familiar, which surprised Elizabeth and reminded her that she was now, after all, wife and mother and not so often in the places young men might frequent.

At the edge of the stage were portable stanchions tied together by rough ropes of the sort found in barns, separating Colton from his audience as if one needed protection from the other. Colton was explaining about the gas to be used. As in his advertisement, he quoted the British poet Southey, then spoke of how the potion was prepared. "En-two-oh," he proclaimed in a voice dark and thick as creosote pitch. "Discovered in the earth, particularly where livestock evacuate themselves. Most commonly prepared in a laboratory by heating ammonium nitrate, which I myself have done, despite risk of explosion. Such danger can be mitigated by the application of certain phosphates at just the proper moments, and these phosphates have the added benefit of purifying the gas to improve its efficiency, making it wondrous as Gabriel's own breath in the horn come the day of reckoning. I have prepared the gas for more than a dozen of these engagements, and to prove its safety and efficacy, I shall be the first to inhale."

Peg leaned near. "As names go," she said, "*Peg* is always a suitable choice."

"Pardon?"

"For a practical-minded daughter."

"There is no daughter," Elizabeth said, and she smiled in a way she hoped would encourage Peg's retreat from the subject.

"From the moment a girl holds her first doll," Peg said, "there is always a daughter."

Meanwhile, Colton paced the stage, describing his first encounters with nitrous oxide when, as a medical student in Manhattan, he found himself astonished by the transformations of people who inhaled the gas. The meek became bold, the bold sensitive, clumsy men danced jigs, and the quiet sang hymns to make angels weep. "It struck me," he said, "that this magic, which is truly science, ought not be the purview of medical men alone but must be available for the benefit of all. This is an age, my friends, in which science ought to be our chief occupation. Through its mysteries we may one day descry all that Divine Providence has planned for His creation."

And Elizabeth, who had been trying to remember her first doll, reminded herself to be grateful for Charley, to trust the Almighty's plan for her family whatever it may be. If time to come brought a daughter, so be it. Trust God, she told herself. Trust.

Now Colton asked the hired young men in the front row to prepare themselves, to unbutton their shirt cuffs and roll up their sleeves, because there was no telling how men might behave after they breathed the gas. "Do not hesitate," he commanded his stalwarts, "to subdue any subject of the gas by whatever means required to preserve the security, modesty, and honor of the good people here present."

Then he turned to a small table beside him, a drape covering some object set on its top. He yanked at the drape (*con brio*, thought Elizabeth, as every traveling charlatan performs), and revealed a rubber bag the size of a man's head, and attached to one end was a device like those used to tap cider barrels. Colton lifted the device for all to see.

"Herein," he said, "the gas. Of every benefit possible to mankind. An entertainment, a joy for those who breathe it. Even ones whose merrymaking is grotesque report a panoply of pleasures. Now, observe as I turn the faucet's key and inhale. Each time I breathe the gas, I will hold the mixture in my lungs for a ten count before exhaling. And when next you hear my voice it will be deeper, more sonorous than what you have heard before. I cannot predict what I will say. Each time, my reaction is different. Once, I promised refunds to my audience!"

Chuckles.

"Tonight, who knows what might occur? I may climb into the rafters and chatter as does a monkey from inky-black Africa. I may beg you as a vagrant to feed me hardtack and rye whiskey. Do not be surprised if I remove my shoes and stockings, roll up my pant legs, and stroll through the dew of a meadow no one else sees."

He inhaled, a deep pull on the bag's faucet, then turned the key and stepped near the front of the stage. Then, as if his own weight were too great to bear, his legs gave way and he landed on his buttocks, his fall punctuated by a great belch.

A moment passed, and he crept back to his feet, staring darkly at his audience. He began to mumble, his voice deep and scratchy, but what he mumbled none could understand. Then he leapt forward, cried at them, his voice pitched low, a howl or ululation, and he crouched as if menacing all with a spear.

"I am a Cherokee chief!" he yelled.

Elizabeth barked a laugh. So did Peg.

Colton stepped about the stage, his footsteps exaggerated and long as if with each he cleared some brush or fallen log. Never did he take his eyes off the people in his audience. "Chief T_____," he yelled, but the word that followed *chief* was a jumble of vowels and consonants none could make out or even repeat, something unintelligible and suitably wild, Elizabeth thought. She tried to see him as an Indian, but his suit was too dapper, the tails of his coat too long.

"Horace plays games like this with Charley," she whispered to Peg. "Given the boy's church-mouse ways, we encourage him toward noble savagery."

Colton rushed now from one edge of the stage to the other, brandishing his imaginary spear, growling and baring his teeth, until finally, near center stage, he lifted his weapon with two hands over his head, the imaginary tip pointed earthward, and plunged it into the floorboards. "White maggots," he said. "You crawl about the land, pale, an infestation, eating out the substance of my people's being. If you were warriors, I would kill you all."

The women laughed. Now the men laughed, too. They clapped politely. Colton snarled. He staggered, ran his tongue over his teeth, breathed deeply two or three times, closed his eyes, raised a hand as if to quiet his audience, then said, "The effect now is nearly gone." He asked a young man in front for a cup of water. After he drank, he said, "After a turn at the gas it is often the case that one wants a swallow. Who would like to be next, to find himself and his very world transformed?"

Mr. Cooper the widower breathed first from the volunteers, then danced a round with an imaginary partner he called Hester (his wife had been Winifred), whom he praised for the skillful way she touched her tongue to the tip of her nose. Mr. Palmer followed, and with a lungful of gas tried to dive headlong into the audience, and he might have, too, but after he'd shed his clothes to the point just before immodesty, the thickset stalwarts covered him in a blanket and brought him off stage. When he came back, returned to sobriety and fully dressed, he allowed, loudly, how "the pond had looked so tempting and the day seemed so hot." After Mr. Palmer came several who merely giggled, and then Mr. Wingfield, who sashayed as would a lady of the French court, batting the air with an invisible hand fan as he repeated the phrase *"Je suis mouillé."*

And who succeeded Mr. Wingfield?

Elizabeth's own Horace.

He looked small to her there, vulnerable. Colton stood a foot taller, and with his granite face and hair of a lycanthrope he seemed every bit the predator; her Horace, the tender prey. His eyes were eager, his manner shy. Had he planned this? She remembered their conversation about how college students forgot themselves by inhaling the gas, and she realized he had been looking for an opportunity such as this. This had been his plan all day. But he'd not said a word. The secrets he kept!

Horace looked deeply at Colton as Colton asked questions about Horace's lung capacity, about the universes he dreamed of at night, about the readiness of his soul to escape into a land of mist and mystery. Horace blinked a bit, seemed to smile, though the expression might also have been a wince at a tight collar. Colton asked Horace's profession. When Horace answered "Surgeon dentist," Colton thundered, "A man of science! You, then, must appreciate all the natural wonder we've seen this evening."

"I have noted it carefully," Horace said.

"And will take the gas of your own volition, in the interest of science?"

"There is no other reason."

With a handkerchief, Colton wiped the mouth of the faucet. Horace took it between his lips, and when Colton turned the key, Horace inhaled.

Elizabeth found that she was worrying one hand with the fingers of the other, pushing and kneading with a nail, picking at rough flecks of knuckle skin. She fumbled her opera glasses twice before getting them to her face. Now she could see his lips, pursed, holding the gas until Colton waved a finger under his own chin, a signal coaxing the breath from her husband's chest. Horace exhaled, then stumbled back, Colton catching him. He closed his eyes, squeezed the lids so lines appeared on the sides of his face, then smiled, but with lips sealed and no teeth showing. She'd never seen that smile from him before, and something about it made her set her opera glasses in her purse with great care.

"I-I would like an ale," Horace said. "Yes. Thank you." He cocked his head and grinned, and he asked Colton if he often visited the Dutch Point

Tavern. When Colton hesitated to answer, Horace waved his hand to encourage play acting. Colton allowed as how it was his first time at the Dutch Point Tavern.

"This is a fine . . . place," Horace said. "Good people. A sort you won't meet in church, if you get my meaning." He winked in a slow, exaggerated way, and gentlemen in the audience laughed. Harmless, this entertainment, their snickering seemed to say, but there was unease, too, a disquiet that kept these restrained and sober men of church and property from fully embracing the scene. Elizabeth sensed Peg Trumbull lean away from her.

"Take Evelyn there," Horace said, pointing into the audience at Mrs. Morgan, whose given name was not Evelyn, "and that fellow beside her. The Earl of Bilgewater, they call him. They say his father was a pirate and his mother a slave. Thus his dusky skin. They're fiercely loyal to each other, Evelyn and the Earl, though never married."

"Really?"

"Yes! And he doesn't mind all the men she takes to her bed so long as she pays for his rum."

Her eyes burning, Elizabeth turned to Peg. Could Horace be stopped? He committed no crime against God or man, not murder nor adultery nor robbery. But he was laughing his way toward public disgrace, a downfall of reputation that could exclude him and his family from Hartford's social circles, perhaps even ruin his dental practice. Peg looked back at Elizabeth with a face full of apology, then turned away. So Elizabeth knew it was too late. In this Union Hall she sat alone. Those around her were united in communal revulsion. At the very least, they now had an opportunity to extend a pious, condescending pity to her and her husband.

"Let's sing along with the river men!" Horace said to Colton, and he reached an arm over the big man's shoulders, so that Colton needed to hunch to keep the pretense alive. "Follow me on this, man. You'll get the hang after a verse or two."

When Horace sang, his voice was surprisingly clear and loud, a choir soloist's. A tenor one expects to hear singing hosannas.

Clara Bliss is my true love, Oh! Clara's so dear,
And together we travel to ports far and near;
Of all the young beauties, she has the best luck,

All days we're in taverns, all nights we do fuck!
This way, that way, which way you will,
I'm sure I sing nothing that you can take ill.

"Pray God, stop," Elizabeth said, meaning her husband, meaning time, meaning whatever divine decree played out this night. Because what had started as a crass breach of decorum had become vile, perverse. Men hurried to their wives' sides to hold their trembling hands or to rush them, bloodless, from the hall. Colton himself seemed torn between laughter and some pretense of horror. What to stop? What to allow? Horace kept on, filling the theater with his voice, louder than the protests from the audience. He laughed and sang and swung his arms to and fro like some mad metronome of obscenity.

Clara's born of a good priest and his saintly wife,
Clara fled home to vouchsafe them days wi'out strife,
Had they known how she lives she'd weep in the stocks
'Stead of drinking down ale and swallowing cocks!
This way, and that way, and which way you can,
For the fairest of women who lies with a man.

"Enough, enough!" Elizabeth whispered. But everywhere the same faces, the same sour, pleased looks, until she saw Sam Cooley. No longer smiling, but on stage beside Horace, young Cooley pushing Colton away and clamping a hand over Horace's mouth. Cooley shook Horace some, as if wrestling him, and let him go only long enough to yank at Horace's muttonchops to get his attention. When Horace began another verse—"Clara's church is a . . ."— Cooley slapped him, but Horace only giggled, then kissed Cooley on both cheeks and said, "Try the gas, Cooley. Prithee. For science's sake."

Cooley signaled two of the hired stalwarts, who led Horace back to his seat. Colton then made some stumble toward an apology, but Cooley was waving him to get on with it, that he wanted to take the gas, to keep the entertainment a-moving and shift attention from the dentist in the third row with the whaler's salty mouth.

Elizabeth hardly noticed. She could only look down at the brooch that had fallen from her breast somehow and landed in her lap. She wanted to take its pin and prick her hands. She wanted to be sitting at home as

Horace read to her from the advertisement in the morning's paper, and to say, "Horace, let's stay home. We've no money for this nitrous oxide show." She wanted not to hear the gasps from all around her, the murmurs and footfalls of people leaving the Union Hall. At the sound of each, she imagined the weeks to come: the sideways glances, the scolding chatter from people who would not suffer a moment in the chair of a dentist so odious.

And worst of all: this was, after all was said, her husband. The man she sat beside in church, who so devotedly praised God and His creation, industrious man who labored long hours in his workshop, who so despised the pain he caused his patients that he would foreswear his livelihood, this man also held, deep inside him, a vein of depravity that she did not recognize, that made him a stranger.

When at last she raised her eyes, hopeful that he would have found her in the now thinning crowd, would have come to sit by her, come with apology, or with support, or to escort her away from this gross humiliation; instead, he sat where the stalwarts had placed him, in a third row seat, one in from the aisle, watching—what word could describe him, *fervent!*—as he studied how Cooley took the gas. And when Cooley lost his mind and ran about the hall chasing poor Mr. Eaton, Elizabeth watched the man who was her husband and a stranger, who seemed to have forgotten she was in the room, forgotten that he had mortified her with his vulgar song. She had never felt less important, less necessary. Now, with her mouth opening and closing, her fists clenched as if they could never let go of the shame he caused her, she wondered at the cruelty of becoming, to someone you love, no more than an accessory in some grand scientific investigation. "We should go to this exhibition," he had said earlier that day, without revealing his plan. How awful, she had thought then, to forget who you are, not at all foreseeing this darker veil.

6

In his seat in the Union Hall, Horace Wells scrunched his nose and sneezed out the stink of Monkey-Face Pete's clam breath. The Union Hall—"You are in the Union Hall," he told himself—tilted left, then right. When he tried to shift his legs they felt porridgy, which made him giggle. He fingered his pockets for a pencil (*Pencil for a pockets* are the words he thought) because he wanted to write down what he remembered while he remembered: knock-kneed on stage, studying the serious faces of Hartford's better sort, then blinking as those good people became others: Levi Knowles, Monkey-Face Pete, Evelyn, and the Earl of Bilgewater, all rum-happy and back-slapping. Levi started them singing a full-throated drinking song with words that were, well, *Caribbean* is the most polite way to say it. Horace had never sung when the company in the tavern launched into vulgar ditties, but now he gave full voice to the tune (something he'd not even done when singing *Hallelujah!* in church). What a lark! He felt himself a new man, and he saw no reason why the old Horace had with such care avoided the fun of the taverns. It was as if a hooded cloak had been lifted from his shoulders, taking with it the burden of discerning sin from virtue, moderation from intemperance. Those qualities no longer existed: all life was a song. So sing, Dr. Wells! Sing!

Still no pencil in his pocket. No paper, neither. Either.

He shook his head to clear the moss. Tried not to giggle.

Colton's gas works itself in wondrous ways, he thought, on mind and spirit. An inventory: first, the woodsy taste of the faucet, like bark; second, the gaseous mist that lingered in his mouth, cool as a waterfall's spray. The ease with which he held his breath. The beginning effects: how he closed his eyes and the darkness behind them seemed deeper than any he'd known, how he probed that darkness, curious as to how far it led, whether places in it might reveal a thread of light he could follow. How soon thereafter, light or dark, he no longer cared. How he let go of all curiosity.

(Horace paused here to mark the memory, because he could not recall any other time when he'd stopped being curious. His mind, that supple companion, that perpetual machine, had always wondered about the goings-on behind this door and that, contemplated the trivial and profound in equal measure: what chemistry led bricks to fire into the colors of bruises, how the human gum secured teeth in place, or what mechanisms of the nervous system allowed pain to travel its length. He mused over why God separated the heart and mind and spirit, if Descartes was correct, and whether in heaven all three became one. And was that unity the source of all bliss? He questioned why he questioned, why his mind could not keep still. Except, in the nitrous oxide dark, he had felt no need to think. Awake, his mind focused, and he sang.)

Was that relief from curiosity third or fourth in his inventory?

When he had inhaled Colton's gas and the limits on his perceptions vanished, the Union Hall waxed in particular and vivid ways. He could count the threads of each rope between the stanchions without leaning near, notice dandruff spread on Peg Trumbull's shoulder though he stood on stage and she sat so many rows back. The lamplight pulsed as if alive. He'd never thought a brown hue could look bright, but Colton's coffee-colored coat had then cast light. He heard Colton's young men breathe, heard their heartbeats mingle in wet rhythms, and then that song, distantly: "This way, that way, which way you will, / I'm sure I sing nothing that you can take ill." Colton encouraged him to breathe deeply, so he did, and now Colton sang along, as did Riggs, and Levi Knowles in the second row, who would not usually belong to this crowd but who did not seem out of place. Up farther, Elizabeth sang, too, as did her dandruffy friend, Peg. So did Monkey-Face Pete, with Horace's long-dead father beside him, robust now, a purplish glimmer in his eyes. And Morton, of all people—clean-shaven Morton—laughing with a woman in his lap. . . the mad girl's mother, Nan, who sold eggs, whose whole person seemed so *of the world*. They did not sing, Morton and Nan, and their not singing sounded perfect. But the rest did, and Horace, too, pitching his arms as would a Bedlam-bound orchestra conductor. "Ooooooh! Clara is a . . ." and so forth.

Then Colton winked at Horace, and Horace's tooth no longer ached, and well, what do you know? As there was no sin nor virtue in Colton's gaseous realm, so, it seemed, there was no pain—all of those former things vaporized by the vapor.

Monkey-Face Pete had come from the audience to grapple with him, breathing clam breath, and slapped him—the slap didn't hurt—and the nitrous oxide party stopped. In the same way he could never remember the moment of falling asleep, he could not now remember that moment of waking. He was singing, then not. Monkey-Face Pete stood with him, and Pete became Cooley. Morton and Nan vanished, and Peg Trumbull stopped singing. He existed in a new paradise, then his head felt full of moss. The stalwarts led him by the arms off the stage, and Horace heard mutterings as he passed his neighbors.

What was Cooley up to now? Shouting? Yes, at Mr. Eaton. And Eaton was on the run, galloping up the aisle, Cooley behind him spitting accusations.

"Contract!" Cooley snarled. "Pistols at fifteen paces!" The men in their rows laughed particularly hard. The women yelped. Eaton, gray-haired and bovine, somehow stayed ahead of Cooley, whose legs worked but not as designed. He stumbled as he chased, sometimes bounced off a wall or tumbled into a chair. And when he scrambled over a sofa, it teetered and he fell and upholstery ripped. Protected now by the stalwarts, Eaton crossed the stage and made his case: "I buy my tallow from Mr. Glassen. Cooley doesn't even sell tallow!"

Strain showed in the dampness of Cooley's shirt. Hands clawing at the air, he groped toward Eaton, but a stalwart had him wrapped up. Then, as if a magician had snapped a finger, the effect of the gas wore off. Colton corralled groggy Cooley and flummoxed Eaton to shake hands and to raise clasped fists as if they'd been crowned king and crown prince of Hartford. Colton's men helped Cooley to a seat next to Horace.

"How did I get past the ropes to chase Eaton?" Cooley asked. He panted, his eyes glassy. Horace felt similarly out of sorts, though his tooth and jaw had begun to ache again.

49

"I was in no condition to notice."

"Did I make as much the fool of myself as you?"

"There will be talk, won't there?" Horace said.

"Sermons." Cooley glanced at the crowd. "The faces of our peers aren't kind."

"I'd do it again."

"Immediately."

Cooley's pant leg, Horace noticed. Torn. He leaned near. Blood there, oily and dark, on the leather of Cooley's shoe.

"My heavens, Sam."

"What? Oh."

Cooley rolled his torn trouser leg to show that a stocking had been ripped, skin under it shredded. Shiny white flesh and shiny red blood.

"That's an awful mess," he said, sounding weak.

"We've got to get you fixed up. How did this happen?"

"I've no idea. It's the first I knew of it."

"Can you walk?"

"Maybe. It's starting to smart some."

The men stood, Cooley tenderly, his foot cocked so he could better see his leg. They staggered together up the aisle, each pretending not to hear the opprobriums spoken in their wake.

"You didn't feel it before?" said Horace.

"Not at all," said Cooley. "Just now a prick."

In the lobby, with Cooley sitting on a bench near the men's washroom, Horace ripped back the trouser cloth. He felt a quick elation, spurred by the violence of the wound and Cooley's testimony that he'd felt nothing. A small group had gathered to watch and murmur, Riggs among them. Elizabeth arrived and squatted near to Horace. He sensed her at his side, said, "Cooley didn't feel this at all."

"Horace, a word, please."

"But, you see, he felt nothing. And when I was under the spell of the nitrous—"

"You covered our good name in shame, is what you did."

He had not noticed her face until that moment. Had he met her on the street, he'd have thought she was not his wife, but some blacksmith's creation hammered to look like his wife. He saw no softness in her, nothing vulnerable. Had he done this with his antics? He reached for her hand, but Cooley interrupted. "Now the leg hurts a piece," he said, and Horace turned. Cooley gritted his teeth. "Will it need sutures?"

"Not likely. The wounds run vertically. You'd have bled dead by now had you caught an artery. A tight binding should do it. Let's raise the leg. Lie back."

"Horace."

His predicament came clear. Worse, he knew that what ailed Elizabeth could wait. In fact, her concerns should wait, given the time and attention and privacy they would require. Cooley needed care here, now. And his situation carried the tantalizing possibility of an insight. Horace said to his wife, "I wish it were otherwise, but I must have water for Cooley's leg. Would you?" He meant for his voice to sound even-tempered, but when he heard his tone he feared it sounded cold, uncaring.

"A fine night's entertainment, Elizabeth, don't you think?" said Cooley, his wide smile returned. "We're all clowns through and through."

"I'm no tavern wench you send to fetch a pint."

Her pique, Cooley's leg. Two sorts of bleeding needed to be stanched. Horace shifted his position so she could see Cooley's wound. She gasped— her anger, he hoped, tempered by the sight.

"Isn't that an awful lot of blood?" said Cooley, sounding proud and scared.

Elizabeth left then to fetch water, and Horace, relieved, closed his eyes, the reckoning postponed. To Cooley, he said, "You really felt nothing? All that time we sat together. No pain in your leg. Not even when you cut it?"

"On the Holy Gospels, Horace. I felt nothing."

When Elizabeth returned, her hands trembled as she set the bucket beside her crouching husband. He dunked a rag into the water, surprised at its iciness, a quick ache stiffening his fingers.

The sleigh runners rasped over ice patches, and the mare, Newton, coughed in air become even colder. Elizabeth crowded the far edge of the sleigh's bench, leaning so far from her husband a bump might have tumbled her into a snowbank. He made no comment as he drove, did not ask her forgiveness. At Lord's Hill, he kept his coat buttoned. His boots left snow on the floor. Elizabeth hung her coat on a peg, slipped into her house shoes.

She noticed that he stayed dressed for the outdoors and took it as a sign of his chagrin and sincerity, that his desire to be forgiven and the conversation awaiting them was of such importance that nothing else—especially not what he wore—mattered.

"You have ruined us," she said. *Ruined.* It was the word that had echoed through her head since they left the Union Hall.

"No, no. Not at all."

"We shall need to start again in another city. Who will seek your services now, so foul a man?"

"The gas erases pain. I'm certain of it. Cooley felt nothing. The exhilaration—"

"We are not talking about the gas!" A large snow clump from his boot had begun to melt into a pool, she noticed. She did not want to be angry. Her anger was a pain to her. She calmed her voice. "We are talking about how you have brought us low."

"People will forget," he said. "If my theories are correct, patients will stand in lines from my office door all the way to Boston. All the way to London! What happened tonight won't matter."

She bent near him, and he startled backward, and she rose with the snow from his boot, now a small ball of slush in her palm. She let it fall atop the heating stove, and it sizzled, steamed. She had asked for his contrition; he gave her science.

"You keep secrets," she said. "You never spoke of your intentions. I lie beside you, and we are strangers. The words you used."

"People will forget."

"I will not."

Such a hard crystal phrase, brittle in the cold air. She sensed a hardness thickening in him to match her own.

"Are we done?" he asked, standing. "Colton may leave on the first morning train, so I must speak with him tonight."

Astonished, she gave no answer. Then the door clunked shut behind him, and all her hardness softened. At first, that change felt a relief, but she stayed still for many minutes, and soon that softening became a rawness and then a vulnerability. The cottage walls fell away, and the cold crowded her, and Elizabeth could see far into the night-black city and beyond, the world so large and hostile, and herself small, much too small.

7

Not a bad evening's entertainment, Colton thought. Upsetting about the young fellow's leg. But the surgeon dentist's singing! His gutter-bird warbling! A highlight.

He dimmed the lamp, and with a dull knife cut a ham slice from the room's sideboard, though it was hardly that, more a shelf with a bit of dried-out meat, moldering cheese in a crate underneath. He sipped hard cider from a mug and imagined the visit from a town sermonizer that would surely come tomorrow. "You're right, Reverend. Endangering morals of the flock. Very concerned, yes. Oh, Reverend, my gas isn't what devils breathe in hell. A little air from the shit fields? Ha ha. My gas—and this is what the poet claims, Reverend, not myself—is the atmosphere of heaven. Would you like to explore those Elysian skies? No charge. As the Psalmist sings, 'Let everything that has breath, praise ye the Lord.'"

Now, Colton breathed pipe smoke, and sipped cider, and let the knotty muscles near his tailbone relax into the back of an uncushioned chair. *Clara who sucks cocks.* Wonderful. He'd like to meet this Clara.

He rested his pipe in a bowl and pulled the tank near, leaned over the faucet, intending to take some gas. Three quick raps on the door stopped him.

The surgeon dentist gutter-bird stood there, flushed as if he'd sprinted up the stairs. "A moment of your time," said he between gasps. Some gurgle in his pronunciation, as if his tongue were working to avoid that nob on his jaw, more inflamed now than it had been at the exhibition.

"No refunds," said Colton, "but I can sell you another tug on the pipe for ten pence." It wouldn't be the first time a man returned wanting more. "You can join me. I was about to partake."

"My concern is not your entertainment. My concern is science."

"More money in entertainment, but come in."

The dentist stayed outside the door. "I need you to administer the gas for me in a larger dose than you did tonight. Tomorrow would be ideal. At my office. My name is Horace Wells."

"Come inside, Dr. Wells. Sit down, please. Allow me to sit. The evening lasted too long for my back, and its argument with my legs is more than I can bear. How's the lad who raked his calf?"

The dentist quick-stepped into the room, not so much sitting in a chair as landing birdlike at its edge. He seemed unwilling to commit to sitting, leaning forward, elbows on knees, with just enough of his backside on the chair to keep both from sprawling.

"At home. Sleeping, if the pain won't keep him awake. I prescribed a whiskey."

"What a spectacle, his chasing the other fellow about the room! But you, my friend, you were the highlight of my evening. Whatever place you visited in your gaseous dream, I'd like you to take me."

The dentist's half-smile suggested ruefulness. Without asking, he carved a wedge of ham the size of a piglet's hoof and bit into it, chewed only on the side of his mouth opposite the bump.

"Would you like a slice of ham?" Colton said, but the dentist seemed too engrossed by his thoughts to notice the gibe.

"My theory," the dentist said, and Colton heard something unyielding in the man's voice, "is that exhilaration of all sorts alters sensibility and interferes with the mind's perception of pain. Think of the wounded soldier fighting through his agony. The mind that is bored or at rest, I think, experiences pain more acutely, having nothing else to occupy it. Young Cooley said he felt nothing of his wound until the effects of the gas wore off. His sprint around the theater could also have annulled his pain—as with that soldier in battle—but, having breathed the gas myself, I believe something in its exhilarating quality separates mind from body. Could that quality be potent enough to separate the mind from the most severe pain? Say an amputation? Might we control that exhilaration through careful application of the gas? Perhaps you already know."

"I'm not in the habit of hurting myself while undergoing the gas's effects, nor subjecting anyone else to pain. Why interfere with the good life?"

"You think my preoccupation to be morbid. Perhaps. I go where my profession leads me. Thus, I study pain."

"That's a life's work. Three lives, even. The poet's, the priest's, and the scientist's."

"I have approached the problem as the scientist. Now I need your help. Will you come to my office in the morning at ten o'clock? I ask that you administer an excess of the gas. I'll arrange for my colleague Dr. Riggs to extract a tooth that has been causing me discomfort. We shall see how I react. Please understand the implications of proving my theory. Surgery without pain. And then after that? Painless childbirth? Battlefields where soldiers are spared the agony of their wounds? An end to cephalalgia, cardialgia. Another generation might even eliminate every species of suffering."

The dentist had stopped looking at Colton as he spoke, staring instead at the bladder holding nitrous oxide and its faucet. His aspect had grown fervent but his voice strangely calm, as if he were reciting docking schedules at a harbor or detailing the mating habits of a thrush. The sincerity of the man's grandiosity troubled Colton, who preferred his dramas false and harmless.

"What I know of pain," he said, "is that it is best avoided, and when it can't be avoided, it is either endured or it kills. Were I to allow you a hearty inhalation of nitrous oxide and some harmful thing resulted, I, too, would suffer. Say the gas leaves you mad or makes your wife a widow. What would happen to me? Have mercy, Dr. Wells. I'm an entertainer. A clown."

"But, you must be a scientist, too?"

"No, sir. I am not. I ended medical studies after I observed my first surgery."

"Look, Colton, I'll sign any contract that holds you harmless. Write one up. My signature is good. I am in my right mind."

"You have a wife."

"And a child. A son."

"Who will take responsibility for your family? These are not small questions. As you say, the gas is an exhilarant—"

"Pain, also, is an exhilarant."

"Say your heart ruptures. Say your eyes open but your mind never wakes. What happens to your wife and child then?"

The dentist had cut himself another lump of ham. He chewed with care. "Widows marry again," he said softly. "My mother did."

He stood from the chair and stepped nearer the pouch of gas. With the fingertips of his left hand, he touched it and kept his fingers there as if he could feel something—heaven's faint pulse? He said, "But it's not my aim to make my wife a widow. You allowed me how many breaths of the gas? Two? Three? How many more can a man survive? When you started this business you must have pushed the limits."

"I have not. I allowed you three good breaths."

"We'll not go past six. Three big mugs of ale make me drunk. Six make me sick but won't kill me. There. Now my risk is limited. Ten o'clock. I will pay you for the gas and for your time."

Colton considered. Among these Puritans, the wall that divided seemly titillation from scandal was constructed of wet paper—easily broken. He'd not likely draw a crowd in Hartford for a very long time. This dentist whose singing cost him money might as well help square Colton's balance sheet.

"No contract," he said. "I'll not have any evidence exist that I participated in your death. But I want an oath, sworn on the Gospel by both you and this colleague of yours, that you will never connect me to this foolishness if it turns out badly. And ten dollars. I require ten dollars and that oath. Then, we'll pursue your science."

An enthusiasm flashed across the dentist's face, bright and keen. "Agreed," he said. "But believe me, Colton, because of what we do tomorrow, you will someday see your name in every newspaper and magazine. Europe's leading scientists will praise you. Children will sing hymns to you in their school rooms."

Then he was gone. Colton bolted the door, swallowed a gulp of cider, a bite of meat. He could not sit comfortably in that hard-backed chair. He arched his spine, tried twisting a bit to the side, lifted a leg over the arm. The pain would not diminish. No, not *pain*. The word was too strong, tossed about too easily in this room this night. His back ached. He knew the difference between an ache and a pain. His father knew true pain, what he'd once called a hot curl of ash inside his ear. The man had endured. Attended his fire and his molten iron every day, hammering nails and shoes for horses. Swung his tools even as that worm of pain burrowed and squirmed. No doctor could explain it, nor any minister. Old women made tinctures of root and herb; doctors prescribed calomel. Nothing worked. And here came Papa into Colton's head, a clear picture, half his face a grimace, probing his ear with a finger or with a swab of cotton on the end of a stick, digging around, trying to kill the pain. Always, every day. His night moans, his sudden whoops at the dinner table as if he'd been bit. How he, a pious man, gave in to the vilest oaths. The skin around his eyes grew sallow from sleeplessness, his nocturnal roaming. Then came the day young Colton found his father in the barn, sprawled in the hay, a red and brown halo where his head lay, his eyes open but his skin cold, a bloody hole where his ear had been, and still in his fist that knife he had used to kill the worm.

Colton's back felt sore but that was not pain.

He pulled the bladder into his lap, cradled it as he would an infant. The dentist believed in its properties, and he'd pay the high price. So why not? The wick on the lamp had burned down to a blue glow. Colton's mouth tasted bitter and velvety from the cider. He took the faucet between his teeth, pinched his nose shut.

8

If she had been dreaming, Elizabeth did not remember. She woke in morning's dark, gauzy with sleep but only for a moment. Then the previous evening returned to her, muscle cramp, hard pulse, a fragility in her belly. She untangled her feet from the sheets, sipped water from a cup at her bedside to moisten her lips chapped by winter, moved so as not to wake Horace—but no need for that. She lay in their bed alone.

The bite of cold floorboards underfoot. She shivered as she hung her nightclothes in the wardrobe. Horace, if home, made no sound. Tinkering in his workshop, perhaps, or nibbling in the kitchen. She would not eat with him. The thought of a cheddar slice or a cake with jam weakened her legs, curled her lip. Disquiet filled her now, coming with the memories of her husband's sickening performance, his disregard after. She hugged herself until her arms trembled, and then she stopped.

She *had* dreamed. What was it? The sense that lingered was of something better than this morning's reality, so she reached for it. Horace had been with her, and she'd been furious, yes, but he somehow—

The dream left her.

She relieved herself in the porcelain bucket, then returned it to its small closet. After raising a lamp wick to brighten the bedroom, she washed, brushed her hair, and twisted it into its bun. She opened the bedroom shutters to the cold morning and to bright stars winking out of a serene sky. A small mercy, and she thanked God.

In the kitchen she brewed tea, then carried a tray with cups to his workshop. Still a wife no matter how aggrieved, still concerned with her husband's care. She found him hunched at his worktable, his body shrunk into itself as an old apple, pencil scratching across a design of some new invention. He had not heard her footsteps, or if he did he pretended otherwise. She would not interrupt. He had asked her not to question him about his devices until he began to tinker, to put screw to bolt or clamp to flange. "When idea becomes object," he had told her in the first days of their marriage, "and not before. I am nervous about my inventions until my hands start to work."

She watched him, this man, her husband, and studied the ferocity of his concentration, saw also how his reddish forelock fell in a loose curl across his immense brow, noted the fingerless gloves he wore against the room's cold, the paleness of his fingertips. Her heart felt that pale and cold, like a windowpane in winter. She had not imagined marriage could lead to such a moment as this, to such a life. But there was much she had never dreamed possible in marriage. She had thought there would be more children, at least a daughter. She had thought there would be regular joy in their bed. But something changed after Charley's birth, which had brought her so close to death that the midwife called for Reverend Hawes to say a last blessing. Not that prayer but some other—Horace's, she liked to believe— returned Elizabeth to the living, though for months her blood ran so thin she shivered unless wrapped in blankets, and her eyelids weighed so much she twice fell asleep with Charley nursing at her breast. So weak, so intent on her son, she had needed months to notice how in bed Horace no longer pulled at her nightgown's collar to kiss her bare collarbone, how instead he kept his hands fisted around edges of the quilt. When at last she felt herself recovered and Charley had been weaned, the long silence between their bodies had already become a habit, and though she had tried to provoke that now unfamiliar passion in coy, coded ways, Horace seemed not to understand, or had a quick errand to run, or a need to visit his workshop. The expressions of their affection became like those of siblings or best friends, each night a shared prayer and a hand squeezed in sincerity, the lamplight extinguished, the quilts kept orderly.

Horace made notes now with his left hand and tugged with his right at the small curled whiskers growing in a muttonchop on that side of his face. Crossed his slippered feet. Cocked one at the ankle and tapped the toe against the rug. Then he looked up, looked right at her, blinked. He had such long eyelashes. Such tender lips.

Out of which had spewed gutter words. Were there actually women in the world, she wondered, like that Clara of song?

She placed the tray on the table near his desk, poured him a cup. A small stove in the corner remained unlit, and the room chilled her. "Your tea will freeze in here," she said. "Have you slept?"

"No, no, I've been here." He scratched his nose with the dull end of his pencil, looked again at the papers on his worktable. He said, "I wanted to be here when you woke. I need to apologize to you. Please sit."

He cleared a crate from a chair, then watched her take the seat. He still watched her even as he returned to his place behind his desk, and the intensity of being his subject unnerved her. It always did, had even on that first day he came into the parlor of her aunt's house and looked on her with such longing and terror as to force hydrangeas to bloom and wither all at once.

"What you heard," he began now, "was not my voice but the voice of the gas. It overtakes the mind. Much like a fever, the hallucinations that can accompany fever." He pushed papers about his desk, and when he'd found a book he flipped the cover and paged through. "You remember how your cousin witnessed visions while feverish with the Asiatic Cholera? His was a common reaction. Angels, devils, long-dead companions, all appeared to the afflicted. Here," he said, and he read, "*among acute patients their visions included cities built of glass, winged cats, blue flames, and, most commonly, worms upon the skin and in the bed.*"

"Do not lie to yourself nor to me. The gas does not lounge about the Dutch Point docks and memorize vulgar songs."

"Elizabeth, I will make this right, whether with neighbors or with God. You needn't—"

She rose from her chair to light the cold stove. A good wife even now, she would warm him if he would not warm himself. Why must he pretend he had no need for food, nor heat, nor drink, nor any human want? When she turned to chastise him with her glance, she saw an anguish in his face she could not explain, watched how with both hands he scratched at his whiskers as if he wanted to rake them from his skin.

Elizabeth set a long, lit match to the kindling she'd stacked in the stove. Then she shook out the match, placed it in a tin box, and, with no warning, saw again the prior night's dream. It was there, clear as the tongues of flame that filled the stove. Horace's sweet breath on her lips. The strength she felt in his body, her one hand on his shoulder, the other squeezing the small of his naked back. The furious ease with which their bodies joined, how she lifted herself toward him, the bedclothes a disheveled consolation.

When she turned to her husband, knowing that shame and joy and longing must be plain on her face, he only gathered a pen and a knife, some coins and a kerchief from the tabletop, and stuffed them into his coat pocket. Off again, she thought. Not to tarry in the warmth she made and wanted.

As if he sensed her mind, he fingered his jaw.

"Riggs," he said, "and this foul tooth."

9

Late on the Wednesday morning of December 11 in 1844, Gardner Quincy Colton splashed cold water over his face and toweled his skin dry, smoked a cigar, then tongued a pinch of dried mint around his mouth. On the street, because he liked crisp air in the morning, he walked wearing neither hat nor gloves. He relished how the chill reddened his knuckles, and how those same knuckles stung when he knocked for attention at the counter of a bakery. "Two johnnycakes with apple butter," he said. The baker asked, "What's corked in that bladder?" and Colton replied, "My fortune." The baker said, "I take coin and paper only."

Colton paid out of his purse, then set the bladder on a shelf near the window while he ate. The baker's clock showed nearly ten, but Colton thought it prudent to dawdle. Possibly the gutter-bird surgeon dentist would reconsider his course. Ten dollars was ten dollars, and Colton would be glad for it, but the business unnerved him. In morning's light and sober now, he realized that should the dentist die from this experiment and word spread, the market for laughing gas entertainments would die with him. What right-thinking person would pay to inhale the stuff that had killed a clever young medical man? For a moment, Colton thought to miss the appointment, head for New Haven and a performance scheduled there.

"Another cake?" asked the baker, waving to Colton, who noticed for the first time that the man had only half a pinkie on his right hand. The baker smiled at the attention paid to his nub. "Calm yourself," he said. "That piece never made it into the dough." He presented the hand as would a rich man showing off an emerald ring. "My father took it when I was a boy. Gave him good reason, too. He fed the bit to my dog, Mips. Then we prayed together, yea, even Mips sitting right and proper by our side. 'Fear the Almighty,' my father bade me, and that was love, I felt it, and to this very moment I cherish his lesson and the Almighty both." He gestured with a bread loaf toward the back shop. "Should my own boy profane the Lord, I'll flatten his palm against one of them ovens. He'll have his taste of Hell and know to want the better place." The baker smiled. "So. Another cake for you?"

Colton gathered his bladder to his breast, shook his head like a horse shaking off flies. "Grind more cinnamon into the apple butter," he said as he opened the door to face the wind-thrown snow. "You'll sell more cakes."

Arriving at the south corner of Main and Asylum Streets a few minutes past the hour, Colton tramped to the dentist's second-floor office. At the threshold he smelled a wet sweetness, the slaughterhouse odor he remembered from surgical chambers in medical school. When he knocked, the door swung open and a young man waved him inside, the same grinning rascal who'd scraped his calf at the previous evening's entertainment. Cooley, wasn't he?

"How's the leg?" asked Colton.

"It's no war wound." Cooley rolled his pants cuff and peeled back a dressing to expose the skin—green and yellow with brown streaks where the blood had dried. "But this morning it inspired the kindness of my neighbor's daughters, and between their prayers and gentle touches, all discomfort washes away."

Inside the office, a wooden curtain separated the surgery space from a waiting area and its three cushioned chairs. The décor was spartan, with two live songbirds in a cage, though Colton didn't know what sort. He followed Cooley around the curtain, where he found Wells in a dentist's chair, swinging his arms and jabbering as if in debate with the fellow who crouched at the hearth and worked a bellows to draw a healthier flame. Wells's jacket lay open, and his shirt was unbuttoned to below his sternum. That crab-apple lump still swelled between cheek and gum. Beside him stood a taboret, on which rested a polished silver pitcher and a silver cup sitting atop a book. Behind him, burning wood cracked in the hearth.

"Colton!" said Wells, pointing across the room. "We have the Holy Book for my oath, and here: your ten dollars."

The man who worked the fire wore an apron. His eyes were deep-set and heavy with what might have been concern or religion or both, and he wore something on his face that wanted to be called a beard but wasn't quite. Trimmed and shaved in a strange way. All chin and no chops. Some new fashion. Colton wouldn't dare it.

"You've made no record of this?" he said. "Nothing in a journal or a day-book?"

"Not a word."

"Hands on the Bible, then, all of you. Swear that my name not be connected with you tomfools."

So they did. Then Wells introduced the man in the apron, Dr. John Mankey Riggs, Wells's one-time student, who now owned his own practice.

"Riggs's progress in periodontitis is excellent," Wells said. "And he is a finer general dentist than he knows. I trust him in all things. He will remove my afflicted molar while I lie here entranced through the properties of your gas."

Colton sparked a match and lit his cigar. "Do you have oxygen on hand?"

Wells's look showed his confusion.

Colton said, "Haven't you read Davy's notes? On nitrous oxide?"

"I'm not a chemist, Dr. Colton."

Colton spit a tobacco leaf. Provincial men. "Oxygen speeds recovery from the effects of the gas," he said. "Should you breathe too much and your life become endangered, oxygen could save you."

Wells looked from companion to companion, agitation evident in the way he squirmed in the chair. He lifted a hand as if to scratch at his cheek, then lowered it. "We don't have time for that," he said.

"Let me repeat my warnings. You could become violent," said Colton. "Your intellectual capacity could be permanently limited."

Wells nodded.

"And you," Colton said to Riggs. "Davy's studies weren't exhaustive. We can't fathom all that might happen when a man fills his lungs with so much nitrous oxide. Perhaps his gums will bleed until his mouth is a cup of blood and his windpipe a siphon to his lungs. Perhaps he falls into a catalepsy, muttering and delirious, to all appearances awake but his eyes unseeing. You don't know." He laughed. "Maybe he'll piss blue."

Cooley chuckled. Riggs straightened his apron, untied and retied the knot in the back to a tighter crease. He said to Wells, "It needn't be you.

There is the charity hospital. Negroes. We could begin with the incurables at the Hartford Retreat."

"My gum swells, Riggs, and the tooth aches. It must come out anyway. If there are dangers associated with my theories, no one should bear them but myself. Would you measure my pulse?"

Riggs hesitated as if waiting for words, but none came, and he touched fingers to his patient's opposite wrist. "Strong," he said. "A little fast. Write that down, Cooley."

"No record," said Colton. "If he survives you can take notes."

Wells motioned with the fingers of his upturned hand as a scholar demands a theme from a student. "What lines from the poet did you quote in your advertisement?" he asked. "The atmosphere of the highest heaven? Right and good. Make me a temporary angel, Mr. Colton."

Colton handed him the bladder. He explained again how to use the faucet, but even as he did, Wells seemed to forget him, smiling instead at Cooley. "Open the office door, Sam," he said, his face transforming itself into a mien of mock terror. "Should the gas unhinge me and I sing bawdy songs, you must all be ready to flee."

Riggs frowned. Wells saw the expression and looked to his lap. "I know, Riggs. I misbehaved. But please agree with me that my actions are not so bad as my wife fears."

"Never take a man's side in an argument with his wife," said Riggs. "My father told me that."

"Wise men, our fathers," said Wells. He winced and jerked his head, as if trying to move it away from the pain in the jaw.

Colton stepped to the side as would an actor who has finished his role. For the first time, he considered the possibility that the dentist's theory might be right. Wouldn't that be something? He found, to his surprise, some admiration for the man's gumption. He seated himself near the caged birds. Leaning close enough to see light reflecting in their dark eyes, he softly sang, "Clara Bliss is my true love . . ."

The door would not stay put, so Sam Cooley—age twenty-two, an extra hand whenever his friends Wells or Riggs needed one—swung a tall, loop-handled brass doorstop to rest against it. Then he rummaged through his satchel for his charcoal pencils and sketchbook. Admittedly not much of an artist, he nevertheless understood how to shape a scene, to frame a vision. The visual relationship of objects, the juxtaposition of contrasts, these he saw with the clarity of a European master. He could not draw, no, not as the masters drew, but he was sought as a companion for those rare gallery showings in Hartford, because he could explain why an artist's work looked right. He valued imbalance in a composition, and he recognized tensions made by shapes, color, and light. As he blocked in the scene before him, he wished he could rearrange the lot, turn Wells and his chair to an angle against the hearth, and push Colton and his cigar farther toward an imaginary edge. He almost spoke his suggestion, but instead turned to a fresh page and started a second, more appealing version of the scene. He paged between two sketches, creating one picture that was true to physical reality and another that would best flatter the heroism of the moment. No wonder, he thought, that Reverend Hawes warned against art as the devil's tool. How many lies exist in historic canvas? Franklin in the field with his kite. Newton reposing beneath an apple tree. Horace Wells and his afflicted molar. Sam smiled. Well, perhaps not so grand as those others.

He knew he should be serious about the stakes, given Colton's warning about bloody suffocation and blue urine, but he couldn't bring himself to the proper state of reverence. On stage he'd inhaled the gas more than twice—how could a few more puffs kill a man? His father dispensed potent medicines in the apothecary where Sam clerked, and people often took them in greater doses than prescribed, and none had died. Reasoning by analogy, then, it seemed unlikely that the gas would kill Wells. Whether it would work as Wells predicted? In Abial Cooley's shop, customers could buy cocaine and laudanum, clove poultices, creosote sticks, lotions and rubs, opium—all proven to alleviate gout or intestinal cramp or a burning gullet. None destroyed pain as if pain had never been. Sam doubted such an analgesic existed. But Wells pursued the idea as if he were de Leon chasing the waters of youth or Magnus wanting gold from lead. Sam himself had been subject to Wells's exploration: an experiment intended to quash the pain of a sore molar via magnetism as championed by that European quack, Dr. Mesmer. "There might be something to his theories," Wells had said as he tied dangling magnets about Sam's body, squeezed his fists around Sam's erect thumbs for a ten count, then waved his fingers over Sam's brow, near his temples, close enough to touch but never touching, the motions slow and precise as a man might caress a woman. All the while, Wells spoke in a singsong whisper, words too soft to hear. Maybe he had said "flow"; perhaps "vitality" and "relief." The whole effort seemed silly and desperate, but Sam allowed it for friendship's sake and for a tooth pull without charge. But when Horace's tooth key gripped Cooley's molar and ripped, yes, Sam screamed. Flew right up out of the chair, body jerking as if gravity mattered not at all, an animal's instinctive leap, his conscious mind made irrelevant. Magnets bumping against his jaw, the animal that had been Cooley grabbed a poker from near the fire and smashed six times against the hearth bricks, chips cascading about the office. Some guttural sound barked from Cooley's mouth, and it was all he could do not to shout profanities. Pain charged through him like lightning, and like the lightning its spark proved furious, unsparing, irrepressible.

Quickly as it rose, the temper passed. "Rinse with this," Wells had said, offering Cooley a cup. His open hand on Cooley's back comforted.

Riggs cradled the Bible against his chest, closed his eyes, moved his lips in prayerful silence. Wells closed his eyes, too, dropped his head, and folded his hands, whispered, "Amen."

Then he adjusted the bladder in his lap as if wanting the gas itself to feel at ease. He placed his mouth over the faucet, turned the key, and inhaled.

"Count ten," said Colton.

Wells did, then exhaled. He inhaled again. Another ten count.

Then Wells stopped holding his breath or turning the key. He breathed back into the bladder, inhaled from it, breathed again into it, his mouth tight over the faucet. Colton counted breaths, and at six jumped from his chair.

"That's enough," he said. "That's enough! We agreed to six." He seized the bladder, cranked the key to shut the faucet. With a hand to Wells's brow, Riggs lifted the heavy head away from the spigot and set it to rest against the padded pillow of the chair. Colton noticed Cooley at work and seized the sketchbook. "No record, I said!" He tore at the pages, taking half of one and almost all of the other. Then he gave the crumpled mess to the fire. Cooley recovered his book and made an obscene gesture at Colton's back.

Wells's skin had blanched like the scales of a fish belly, so his red hair seemed even more like flame. He blinked, his blue eyes shifted, lids half closed but the eyes still seeming to see. But see what? The pupils lazed about, sometimes settling on an object, then moving in the direction of another: from open drawer in the tool chest to a green-glass bottle of chemical to a fleur-de-lis pattern in the wallpaper. Riggs placed a fingertip against Wells's neck.

"His pulse is tranquil," he said. He counted. "The beats spread widely but with regularity."

Colton pushed his knuckles into his own brow with such force he left his skin mottled pink. "Is he awake? Is he asleep?"

Though Wells's eyes remained open, he appeared unaware, helpless. His vulnerability troubled Riggs with a sense of responsibility he'd not experienced in all his days as a dentist. He glanced out a window and saw that snow still fell, layering the shingles of the tobacconist across the corner. "Neither asleep nor awake, I think."

Colton waved his hands in front of Wells's placid face. "Open your mouth!" he shouted.

Wells opened his mouth.

"He's not deaf," said Riggs, less reproach to Colton than a note to himself. He reached for the tooth key, crouched near Wells's face. "Open wider," he said. Wells did.

In the next moment, Riggs found the tooth, secured the key. He felt his own pulse jump. "Shouldn't someone hold his arms?" he asked.

"Just pull," said Colton. "Now."

Riggs tightened his fist on the handle, gasped as he yanked.

Nothing else happened. Wells lay in his chair, his expression unchanged.

"Not even a flinch," said Cooley.

The men stood a moment, watching for some other reaction. As if by reflex, Riggs wiped Wells's blood and saliva from his fingers onto his apron. Then he presented the bloody molar to Colton, showed Cooley. Riggs's whole arm trembled, and the molar shook in the air like some strange moth in a light.

Riggs whispered near Wells's ear. "What do you feel?"

Wells's lips moved like an infant's in its sleep.

It had begun, Horace would later remember, with a tingling. He had made a mental note.

Tingling.

Tips of fingers.

Tips of toes.

Then numbness overtook his limbs. He thought to tap his foot, to lift it at the ankle and tap his shoe sole against the floor. Strange, this part, because he sensed no subsequent movement. Given that his mind was a scientific mind, he did not assume that an absence of a sense of movement proved failure to move. Perhaps his foot had tapped but he hadn't felt the sensations of tapping. Perhaps absence of pain required absence of all feeling. Perhaps. Perhaps Charley could learn to tap dance. He should ask Riggs. He thought to say, "Might Charley make a good tap dancer?" but again, he sensed no movement in his mouth. But he felt something. Or his head did. Whichever it was, he approved. His body became waves— waves instead of legs, waves instead of arms, waves instead of lungs, the weightless pleasure of waves. He experienced something like a laugh, but it was the laugh of soul rather than body. So the two—soul and body—are separate after all! What a thing to discover! What else? He could hear. A pulsing beat, a sound the color of gold. A beat that sounded as if it rang from inside the bell of the world. Ah, the church bell of Creation. The heartbeat of God. He looked around. Cooley tap dancing! A delight. Riggs a delight, too, and Colton, and teeth, and gums—all a delight! The room expanded. Or rather, Horace shrank. Or rather, the room expanded. Somewhere he heard a sharpening wheel, and he saw its sparks spray into the air. What ecstasy to be a spark in this universe, one of an infinity of sparks, all brilliant, all in flight. A spark streaked by his face, and it spoke to him in a voice like God's. "Open your mouth!" said the spark, and Horace imagined his mouth opening, and perhaps it did or did not but did it matter? Brilliant and humble and in flight! Rapture!

And then, he felt himself breathing. His lungs, no longer waves, had become lungs again. He blinked and saw blinding brightness. He felt the blink. He held his eyes shut a moment. The pulse that had been God's heartbeat seemed now to be a throbbing, as if it were a visitor knocking on his forehead with two knuckles. His mouth tasted of iron. His tongue felt leaden. Still, it moved at his bidding, sort of, so he explored his mouth and found a hole along his gum line where he remembered no hole. He opened his eyes with care, and in the brightness he saw Riggs in his apron. Riggs held a tooth key, and lodged in the key was a tooth. It looked to him white as could be, as if polished, as if it were the tooth of an angel.

"Did you feel it, Wells? Did you feel the tooth pull?"

He had not. He had not, and even as he felt tired, wanting to sleep, the awareness that the angel tooth Riggs held was his own sparked through him like some celestial fire. He tasted blood and tongued the spot where his sore tooth had been, felt its emptiness, and even the pressure of his tongue in the hollow space felt as no more than a caress.

He clapped his hands once, then let them fall, benumbed birds alighting in his lap.

Thus does the map of the known world widen and its mysteries multiply. Giddy with discovery, a dentist staggers to and fro, laughing as he upends a tool tray, caught by a companion as he tumbles into a bird cage, spilling seed and litter. "Oxygen!" one fellow yells. "Open the window!" But no one does. A more momentous thing has opened, and in this second-floor office above a frozen-dirt main street in a provincial capital, men gape at a new panorama, knowing they are first to see. Being men, they want to speak of what makes them whoop and cheer, but words have yet to be invented for the unknown that demands to be explored. "Pray, keep this secret," mumbles the dentist (his mouth packed with cotton) as his fellows leave to return to their commonplaces—a bill to pay, a floor to sweep, a bench seat on a train beside a boy crying over his stubbed toe—all that humdrum which will buoy them as it never has before, its monotony lightened by their new hope for humanity. "Hold your tongues," says the dentist. "Not a word. Not yet."

10

From butchers on Market Street, Horace Wells bought a half dozen hog bladders and a few of sheep. The sheep organs held the gas just as well but crackled like parchment as he filled them. "You see, Elizabeth?" he told her that Friday she and Charley visited his office. "Who imagined there could be a qualitative difference between the bladders of hogs and sheep?" She stared into the wooden tub full of inflated animal parts, each corked shut, and allowed that she had not. Charley nodded as if it had always been plain to him, then leaned against a wall to draw on a fogged window pane with his finger.

Horace made a spot for her to sit on a crate, which smelled strongly of cedar. "To forestall moths," he explained. "That's where I've stored my business records."

Then he told how in recent days he'd learned to measure lung capacity—"Mine's not so good," he said—and showed her the table where he blended chemicals and heated gases, the tubes fashioned from the arteries of livestock and sewn with sinew. The ventilation system he had made from a bellows, a board, and a length of stovepipe leading to the window. "You broke a pane?" she asked.

"With a tiny hammer."

At the window, Charley had finger-drawn birds on the wing, which with a few lines he turned into angels. Then he gave each a sword to wield. Elizabeth, watching him, noticed small nests of dust drifting under his shoes and realized furniture was missing. She smiled and reached for Horace's hands so that he might stop scampering about the room like a hound in a field of rabbit holes. The week since Mr. Colton's exhibition had been too much, too fast.

"Where did you put the settee?" she asked.

"Not to worry," he said. "When I'm ready again for patients, I'll buy it back."

He pulled away his hands and began whistling the song of a meadowlark—*chee-chee-yoo chee-yoo, chee-chee-yoo chee-yoo*—so that Charley turned from the window and tried to whistle, too. They met at the middle of the room, and Horace lifted the boy and swooped him about, Charley's arms beating the air as if wings.

After, Horace arranged illustrations and beakers just so, then recounted to son and wife how he'd felt nothing when Riggs yanked his tooth. He showed his notes and explained that very soon he would introduce his discovery to the medical establishment, and physicians and surgeons could see for themselves how it would change the lives of every man, woman, and child.

"All this from a pulled tooth?" Elizabeth asked.

"It's possible," he said. "We could live in a world with no pain. None. Not after a scrape or tumble, not with a broken bone or the worst disease."

"Not even in childbirth?"

Her words—carefully chosen to open him to a new subject, to a new possibility—took away his smile and buoyancy. He looked over to Charley.

"Perhaps not even," he said, as if he understood her secret desire for a daughter. "Life will change in ways we can't divine."

Charley applauded. Then Horace waited, relying on his wife's love to confirm the reality of his hopes. She laughed once, and her face glimmered with what he took to be assent. "You are becoming a wizard," she said.

"It's no dark art," he said. "I am becoming happy."

"That answers my prayers." She kissed his cheek, then left with Charley to visit the bank and confirm her worries about their debts and balances.

Of course, childbirth is pain. But for Horace, his son's arrival had been a nightmare of silences and screams, an unpredictable and awful pairing, hour after hour. Pain seized Elizabeth's body with its own whims, and the helpless body did pain's bidding. Excrement on her bedsheets. Her face purpled. She beat her arms against the headboard until her hands bruised and swelled. A film clouded her eyes. Thursday. Friday. Saturday . . . "Pray," said the midwife and the neighbor women, repeating the word. *Pray. Pray.* Elizabeth's screams wormed their way into his head, his heart. At the church, on his knees, he beseeched God as Reverend Hawes recited the sixteenth verse from the third chapter of Genesis: *Unto the woman he said, I will greatly multiply thy sorrow and thy conception*; *in sorrow thou shalt bring forth children.*

Throughout the long plod home, snow-white worms worked at Horace's heart, left a cold cavity, until he who arrived at the house was not Horace Wells at all, but a ghost, a shade; the worms had eaten him empty. He sat outside Elizabeth's room, a hollow man. Had you asked his wife's name, he would have answered "Elizabeth Wells." Yet he felt nothing of the husband he had been those months before, who had shed tears and kissed his wife's belly at the happy news.

This man, this *not*-Horace, executed his duties, stationed just outside the door, fetching what the women asked, and they praised his courage, marveled at his stoicism. Then the hour came when they told him he had a son and with the same breath that his wife would soon die. He offered no reaction, made no remark—only nodded and took a shovel to the yard, and the women no longer thought him praiseworthy. They whispered to each other about his monstrous indifference.

Driving the shovel into the earth, his body was not his own, but some other weighted thing that he could sense but not feel. August's muggy air slicked his skin with sweat so dirt clung to his hands and forearms. His eyes burned. But of these irritants, he had no concern. He worked as if in the world and out of it. The pile of soil and stone grew to his knees, then higher. The grave deepened. When the hour came that his work was done, he returned to where his wife slept, each breath coming from her mouth as if torn. "I want my son," he said and took the boy from the arms of a neighbor woman.

Outside, he set the infant on his back at the grave's edge, then climbed down. When he again took his son, it was to cradle him against his chest, then to sit with him at the pit's bottom. He studied the mottled forehead, the half-open eyes, and only then did his heart grow back. "Little murderer," he whispered, that new heart ripping, one part grief and the other joy. "Son of mine."

But Elizabeth did not die, and Horace refilled the hole. When she slept in bed with Charley on her bosom, Horace kneeled beside them, unshaven, his vision blurred, his soul bursting. He had suspected that her affliction was his fault, Heaven's judgment against a sin from his past (he knew which one), but he had prayed, and God had given back his wife. Thereafter in Horace grew an apprehension that such mercy must not be taken for granted. So, to his sleeping wife and to his ever-living God he swore an oath: never again would she suffer childbirth. Not ever.

A difficult promise to keep, because he was young and yet a man. In years since he'd sometimes revisited his response to Elizabeth's trial and thought it extreme or unreasonable. But when he had offered that sacred oath, it was fitting and right, born of gratitude and love, and once made how could a promise to God be unmade?

Now, on those nights when he woke because Elizabeth moaned from a dream, and her leg brushed the soft spot behind his knee or she snatched a deeper breath, his awareness of her parted lips, of her fingers curled at her collar, grew so sharp that the only way he could not place fingertips against her neck, not lay his lips to the edge of her ear, was to steal from their bed and to think about some problem of nitrous oxide. Whether a person's size might alter the efficacy of the gas, whether the young would prove more or less susceptible to its exhilaration than the aged, whether Horace would experiment on himself before a meal or after, what might serve as counteragents, and also such mundane matters as how to organize notes. Through work, he kept his oath.

At the office in daylight, he filled notebooks with his observations and a precise record of his actions. He tested the potency of gas freshly manufactured against that which had sat a day, then against that which had sat two. He counted the breaths of nitrous oxide required before he began to feel the waves of pleasure that signaled its effects. Sitting in his dentist chair, a bladder and a notebook in his lap, he marked a single line for each inhalation. Generally, five breaths brought the pleasure-waves. They moved from his toes, pulsed along his tendons, and then nestled as a kindness against his skull, just below the epidermal layer. He heard waves as he had when on their honeymoon he breathed in the summer tang of Elizabeth's skin, and she held a seashell to his ear, and a quiet, personal ocean echoed. The nitrous oxide waves from his toes and the waves just below his scalp moved through his body toward each other—as soul mates find each other in the dark, he remembered thinking—and how miraculous that the waves moved in a dance, oceans meeting in perfect rhythm! His vision sharpened. Looking into his lap, thinking, "I must look into my lap," he turned the spigot and breathed again. What was he breathing? What was he? What was? Waves waltzed inside him. He could waltz, too, though he never had, had never really danced, but now he perceived his own grace and rhythm. God meant for him to waltz. He had only to stand up out of his chair.

He could not stand up.

Fine and good. Seated in his chair he waltzed, and seated in his chair he dreamed the interior of a great ballroom such as he knew existed only in Paris, and then Elizabeth waltzed with him, in the chair, his arm about her slender waist, her eyes wet with admiration, and his with happiness.

What had been a fresh dusting of snow the week before had become dirty, crusted, crushed by footfalls and yellowed with the urine of livestock and, Horace supposed, a few crude men and boys. He craved warmth and rain, a cleansing. Or a blizzard. Then bright blue sky and icicles glistening from every eave.

"We need more color, don't you think?" he said to Elizabeth one evening as she prepared supper. "Silk flowers. Gold curtains. I'd like you to wear blue, something like July in your scarf."

Elizabeth looked at him through eyes red and damp from the onion she'd chopped for a stew. She said, "Bring me that water heating on the stove, would you?"

He did, then wondered whether a chemical property in the gas could be distilled into drops that might dull the onion's sting. He rubbed the bump on the side of his noggin. That day, while under the influence of the gas, he had fallen out of the chair and knocked his head against a footstool. He hadn't felt it then. His body remained on the floor, that was true, but his five senses traveled, left him. Or perhaps the gas peeled apart whatever thin membrane separates this dull earth from heaven. Heaven is not above, he thought. It is around us, angels in every room, hidden to our sinner's eyes. Onions cloud our vision. The gas reveals brighter colors.

Elizabeth tilted her face to the ceiling and squeezed a rag to sprinkle her eyes with warm water, and she blinked so wide her brow wrinkled. He turned the bacon sizzling at the bottom of the otherwise empty soup pot. "Should I add the onions?" he asked.

She nodded, then reminded him to make time for their son, that Charley wanted to go sledding. "The boy needs outdoors activity," she said. She snapped the towel and hung it again. "My aunt Dorothy tells me that a physician from Boston conducted a study regarding frail boys. Contrary to expectation, their frailty did not make them vulnerable to the elements. In fact, activities held out of doors—play or work—strengthened them. A good sledding trip could inoculate Charley against fever or the mumps."

Horace put his face into the pot to breathe in the smoky bacon. His voice echoed back on him out of the sizzle. "You say *Boston* as if it is the Athens of the medical world. A residence in Boston does not make one privy to every secret of science and human physiology."

"We are not talking about you," she said. "We are talking about Charley. So, now. Sledding?"

Half a mile from the Wells's house, Governor Ellsworth owned a dozen acres that included a logged slope, and when the snow lay deep—as it did now—it covered the stumps. Horace and Charley marched toward that place, over hard-packed roads and then off into the glare of icier stuff in a copse of birch trees. Horace led, breaking a path to make it easier for Charley, who pulled his sled by a rope. The father pointed out animal tracks as they walked, and he identified deer, hare, and muskrat, but the son made few comments about the tracks and found none on his own, even when he walked right through them. In the cold, the boy's cheeks had reddened so completely Horace could hardly imagine them any other way. The sky seemed equally static—gray.

"If a boy holds his privates in his fist at night, will that keep him from wetting his bed?" Charley asked.

Horace thought maybe the boy had asked this same question of his mother, thus her insistence that they go sledding together.

"I've heard that," Horace said, "but there are other dangers to the practice. Best to use the chamber pot and relieve yourself properly."

"My line for the Christmas pageant at school is 'No! I would rather see Jesus!' and then I die."

"That's high-minded."

When they noticed the steeple of the asylum for the deaf above the trees in the distance, Charley said, "I wonder if it is better to be deaf or blind."

"Maybe we should put wax in your ears for a day. Send you down Governor Ellsworth's hill in a blindfold. Wouldn't that help you decide?"

"I want to know because I want to know which person to pity more. Who should get the most prayers? The deaf or the blind?"

"Pray for all equally, Charley. We are each unfortunate until we arrive in heaven. Has your school teacher changed his views about tooth-brushing after lunch?"

Charley changed his voice, made it squeak. *"That's a domestic lesson. Not a schoolhouse lesson."*

"You erode your own dignity when you mock your teacher's voice. It is important to respect him."

Charley hung his head, but Horace pointed to fox tracks, and the boy's thrill of adventure returned. Later, at the top of the slope that was their destination, Horace turned his son by the shoulders and looked into his ruddy, smooth face, fresh as an October apple. He said, "Charley, listen to me. This is important. Brush your teeth after lunch regardless of what Mr. Reed says. Do so in secret if you must. Encourage your schoolmates likewise."

Charley fell off his sled on the first run, his mitten filling with snow, and though Horace turned the mitten inside out and beat it against his thigh, Charley continued to complain about his fingers being wet and cold.

On the third run, a dog startled them when it charged barking from the wood toward Charley on his sled. White and grand, as if bred for some glacial European Alp, it wagged its tail, and when Charley tipped, the dog continued after the unpiloted sled as it crashed into an oak tree. The dog then coursed the slope with its nose to the snow, and father and son conferred as to whether Charley should tempt it with another run. When Horace said, "All right," Charley launched himself, the dog galloping alongside, barking low and full as the echoing report of a rifle, again ignoring Charley when the boy tumbled. Soon the dog became as much part of Charley's game as crashing, Charley calling, "Chase me! Chase me!" at the start of each run. The sled struck trees again and again until Horace, peeling slivers from where its rail had buckled, declared sledding to be at an end: "You enjoy the ride less than you do the fall."

As they trudged home, Charley said, "He always knows where we are," and it was true, the dog stayed with them as they walked, sometimes nuzzling under their hands, more often ahead, anticipating their path. The animal had chestnut-brown eyes and a tar-black nose, and it carried its long-furred tail upright as a flag. Powerful, when deep in a drift, the dog kept its head high and pushed through. It was in just such a drift, near where they had earlier seen fox tracks, that they heard something like a tree branch crack. The dog yipped, then spasmed, then turned on itself to twist in the snow. Its bark lost force, became high pitched, quick, yelp after yelp. Charley stepped toward the dog, but Horace stretched out an arm and yelled "Back!" even as something in him leapt forward, a familiar urge toward pain. The cold air grew colder.

Red stained the snow near the dog, which snapped its whole body, awkward convulsions that kept returning it to the same spot. The stain spread as if from the snow into the dog's fur, its underbelly, and especially around the right foreleg. That was where the jaws of the trap had bit.

Though his own blood pulsed powerfully in his temples, Horace worked to stay dispassionate in the face of the dog's plight. He recalled his encounter with that eviscerated bird trapped in a bush outside his home, how he calmed himself to free it. But these fangs, these claws, threatened greater harm. Horace moved in a half circle about the animal, crouching, studying. The dog kept at its frantic leaping until the stubborn trap had peeled away skin, bunching it as a man's shirt sleeve bunches above the elbow. The leg turned in an impossible way, bone broken, white tendons glistening. Yips became growls, and the growls became weary, and Horace noted that. Was it pain or surprise that caused the dog's first cry, he wondered. Now its primary concern appeared to be captivity and not pain, panic trumping its physical suffering. That matched expectations. Panic was a kind of exhilaration, such as that brought on by the gas.

Behind him he heard a whimper. His son, standing back as he'd been told but with eyes shut and his hands over his ears, his feet stamping at the snow. Would you rather be blind or deaf, Charley?

He called, and when Charley reached his side, he turned the boy by the shoulders to face the dog, steadied Charley's arms at his sides. "Do you see the problem?" he asked. "Look carefully. Do not guess. Speak with precision."

"I want to go home."

"Not yet. With precision. Tell me."

"The dog is caught in a trap. The leg is hurt."

Horace unwrapped his scarf, unbuttoned his coat. "How do you know it is hurt?"

Charley thought. "The blood. There is an awful lot of blood." The dog turned a circle, snarled. It gnawed at the metal trap.

"Blood indicates injury but not necessarily pain. Men gashed on the forehead sometimes feel next to nothing, though their faces be daubed with blood. So how can you tell the dog is hurt? What is different now than a few moments ago?"

Charley thought some more. His fingers played with the hem of his coat. He said, "It forgot us."

"Utterly."

"We don't matter."

"We don't," said Horace. "Even if we could make the hurt go away or make it worse, the dog is past caring. Its one concern is its own suffering."

Charley gasped, some sorrow greater than sobbing could describe. Horace whispered, "If it can remember we're here, regain awareness despite its pain, it might let us help. We'll wait."

He checked his pocket watch to count the minutes—he would make a note of them back home. The clouds remained leaden, and the gray allowed no shadows, though Horace still squinted against light flashing off the snow. He recalled a brighter morning from his Vermont boyhood, spent with his father placing wolf traps around the sheep meadow—his father's bare hands big as a giant's, knuckles pink against winter's white, and how deeply they buried the chains. Could Horace yank this trap loose? Unlikely. The ground must be frozen fast, or the dog would have pulled it himself. Those long-ago wolves had—or chewed their way free—and now Horace pondered whether they'd overcome pain through will, or—because life depended on it—shut down their capacity to feel? Was that, somehow, related to what Charley noticed? In its suffering the dog had forgotten them, secluded itself in a desolate cave dug out of its own agony. Reverend Hawes often said that through sin we separate from God. But what about pain, Reverend Hawes? Have you noticed how pain separates us from all God's creation? A hypothesis only, but consider Charley, who now wanders to lie curled against the rough base of an oak, hiding himself and his sympathy behind his broken sled. Consider the first pain of living, how it separates child from mother, and how other agonies and aches lead to separations. Blood from a vein, a tooth from its seat, heart from mind, thought from action.

Horace from his father. And nearly from Elizabeth.

Horace from himself.

He thought of the Gospel, how in His anguish even Jesus felt alone, forsaken. Yet He never separated from His essential self. He forgave when He could have destroyed. Perhaps that was the miracle—wracked with human pain and capable of anything, all the violence He didn't do.

Twelve minutes, and the dog stopped working at the trap, settled itself in the snow, and looked Horace's way. A beautiful animal, truly. Horace thought he could admire the dog a long time. He stuffed his gloves in his coat pockets and, in a crouch, offered a hand for the dog to smell. The dog sniffed at Horace's knuckles, the black nose wet and nostrils flaring, white breath puffing, the ribs' long cage swelling and shrinking. When Horace sat close enough, he reached with both hands and grasped the trap's jaws. Blood made the grip slippery, and searching for a release mechanism (he remembered such a mechanism from boyhood), his fingers fumbled, his hand striking the dog's shoulder, so the dog fell on him—teeth and claws and snarls. Horace's throat shut, though he made a noise like a scream, and he raised his arms to cover face and neck, kicked his legs. He might have closed his eyes; he saw nothing. In a moment he had scrambled free of the dog's reach, though it lunged until the trap's chain stretched taut.

Charley's cries sounded louder, and Horace remembered in distant images as if through a spyglass how the day had started: a sled, the buckles on Charley's boots, Elizabeth's kisses as they'd left her behind, men off on an adventure. Now that cavernous bark had returned to the dog, and Horace—disoriented from sudden nausea and a weakness throughout his legs—staggered to where Charley hid, and then, letting the boy sit on the broken sled, he pulled Charley away from the deep of the darkening woods until they could no longer hear the dog, and then they were home.

11

Levi Knowles, the tavern keeper, spread word among Hartford's penniless sort that any person requiring a tooth pull ought to visit the surgeon dentist Horace Wells, office at Asylum and Main Streets, for an operation without pain or cost. They came, did the poor—tannery workers, their children, an old man with no hands, a blind vagrant, and a half-dozen delinquents, including a gaunt Irish boy of twelve or thirteen with pox scars, who arrived at Horace's office that January day in 1845 already drunk on cheap applejack. Wisdom teeth.

"I'd like to keep 'em," the boy said, straightening up tall. "Drill holes in each. Make a bracelet. Wisdom's precious, right?"

Horace fingered under his own shirt collar, showed a charm Riggs had given him: the molar pulled while Horace slept the nitrous-oxide sleep, now fastened to a chain. "Wearing teeth is the newest fashion," Horace told the boy. "Like a whaler's tattoo."

With the help of his new clientele, Horace learned that the gas could erase the pain of tooth luxation in even the worst cases. An ox of a man, a drunkard heavy as three molasses barrels—if not four—came with a jaw so swollen he couldn't take rum except with a dropper. A few breaths of nitrous oxide put him to sleep. A woman, mother to seven, brought a mouth so ruined her oldest daughter had to tell her tale; how, exhausted from factory work, the mother had drowsed while sitting on the eave of a second-floor window and fallen into the yard on her face. Interrupting the surgery now and then to give the woman another breath or three of the gas, Horace worked for fifty-seven minutes to remove three incisors and reposition others. Later that same day, a teenaged girl with a chipped tooth admitted that she had once picked Dr. Wells's pocket on a night he'd visited Levi's tavern; after surgery she woke confused, mumbling about a golden horse that nudged her with its soft nose and huffed and puffed at her ear.

At first he approached each surgery as he always had, with locked jaw, expecting to change in that way he'd described to friends and Elizabeth the night of Colton's exhibition, the way he'd changed so often since the night his father died (he turned his mind from that), to become *not*-Horace. But no change came. Now, as patients slept, he could cut a gum without any deadening of self. He could pat a shoulder in kindness, whisper an assurance. He gave his patients gifts: a hard candy, or a Bible verse printed on a slip of paper. He could look in a mouth and see it as he would any machine with broken parts—a plow on his father's farm, or a meat grinder—something he could fix, and by fixing feel accomplishment and satisfaction. He remembered his patients' names: Desmond, Cornelia, Albert. Malachi did indeed keep his wisdom teeth.

With each surgery a foolish hope grew in Horace, one he knew to be grandiose and perhaps cloying yet one he prized, nevertheless, as Malachi prized wisdom. He dared not speak of it aloud even to Elizabeth, even to the caged songbirds in his office, for fear it would prove fleeting. Only on his knees, by candlelight and with folded hands, did he admit to a wish that it might be so. Could it? Could this discovery—the miracle of painlessness—prove a counterbalance against what suffering and injury he'd caused? Not just in his dental chair, not just pains he recalled, but also those he'd forgotten, those he'd visited on strangers and on loved ones, those accidental and those intended, from farm to city, from boyhood to today, as son and as husband, all the griefs, the heartaches, the quick or lasting agonies? If for generations to come his discovery erased humanity's torment, might what pain he had inflicted be redeemed?

Please, Lord. Let the uplift of your miracle exceed the weight of my sins, ease my burdens, and grant me peace. Through your Son, I pray.

Amen.

One January evening in 1845, when at last he'd convinced himself that nitrous oxide worked according to his theory, Horace sat at his desk, giddy with the exhilaration particular to success, and by the light of two candles he scratched out a letter to the person in Boston he knew best.

Dear Will,

Please recognize the URGENCY of the matter I will heretofore explain, and act with haste. I have discovered a process that makes pulling of teeth painless, and I wish to present this discovery in Boston. I do not write details here but I have learned that an Exhilarating Gas in precise doses renders the patient dead drunk deader than alcohol or laudanum. Fifteen operations under these conditions and every patient recovered and testified to having felt _NO PAIN_. Said operations have included simple extractions, exc. of collapsed roots, and shaving of spongy gums. All pain is erased as if by Divine Hand!

In Hartford word has spread of my success, but this discovery must be tested and established in Boston for the same reasons that led you & I to test our previous discovery there Fair or not Boston is where medicine in New England most matters. Thus, in Boston I'll make my case. Will you make arrangements for a presentation? I'll require a volunteer with a troubled tooth, but also witnesses. A class of medical students, maybe? Perhaps you can engage Dr. Warren of Mass. Medical College in this effort? Imagine the license his approval would afford!

Likely the principles of my discovery will apply also to Gen. Surgery. More about the gas when I see you.

Assure interested parties of my resolve that this discovery provide for the general benefit of mankind. I have no expectation nor desire for pecuniary benefit.

I am eager and I rush, thus the scrawl here that must pass for handwriting. Let us forgive one another and move forward. Good wishes to you. Regards to your Elizabeth.

Wells

II

BOSTON

12

On the morning her husband meant to leave for Boston, Elizabeth Wells lay awake in the silvery dark, listening to the neighbors' cows lowing for their feed. When the cacophony grew loudest she knew Mr. Larkin had arrived on his hay wagon. Then the sounds of dumb hunger faded as the cows ambled to the pasture's farthest fence. Horace slept through it all, strangely enough, Horace for whom insomnia was a talent—and today of all days. On his side, facing away, he made a breathy gurgle that put Elizabeth in mind of Charley as a dreaming infant, and with that thought, something inside her tipped out of balance, something she wanted only her husband to make right. Moonlight fell on the back of his neck where his hair curled, and she watched him until watching him hurt. Then she rested the palm of her hand on his shoulder; his wool nightshirt itched her fingertips. She moved, let her fingers fall from morning's darkness into that small strip of moonlight, let her knuckles brush his red curls.

She breathed him in, and she wondered, is this what a great man smells like? Could this be a man history will remember?

She shaped herself to the curl of his body until her breath crowded back on her from his neck, and she reached to touch his hip. She pictured in her mind a daughter with his reddish curls. She waited, and he didn't stir. Her motions against him were at first so slight she might have been moving only within herself. But she grew bold. Eyes closed. Breath calm. Her own pulse loud. Pressing herself against his back, a slow rub, she dreamed him rising above her, imagined her hands on his bare chest, her legs opening to welcome him.

Her body moved with such subtlety, he slept on, undisturbed.

In the carriage of a crowded railcar on its clanking and coughing way from Hartford to Springfield, Massachusetts, a woman and a girl of about fourteen talked louder than anyone else, louder even than the train's racket and the screeching baby in the woman's lap. "What is your favorite word today?" the woman asked the girl. "Obviate!" came the reply, accompanied by definition and etymology, even as the woman shook a rattle at the infant, singing in a high-pitched voice, "Baby, baby."

With a pencil, Horace scribbled a question in his notebook about infants and the gas, a theory about how much might stop a crying child. In Charley's first months, Horace and Elizabeth walked the house like ghouls as their son shook the window panes with his shrieks. During teething, the sleeplessness was worse still.

Now the woman was making motions with her hands, the day's low southern light bright on her fingers, long shadows flitting across the railcar, and when the train leaned into curves, those shadows touched Horace's lap. He'd seen such gestures when children from the deaf asylum came into Hartford for Sunday services. The hand motions were their language, precise and quick, powerful with intention. Watching the woman, he recalled the beauty of Elizabeth's hands as she arranged evergreen clippings in a vase, her long fingers so quiet and eloquent.

The girl made a fist of one hand and smacked the open palm of the other. She brushed fingers against her chin. The woman took the girl's hands and manipulated them to refine the gestures. But these two weren't deaf, were they? Hadn't they just been talking? The train leaned into another curve, and the baby leaned with it, the woman gasping and catching the child before it tumbled from her lap. The girl laughed, and the woman did, too, the disaster of the baby on the floor averted, oh happy blessing! The baby wailed as if upset by their giddiness.

When he approached the family, the woman frowned. "She's not disturbing you?"

Horace smiled an assurance. Now the girl had the rattle in her mouth as if she were a dog with a bone, and she growled to get the crying baby's attention. When that failed, Horace tongued his lips wet and whistled a passably accurate robin's call: *cheer-y-o, cheer-y-o, cheer-i-up!* The baby stopped crying, looked right then left, its face all curiosity. Horace whistled again, *cheer-y-o, cheer-y-o, cheer-i-up!* The baby grinned. The woman clapped.

She introduced herself as Mrs. William Sidwey of Holyoke, and these were daughters, youngest and oldest. The middle child, deaf since birth, now received her education in Hartford at Reverend Gallaudet's school. "Our visit done, we're homeward," Mrs. Sidwey said. She asked about his family.

"A son," he said. "No daughter."

"Mr. Sidwey and I have no son," said Mrs. Sidwey. She grinned at her oldest and pinched the girl's cheek. "Perhaps I should trade this one." Her daughter made a disgusted face with her mouth and motioned a hand response so the mother laughed before asking Horace, "Would your wife like this girl?"

He did not know how to answer. Something jovial was called for, a quip, but this was not a subject about which he could joke. He wondered at life's capriciousness, how one had a son, another daughters. How some gave birth with ease and grace; how others died. Or nearly did. Cribs and graves had its limitations.

"Is your baby teething? I'm a dentist. Shall I have a look?"

The train's brakes rasped, and in the sound he heard echoes of Elizabeth's confinement. Perhaps the gas could relieve childbirth's agonies as Elizabeth herself had hypothesized. But his gas annulled pain and only pain—not Death, greasy and long-fingered under the bed. Every miracle, he supposed, had its limitations.

Mrs. Sidwey held the babe toward him, and he probed the mouth. Emerging white pebbles. Teething, yes. "I've got some clove oil," he said. "A small dab won't harm her."

As he touched a cotton swab to the baby's gums, he asked, "How do you suppose it shapes us that our first knowledge of life is pain?"

The woman looked startled, but the conductor called, "Springfield!" and she began to collect belongings, to instruct the oldest daughter, and to hastily thank Dr. Wells for his help.

Buttoned in his warmest overcoat, cravat knotted high on his neck, he waved goodbye to the Sidweys as he stood in the bright sunlight on the platform waiting to continue his trip via the Boston-Albany line. He stamped his feet against the cold, though he wore his warmest boots, lined with wool. Elizabeth had packed in his trunk a few days' clothing and a pair of dress shoes freshly buffed and wrapped in tissue to wear at his presentation. "I would like to be there to see you," she had said. "You have earned this happiness." Amid his clothes he had placed his notebooks so that interested parties might review and invite publication of his science, and around his neck he carried that gift from Riggs, the upper molar yanked on the historic day, now a traveling charm. On his person he also carried an envelope with the reply letter Morton had sent explaining how Horace would make his presentation to Dr. John C. Warren's class in surgical medicine at the Massachusetts Medical College, and that it would involve an amputation—not a tooth pull. Unnerving, that, because it would be a first, but also thrilling. What better proof?

Steam from the train's engine hung low and obstructed Horace's view on the way to Boston. With the toe of his boot, he tap-tap-tapped the traveling trunk sitting on the cabin floor, considered the bladder inside, and the gas. Curious, this tug. Like the slightest hunger. He'd always been a man to snack, to steal a shred of bread or crunch an apple between meals, answering a bodily desire he saw no reason to resist. This was the first time he'd felt so about the gas, and when he considered why, he thought about waves and ease. A breath or two would do it. But on a train? Among his fellow passengers? There was no law against such a thing, yet he felt a vague reluctance. It seemed bad manners or something. So, as a distraction from that gas-hunger, he amused himself by imitating the gestures of the Sidwey mother and daughter, inventing movements and giving them invented meaning: drawing lines on the palm of one hand with the other's thumb (to say *I'm sorry*) or wiggling fingers near his skull (to mean *imagine*). Imagine, he thought, and did: Elizabeth with daughters.

He rubbed his eyes. He'd not meant for his thoughts to arrive here, reminding him of the oath by which he had spared Elizabeth another birth, an anguish she might after all want. He knew his vow was no kindness. He understood the cost, that after all these years some part of their marriage had dampened.

Yet she lived.

Miles ahead of the train's arrival, Horace smelled Boston. He could not say how much of the stink was rubbish burning and how much was hog butchery, nor could he say what part was excrement or cat urine or shoe black. It was all of a piece, so pungent that even through the train's closed windows it punched him in the nose, gagged him into a cough. Familiar, that smell, and with it came an old wariness. Twice the city had hurt him, when he lived there as an apprentice and again with that Morton business. "Do not trust Morton," Riggs had said before this trip began, a concern Horace waved aside. Morton he could depend on; the man was predictable in his vices. Horace could divine his smells, perhaps too well. But Boston confounded him.

This time will be different, he decided. This time, Horace Wells brings a discovery to change the world.

Morton met Horace at the Boston station, and he'd brought along a chemist, for what purpose he did not explain. None of the men shook hands, but stood stiffly, a quick nod their warmest greeting. In the days since Horace and Morton had met at Coles Barber Shop, the latter had grown a beard in the manner of a Nantucket whaling captain, chin and cheeks covered but the upper lip shaved, and the chemist wore the same style, though with eyeglasses. A Boston fashion, Horace decided. On Morton, the beard suggested an underhanded banker, especially when combined with that sharp nose and his underbite. On the chemist, however, the beard seemed an accident, a failure to shave properly. The chemist's eyes, magnified behind his lenses, seemed always to look where Horace was not. "My home is humble," Morton was saying, arguing for Horace not to stay at an inn as he'd planned. Morton bent over to retie a length of twine that kept the sole of his left shoe from flapping. "Cats scrap nightly over the alley trash, but the lodgings come at no cost to you. More importantly, my Elizabeth insists."

Later, in a tavern over a lunch table, Horace leaned toward Morton and the chemist and their beards, gesturing with a chicken leg, explaining his discovery. The chemist frowned. By now Morton had explained that this man, Charles T. Jackson, had at one time been Morton's landlord. He served Boston's top medical men, so had the associations by which Horace's exhibition had been arranged—though Jackson anticipated failure. Never had the chemist heard of a gas to annul pain. "Nitrous oxide has been studied for decades," he said. "If it works as you say, why has no one else realized your discovery? I formulate nitrous oxide, Dr. Wells. Nothing in its makeup suggests an application as you describe. Tuberculars inhale it to stimulate their lungs, you know. It creates excitability, not insensibility. Surely you've read Davy on the subject."

Horace remembered that Colton had also mentioned Davy. Upon return to Hartford, he decided, he'd find and read the man's papers. But to Jackson he said nothing to reveal his ignorance, only leaned back in his chair and spread his arms, as if welcoming whatever Jackson might say next. Jackson took the bait.

"If Davy didn't find that nitrous oxide annuls pain," he said, "then it doesn't."

Horace fingered beneath his collar, showed them the chain with the molar. "My own tooth—," he said, "and I felt nothing. Not a prick!"

"Perhaps you managed a tooth pull," said Jackson, "but what is that compared to a leg amputation? Imagine it, Dr. Wells. Would you inhale nitrous oxide and submit yourself to the saw?"

"No reason to consider it. My limbs require no alteration."

Morton helped himself to a chicken leg from Horace's plate and gnawed at it, and Horace again marked that old suspicion on Morton's face, a permanent expression that said, *We are an earth full of devils and antagonists.* Morton swallowed. "Warren doesn't believe your claim, either," he said. "He is as mighty a skeptic as God ever made."

Horace dropped a bone and the tin plate rang. He wiped grease from his fingers on the napkin tucked into his shirt, then scratched at his cheeks. "You believe it, though, don't you, Will." He hoped not to sound questioning, but definitive, master to apprentice.

"You were my teacher, so I asked Jackson to arrange things. But we are scientists here, and our profession requires proof. Your claim—"

"It is no claim," Horace said. "It is a discovery."

Jackson rapped his soup spoon against the tabletop, and Horace looked to him, but the man's eyes stared left toward a table of solicitors.

"Horace," said Morton, "out of respect for our shared history, I'm asking you. We've not advertised this event. If you return to Hartford and your practice, no one will know. Your reputation remains intact."

"I've read your essay on teeth cleaning," said Jackson. "A career can stand on such work."

Horace placed a bit of chicken from his own plate on Morton's. A gift. He smiled. "Your pessimism is misplaced. Your imaginations are limited. A world that is no vale of tears—how can anyone argue against such a thing?"

Jackson covered his smirk with a fist. "A painless world? Don't you study history, Dr. Wells? Even if your method relieves all pain, someone else will invent new ways to inflict it."

That evening, Horace was reacquainted with Morton's Elizabeth, her eyes shrouded in melancholy as always and her dress still tightly laced. Once she had been Miss Elizabeth Whitman of Farmington, Connecticut, daughter of Mr. Edward Whitman, a farmer widely admired for his lack of humor. She had met her future husband when she brought her bad tooth to him in Hartford. Though Morton healed her mouth, she steadfastly refused to smile, as if she'd inherited the family aversion to gaiety, a trait that seemed to appeal to Morton as much as did her pretty brunette ringlets and the dresses she wore immodestly low off the shoulder. It was because their wives shared a first name that the men, to avoid confusion, referred to "my Elizabeth" and "your Elizabeth." In a playful moment, Horace had once joked that Morton seemed eager to replicate Horace's life detail by detail. "First you take my knowledge of dentistry, then my manner of managing a practice, then a woman with the same name as my wife! When your Elizabeth bears you a son and you name him Charles and move to Lord's Hill, then I'll know that I've never been more than half my true self—and you the other part."

The hour was late, candles tossing light across the plates left greasy after the day's last meal, though when Horace yawned it came from nerves rather than fatigue. A thrilling and daunting day, traveling from Hartford, and then a Boston ramble, including a scouting trip to the Massachusetts General Hospital ("Where history awaits you," Morton had said, grinning), and to a post office so Horace could mail a letter to his Elizabeth. Then back to Morton's apartment, where now Horace with his host and hostess each quaffed rum from mugs.

Morton's Elizabeth grasped Horace's coat sleeve, canted her head toward him, her movements liquid and lazy. "Take me home with you," she begged, a little whine in her plea. "Boston will kill me yet. How can people endure such crowds? And the stink! A little rose-scented oil dabbed under my nose and the city becomes bearable, but only that. I miss Farmington. Air is breathable there. Please, Wells, take me home when you go."

"You stay with me," Morton said as his arm encircled her, pulled her so she nearly tipped her chair, and her laughter was a squeal. Her skirt bunched, and Horace let himself look at her ankles, the flex and turn. Morton spilled his mug of rum into her lap.

"Ah!" she cried. "Will nothing civilize a man from Ohio?"

Horace looked for a towel or rag to clean the spill, but stopped when he saw that Morton and his Elizabeth ignored the mess. Instead, Morton nuzzled his wife's neck. "Pshaw, girl," he said. "I'm ill-mannered but not a bad man. And you know it, too." Then he pointed across the room at the bladder Horace had unpacked. "What do you say, Wells? Shall we? Better than my Elizabeth's Farmington air from what I hear."

So this was why Morton had wanted him to stay here rather than at the inn. Horace did not want to share, no. But in the letter to his own Elizabeth he'd confessed fears of failure, admitted how moment by moment his heart lunged between despair and exhilaration. The gas, he knew, could settle him.

"I'll leave you men to your science," said that other Elizabeth, who kissed each on the cheek and retired to the apartment's bedroom. Horace followed Morton behind a dark blanket hung as a curtain across a doorway and into a space a bit smaller than the pantry at Lord's Hill. Two short stools, a circular table not much broader than a stool, cabinet shelves crowded with journals and books and half a dozen human jawbones, teeth intact. "Models for my plates," Morton said. "Too ghoulish for the office. The patients would rather not know." Roaches scurried as Morton pushed aside a tin plate littered with cheese rinds and peeled egg shells. He motioned for Horace to put the bladder where the plate had been.

Horace said, "Jackson's cock-eyed way of looking is disconcerting, isn't it?"

"He's an odd one, sure. Do you know, he insists he had the idea for the telegraph? That on some cruise to Europe he met a fellow passenger. Gave him all the details of his theory. 'That passenger was Samuel Morse!' he told me. 'Stole my invention!' He's mad. I'm convinced he'll die in an asylum. But he's a top-notch chemist. I pay him for the materials I need for my solder and plates. He thinks you're daffy, too, with this theory about nitrous oxide."

Horace checked the bladder's faucet, touched his lips to its spigot as does a man testing a pipe. "I wouldn't have come if painless surgery were only a theory," he said. "I've proven it on man, woman, child, portly or emaciated, Congregational or Episcopal."

"Episcopal? Then let's toast the sanctified genius of Horace Wells! Tomorrow's eve, all Boston will be alight with bonfires celebrating you."

One of Morton's dependable vices: to mock another's better qualities so they seemed shameful. But Horace paid no mind. Instead, he calculated the number of inhalations needed for the next day's exhibition, and given the volume of gas per bladder, arrived at a sum they could breathe this night. "Three each," he said, "should do."

Not long after, Horace found himself strolling through his house on Lord's Hill feeling the weight of his full bladder, more concerned with where to relieve himself than how he found his way from Boston back home. He opened doors in a long hallway—a dream hall, he knew—but none led to the closet where he could piss. One door opened to the bedroom he and Elizabeth shared, and behind another lay the Boston office where he and Morton had argued about a woman in Morton's dentist chair and liberties taken. Behind a third door, he found his father at a sink basin shaving his cheeks clean, and his father said, "Tell no one. It's our secret." He opened doors to Charley's bedroom and to the workshop and, at last, to a water closet. The closet had three windows, and through each he saw a bright blackness, a darkness that somehow illuminated. He pissed in a pot, and the ringing in the pot became a tune he recognized. He sang along:

Yankee Doodle went to town
A-riding on a pony
Stuck a feather in his hat
And called it macaroni.

Yankee Doodle, keep it up
Yankee Doodle dandy
Mind the music and the step
And with the girls be handy.

Father and I went down to camp
Along with Captain Gooding

And there we saw the men and boys
As thick as hasty pudding.

And singing along with him there in the water closet was Charley, who gestured to him as the girl on the train had gestured. And Charley's gestures made perfect sense to Horace, who understood that what the boy was both motioning and singing was a song about his mother, about Horace's Elizabeth.

Father and I peeked in the room
where mother was in labor,
she breathed the gas and felt no pain
"A girl!" cried out the neighbor.

Yankee Doodle, keep it up
Yankee Doodle dandy
Mind the music and the step
And with my girl be handy.

Boy and girl, husband and wife, four corners on a perfect square. Horace woke, ecstatic, on the floor in Morton's cold study, and he leaned against a wall and enjoyed the heat of his tears and understood that his daughter's name would be Helen. A few steps away, Morton sat unbalanced on a stool, tipping this way and that and laughing at something Horace could not see. Then Morton clapped together two naked jawbones from his collection as if to shape a mouth, and he fit that mouth over the spigot, opened the faucet, and let the jawbones inhale a share of the gas.

13

Morton had called the building Warren's Castle, and his naming was apt.

The Massachusetts General Hospital imposed itself on the cityscape, a pillared fortress realized through the willpower of New England's pre-eminent surgeon, Dr. John Collins Warren. At its peak, a dome sheltered the surgical amphitheater, Warren's Roost, the high point physically and figuratively for the country's medical profession. A surgeon's heaven, all light and space.

In the building's bowels, however: a charitable hell. Even outside, passersby could hear the cries of the destitute therein. Shake the poor house and out fall its infirm, its crippled, and its decrepit, gangrenous, yellow-skinned, gouty, shrieking with syphilis—and here they land. A rich man's doctor visits him at the mansion; a poor man's doctor works here.

To this place came Horace Wells, taking two stairs at a stride, his eyes bloodshot and his head light with laughing-gas dreams, a hog's bladder full of relief tucked under his arm. He coughed to clear his lungs of some papery sensation, peelings from a wasps nest, sped his step to outpace the ghastly chorus of ailing poor. But the sound pervaded, mingling with the complaints of crows perched on the roof's edge. Horace stopped, craned his neck to better see the birds, dark and healthy, their feathers shining violet and blue in this new day's light.

Something was amiss.

Those painful cries? They recalled for him the white dog, the disembowled cardinal outside his cottage door, the mad girl at the institute whose tooth he pulled. Expectant, he waited for the change he'd only ever been able to describe as *not*-Horace. But nothing happened.

Listen again, he told himself. So he closed his eyes. The crows quieted. The cries from below grew louder. Those human griefs. Merciful Lord, he thought, how pure they sound.

Still, he remained himself.

At the third floor landing, he caught up with a slow-climbing, ancient fellow. The older man stooped, and he wore a chaotic spray of thin gray hair, some of which had fallen out and lay squiggled across the black wool cape that covered his shoulders. He rubbed the back of his hand across his hooked nose. Lines creased his face the way fissures crease granite cliffs. Horace had the sense that he walked beside a mythological creature: a gryphon, perhaps—lion and eagle and man.

"Dr. Warren?"

The man canted his head without breaking stride, and a quick change in his countenance suggested that the name had a bitter taste.

"Yes," he said. "I'm Warren." At the fourth floor, he said, "You are the dentist."

Warren opened a door that led into the amphitheater, a chamber with room for several surgical tables but containing only one, and, higher, a surrounding gallery of four rows, at the moment empty. Bolted into the walls were a tangle of pulleys and hooks and rings, heavy iron and black, to stretch the intractable patient until all fight ended and the muscles relaxed enough to be cut. Sunlight dazzled Horace, an enchantment sifting through the vast skylights, by some optical science cleaner even than that outside on the street. Warren hung his cape in a wardrobe, which itself stood beside two unusual furnishings and figures: a glass case in which dangled a human skeleton, and adjacent to that an Egyptian sarcophagus opened at its top to reveal the head of an unwrapped mummy. Horace had never seen a mummy. Its skin had become a gray, shriveled substance like leather. Details in the jaw suggested that the teeth were intact.

"Following my lecture," Warren said, "I have a surgery scheduled during which I intend to remove a man's arm from just above the elbow. A sawyer. Caught the arm between a log and a brick wall. Shattered the bones, infection set in. We'll let the poor fellow breathe your gas, see how it works."

"I admire your book," Horace said. He wanted to smile but nerves prevented him.

"Which book?"

"*Comparative View of the Sensorial and Nervous Systems in Men and Animals.* I found your conclusions proving God to be particularly satisfying."

"I did not prove the existence of God. I was very careful in my wording. 'A single, omniscient being.'"

There. Again Horace felt it. That wasps nest in his lungs. He coughed. "I took that to mean the Almighty."

Warren puffed, and his breath lifted bangs from his forehead. "I have faith," he said, "and I have science. Each heartens me, but I never mistake one for the other." He pulled notes from his briefcase, then fell silent, reading, and for a long moment as he read he lay his hand on the surgical table as if offering it comfort.

A decade or so earlier, while apprenticing with a dentist in Boston, Horace had attended two surgeries, both in a small dismal room where his cheap-soled shoes had made an unpleasant peeling sound as he walked the floor, tacky with blood. Here in Warren's Roost, someone had soap-scrubbed the boards. Sawdust littered the floor thickly. Knives and saws were arrayed on a white linen cloth draped over a table; beside them a deep white basin of clean water awaited the surgeon's smeared hands and tools. Near the table was a stove for firing iron pieces into white heat to cauterize wounds.

Through doorways high above, students now shuffled, chatting, descending the rows of the theater, choosing seats. Horace smelled the sweetness of a lit cigar. Many of the students wore sea-captain beards in that style favored by Morton and Jackson, and perhaps their ubiquity explained why Horace didn't notice Morton until he heard someone call "Wells!" and saw his former student waving from a topmost seat.

Horace waved back. Then he noticed a student point at him, comment to another, who turned to hide his laugh. Feeling conspicuous with an animal bladder clutched under his arm, Horace sought Warren, who had moved with his notes to an alcove. He whispered, "Where, sir, may I place this?"

"Nowhere. Hold it until I summon you."

Horace shifted the burden to his other arm.

"This is a Bulfinch building, I hear," he said. Warren grunted, his attention on his notes. Horace said, "He also designed the state house in Hartford."

"And the United States capitol building," said Warren. "What is your point?"

"That there are connections between our cities."

"Obvious on its face." Warren put aside his notes and addressed Horace directly. "I stopped in Hartford once. En route to Yale. Ate at some inn where the cook charred the steak. Did I mention that you'll speak about your theory following my lecture?"

"You did." Horace paused, unsure whether to speak what was on his mind. "It's not a theory, doctor. It's a discovery."

"The human brain works efficiently and with its own secret genius— of which pain is a part. It is a complicated phenomenon. I doubt you've solved it."

"I do not claim to understand pain—"

"Morton showed me your letter. You think you've come upon God's own breath, but you mustn't romanticize scientific inquiry, and you must consider history. Physicians once believed opium would erase all pain. Then there was that Mesmer foolishness. We're all looking for heaven on earth, Dr. . . ."

"Wells."

" . . . but we left Eden long ago. I doubt our banishment ends because of what's inside that sheep sack."

"This is a pig's bladder."

Warren nodded. "Apparently, I need more study in barnyard anatomy."

Then he retrieved his cape from the wardrobe, fastened it off his shoulders, and stood straight as his stooped back would allow—becoming again the lion-eagle-man.

Stepping out to his stage, he roared a lecture about organic diseases of the heart. Horace tried to listen, but he could not concentrate. First Morton and Jackson, now Warren, had attempted to make a chimera of his prospects. He reached into his shirt and touched his own tooth, squeezed the hardness of it between his fingers, assured by its familiar jaggedness. Looking up, he found the mummy staring at him—its settled features, its immortal face, coaxing him near. He stepped closer and with a finger in the air traced the sharpness of the temporal line and the sunkenness of the sphenoid bone. At the cheeks, he noticed, the zygomatic bones sat wide, and the nose flattened at the tip, and the lower jaw sat so far back as to make an overbite. The lips receded to show brown teeth, a gentle eternal smile that seemed to say, "Death isn't so bad." Horace whispered without expecting an answer, "What killed you?"

Had the mummy wanted to reply, and had death allowed such a thing, had priests not removed his tongue, and had his larynx not been calcified for centuries, he would have said, "I asphyxiated. A need to sneeze. I aspirated an almond."

Horace whispered again.

A bee sting is what the mummy recalled, that first memory of pain. At wheat planting, in the third year of boyhood. Though dead these centuries, he felt certain of his recollection; he had always used painful episodes as a way to mark his personal history. Knifing, bright pains inside his skull had coincided with the summer his brother was born; the day when a hard knee to the testicles liquefied his intestines was also the day his father said, "You've become a man." What the mummy most wanted to tell Horace was that in anger he once clenched his wife's hand and broke three of her fingers. Her knuckles healed crookedly and ached thereafter, making her useless and a discomfort to him every time he watched her eat, so he sent her away and married another. That was during pomegranate harvest; his sixteenth year. He had felt so old.

The mummy's face seemed to turn upward a bit, as if in prayer. Horace wondered if it was a trick of the light.

The mummy wanted to say, "We dead can't hurt anyone. That's a comfort." But because he could not speak, the mummy turned his attention back to Dr. Warren, who was about to finish his lecture on hazards to the human heart. The mummy had heard it before. It was his favorite. He wanted to explain to Horace what harming people—even to preserve their health—does to a man's heart. He'd seen Dr. Warren change over the years, become steel. "His work," the mummy wanted to say, "has scraped off his soft spots. He is all hardness."

Then Warren was calling, identifying Horace to his students only as a surgeon dentist from Hartford, so that Horace felt the need to present himself by name and to establish his authority by listing his credentials. Speaking too quickly, he enumerated what he knew of nitrous oxide, what he'd learned from Gardner Q. Colton's exhibition coupled with his own observations. He showed his tooth on a chain; a few students clucked. He spoke of how when breathing the gas he'd heard heaven's bell tolling. He said that he'd felt nothing when his tooth came free. When he finished, some students coughed. The cigar smoker tapped his ash. Asking for questions, Horace received none.

Warren tugged a tasseled rope affixed to the wall, and somewhere outside the chamber a bell rang. After a few moments the door near the mummy opened and in shuffled a man, barefoot and trembling, wearing only a muslin robe, his left arm gathered in a sling: the sawyer with his shattered bone. Blood and pus had stained the cloth brown, and with the man came a pungent, nauseating odor, something like a drunkard's vomit. The man startled when he saw the mummy, backed toward the door when he noticed saws and knives. Warren took him by the arm that was whole and whispered to him. Horace smiled as if he and the man had just met at church choir rehearsal, but he felt embarrassed by the falsity of it.

"Dr. Wells, will you explain the procedure to the patient?"

As Horace spoke, the patient stared one by one at each pulley and iron ring, each hook. His skin shined with fever-sweat, and his whiskers needed a razor. Green and yellow bruises colored his skin from damaged arm to neck, and he stood so as to give his good shoulder to the world, to let it receive the blows the other could not bear.

The man cocked his head toward Horace, then spoke, his voice a scrape in the air. "I'll not feel a thing?"

Horace nodded.

"You go first."

Some laughter from the gallery. Horace noticed the grins, including Morton's. And now that of Jackson, too, who had arrived and sat by Morton, his eyes looking nowhere, mouth open as a fish's.

Horace said to the man, "I had a tooth pulled and felt nothing."

The patient barked. He inhaled as if it were his last breath, then rasped, "I'd rather take a pistol ball in the ear than lie on that table."

Warren touched the man's good shoulder but was shrugged away. With a last sad look at the mummy, the sawyer stepped from the amphitheater, closing the door behind him as if on a room of sleeping children.

"Time and again, this happens," Warren said softly, for Horace only. "I don't begrudge any of them." He stepped back out before the gallery.

"Gentlemen, we have no patient. Thus, we have no exhibition."

The response was immediate and mundane: notebooks shut, leather straps buckled, a general shuffle and murmuring. Horace watched the students turn from him as if he'd never been, and he felt that wasps nest in his lungs flake apart into dry bits. He coughed twice, but the sensation still plagued him. What now? All this way to Boston, and for nothing? "But Dr. Warren!" he was saying, "but Dr. Warren!" though Warren didn't seem to hear, was instead answering questions put to him by a crowd of students.

Horace clutched his bladder, fought the urge to find a quiet spot where he could breathe the gas, calm himself, forget how his discovery—and he himself—had been dismissed.

Then he noticed Morton pointing to a student sitting near him and motioning for Warren's attention. Even from Horace's distant vantage, he could see that the student's face was swollen along the left jaw.

"This one," shouted Morton. "He needs a tooth pulled."

Soon, Horace was peeking into the young man's mouth. The student sneezed, then groaned and complained about the combined misery of head cold and toothache, but he declined immediate surgery because he needed to keep a social appointment. Perhaps later? Talk of schedules followed, and Warren declared that if an exhibition could be arranged for after his supper, he would attend. Hearing that, most students agreed also to change their evening plans. The amphitheater had been reserved for later that night, but Warren knew of a hall on Washington Street and agreed to see to the details.

"A tooth offers less drama," he said, "but that's fine. I prefer a quiet evening."

A half hour later, Horace and Morton walked through the coal-smoke dusk of a winter's late afternoon, heading in the direction of Morton's lodging. The latter walked with fists in his coat pockets; Horace kept his hands busy, fingers alighting on the bladder's faucet one moment, scratching at his cheeks the next. He worried that Morton might think him apprehensive about the evening, and he did not want to show Morton any weakness. Though perhaps he was apprehensive, a bit. The bladder he hugged against his body carried so many of his wishes. Courage, he told himself. Delay does not foretell disaster.

"But Warren—you were right, Will. He doesn't believe me."

"I'm convinced, though. Last night I lost all doubt. The gas is a miracle."

Around them, Boston was in full roar. Mongrels barked at lowing cattle, bells tinny and loud around their necks. A Negro house servant dumped broken lobster shells in the gutter and with a shovel buried them under dirty snow. Drunkards cheered as tavern workers rolled rum barrels down a ramp into a cellar. From up the street came a one-eyed man hauling a cart through the slush, and in a clear tenor he sang out his wares: pots, pans, ropes and twine, horseshoes full of good fortune.

Horace stopped in front of a building newer than its neighbors. Morton turned back. "What?" he asked.

"This bookstore," Horace said, pointing. "When I apprenticed, a lodging house stood on its site. One evening on my way home, I joined a crowd to watch it burn."

"I know the store's owner. I've filled a cavity for his wife."

Horace peered in the window at his reflection, then past it to the books on display. "It's a thing to see, a big building like that aflame. Even in November, its heat made me want to shed my coat. But a woman stood among the crowd, and I couldn't be so immodest."

Morton chuckled. Horace glanced over his shoulder at him but didn't smile.

"She kept shouting a name, voice strong at first, though growing shrill. Timbers exploded, cracking like musket fire. We could still hear her scream the name, her shrieks. Her son's name, we later learned."

"What was he called?"

Horace meant to speak, but when he inhaled cold air seized his lungs. He coughed, and one hack led to another, such a wracking that his eyes teared. When he recovered, he said, "She rushed in. A wall collapsed, eased itself into the rubble. A great flame erupted, and at last we took action, seeking water and buckets. But no one followed into the ruin." Now the store window showed him bent as if the woman's pain yet burdened him. He supposed it did. Straightening his back, he said, "I should purchase a book."

Morton spit on the sidewalk. "A strange atonement." He tapped the bookstore's wall with his boot toe, and when next he spoke his voice had the practiced hush of a conspirator. "Wells. That business . . ."

"Which business?"

Horace knew but had decided not to make this conversation easy, and Morton, as if he understood, smiled a mean smile. When he spoke again he raised his voice so even passersby could hear. "The woman in my chair that day. My own immodesty." Horace gave no reaction. Let Morton lift himself up from the gutter.

"I'm grateful for your continued discretion," Morton said, "especially around my Elizabeth. But a contract is a contract, and I have felt obliged to follow ours. Your early leave-taking damaged the business. I should be the party demanding restitution."

"I left with cause: my partner's turpitude. Thus, I am owed my investment."

The look on Morton's face suggested that he took the thought seriously. He nodded, tugged hairs on his chin. "*Turpitude?*" he responded, his tone grave. "How can you say that word without giggling?"

The medical student with the abscessed tooth and head cold did not practice good oral hygiene. This was clear to Horace that night in the hall on Washington Street when the student opened his mouth. Two teeth showed hints of cavity decay. Perhaps there would be time for that. The abscessed tooth—the mandibular second premolar—needed to be pulled and the root bed cleaned.

"You have weak teeth," Horace said, checking the arrangement of his tools. "Do them a favor and brush more often."

The student mumbled, "My father also has weak teeth."

"Some people have the teeth of horses," Horace said. "Others have teeth like chickens."

"Chickens don't have teeth."

Horace smiled. "Because they don't brush."

Other students crowded near, some standing on chairs or stools to see. Warren loomed behind the patient, who sat in a bentwood chair, there being no dentist chair with a proper headrest. The patient tilted back his head, and Horace asked for light. Morton, who held the hurricane lamp, adjusted its position. "My arm tires, Wells," he said. "Speed your preparations."

"Hand the lamp to another, if you must," said Horace. "I'll take my time."

Horace rubbed his hands on his apron to hide how they trembled. He coughed, that papery crinkle in his lungs still plaguing him. With his tongue, he worked the empty space where his molar had been. The patient sneezed, and Horace took the moment to offer a fast, silent prayer that he be worthy to convey the Almighty's blessing of surgery without pain, that here and now the Lord would make this miracle known. But the prayer failed to calm him; his hands trembled still.

He undid his cravat and removed his jacket, pulled at his shirt to allow air against his clammy skin. "Don't crowd so much," he told the students, who managed half a shuffle back at most. The patient's eyes flitted from this face to that. Horace once more checked the order of the tools on his tray. He raised his arm to wipe his shirtsleeve across his forehead.

Morton asked, "Are you ill, Wells?"

"Just hold that light steady."

Warren, the gryphon, from his perch behind the patient's head, had said little since arriving, only a comment about how his wife had prepared that night's beef with dried corn and rum, "an odd concoction."

The boy's name. The boy who died in the fire. Outside the bookstore, Horace had wanted to tell Morton. The boy's name had been Will. His mother had called it. Will. Will. And the woman in Morton's dentist chair—she, too, had cried Will, Will.

Three breaths of the gas, and the patient giggled. "Dr. Wells," he said, "everyone has the face of a mouse."

Horace opened the faucet again. He counted the patient's breaths, and with three more shut down the faucet. Students again drew close, their sour smells and snide murmurs, and he shouted to give him room. Boston! How he loathed this city! His pulse hammered out an urge to inhale the gas himself.

When the patient's eyes shut and his head rolled, Warren caught, held it steady. Horace blinked sweat out of his eyes, fingered open the patient's mouth, fit the tooth key in place. A quick yank, and the tooth came clean.

But the patient yelped.

The wasps nest in Horace's chest broke apart.

"Not asleep?" said Morton. "What—?"

Horace stood still, arms weak and at his side, the premolar bloody in his tooth key, the room silent with confirmation of what everyone knew all along.

"What a wasted night," a student said. "Just a humbug."

Warren let go the patient's head, which lolled to the side, blood trickling in a crooked line from mouth to cheek to neck. The patient blinked in sequences, twice, then twice again. Groaned. Horace struggled to breathe. Flakes of wasps nest choked him. He listened with all his concentration, as if he might find that the whimper came from someone else, not his patient.

"He felt something," someone said.

"Imagine an amputation."

Horace looked to Morton, whose face had reddened, who shook his head at Horace, then turned on his heel to leave the scene—let flames of failure consume the building. Someone laughed. Another shouted, "Hartford! Hartford, of all places!" and another guffawed. Horace lunged forward, his ear near the patient's lips. In the giddy bustle, Horace tried to hear, tried to make sense of the roar in the room, a strange new sound above all that. Like Warren's voice, like Morton's, like all Boston's voices gathered in a low, dizzying chant: *Humbledy-hum. Hum-hum-aroo. Humbuggery. Humbughum-bughumbug!*

And above them all, Boston's loudest voice, the shriek of a mother, drawn by pain to death.

14

January 20, 1845

Tonight, I admit error. I failed a promising young dentist.

I will not name him in this journal, because posterity has no need to immortalize every philosopher of science who has fallen short. We are legion.

He believed, wrongly, that the exhilarating gas nitrous oxide could render a patient insensible to pain, and he hoped to make an exhibition of his theory here. I granted permission, and assembled students and other fine physicians at a hall on Washington Street. I permitted this gathering though the dentist's theories struck me as fallacious. Now I know that a private exhibition was in order. If convinced, I might then have let the dentist present his findings to the larger medical community. But I was distracted—as I am too often these days—by diminishing time.

Already I have exceeded my father's allotment of years by seven. How long before I am called home? Sinner that I am, I overspend what hours remain. I read while walking, teach while eating, write my books on the Sabbath days. I demand efficiency! Efficiency, I have this evening learned, is itself a sort of malice.

The dentist failed, as I noted. The patient showed evident pain.

What happened next troubles me still.

We should have all been saddened that the young dentist was wrong. Imagine the boon to mankind had he discovered how to impair pain and allow for surgery without suffering! For me? What a strange peace it would grant, one I've not known since my youth, before I took up the scalpel and saw. That is a peace the nature of which I no longer remember.

But our medical students, of the highest quality, are yet too young, are yet strangers to failure and impatient in its presence. One spoke the word *humbug,* and another took up the chant. The students had rearranged schedules, canceled appointments, taken time from their studies to witness a promised miracle of apostolic proportion. Instead they saw quackery, so hissed their irritation. "All's not so well that Wells ends," shouted one, making a play of the young dentist's last name (and there, I have identified him after all). One crumpled the notes he had jotted, then tossed the balled paper at the dentist's head. I glared; he'll hear from me tomorrow.

When I had met the dentist earlier that day, what I saw in his face was conviction and possibility, a sense that the universe had an order he understood. Now all was chaos. The gas had betrayed him, and nothing could be trusted. Perhaps a chair would break under his weight, or a ladle of well water fail to quench his thirst; in a storm an umbrella would let through the rain. I saw all that on his face. "Another patient!" he cried. "I shut off the gas too soon. You see, he sleeps even now. That groan—it was not from the tooth pull but from something he saw in a dream. Stay! We'll do it again. Watch—"

He lifted a scalpel from the tray of tools, and as if lurching from some nightmare, he poked its sharp point into the patient's left cheek. I did not see the patient's reaction, only that blood spurted and spread across his jaw. The dentist shouted, "He sleeps, you see? He feels nothing!" He stabbed again toward the patient, who sat defenseless, his head hanging like a ripe pear. I caught the dentist's arm, called for help, and in a moment three of us held him. His eyes clouded as if with tears, and he panted. His face flushed. He had not seemed insane to me in the hours before the exhibition. He seemed insane now.

Two men wrestled him from the building. I've not seen him since, and I suspect I'll never meet him again. I left the patient in the care of his fellow students and hurried home. Perhaps putting this memory to paper will help me forget, even if by small degrees, and thereby get on with my work.

15

In his dark study, among spiders and flickering candles, Morton—drunk—plays with a pair of human jawbones. He laughs and love-pecks them. Then the yellowish jaws open and close, teeth clacking, speaking to Horace, who sits on the floor nearby. "I miss the gas," say the jawbones, a desiccated mockery of Morton's mouth.

"It seems not to work so well anymore." Horace coughs, and rum sloshes over the side of his mug to wet his lap. His cheeks are wet, too; his scalp feels hot at the follicles.

"Why only one bladder?" Clack go the jawbones. "You should have brought two." Clack. Clack. Morton tips a mug toward the jawbones. "Rumbug-a-roo." The bones drink up.

What Horace knows about bones is that when exposed to air they will yellow. When exposed to sun they will bleach. Also, bones do not doubt. Bones do not worry about hell or heaven. They never reproach themselves. Bones dance in the mountains of New Hampshire when the devil plays his fiddle, his father used to say. Jawbones sitting in Morton's palm drink from Morton's mug and endure his kisses. While Morton's own Elizabeth—she of the brunette ringlets—snuggles in another room under a patched bed quilt, the jawbones sitting in Morton's palm drink from his mug and endure his kisses. Ill-mannered adulterer.

"I didn't plan to exhaust the bladder," Horace says. "My discovery concerns pain—not . . . not . . . clairvoyance. Is it still so noisy outside? How this city shrieks!"

The yellowish jaws reply with a question, something about sulfuric ether, but a nail has come loose from the floorboard and pricks Horace's hip through his trousers. Time to stand, says the nail's point. Time to board the train. Home to your Elizabeth. Except he must avoid the tracks. He considers whether he might prefer to lie face up or down. The idea of suicide tempts, though he sighs it away. A vision of Elizabeth robed in black—alone at graveside—troubles his heart back to the living. If he misses her now, from so near as Boston, how much more so when soul flies and body molders?

The jawbones say, "You've ripped your trousers."

He has? That nail. He turns like a dog trying to bite its rump, fingers the tear, then loses his balance and turns some more. "Will," he says. "Will Morton." Standing, he turns about the study, touching his fingertips to each wall to prove a theory. Four walls, a complete inventory, and yes, it is true: no windows. How does Morton work in a room *sans*, as the French say, windows? You can't watch birds if the room has no windows. Birds with their songs and their fluttering wings.

"The papery flutter in my chest is gone," Horace says. He claps his hands twice, then wiggles his fingers as if they are bird wings flying off. Make a note, Horace: failure cures flutters. Or humiliation does. Scissor-edged humiliation has shred the paper in his lungs, and Horace has coughed out the tatters. He's still coughing now, which is curious, and Morton throws him a kerchief, which falls to the floor and is lost among the books and stew bowls and a broken jar of blue pottery celebrating the accomplishments of George Washington. *Humbughumbughumbug-a-roo.*

"I'll find it," Horace says, doubling over, eyes squinting in the dark. "I'll find it."

"You embarrassed me in front of Warren," the jawbones say. "Stabbing that boy!"

"Six breaths. I counted. He should have felt nothing. Are we friends, Will?"

"We need to leave soon for the train."

"Yes, but are we friends?"

"You're as good a friend as I'll ever have."

A puzzle, that answer. No answer at all.

Morton stokes the stove with a wedge of dry maple. Pawing through the debris on the floor, Horace finds the kerchief. He also picks up the broken George Washington jar, waves it at Morton.

"All men of conviction are great men," he says. "A drunkard who drinks without regret—a great man. An adulterer who fornicates without regret—a great man. You, Will, are a great man. A truly great man."

"In centuries to come, schoolchildren will sing my name."

"A man of conviction! Blessed by the stars, by the alchemy of his humors. The blood of kings runs in you, Will, the wisdom to know when to open a bottle of rum. May you never doubt yourself."

"I never doubt myself. We must leave for the train."

"May you never."

Four walls and no windows, and Horace can't hear anything outside the room, which is good because he's had enough of listening to the shrieking city. But then Morton has him by the hand and is leading him out of the study, out of the apartment, with no farewell to Elizabeth of the ringlets, and the two stumble downstairs to the slushy streets and harsh sunlight, and Horace says no, thank you, I'm comfortable with your windowless study and your rum. A goat shrieks at him as they pass, and a cat shrieks, and a school teacher shrieks, and also a book binder, and a fellow who looks as if his only skill is at cards, and a livery boy, and a warden. Shriek. Shriek. Shriek. Morton shrieks, and Morton, you are no friend of mine to remove me into the streets of Boston, you are no friend! The train at the station shrieks to a stop. Nothing to be done about it anymore, and there's an emptiness in his lungs where paper once fluttered, and as with all emptiness it wants filling. A shriek louder than all the others sounds through his blood and along his nerves, following marrow, sloshing through the liquid spaces of his body until it finds those empty lungs, and that's where the shriek nests. Followed by another. The noises deafen him so he doesn't hear what Morton says, nor does he hear the lunges of the train as it steams away from Boston, nor the woman passenger who sits across from him and keeps asking questions and who looks like neither his Elizabeth nor Morton's but instead like a wading bird, a bittern, and he doesn't hear the command to switch trains in Springfield, but that doesn't matter because he knows he is supposed to, and when at last he arrives in Hartford, he doesn't hear his Elizabeth gasp as she meets him in darkness at the station, and he doesn't hear her ask where are his boots, where are his boots because it is January and the slush and snow cause frostbite, *humbughumbughumbug-a-roo*, nor, when he reaches home, bare feet wrapped in a wool blanket, does he hear the strangled combination of bark and howl issuing from a solitary white dog which is missing a leg and balancing on the three that remain, distant, under a leafless oak tree where the cleared property ends and woods and darkness begin.

III
SEDGEWICK HOUSE
HARTFORD

16

In the well-appointed parlor of a three-chimneyed house on Wethersfield Avenue in Hartford, Elizabeth's aunt, Dorothy Sedgewick, welcomed her niece with a long embrace. "Would you have an ale?" she asked. The clock showed six and fifteen on that February evening in 1845, and lamps cast halos throughout the room. Elizabeth had not visited her aunt since Horace's Boston trip, about which Dorothy had heard rumors. Though Elizabeth had yet to mention her sorrows, they were plain given how she sat with such rigidity in that velvet-upholstered chair. Straight back. Chin out. The last clutching at composure. She needs a pick-me-up, Dorothy thought, but Elizabeth declined.

Dorothy said, "You haven't joined the temperance gang?"

For Elizabeth's favorite aunt, ale was a nightly ritual: only after six o'clock; two mugs—never more or less; always in the parlor and usually in the company of her friend and house guest, Frannie Steele. Frannie had lived at Sedgewick House for twelve years, and, like her host, was a childless widow. At the moment, she bustled in the kitchen, heating water and arranging a tea tray. Frannie had forsworn spirits after her husband died—he'd been a drunkard—whereas Dorothy had been inspired by her husband's tippling. Her fondest memory put Mr. Sedgewick back in this parlor, sipping as he snickered at witty passages from some book. Not too long after his death, Dorothy poured two mugs (one for him, one for her), adjourned to the parlor, and toasted him. After the first mug, she savored the second. Each night thereafter: "To Mr. Sedgewick, that he may find an ale drinker among the angels," or, "To Mr. Sedgewick's taste in women and in drink!"—and by this ritual the pain caused by his absence both sharpened and diminished. It was also about this time that her chin sprouted whiskers. The beard grew only an inch, but she had reached an age at which her body's quirks no longer surprised. Perhaps the whiskers were connected to mourning or to ale; no matter: she still drank and grieved. In the last few years, the whiskers had turned gray and brittle, much like those Mr. Sedgewick wore at his death, and they comforted her.

"Frannie believes in temperance, don't you, Frannie?" She shouted this over her shoulder toward the sound of thick-soled shoes clumping in the hall.

Then Frannie arrived, accompanied by two waddling cats—one black, the other orange and white—each fat enough to stuff a bushel basket. "Drink disagrees with so many people," she said. "The bad seems to outweigh the good."

"If every disagreeable thing were to be prohibited, our legislators would pass a law silencing themselves. Such a bother these arguments about spirits. Jesus turned water into wine. Heaven's bias is clear."

Elizabeth whispered, "I've not joined the temperance lot, but tea will do."

Dorothy and Frannie served in tandem, as people do who have shared harmony and years: Frannie placing the doilies and saucers, Dorothy arranging the blue china cups; Frannie offered molasses, Dorothy the spoon. Before their husbands died, the women had only a churchgoing awareness of each other, but after the deaths in quick succession of Mr. Sedgewick (Asiatic cholera, 1830) and Frannie's Mr. Steele (riptide off an East Lyme beach, 1832; drunk), Dorothy opened her home to the widow whose intemperate husband had left little money and no property. "Just common sense," Dorothy had told those townsfolk who praised her Christian charity. "She needs a home; my house has empty rooms." Being Puritans, they admired her practicality even more.

"This is a cheerful brew," said Elizabeth.

"Do you taste the rosehips?" said Frannie, scratching between the black cat's ears.

"Very nice, yes."

Dorothy stroked her beard. She was, in fact, a woman of prodigious charity—her own work at the insane asylum had marked the path Elizabeth later followed. But (and this she would not admit to anyone) her character also included a greed for the company of misfortune; woeful tales delighted her. At the asylum, she had heard stories to make marble statues weep, and she'd learned that to hear more she must not ask too many questions nor appear eager. Rude questions beget silences. But silences often beget the most miserable revelations.

Alas, Frannie, bless her soul, was a chatterbox.

"Just the other day," she was saying, "I had a very interesting conversation with a neighborhood boy." She poured again, gauzy steam rising. "He brings firewood, and we adore him—he stacks so soundly you'd think he were rebuilding the walls of Jericho. The other day, he says to me, 'I'm dying, Miss Frannie.' I ask, 'Why might you worry so?' And he shows me his teeth the way a dog would, and the teeth had all turned orange. I thought I'd like to ask your husband about that."

Dorothy lay a light hand on Frannie's lap. It was enough; Frannie quieted.

Elizabeth held her breath until the skin on her face flushed pink. "My Horace, as perhaps you have heard, cannot maintain his practice. He suffers from ill health."

Dorothy frowned her sympathy. With some effort, she lifted the orange-and-white cat to her lap. Elizabeth placed her teacup in its saucer and watched the cup.

"Dr. Taft identified a problem with Horace's lungs. There are other concerns, discernable to one who loves him, which are not likely noticed by acquaintances."

Dorothy had liked Horace from the day he came to woo Elizabeth at Sedgewick House, which offered a more charming parlor than that of Elizabeth's parents, who used theirs mostly for Bible study. A quick mind, that young man, with an adorable blush.

Elizabeth said, "These days, he is much concerned with birds."

"Birds?"

"He practices whistles, keeps a dozen or so cages in the house, amasses stuffed examples of rare and local species, collects nests, and makes notations of bird habits. He is particularly fond of the *Sylvia coronata*."

"It is my favorite also," whispered Frannie. She turned to Dorothy. "The yellow-rumped warbler."

"A bird of fine character," said Dorothy. The orange-white cat began to knead her lap with its claws, so she shooed it. Elizabeth continued.

"Dr. Taft says the pursuit of ornithology is in Horace's best interest and that he should give up his dentistry. But birds do not pay him for his attention, and we cannot afford the cottage at Lord's Hill without an income. We don't want to sell the cottage either, as we believe Horace's lung ailment to be temporary and that he'll soon resume his practice. At the same time we cannot predict when he will recover his former self. We can let the cottage, but then where do we live? As you can see, we're in a pickle."

Dorothy hoped that her face showed her concern, which was real. Still, she kept silent, and when she heard Frannie inhale as if to speak, she placed a careful hand again.

The three women sat in the weighty silence. Elizabeth's teacup pinged against its saucer as she set it down, picked it up, set it down again.

"Something happened to Horace in Boston," she said.

Dorothy nodded.

"But I don't know what," said Elizabeth. She looked at the women in turn, as if each might be able to tell her what ill fortune can fall upon a man in Boston. Her voice rose. She whiffled her hands about her ears as if to clear cobwebs. "I've asked him—dozens of times!"

Dorothy sipped her ale and with a napkin dabbed her lips. She waited a moment, then three, until certain that Elizabeth had no more to say. Then she leaned forward and squeezed her hand. "Dear niece," she said. "If you want an answer, you must never, never ask."

The Wells family moved from Lord's Hill to the three-chimneyed Sedge-wick House on a bright April day. Charley's face showed his concern about the change, and Frannie kept him busy with twenty-three games of check-ers, of which Charley won fourteen. All that day, Elizabeth's eyes showed a whirling combination of fear and relief, as if she were glad for the new situation but concerned to nausea about what might happen next. And Horace? He was furtive, polite one moment and in the next wary as a beaten dog.

Dorothy and Frannie had reorganized the attic, which had been home to objects that recalled their husbands—coats and cufflinks, property deeds and spittoons—and made room for Horace's newest preoccupation. He carried his collections himself and let no one touch his cages or his array of tail feathers, nor the dissected and pickled larynxes of songbirds (which, he told Dorothy, illustrated their superior musculature against those of birds that croak or caw). Nor could anyone else place a hand on the mounted remains of a creature with a hawk's wings growing from the shoulders of a large tabby. Horace had bought the cat-hawk from a ship's cook, a man missing both eyeteeth. The cook described for Horace how he had shot the creature while hunting on an island off Egypt's coast. These cat-hawks, said the cook, fly about seizing squirrels from high branches, then make nests of the tails. Horace did not believe squirrels lived on an island off Egypt's shore but purchased the cat-hawk anyway and named it Warren.

Only a week after the move into Sedgewick House did the sounds begin. From the attic, in the empty hours after midnight, came coughing and scraping that startled Frannie Steele out of teacup dreams, and which roused Aunt Dorothy so she covered her head with a pillow, and which gave Charley nightmares so that he fled crying to Elizabeth. She pulled him into the bed where her husband seemed never to sleep, and where she lay awake fretting over Boston and Clara Bliss and those who sang about her. Together mother and son comforted each other amid the nocturnal noises.

April became May, and one afternoon Horace stepped into the parlor and interrupted Aunt Dorothy in the midst of a toast to Mr. Sedgewick. "Why are the hairbrushes in this house so clean?" he demanded. "Why is there no soot in the cook stove?"

Dorothy did not know how to answer. When she did not reply, he said, calmly:

"Answer me."

She said, "The stove contains soot, nephew. The brushes do indeed collect hair."

She could see in his face that the response made little sense to him, but rather than struggle with the riddle he announced that he would be in the attic, tending to his birds.

Dorothy put aside her ale, then sought Elizabeth, whom she found in the cellar, putting up canned rhubarb and seeing her way by guttering candle flame. She wore an apron, and a smudge of sauce colored her cheek.

"Are we in danger from your husband?" Dorothy asked.

Elizabeth set down her tray of jars and smiled at her aunt, then shook her head to indicate all that she didn't know. She lifted the candle's tray and cupped the flame as if to find a place where there might be shelter from drafts.

"His mind is lost," said Dorothy.

Placing the tray on a moldering ledge of foundation stone, Elizabeth looked from her aunt to the flickering flame, from the flame to her aunt, a twitch making her mouth ugly. Then she pinched the wick. In the space the darkness made, Dorothy heard Elizabeth gulp and choke. She gasped when her niece's body nestled against her own, a sensation she hadn't known since Elizabeth was a girl of nine or ten. Elizabeth pressed harder, head against Dorothy's breast, hands grasping at her blouse, her body small as a child's. Dorothy lifted her arms to girdle her niece, whose name she whispered as she would a prayer, holding fast out of fear that if she let go the girl would splinter into uncountable fragments.

In Elizabeth's nightmares, it was always cold on Colton's stage, and Horace stood shoeless, his toes frost-blackened and curled, the whites of his eyes scratched red as if roughed with sandpaper. With trembling hand Elizabeth clutched his stockings, worn with holes. "Husband," she said, "where are your shoes?" And he replied, "Are you my sister in Christ?" Her voice broke when she said, "I'm Elizabeth," but he looked at her as if she were a carrion bird he was seeing for the first time.

"What do you hear?" Horace asked.

He sat with Dr. Taft in the kitchen, the two alone. Charley was at school and the women out helping to prepare the church for Holy Week services. Dr. Taft pressed the right side of his head to Horace's shirtless chest. The physician hadn't shaved, and his cheek stubble tickled Horace's skin.

"Quiet, please," said Dr. Taft, a small man with thick-lensed spectacles and a jaw that disappeared into his neck. "Now: full breaths. Imagine your wife on your wedding night. That sort of breathing."

Horace asked Taft to repeat himself, but louder. What he did not tell Taft was that the blue-winter shrieks had remained in his lungs since Boston, and because of them he could not hear a mumbler such as the doctor. He wondered whether Taft heard the shrieks, too.

As a child on his father's farm, Horace had heard rabbits scream when torn by dogs. Now, if he concentrated, he could hear those same rabbits. Also, when he concentrated, he could identify among the shrieks those that had broken from Elizabeth when she gave birth to Charley. And those of Charley himself, fresh from the womb as he breathed his first breaths. But was it fair to call Charley's cries *shrieks*? Those might be wails. The rabbits certainly screamed. Horace listened, and amid the shrieks he heard the Boston woman's lament rise above the roar of the fire. Wails, screams, laments. When joined in his lungs as a chorus, they became a single everlasting shriek. Sometimes he took notes, a catalog of the sorrows he heard, because he theorized that the clamor contained a message he was meant to understand. Fated, perhaps, to hear. Something to do with breath? Because one night in the Sedgewick attic, he'd discovered that when he held his breath the pitch of the shrieks grew low, almost bearable. Take air into his lungs and the pitch rose. Empty his lungs and the pitch fell. As pitchforks fall into hay. As pitch black falls with night. Pitchpoled, ships sometimes are, stern over bow. When the ship is pitchpoled, sailors shriek.

"When you cough into a handkerchief," asked Dr. Taft, "what color is your sputum?"

"Yellow. Now and then a thread of blood. Size and shape of a burned candlewick. What do you hear?"

"I'm confounded. Given the blood, I'd expect the lungs to crackle, a sound like foil as it's balled in a fist. But there's nothing."

"Nothing?"

"Breathe steam twice a day from water boiled with herbs. I'll leave a list of the herbs at Cooley's apothecary. Do you smoke?"

"No."

"Consider taking up a pipe. Tobacco excites the lungs."

"You heard nothing?"

"What did you want me to hear, Horace? A circus band? It's better that I hear nothing. When you hear noises from the lungs, that's when there's trouble."

The shrieking kept him from sleep. He trudged through the minutes of each night, nauseated with exhaustion—but as soon as head fell to pillow his thoughts sharpened, his senses hummed. Sometimes he curled himself into a ball and felt as if he should weep, but he had not the necessary vigor. Awake overlong, he filled notebooks. Maybe the shrieks were a trick of the brain, some reaction of memory in the pineal gland, as Descartes described. Perhaps they reflected his history of pain—suffered or caused—every tooth drilled, every violence done. Unabsolved and unredeemed, because he had failed with the gas. It followed, then, that he not hurt anyone ever again. Must not add a new voice.

Ornithology helped. When he listed bird taxonomies, or examined under a microscope the facets of a cardinal's eye, or even wiped canary turds from cages, he was not so bothered by the shrieks.

But when he stopped.

But when he listened to stories about Charley's day at school.

But when he prayed.

But when on his way to the chamber pot he met that woman with a beard.

Sometimes, studying birds, he held his breath. Delicious lung-quiet times. Bird claws and beaks (no breathing), their songs and nests and eggs, the gentle flap or the frenetic drive of wings, birds in water and birds on land and birds in sky, their nestlings, their dead eyes under the knife on his examination table (no breathing)—every happiness in birds.

17

John Mankey Riggs, surgeon dentist
43 Pearl Street
Hartford, Connecticut

June 12, 1845

Dr. Morton—Dear Sir:

Let me be blunt. Had you seen, as I did this night, Dr. Horace Wells, our esteemed mentor, you would see a stranger where you expected a familiar face. On behalf of his family, I ask you to send word of what happened to him in Boston. If we can understand, perhaps we can help. Otherwise, I fear the worst. We have had our differences, you & I, & I suppose a plea from me bears little weight with you. But as Wells has always spoken of you in good regard, please respond with haste for his sake.

Since his return he has surrendered his practice & the family has no income. He has occupied himself with ornithology & in an effort to make money from what can best be described as a hobby, he scheduled a 3-night exhibition at Hartford's city hall. This "panorama of nature," he told me, would show that his engagement with birds was not "loafing," that his understanding of avian life was no "humbug."

He constructed showcases & displays meant to educate ticket-buyers about the wonders of birds, & he hired a brass band to entertain. He visited a barber for haircut & shave & he dressed neatly but still seemed out of sorts that opening night. A handful of people bought tickets for the debut, myself included & some of his former patients, among their number a woman who brought a carrying coop with a pair of laying hens, & who sat in the first row. He remarked on her birds & thanked her for adding live domesticated fowl to the exhibition. That moment proved to be the night's high point. Afterward he stuttered through lectures, losing himself in a thought & then arriving at a new idea unrelated to what preceded. Three times he was overcome by coughing, though he never left the room to recover— only stood & forgot his audience.

I did not return the second night but heard he had dismissed the brass band. On the last night, Wells & Elizabeth waited alone in the hall, & I alone with them. When it was clear no one else would come, Wells rose from his seat, arms in slow mimicry of a bird's wings against the air, turning himself softly amid the rows of empty chairs. "So elegant," he said, "so stable in flight. How is it they never stumble in the sky?" I held Elizabeth's hand as she quietly called him back to her side.

Yesterday—two weeks since the panorama—Elizabeth sent a note asking me to visit at the address where they now keep house as guests of her aunt. "Urgent," she wrote. I arrived that evening & the aunt met me, saying that Elizabeth was occupied with her son's scripture lessons, though I think, perhaps, Elizabeth could not herself bear to show me what her husband has become. The aunt pointed me to the attic entrance, explaining that her nephew seemed neither to eat nor sleep, but at all hours secreted himself behind that upstairs door. "It's like living with a ghost," she said, "except one we love."

In the dark outside the attic, I stooped to scratch the ears of two giant cats, each yowling to be let in. From behind the door, bird calls sounded: some sweet but also a heron's croak, a jay's shriek. It was hot & damp in the stairwell & breathing proved difficult. I tapped the door, heard no response, so shooed the cats & opened it. Heat rushed out—I staggered backwards. A miasma engulfed me, an odor I can't describe except to say it gagged me as a whiff of the tanneries sometimes can. I recovered myself in time to hear a loud beating & I jerked my head low as a pigeon winged past to perch in the stairwell rafters. It was then I saw: the attic seethed with birds! Jays & meadowlarks & grackles, crows & kingfishers. Some caged, some not. They cooed, cawed, cackled. An owl stared at me as if I presumed much by being there. At the center of all, Wells sat at a table, his shirt stained yellow by sweat, and he used the unbuttoned cuffs to wipe his brow & neck. He did not mark my intrusion, occupied as he was with what appeared to be a dead carrier pigeon. He picked at it with forceps, in the midst of dissection, I think, exhaling & inhaling at odd intervals as if trying to hold his breath. Excrement lay everywhere, gray & green & black on the attic floor, on the table where he worked, dried along the back of his chair, even, it seemed to me, clotting in his hair. He was unshaven, a condition you'll agree is alien to his nature. Blood was smeared across his forehead & I could not tell if it belonged to the dissected bird or to our friend himself. His eyes: raw, rimmed red. He chewed his top lip.

"Wells," I hissed, "what has happened to you?"

He looked up from the corpse at his hands. I saw that he recognized me, but he studied me as if I were that dead pigeon prodded by his scalpel. He waved the blade in my direction. "You use the gas in your practice, don't you, Riggs?" he said. "Your patients wake having escaped pain?"

"I do use it, Wells," I answered. "It works. As you proved it did."

"Did you bring any?"

When I answered that I had not, he turned back to his dissection.

"It's all a humbug," he said. "A humbug from womb to grave. Morton understands this & lives without cares. He moves through this world with the ease of an eagle on the wing. So I admire him. Next visit, Riggs, bring a bladder filled with gas."

For the love of God, Morton, can you tell us what will make him whole?

John Mankey Riggs

18

Mosquitoes hovered thick in the afternoon air, while gulls swooped low and splashed in black pools along the railroad tracks. Lightning played over the western hills, a storm moving closer. On the Hartford station's platform, John Mankey Riggs shifted foot to foot as if uncertain where he stood. Now and then, a buzz against his ear triggered a twitch and slap, interrupted the persistent and awkward heartache of having seen Horace Wells, his teacher and friend, so troubled. Such concern had preyed on Riggs for several days and become a brooding that kept him awake as many nights. He was tired, the air was dank, mosquitoes hungry, and he felt soul-sick about a man he admired who was broken, whom he couldn't fix. He rocked foot to foot on the platform as he awaited help in the person of that other fellow who had studied dentistry with Wells, a man Riggs disliked and did not trust and despite himself had summoned. No wonder he felt tetchy.

A train lurched into the station, steam whistles complaining and steel screeching against steel. Men on the platform shouted halloos at passengers waving from behind windows, and a small black dog in a girl's arms started to yap. Riggs felt an itchy welt swelling on his chin, aggravated by his scratchy beard. He wished he'd not written so dramatic a letter. He only wanted to get Morton's attention, to make clear that an urgent reply was needed. He'd not intended for Morton to descend on Hartford as if he were some knight errant drawn by distress, bent on rescue. He knew Morton well enough to know that wasn't true; the man never suffered a noble impulse. Something sordid lurked in his motives, of this Riggs was certain. And that meant the letter, intimate as it was about Wells's indignities, had divulged too much. A worry that he'd been a disloyal gossip puddled cold and oily in Riggs's belly.

Passengers began to disembark, and he saw a toddler stumble down a train car's steps to smack against the platform. Behind the child came Morton, scowling, lifting his suitcase high and taking an exaggerated step so that for a moment his storkish legs straddled the wailing boy. Then he marched on, straight to Riggs, even as the boy's mother lifted her child to his feet and chastised him with harsh words and open-handed slaps to his trousered caboose.

Morton turned back to watch. "Brat," he said, spitting something dark. "He raised Cain all the trip, cut past me in the aisle as we waited to disembark, and nearly tripped me just now."

"How did he come to tumble?"

"I didn't push him, Riggs, if that's your implication."

Riggs clasped his hands behind his back to avoid a handshake and rose on his toes so that for a moment he stood taller than his visitor.

"Not at all. It's too bad you endured an unpleasant journey. A letter detailing Wells's Boston trip would have spared you the trouble."

"I owe him money," Morton said.

"January was not so long ago. You could have paid him then."

"My lawyer says now. Why so much argument, Riggs? Perhaps I've other business here that doesn't involve you or Wells."

Other business? Riggs hadn't considered the possibility. So single-minded had been his concern, he'd not allowed for any purpose but Wells to explain Morton's visit. It was a small slip, yet it dumbfounded him. Morton turned and marched toward the lodging district, but Riggs lingered as if just shaken awake. Since he'd been faced with his mentor's suffering, his wits had scattered. His brain—despite years of training in scientific inquiry—had reverted in its thinking to that of a schoolboy.

"Riggs?"

He felt Morton pinch his jacket sleeve. Exasperation seemed to be turning the man's shaved upper lip cherry-colored. "What's the delay?" he said.

Riggs looked at Morton now as if through a glass wiped clean of soot. Science required disinterest, and here was a man without love for Horace Wells. He'd not be distracted by pity, as Riggs had been. Morton, Riggs realized, might well be their mentor's best hope. So he offered his hand, which Morton looked at, cockeyed, then took. "I only wanted to tell you," Riggs said, "before we left on our mission, that I'm glad you are here."

Morton let go Riggs's hand to slap his own neck and grunt. He showed Riggs the bloodied wings and legs before wiping mosquito remains on his jacket. Morton's sleeve cuffs, Riggs noted, were frayed.

While Morton settled into his lodging on Allyn Street, Riggs—in the lobby—recalled that wintry morning not so long ago when he'd pulled Wells's tooth and Wells had felt, as he said then, not a prick. But what occupied Riggs was the moment before: *We can't fathom all that might happen*, Mr. Colton had warned, his face grim, humorless. The phrasing suggested endless possibility, effects in the short term and effects over time. Because Wells's breakdown manifested after he returned from Boston, Riggs had assumed Boston was the source of the trouble. But what if Boston were not? Could his friend's affliction be traced to that snowy morning's inhalation of nitrous oxide? Could Riggs himself, a participant in the experiment, have been an unwitting factor in Wells's later collapse?

He hurt to think so.

When Morton returned, the men hailed an open buggy, taking seats on the bench behind the driver, who wheezed and kept his horse at a trot and who, as they approached cavities in the road, called out, "Mind the hole!" but always too late.

"In Boston, Wells seemed more nervous than usual," Morton began, "stuttering and doing that funny thing where he scratches at his cheeks. You know—" Morton scrunched his eyes as he clawed his beard. "Afterward, he proved inconsolable. We spent the night chugalugging cheap rum. Wells drank like a friar, and it was all I could do to get him to the train station. The man's nerves break like straw. You'll concede to his erratic nature. Made for a poor business partner. One can't count on him."

"That's a slander."

"Not if it's true." Morton pointed to the sullen clouds now overhead. "That Wells, like the weather, is inconstant is a fact, and no more an insult to him than to the weather."

The driver reined his horse at the Hog River bridge, taking its rise at half speed, and at the bridge's apex, Riggs caught sight of clouds flashing; thunder rumbled soon thereafter. All over the city, shopkeepers shuttered their windows, and near the south pasture, Riggs marked a farmer with a switch flicking his pigs toward shelter.

Morton elbowed Riggs. "Help me understand Wells's experiments. Yours, too."

Because he knew such facts might aid his teacher, Riggs answered precisely as he could Morton's questions about the nature of the gas, the time between applications during longer surgeries, whether Riggs or Wells had tried any other vapors—alone or mixed with nitrous oxide—how often Wells himself had experimented, whether either dentist had attempted methods of application other than the bladders with faucets, whether they'd given the gas only to people of sound mind, whether they'd tried it on people whose dispositions proved delicate.

"A chemist friend," Morton said, "theorizes that laughing gas is an unreliable agent."

"Do you suppose it is at fault here?" asked Riggs, his voice softening. "Might the gas prey on a certain mind? A certain disposition?" He felt the question like a cramp near his heart and wished suddenly that he'd not asked. He recalled as a student watching Wells work with patients, the hardness that overcame his teacher that seemed also like a fragility.

"Mind the hole!" bawled the driver just before a jolt shivered their spines. After the buggy regained its rhythm, Morton shouted over the rising wind and thunder claps: "How goes the battle against spongy gums?"

Had Morton not heard the question about the gas being to blame? Riggs sighed, relaxing against the side of the wagon with gratitude for having escaped a knowledge he'd rather not face.

Inside Sedgewick House, Morton scowled at Charley as if here were another boy to tangle underfoot. Elizabeth in turn gave Morton the full power of her eyes, but Morton did not wither under her gaze, saying that whatever Elizabeth's misgivings he had indeed come to help, that after Boston he owed Wells his presence. "Also," he admitted, "he's a curiosity to me, how his admirable qualities so often conflict with his interesting ones."

"Likely we'd disagree over your definitions of admirable and interesting," Elizabeth said.

Morton shrugged. "A discussion for a more quiet time," he said. "May I visit him now?"

Elizabeth looked to Riggs for an answer, and he nodded. So the widow Mrs. Sedgewick, Elizabeth's aunt, led the two men up the dark stairway to the attic, waiting with them as Riggs knocked and spoke into the door, announcing them.

They heard footsteps, and Riggs straightened, preparing for both Wells and a flurry of birds. But instead a door's bolt crashed into place, and fast as a finger snap went a second, and then the rasp of a chain. Mrs. Sedgewick yelped and remarked that the door had never locked from the inside, that this was new, and moreover, inhospitable! Riggs pummeled the door with the fleshy side of his fist. Morton shouted, "All the way from Boston, Wells, and I'm not leaving!"

"An axe!" called Mrs. Sedgewick, who turned and jounced down the stairs.

"Isn't that extreme?" said Morton.

"You have not lived with my nephew these two months!" she yelled back.

Then came muffled shouting from within, and that started a cacophony of bird cries. Riggs threw his shoulder against the door, and Morton told him to stop, that they should think this through, but before either could utter another word Mrs. Sedgewick panted up the stairs, handed over a maul, and Riggs swung in the tight quarters until he'd broken the door around the knob and locks. "Kick with me now, Morton," he said, and on a three-count they did, and the door opened. That awful smell again! And birds! Those beating wings shattered the air, filling every small space around them, down the stairwell into the house, ever more fluttering, careening, and it seemed there could never be an end to birds. The men and Mrs. Sedgewick raised forearms to ward away beaks and claws, then stumbled through the attic searching until convinced that Wells had vanished. An open window suggested his escape, and when Riggs looked out he glanced first to the sky, envisioning a winged dentist flying gargoyle-like into the stormy horizon. Then his eye caught a spasm of movement on the street. Wells! Stumbling, caroming off the corner of a brick building, sidestepping a pig in his way. The men, without a word, hurried to the stairs and to the chase.

Even as they ran, Riggs didn't know why they ran after, what might be accomplished. It only seemed to matter that they catch Wells, that to let him go would not do. Morton proved fleetest, but Riggs knew the city better. They moved pell-mell, as dogs after a squirrel, heads jerking into this alley and that bystreet. A glimpse! Wells's fiery hair? Yes, him! Scrambling north—

and the chase renewed. Now thunderclaps filled the air, and drops pelted Riggs's scalp. Through a gate they pursued, into a pen where heavy-headed cattle awaited slaughter, past a kitchen woman who tossed supper scraps into the street. A rag-clothed girl selling paper flowers told them she'd seen a man with orange hair, yes, and pointed toward the Hog River. They searched until Morton doubled over panting, yellow in the face. Riggs lay a hand on the man's back in sympathy until Morton recovered his breath and complexion.

When they reached the river, the two scrambled among the factories and tenements and sewage pipes that populated its bank. The air reeked, and Riggs noticed Morton stuff his nose with snuff.

In the muggy dusk, Riggs's shirt stuck to his nape, and a blister smarted on his left foot. He pulled his hat tight against the gusts, unable to tell what spray came from the heavens and what came from the millwheels and spillways along the Hog. He watched for rats and nails, and shut his mouth so as not to inhale any of the bugs that swarmed. Legs wobbly, he seated himself on a pile of broken bricks. That was when he spotted a figure sheltered under the brownstone arch that bridged the river at Main Street. At its foundations the bridge and riverbank vanished into shadow, but the figure's white shirt—he wore no coat—bloomed as an orchid from the shade.

Closer and yes: Wells.

He sat, mud and water soaked into his trousers. With a length of branch he swatted at an encroaching rat, keeping the rodent wary and at arm's length. A shovel leaned against the bridge foundation, its handle and blade caked with green-black river muck. Wells coughed into his fist. Around him, the bank was cleared in an uneven circle, freed of the detritus that lined much of the waterway, and inside that circle stood tiny stones, markers of some kind, as a child's pretend graveyard.

Riggs sat himself a few paces from his friend, hoping distance would prevent Wells from fleeing anew. Then, "The clouds promise a fierce evening."

"The weather," said Wells, his voice hoarse. "When there is nothing to say people speak of the weather. Did you bring a bladder of gas as I asked?"

Again, Riggs felt that cramp near his heart, the joy he associated with pulling Wells's tooth ("Not a prick!") never again so pure. "No," he answered.

"Next time, bring the gas. I must sleep."

Wells looked around him at the markers, then lashed at the rat.

"He wants my birds," he said.

"What say?"

Coughing. Then: "The rat wants to dig up my birds. To eat them."

Now Morton appeared, mud or worse spattered across his face, and a great rip in his coat from shoulder to waist.

"Shit, Horace," he said. "You make nothing easy, do you?" He wiped his sleeve across his cheek and lowered his gaze as if he searched for something lost.

Wells picked up a fallen stone, then jammed it into the mud. "In this spot," he said, hardly breathing, his words smashing together, "I've buried the birds, but the rats dig them up. Each time I return, a gravestone—sometimes two—is disturbed and a little hole in the place where I lay a sparrow to rest, or a flycatcher. I never want to kill the birds, but I need to understand them, and how else to make them keep still but a twist of the neck? My father taught me that when I was a boy, to kill chickens. All farm boys must learn to kill. I have notes I have written." He patted at his chest as if searching for a pocket. "I find I understand these birds too well, and I think I am in a position to say they do not deserve to become rat food." His pitch rose, voice lifting toward shriek.

Riggs noted a red stain in Wells's right eye, and then a chain around his neck—the molar Riggs had pulled. Grotesque now.

"Humbug!" cried Wells, stumbling near to Morton. "Humbug-a-roo!"

"For God's sake," Morton said, "shut up."

Riggs expected an explosion, a wail of some sort, or for Wells again to flee. Instead, Wells rubbed his cheeks—did not scratch—but rubbed. "Will?" he said.

"Christ, yes," Morton grumbled. "Will who never doubts himself. Will, a man of conviction. That's what you said when last we spent time together, Wells, so you'd best listen to me now." Morton began to kick over bird gravestones, grunting as if he were the mad one. "That you understand birds does not mean you speak for them," he said. "They are not *your* birds. They belong to God, or to the rats. Or the ants. Or the beetles. Or the maggots. Let the river rise and carry them to the sea for fish to eat. Don't be a silly man, Wells. You are better than a silly man."

A wind gust tossed Wells's thin hair. It pushed water from an eddy higher along the shoreline, around Morton's boots. Morton looked to the sky. "And now we'll get drenched," he said.

Wells spoke then, a question for Morton, and Riggs heard surprise in his friend's voice, but only surprise—none of the frenzy from earlier. "Will," Wells said, "what brings you to Hartford?"

"I am here to square my debt to you. Also, to ask you a question."

"That's good. I've worried about the money for too long, and it will be good not to worry. Or, to worry about other things." Wells squeezed his eyes shut, then opened them again. "To worry about the right things. So, thank you. Now, what is the question?"

"What other gases have you tested? Nitrous oxide and what else?"

"None other."

"None?"

Wells shook his head. "None."

During the buggy ride, Riggs recalled, Morton had asked him the same. Curious. The old mistrust returned, a fine soot that attached to Morton so well.

Morton fingered the rip at his shoulder. "I'll stop by Sedgewick House tomorrow with a banker's check," he told Wells, "less the cost of a new coat." Then he turned and climbed the riverbank, and Riggs watched until Hartford's lights made Morton a silhouette huddling against what was now a hard-driving rain. He looked back to his old teacher, his friend, who examined his own clothes, said, "I am a mess, aren't I?" Wells used both hands to smooth his hair, then smiled. "I do not want to be a silly man. They are not my birds, as Will says. Their songs are not my songs. How presumptuous to believe that what God gives His whole dominion might belong to me alone. Not true for the birds, nor for laughter nor pain. Not the gas, no. None of it mine."

Riggs swallowed, a softening in his throat. Some flicker in his friend's eyes, some sureness of his footing, hinted at a former clarity. Morton had done it—Riggs could not explain how—but with a few true words Morton had reached deep past the brokenness and awakened Wells. Riggs could not call his friend restored, no. But he appeared to be rescued, a man reacquainted with reality. Pray God that it be enough.

"John."

Wells's voice, calling softly. He reached his hand beyond the shelter of the bridge to catch rain in a shaky palm. "My Elizabeth," he said, an ache in his voice. "How much sorrow have I brought her? How much grief?"

19

For nearly three weeks, Charley sat atop the attic stairs, watching his father kneel with bristle brush and sudsy water to scrub bird dung from floorboards. Trousers soaked at the knees and shirt untucked, Horace swept feathers and seed into a barrel that he lugged to the yard and emptied into a fire pit beyond the shed. He spit-cleaned windows and oiled shutter hinges. The work exhausted him, but he insisted on proceeding without help. "My amends to Aunt Dorothy," he told Elizabeth, just returned from her Monday charity work at the insane asylum. He wanted to see in his wife's expressions a little of the confidence she once placed in him—perhaps even a hint of pride. He told her he would replace the door Riggs had destroyed, but she said Aunt Dorothy wanted the attic to air, which was a true answer if not forthright. *We must watch over you,* Elizabeth thought. "Here's a penny," she more than once told Charley. "Go be your father's tiny shadow."

Though his wife tried to hide her vigilance, Horace detected it and accepted its necessity. He no better understood what he now called "Morton's Cure" than Elizabeth did. It had come without his awareness, like the descent into sleep's truest dreams. Humbug, he'd cried, and Morton twisted his mouth, and rain fell, and what bedeviled Horace—those shrieks—relented. They did not quiet. They did not end. If anything, he might say, they had lifted, let him be. Whether this new clarity, seemingly accidental as grace, hinted at remission from his history with pain, he was unsure.

In the parlor one bright afternoon, Dr. Taft listened again to the wet sighs in Horace's chest. He admitted that Horace's health seemed improved, but he nevertheless prescribed a bleeding. Horace declined. Elizabeth, sitting nearby, poked a needle through an embroidery hoop and nodded her agreement. The doctor's frown showed his disappointment. "If not a bleeding then at least consider this a season of reading and contemplation. Otherwise you risk consumption." Elizabeth replied in a flat, unimpressed tone: "My Horace contemplates with an intensity that would exhaust a draft horse."

Nevertheless, Elizabeth enjoined her husband to measure activities in minutes and half hours. Rest in the between times, she urged. No rough-and-tumble games with Charley. He was not even to read to the boy but rather sit while Charley read to him. And so Charley introduced several books to his father that summer, including one that told stories about great American inventors who changed history, and as Charley read aloud about Eli Whitney and Benjamin Franklin and Robert Fulton, his father often napped, restlessly, and dreamed of his own unborn inventions: dental tools or machines to ease daily life. When he woke, he sketched what he had dreamed and felt calm.

He showed Elizabeth the sketches and with a sharp pencil pointed out their features. She praised when his work deserved praise and offered suggestions when warranted. Mostly, she encouraged his occupation with anything other than "that loathsome gas."

He disapproved of her phrase. To blame the gas for his troubles was like blaming the sea for a boat that sinks under its foam. Better to build a tighter boat. If nitrous oxide had been a kind of poison to him, that meant he needed to improve his processes, tighten up his experiments. Elizabeth might consider the gas loathsome and his hopes for it failed, but Ben Franklin did not harness electricity on his first try. Nor did Robert Fulton's first engine power a ship across the Atlantic.

His mind needed a respite, true. But despite his best intentions, he woke thinking about the gas, and his last thought before he lay beside his wife each night was about the same. If poison, it was one that fascinated and perturbed him, quickened his pulse.

Frannie Steele had lost patience with the new crowd in the house. "Too many people!" she told Dorothy, "too many people!" So now that the troubles had abated, she accepted the marriage proposal of a widower from Manchester named Rothman, whose children were grown and who wanted a companion to warm his bed and wash his socks.

"I'll have the wedding here," Dorothy said. She twisted her index finger in her whiskers, swallowed a big gulp of ale, and put aside Horace's newest drawings of something he called an *improved* shower-bath. "Mr. Rothman wants the wedding at his farm, but I'll not have that good woman married in mud and manure."

Horace pointed to the papers. "It's like bathing in the rain," he said, "except it falls indoors. My improvement involves a foot pedal and treadle action."

She picked up the pages as a dog seizes a rabbit, shook them in her hands and studied them a polite, brief moment.

"Where does the water go afterward?" Her tone sounded as if he'd just handed her a dead bird and asked her to gnaw the beak.

"Into a pot to carry out."

"You'd need a mule to carry the water necessary for my bathing."

He thought a moment. So did she.

"No more than twenty guests for the service," she said. "But a larger crowd for the reception."

"What if I create a closed system? The water circulates."

She turned over the pages to their blank sides and waved Horace to fetch her lapdesk and quill. He pointed to his work, and his eyes showed his alarm, but she waved again. "Quill and lapdesk," she said. "Be quick. I'm inspired."

What choice did he have?

"If we move these tables into the bedrooms," she said, "the company should fit in the parlor." She made a note across the back of Horace's plans. She kept writing and talking until she entered a kind of fury, eyes narrowing, hand punching the quill's nib against the paper. "Coneflowers a possibility for Frannie's bouquet," she said, "but daisies preferred. No. Daisies a *must*. Coneflowers, then, in a dozen vases, including one on the pianoforte. Or gladiolus. I'll invite Honesty Cox to play the music; she knows her voice squeaks and won't be tempted to sing. Reverend Hawes will do the deed, though with strict limits on the length of his homily or I swear on Mr. Sedgewick's grave I'll never tithe again. You'll arrange entertainments for the reception, won't you, Horace? A game of graces for the ladies? Don't look at me that way. Graces for the ladies, battledore and shuttlecock for the gentlemen. And for Frannie's return to wifeliness we'll kill the fatted calf, won't we? Sink forks into its marbled steaks."

Dorothy set aside the quill, shook the papers into a neat stack. She looked straight at Horace, her eyes red and shining wet. "Heaven knows, nephew, that I wanted to salve dear Frannie's grief and, if I am honest, my own. But it seems Dorothy Sedgewick is no lasting balm. And that fact demands its own consolations."

During the ceremony, Charley sat with Daphnis, the black cat, rearranging its dumpling-plump self on his lap, and he insisted his father hold the orange-and-white Chloe. When the couple exchanged vows, Chloe arched her back and circled Horace's lap, pawing with extended claws through his trousers and into the skin on his thighs. In turn, Horace tensed the muscles in his buttocks, lifted himself almost imperceptibly, and clamped his hands in a death squeeze around the edges of his seat. But there was something lovely about Chloe's abuse, the cat purring, the pain precise and delicate: a strange honor, the sense that the cat was making use of him. And then Chloe curled into his lap; his reward.

Later, after the guests had left, he would write that in his notebook, that a little pain heightens pleasure. Does, therefore, a little pleasure heighten pain? He wondered whether that relationship could be expressed mathematically. A cat's claws plus your lap equals what?

Outside, the ripe sun made guests cheerful, and children tried to catch downy seeds as they drifted from trees to the lawn. Farmer Rothman and his new wife won all the games of battledore and shuttlecock, the red-faced groom frightening opponents with his clumsy intensity. After games, the company dined on veal and venison and summer vegetables, sang hymns and cut cake. Elizabeth found her husband collecting the strewn battledore rackets and the hoops, and she took his face with both her hands and kissed his lips. Her cheeks flushed. He felt a liquid rush, a happy coolness to counter the day's heat.

"Have you been drinking Aunt Dorothy's ale?"

She pet his side whiskers. "Playing graces," she said. "Let's stroll."

Hand in hand they walked to where tall lilacs had been trimmed into trees, and she sat with him in their shade. She smoothed her dress, ordered from Lowell, of silk and Alabama cotton, the sleeves banded down, a belt fastened high at her slender waist. Aunt Dorothy had loaned her an Oriental hand fan, and with it Elizabeth cooled herself. Her hair in a bun snuggled at her collar, its decorative braids and daisies done up in a pattern too complicated for Horace ever to unravel, nor did he want to. He wanted only to look at her, girl and woman all at once, who had plucked him from the crowd. She tucked strands that had come loose during graces, and when she turned her head into the sunlight he saw the finest hairs flash on her cheeks. He invited her to lie with her head resting in his lap, and she did, closing her eyes. With fingertips at her temples he counted her pulse without meaning to, and he thought about nothing and then thought how wonderful it was to have a mind full of nothing.

She whispered as if from a dream, "Did you see Charley playing with Farmer Rothman's grandchildren?"

"I saw him giving tours of the cats' outhouses."

Her fingers played with the neck of her dress, revealing a linen corset underneath. "You have your smaller self," she said. "I would like one, too."

He smiled, then didn't, then did again. Spots of sun flitted through the lilac leaves and over his face, and he felt himself blinking too much.

"A daughter?"

She nodded. "If it's God's will. Something tells me it is."

"In Boston, I did dream we had a daughter." He coughed once into a kerchief, tightness just now in his lungs and throat. The midwife's long-ago shouting repeated in his ears. Those strangling sounds Elizabeth made. Her eyes, though open, had seen nothing.

Elizabeth laughed, alive there on the lawn. "Don't look so grave! So, why don't we?"

The shovel biting into the compliant dirt, how he had carried Charley into the hole. Had he lost his senses? He supposed he had. Elizabeth's agony eating away whatever made Horace *Horace*—bringing back that negation born at his dying father's bedside and returned too often since. It was never him, never him—yet he bore the consequences.

As though sensing his thoughts, she said, "I'll take the risks."

He believed her, and that belief brought both pride and fear. He reached for her hand, touched lips to her fingertips. So real, so tender. Her heart, alive and fierce with such courage. But she had only survived her travail; she'd not witnessed it, did not grasp its full substance. He tried to explain. He said, "It is no crime that I love you more than I wish for a child."

Now she sat upright. A few grass blades stuck to the skin near her wrist, and she brushed them away, then settled out of his reach.

"That you love me," she said, "means you would consider my wish."

"I am considering. What if God gives another boy?"

"His will, as I said." She shrugged. "We try again."

She sat straighter if that were even possible, and lifted her chin, and he thought in this moment even angels would admire her beauty. Her eyes fell upon him, bright green with as powerful a gravity as the moon's, drawing answers up out of him like a tide.

"Horace," she said. "Tell me what has happened to us. We have not—it has been so long since you, since we . . ."

A finch alighted so a lilac branch waved and caught his eye. The buds, he noticed, were spent, brown husks needing to be pruned. He knew he must tell her about his oath, because she asked and because he loved her.

It was a relief to him as he spoke. He wondered why he'd kept the oath a secret so long. She would not die, he told her. He would not be the origin of what killed her. But as he explained, he saw that his words created a new space between them, one with both distance and weight. Something moved across her face. A wave, then another, color, then shade, sorrow then confusion. When Elizabeth spoke next, her voice came as if from a wound, as if a wound itself could speak.

"You made that decision alone? Without me?"

He tried to find the words. When he made the oath, she had been closer to death than to life. He'd act differently now—or hoped he would. Who could predict what the tormented soul would do in such a moment. Yes, true, he had made that decision alone. Yet always she was with him. Always.

"A child we have never known?" he asked. "How can that be worth your life?"

Just as when she had lured him into the lawn, she pressed her palms against either side of his head, brought his face close, touched her forehead to his. "Charley's birth taxed me," she said, "but I am here. With God's help, I survived. With God's help, I've endured an unnatural distance you and your oath opened between us. But I want a daughter, Horace. I want you in my arms among the quilts I've sewn, and I want a daughter to come of that."

20

"Of course you must go," Aunt Dorothy said, though even Charley knew she wanted them to stay—especially now that the clop of Frannie's thick-soled shoes was only an echo in the vast Sedgewick house. "It is natural that a man and his family make their own home, just as it is natural that we all someday accustom ourselves to solitude. Now my turn comes round again."

It was a Thursday in September, and a cold snap had broken the valley's summer heat and dampness. Elizabeth hugged Aunt Dorothy to whisper blessings and gratitude, and Charley promised the cats he'd return to help them hunt mice. Once arrived again at Lord's Hill, Horace spoke a prayer of thanks before he thumbed the door latch. Then the family crossed the threshold into their cottage for the first time since winter, like survivors of a banishment now returned safely home.

Since that day with Morton at the Hog River bridge, Horace's head and lungs had cleared so that now a deep breath felt as satisfying to him as a mainsail's whoosh and pop as it unfurls into a stout wind. Consequently, at Lord's Hill he became his old industrious self, resuming dentistry while in his spare time constructing a working model of his improved shower-bath. The model gained the attention of a local manufacturer, who agreed to refine the construction and reproduce the machine it if it were patented, so Horace sent away that paperwork. "A little extra money," he told Elizabeth, "or a wagonful should the shower-bath prove a great success." At his office, he gathered dental patients old and new, and he reread his notes about nitrous oxide and requested that chemists deliver bladders to his office. "Be cautious," Elizabeth said, kissing his cheek. "The gas makes you fragile." Later, when he recalled her words, he pictured himself glass blown, all smooth turns and long, slippery colors, airy as an angel.

So as not to alarm her, he did not advertise the gas that fall and winter as a tool of dentistry. But if a patient knew and asked, Horace turned a key in its padlock and withdrew a bladder from a crate. And if a patient did not ask but suffered pain that made Horace wince—

my gums feel stabbed by pins;

it's as if demons mean to fork the tooth from its bed;

there's that keen fishhook, and the awful anticipation

—he would suggest the gas. When eyelids drooped, the purest relief would wash over him, and he'd work. He never charged for the gas, and he made no marks in his daybook regarding its application. But those operations bolstered his belief in his discovery, in the scientific necessity of the sweet breaths he gave and of those he took.

He wanted to imagine a daughter with Elizabeth's face. For her sake, he tried.

At Lord's Hill one night, the weather tolerable, he carried a mug of Aunt Dorothy's favorite ale to a clearing beyond the cottage. From there he could see the city below and past that the valley's great river with its steamboats and its farms on the far bank. He put the mug to his lips, tasted the ale's tang. A north wind tossed his hair. He liked to think it blew all the way from Vermont, and that breathing it filled his chest with the maple-scented clarity of his birthplace, its black earth and blue-white snow.

A daughter. The question was not yet settled. Just that morning, Elizabeth had put her soft and warm lips to his, and he felt a hint of pleasure from his wife as a husband ought. They were leaving for church, their affection interrupted when Charley asked help to tie his shoelaces. As the family rode to the service, Horace enjoyed watching Elizabeth in that familiar way, admiring the whiteness of her skin, the inviting line of her neck. At the service, he prayed, telling God he loved his wife, and that he knew he ought to love God more, but must his two loves conflict? So arduous, the tension. To love God and keep his vow was to punish his wife, who had done no wrong, and how, he asked God, does that fulfill Your will? Wasn't it possible, he prayed, that Elizabeth survived Charley's birth because Heaven meant for her to bear a daughter? But then, as if offering God's reply, Reverend Hawes announced his sermon's theme: the sin of taking the Lord's name in vain. A growing noise filled Horace's head until it became a roar, and he heard none of the minister's talk, but gripped Elizabeth's hand as she squeezed his own. Afterward, her face gone pale, she trembled as she spoke. "You did not want to risk my life," she said. "How can I ask you to break your vow and risk your soul?"

That night, he finished his ale, his eyelids now dropping, his head too fuzzy to make sense of oaths and daughters. Inside, he dressed in his night-clothes and slid into bed beside Elizabeth, who drowsed and warmed herself against him, and—suddenly a white dog with a mangled foreleg lunged for his throat, and he startled awake surprised and afraid that by flailing he had struck his wife.

And Morton stood by the bed, face sharp with the intensity it showed that day at the Hog River. Morton repeated the question he asked then: nitrous oxide and what else?

Nothing else, Horace said, as he had in life.

Then Elizabeth whispered Horace's name, and Morton stepped from the room, the door closing behind him, and Horace turned his head upon his pillow and let his wife's caresses calm him to a peaceful sleep.

The next morning at his office, Horace recalled his dream and wondered what element Morton might have had in mind. Surely he had something in mind. A man with creditors must always be on the prowl for easy fortunes. Poppies and opium? Might a vapor be distilled from those? Or from ether? In Europe, he'd read, chemists had uncovered a gas called chloroform that suggested itself as a possibility for annulling pain. Perhaps Morton knew about these, too. Or Morton's chemist friend, bug-eyed Jackson. Certainly bug-eyed Jackson.

He wrote his thoughts in a notebook, including suspicions about his failure in Boston and whether Morton or Jackson—the two of them!—could be involved. How could it be coincidence that nitrous oxide failed only that time?

When finished, he marked the notebook's cover <u>Tooth Pulling</u>. A misdirection should Morton return to snoop—via steam train or dream or otherwise.

One afternoon, a tap-tap at the office door, and a hen's muffled chuckle. Though lost in a laughing-gas world, Horace heard it, distantly, and he closed the spigot on the faucet, breathed instead the air of his office and let the world return, which it did, as always, quickly. His legs wobbled as he opened the door to find the woman who was mother to Maggie, the mad girl, and who held a small coop of three chickens at her side. He glanced over her shoulder and saw she'd come alone. She wore a patched coat, and around her neck a black scarf with red tassels. Her dark hair lay tangled at the ends, and he thought to offer a comb for her tresses (and that is the word that came to him—*tresses*). Her back was arched, lifting her breast, straightening her shoulders, giving her a regality, queen of Dutch Point. She held her lips tight, unsmiling, and dabbed a clean kerchief to her mouth near the two pinprick moles at the corner. He invited her in. Her knuckles were pink and chapped.

"You have no gloves," he said and felt an impulse to warm her hands in his. Instead, he arranged tools on his desk.

"You worked on my daughter once," she said.

Nodding. Arranging. "You also attended my exhibition involving birds. I remember."

"I'd hoped you would." Half her mouth smiled. "Levi says you asked for visits. Others who've been told me about the gas. You dream, they say, and you're healed."

He thought the phrasing lovely, and he smiled. "Remind of your name," he said, though he remembered. Nan.

She did, then asked how much she would owe for his work.

"There's no charge."

"Oh, I can't afford that." Her smile filled him with a strange sense of ease, but then she stumbled. He reached for her, withholding his hands when he saw that she'd caught the table and righted herself.

"Haven't eaten in a while," she said. "Can't get food past the pain in my mouth."

She set the coop on a table at which he'd been sitting for lunch. Laying hens, mottled brown and gray. A chicken shuddered, and a curled feather fell from the cage to settle in the sauce of his beans. Nan unbuttoned her coat and untied her scarf, closing her eyes and lifting her chin, as if wanting distance between the knot and her tender jaw. He took the scarf to hang on a peg and noticed wood shavings and bits of feather tangled in its weave. Her dress, tightly laced, had been expensive once and flattered her despite the bygone years since it had been in fashion.

"A cup of coffee?" he asked. She declined. Despite her proud bearing, she looked smaller than he remembered, as if whatever pained her had also caused her to shrink. He noted redness in her cheeks and a pimpling of flesh along her throat. Far off, factory bells chimed the end of lunch break.

He steered her to the patient's chair but hesitated to place the gas bladder in her lap, and when she nodded permission, he arranged it with the care of a housemaid positioning a silk pillow on a loveseat. Her breathing was shallow, and he turned to record this in his notes, but as he put quill to paper forgot what he meant to write. Turning back, he marked again the swell of her breast. *Shallow breathing*, he wrote.

"How is Maggie?"

"Still at the retreat. Nothing to be done, is what they say."

When counting her pulse, he left his fingers overlong at her wrist, feeling the warm delicacy of her skin. He made careful notes regarding an oh-so-slight swelling of her jaw, how it seemed also in her lips. With each letter, he concentrated on shape and line. "Please," he said, "will you undo the top collar button?" He explained, as he had with all his patients, that he wanted nothing to impede the flow of gas to the lungs, but for the first time his request embarrassed him. "I will invite a lady from another office to stay with us," he said. A disapproving frown conveyed she wasn't so fussy. She complied using just one hand—a twist of her fingers—and he realized he still held her other wrist as if counting her pulse a second time. The chickens murmured. The skin beneath her bodice showed fever symptoms as well. Warm pink across her breastbone.

"Could I die?" she asked. The casualness of her question surprised him.

"I've inhaled the gas many times," he said. "It hasn't killed me."

"You own property," she said. "Men who own property can't die so easily. Not like those of us who have none."

He showed her how to take the gas. "Fill your lungs, then empty them entirely. Expand the rib cage. Take in many such breaths."

She practiced. She said she smelled the chickens and the wood stove's smoke. Then she laughed. "It's an attractive quality, isn't it," she said, "a ruined mouth?"

He felt something open inside him and recalled the white dog, how it lay in the woods, magnificent in its vulnerability, more perfect in pain than in health. It wasn't ruin itself that was attractive, no, but some quality of the wounded, and because of it Nan became more beautiful, and he felt tender toward her, a protector; her trust straightened his own back.

"No reason to talk so much," he told her.

But when she was silent, he missed her voice. He heard particular autumn days in its timber and resonance, the days that follow the first chill, when warmth surprises, and sun gilds the leaves of maples and birches, and the gourds want harvesting. He lay a hand across her forehead, felt dampness near her scalp line. "It's nothing messy," he said, "a simple procedure. A trickle of acid to kill the pulp." He let his fingers fall against her tangles. "Are you comfortable?"

"You said I shouldn't talk so much."

He smiled, squeezed her hand; she squeezed back and held his. "You didn't answer truly before," she said. "Could I die?"

Breath caught in his throat. He found he did not want to speak for fear she would let go his hand. Then she did.

"I'll breathe your gas," she said. "But you must tell me what you'll do with my remains should I die. Will you dump me in the Hog River? Or give me a proper burial? Or will you hide my body in some dank cellar?"

"Which do you prefer?" He smiled as he fiddled with the bladder's faucet.

"I'd rather be eaten by fishes than by worms."

She took the faucet in her mouth, and he turned the spigot. She breathed as he instructed. From outside, he heard the complaints of passing goats. He imagined a small herd on the street, a boy with a stick and a dog keeping each in its place.

He took his time as if the procedure were one of leisure, a pleasure to savor. There was reverence as he touched acid to tooth—and later, grateful and wretched and on his knees, he would wonder whether such reverence was a form of idol worship. But for now he only wanted to concentrate, to shift his attention among his senses. He saw that a wooden button at her midbreast was chipped. When she breathed, he listened to a soft whistle from the back of her throat, as if a thrush's nestling hungered there. Leaning near, he smelled cedar and imagined that she'd slept the night on a bed of shavings. Her lips gave against his fingers as he opened her mouth, and he wondered about her age and then decided not to wonder about her age. He adjusted a mirror for brighter light.

With a damp kerchief, he wiped the corners of her mouth and whispered, "Nan?" She nodded, but the spell of the gas had taken hold. The whistle, softer, came again from her throat, so he released one more button, the button with the rough chip.

Whiteness revealed, the gentle curve. He looked away from it, reached again to open her mouth, touched her lips, her chin, paused at her neck. He let his fingertips trace the larynx to the bump of the collarbone, edge the spacing of the high ribs just above her sternum. Then he turned his hand and let his knuckles drift across her blouse where her breast rose with each quiet breath. The whistling thrush. The scent of cedar. His hand back and forth, grazing the fabric. With his apron, he wiped his eyes.

Another button pinched between his fingers. Abrupt, this awful need, and it took hold of him, he yielded to it, his lips grazed the warm swell of her bared breast.

Her eyes opened.

In his mind, he startled away, but when he looked his hand still rested on the fabric, on her breast. She saw, too, smiled a drowsy smile. If he'd had another moment, he later told himself, he might have decided upon the right action. Or if he'd had a lifetime. But he had neither—and never would. Nan shifted in the chair, languorous. Her fingers caressed the faucet in her lap. When she handed it to him, her tongue flicked to wet her lips. He twice breathed deep, shivered. "It doesn't hurt," she said as she helped him lift her skirt.

Afterward, alone again in his office, Horace locked the door, shuttered the windows, and sat in his patient's chair, a bladder in his lap, his skin atingle. So unsettling to feel both weak and bold, to know remorse and gratitude. He wished Morton were across the hall, or at a tavern where they might meet. You could trust Morton's vices. Morton could explain how Horace's life had just changed, what might happen next.

An adulterer who fornicates without regret—a great man. Hadn't Horace said that once? Hadn't he called Morton a great man?

And Horace?

He breathed from the bladder.

A daughter, Elizabeth had said. Bodies coupled again as husband and wife. Husband and wife! Yet here he sat, fresh from a first infidelity. So much for oaths and vows. Perhaps she was right. Perhaps the gas made him fragile. A great and fragile man. Another breath.

In and out. In, out. In. Out.

Inout

and thoughts of Elizabeth

of Nan

of buttons undone

21

The old year surrendered to the new, dry and cold, the skies blue as God's grace. Her husband hurried about outdoors, attending to a fire he had burning under a lidded cauldron. Elizabeth watched him from inside the cottage, through the window over the kitchen basin, where she washed morning dishes. The cauldron, full of water, hung over a fire pit he'd dug the past day, its brace fashioned out of the limbs of an oak tree. She'd always wanted a fire pit out of doors for candle-making and the like, though Horace had been too busy to build one. Now that she had agreed to try his shower-bath, she had her wish.

One wish. A wish. Not *the* wish. It had been weeks since their conversations touched on the idea of another child. What she had thought was a simple decision about family had become tangled: Horace's devotion to her well-being, his oath before God, sin's peril, love's pity. She no longer knew what to say or to think, and it seemed the same for Horace. That he would soon leave for several months of travel removed any urgency to resolve the matter. All that remained was prayer and patience, and the twinge she felt whenever she spied a mother with a little girl.

Horace's hand darted under the cauldron as he moved fiery sticks here and there, crouched to blow into the ash and smoke. Watched pot, she thought, but then steam from the cauldron's lip curled into the winter air. With rag wrapped about his hand, Horace lifted the lid to peek inside. "It's ready!" he called, his voice sounding hollow though the windowpanes. He began ladling water into a pail.

She dillydallied as she undressed in his workshop—where he had assembled the shower-bath—so that when Horace first arrived with a bucket to pour water for the bath, she had shed only her apron and frock. And with the next bucket her stockings. With the third, she had removed her undergarments and stood behind the dressing curtain as natural as Eve, turned in such a way as to hide her belly's sagging skin and what the years had added to her hips.

"A shower-bath nymph," he said and pecked her cheek.

"It looks to be a very fine machine," she said.

"Finer than the working model I built. The manufacturer employs talented craftsmen. It's sure to sell."

Pray God, she thought, let it be so. She worried for him, of course, once more alone and gone from home, three months convincing merchants throughout western New England and New York state to carry the shower-bath. He assured her: the manufacturer had agreed to fund the trip, with particular stipulations having to do with revenue and whatnot. Horace would earn back in shower-bath sales what he lost in those months he gave up his practice. She appreciated and respected his faith in his new invention, but it was not money that worried her—or not what worried her most. It was the memory of his last sojourn and his sorry return from Boston, bootless and muttering. Yes, he'd recovered himself. But birdsong still haunted her, so that even a caged bird's trill stopped her breath. She watched him perhaps too carefully, and for the last several weeks had observed in him a nervous spirit. Quick each day to the office, and once home he shut himself in his workshop. Shut himself, she noted, *away* from her. Shower-bath business, he told her. She listened, yet in a spot just below her heart she felt slippery fear: that it was not his new invention that gripped him but the allure of that loathsome gas.

"Hurry, hurry," he said, his rough hand on her shoulder directing her into the bath.

"Don't scald me."

"No, no. By the time the water is in the pipes, it cools enough. You'll love how clean you become."

"I always love being clean," she said.

She faced the spigot and worked the pedals as he'd shown. Water began to pump out, a trickle at first.

"Push harder," he said.

His eagerness made her smile. "I forgot a wash cloth," she said.

By the time he'd fetched one, she'd pumped the water into a hard, hot rain. It splashed against her breasts, and her skin flushed, and she lowered her head to catch the spray. She could hear gurgling and rushing through the pipes. Horace kept talking, but this small compartment felt too lush, too private, to allow for intrusion, and she said, "Hush now. You want me to enjoy this, let me enjoy it."

The water slid over her, and she soaped up, skin tingling, a saturation at her core, and she thought of Eden and damp, warm moss, and of rivers. She ran a wash cloth up the backs of her legs and inside her thighs. The water sprayed her face, and she smiled, and something in her reached out with a hope. *Wash my eyes, oh God,* she prayed. *Let me see clearly.*

When the water cooled to the temperature of the room, she stepped out. Horace waited, grinning, holding a large towel spread to welcome her. Before she moved into it, she paused to study him: his unkempt air, his swirl of hair, that eminent brow, delight asparkle in his eyes. When she drew close, he wrapped her tight and held her until she thought she might coo, then he whispered near her ear.

"Wonderful," she answered. Her legs became like air or water, and looking down at her bare feet next to his in boots, she felt a pleasant vulnerability. "Eden in a box."

IV
NEW ENGLAND TO
NEW COVENANT

22

The maid—her teeth so bucked they rested on her lower lip—did not know him, a stranger gone twelve years who claimed to be Abiather Shaw's stepson.

"Did you send Miz Betsey word of your visit?" she asked, then canted her head oh so suspiciously, big teeth biting.

This was New Hampshire in late May, a busy village near the Connecticut River, inside a familiar house that for Horace had never felt like home. Through open windows the afternoon's breeze lifted lace curtains, carried street sounds into the parlor. Somewhere outside a girl chided a pup, and chain links rattled and chunked.

Horace retied the ribbon on a box of hard candy. "For my mother," he said. "Your Mrs. Betsey." The maid took the package, asked him please to wait.

His fingertips nudging aside a curtain, Horace looked through wavy glass to mark the boy whom he'd paid a penny to guard his horse and wagon and what it carried: a working model of the shower-bath for demonstrations, and a crate of bladders, filled. The boy leaned against a rear wheel, his eye on a girl—almost a woman—who on tiptoes stretched to wipe a soapy rag over the high points of a bookstore's display window. At the wagon's front end, the mare, Newton, in harness twitched her ears against biting, flying creatures. Horace put his face nearer the window, wanting the breeze and sun. Elizabeth in Hartford would be washing windows, too. He winced. His conscience, that vengeful horsefly, still bit. He'd prayed for forgiveness, but all these months later to wake beside Elizabeth or to sit a pretty woman in his dentist's chair was to pretend that bite didn't sting and to act as if blameless. The deception wearied him. The days seemed ready to shatter and cascade in shards at his feet. The shower-bath had provided an excuse to leave home, and though he wanted its success and the income that would bring, he also embraced self-banishment as useful penance. Separation from Elizabeth might distance him from his failings, a respite during which he'd work to regain the brighter, truer parts of his soul. Failure, he told himself, is handmaiden to hope. Upon his return, he'd be the husband his wife deserved.

Yet he'd not told her about those bladders of gas that he'd packed. Still a man who kept secrets. Must be honest with himself about that, at least.

When he entered his mother's sitting room, she praised God and—as if Horace had left the house only a few minutes earlier to buy tobacco—asked him please to move a sofa to a spot away from the window. "Careful with it, though," she said, her chirping-sparrow voice tinged with its day-to-day hysteria. "You know how your father prizes his floors."

He lifted the sofa high. "My father is dead."

But she seemed not to hear. "Two inches right." Her head cocked, she held her hand as if directing a puppet, invisible strings looped to her fingers. "I couldn't stand this arrangement a moment longer. Everything looked ajumble. Did the new girl ask you to wait long? We didn't know you were coming. That's good. Right there. Now, before we sit, give your mother a hug."

Closer now, on the couch, he noticed that her eyebrows had gone gray. With a fist, she bunched her sweater's collar tightly at her neck. Her hands seemed smaller and less capable than he recalled; he wished it were otherwise.

"Aren't you chilled?" she asked. "Your father likes to keep the windows open. He'll want to smoke with you after dinner. Have you taken up a pipe?"

"I might miss him. I need to make Bennington by nightfall."

"Oh, no. He'll be home soon. And you'll stay overnight."

He leaned near, bumped his shoulder against hers in a conspiratorial way. "I'd fall asleep in one room," he said, teasing, "and in the morning find that you'd rearranged my bed out into the side alley."

Her laugh was sincere. He liked that he still could make her laugh. She glanced over her shoulder to the window as if considering the alley's suitability for a bed. "One mustn't rely too much on things as they are," she said. "It's not good for the elasticity of the mind."

"There must be a best way to arrange things, and once found left alone."

"Not to my view. The Son, I'm certain, would sometimes like to sit at the *left* hand of the Father. Don't look that way." She gazed upward. "It's a joke."

Tea followed, with honey and chitchat about garden blooms, a road washed out near Brattleboro, his brother the physician (for whom Charley was named) still unmarried. He spoke of his shower-bath and the financial security it could provide. "Elizabeth wants another child," he said. His mother chirped and clapped at the idea of a granddaughter. When pressed, she agreed that the Shaws would enjoy a shower-bath. "Though Mr. Shaw will know best," she said.

In the parlor, as Horace fixed in place the shower's pedals for demonstration, Mr. Shaw limped through the front door, arthritic leg thumping the floorboards with each step. His gray eyes leaked when he blinked, and his voice still sounded as if it passed through gravel to his tongue. Something like a smile crippled his face. The odor on his breath suggested loose gums. This was an age Horace's father had never been.

"What contraption is this?" his stepfather said. "I thought you practiced dental surgery."

Horace stiffened. "I do have my kit if you need treatment."

Abiather Shaw waved away the suggestion and circled the shower-bath, his afflicted leg stiff and thumping. "I can't track your enterprises," he said. "Didn't you have a business in Boston? Something to do with ornithology? Your stepbrother lives in Boston, you know. An architect. Worked with Bulfinch. Top o' the mountain. What happens to the water?"

"It drains to this chamber." Horace squatted and pointed. "Then it recirculates via this pipe to the spout, pushed by the force of the feet working the pump."

"Twice-used bathwater? Why do I want dirty water splashing in my eyes?"

Horace stiffened. He noticed his mother across the room, cradling a bowl of potpourri at her waist, looking here and there. She placed the bowl on the pianoforte, seeming as far away from Horace as if he were yet in Hartford.

"Abiather," she said, her voice thin as a breeze, "invite our son to stay the night."

Horace took up a wrench, loosened a nut on the shower-bath wall. He'd practiced disassembling it and could pack it into its crate in seven minutes.

"Make your mother happy," his stepfather said.

"I need to reach Bennington by nightfall. Early appointments with merchants interested in my invention. Perhaps we'll see you someday in Hartford. You might like visiting us there."

But Abiather Shaw was already limping out of the parlor. "Business first," he said. "A sound decision."

Horace did not reach Bennington that night, nor had he meant to. Crossing the Connecticut River, he steered Newton along a road still lumpy with frost heaves, and in the village of Bellows Falls, he parked near a grain mill hard beside a saltbox house in rough repair. "A series of tenants since we moved out," his mother had warned. "They've been unkind to the property. I don't like to see it." Now, on his wagon's bench, Horace leaned to pat Newton's rump by way of thanking the mare for bringing him here, for proving reliable, solid. The house looked meaner than in Horace's memory: the yard all weeds and packed earth, clapboards repaired with scrap, a peeling painted fence behind which a few hens kept company in the moonlight with a scabrous, yipping terrier. Horace expected someone to step from the house, to demand his business or suggest he move on, but none did. Tonguing the space where his tooth had been, he lifted his face and saw flecks of starlight glint in a second-floor window, darkness from the room behind. There his dying father had lain, young Horace—age fourteen—attending. He thought to pray, but that terrible power was not right for him, not now. The bat jerked again through memory, and Horace realized how fiercely he now gripped the wagon's brake handle. Newton scraped a hoof over dirt, and Horace saw a shooting star rend the heavens.

Later, at an inn, he fastened the door latch of his room and made certain the window was shut, turned a faucet and breathed the gas. He hoped for a vision of his father, healthy as when he tapped maples, but instead came a woman strange to him, young, who pressed near, her breath unnerving at his ear. Her whisper: "I hurt."

On he drove, west through mountains and across the Hudson River into New York. A Hoosick Falls storekeeper agreed to sell the shower-bath, as did one in Albany. Too expensive, the rest kept saying, and for this Horace blamed the manufacturer, Col. Roberts, who had calculated costs and set the price. Yet he, the inventor, would by contract owe Roberts money if the bath didn't sell! This knowledge troubled his sleep.

Deep into the Catskills he lost track of the calendar and did not know it was a Wednesday when he and Newton drove a narrow trace into a fen. Branches lashed his cheeks, and the evening air brought cobwebs and mosquitoes and despondency. He coughed—he'd been coughing for days—and a sharp pain surged at the back of his skull. Self-diagnosis: cephalgia, occipital. Headache. Stemming from a chronic cough brought on by morning dampness, prolonged by lack of sleep. He coughed again, so violently that he gagged and spit and sweat broke across his brow, something in his chest hardening as if to petrification. Distant, he heard a panther's scream, and then—closer—an owl's plaint.

Elizabeth and Charley. The worse he felt the more he wished for them. Her with forehead flushed from garden work; the boy in his favorite paper hat. Their voices seemed just at the edge of his hearing—until it seemed not only possible but likely that in the next moment Elizabeth would materialize on the bench to his right, Charley tucked between his parents.

He reined Newton to a stop. Enough sleeplessness, he told himself.

Crawling into the wagon's bed, he unlocked a crate, removed a bladder, bunched his coat as a pillow. With a few quick breaths, he found his way into slumber and dream. Where he found them.

Elizabeth and Charley crouched around a plot of overturned earth, the dingy sky casting a metallic glow—menacing and static. Wet dirt smudged Elizabeth's chin. She held a trowel. Her hair hung loose as she dug, her skirt muddy at the knees. In the dream's unnatural quiet her breath echoed, the trowel rasped with each cut into soil. At the garden's edge, Charley chewed his lip. Redness rimmed his eyes. Elizabeth dug as if she hadn't noticed her son, as if exhaustion allowed her one focal point, which was her chore. Horace watched from sleep, helpless no matter how hard his heart beat.

"My arm still won't move," Charley said, his voice breaking.

Elizabeth drove the trowel with such force her grip slipped. Horace wondered what she meant to unearth. When she spoke, the cold strength of her voice frightened him.

"Dr. Taft said nothing is wrong."

"I can't lift it."

In the dirt, Horace saw root, worms. A spider crawled up the trowel handle toward Elizabeth's bare hand. Charley wiped his eyes with his left. "Papa could fix my arm," he said.

Elizabeth stopped digging, leaving the tool's blade buried. She stared then, not so much at Charley as toward the dreaming Horace. He saw it, straight on, a reproach and a challenge. She yanked the trowel free, stabbed once more into dirt. Why? What to unearth or to bury? He peered hard into the hole. "Why are you digging?" he asked, but it was with Charley's voice. Elizabeth did not answer except to tap the trowel against her left elbow. "My arm, also, is useless," she said. "You must help me dig."

She drove the trowel, waited. With his good arm, Charley made a scoop of his hand and pulled loose dirt from the hole. "Why are we digging?" he asked.

Sweat smarted her eyes, which in the strange magic of dreams had become Horace's eyes. Blinking away the salt-sting, he and she noticed shards of a pot, broken eggshells, a centipede, larvae, bits of paper on which something was written but could not be read.

"Why are we digging?" Charley pleaded, his voice rising.

One eye opened to light. Overhead, a canopy of leaves. Sunlight bright through them. Horace lifted himself from where he lay across the wagon's bed. Coughed. A mosquito whined at his ear. Farther away, bird calls. Goldfinch? Yellow-rumped warbler? He did love the *Sylvia coronata*.

Newton stared up the road. Or was that down? Both views were unfamiliar. Had Newton wandered? Horace considered whether he'd forgotten to set the wagon's brake.

He lifted the bladder at his side. Empty.

A mosquito lit on his wrist, near a prominent vein. He slapped it dead, then returned the empty bladder to the crate, marked that only one full bladder remained. Had he breathed so much gas? He couldn't remember. What remained from the night before seemed fogged, indistinct. He could not discern where memory ended and gaseous visions began. Never before this trip had the vapor brought on a nightmare. He would make a note, figure that out. He needed not to breathe nightmares.

Newton whinnied, and that was neither memory nor dream. Horace verified the proper direction by the sun's place and shook the reins, but the mare refused instruction. He touched her rump with the crop, then swatted, but she only twitched. When he, still light-headed, stood at her head and took the bridle to lead by foot, he noticed swelling below her right rear hip where there ought not be any. When did that happen?

Newton lifted the leg, set it down, a grotesque dance. She turned to him, ears aquiver. He searched her big face, leaned into the shiny fur of her neck, and breathed her horse smell. With her lips she nuzzled his coat sleeves as if they might hide a carrot.

Horace slipped his hands along the length of the swollen leg, over the bone-break. Jaw trembling, he climbed back into the wagon.

Nothing for it, then, but to wait for a man to come by in possession of a musket.

23

First came the hymn—an Isaac Watts tune, Horace guessed from the lyrics, something cheerful and platitudinous about hope wiping a tear from sorrow's eye and faith pointing toward the sky, and so forth. Then up rolled a wagon carrying the man who sang, if the sound could be called singing. That voice clambered from a larynx dry as cork, the tune sounding less warbled than exhumed.

The wagon stopped so near that Newton touched wet nose to wet nose with the other's horse, a raw-boned beast that had more sores than fur along its legs. Horace waved a two-fingered greeting. The other driver set his brake and grimaced, evaluating each detail of Horace's own wagon as if meaning to buy, then muttered, "Frippery." It was true Horace's running boards and cushioned bench seat made the man's own wagon look ascetic with its gray, peeling sideboards, the wheel bands flaked with rust, and the seat upholstered with what looked to be an old potato sack. Still, how odd that the man hadn't first said hello. Horace stepped toward the other wagon and saw in its bed a web of rope and a jumble of broken barrels— "Casks," the man corrected, "firkins and kilderkins"—because he was a cooper, and he was driving the casks to his shop for repair. He wore a wide-brimmed black oilcloth hat; twigs and bits of leaf tangled in his gray beard, long and thick as a prophet's. Then the man called out, a *deenk-deenk* sound like some piano key struck twice, and at his side appeared a Chinese boy dressed in faded yellow and gray rags, head shaved as if by a broken razor, forehead broad and pimpled, narrow chin and eyebrows placed by God as to suggest constant bewilderment, his face a living question mark.

"Today's language lesson," the cooper said, and he pointed in Horace's direction. "Tell me what we're seeing."

"City man," said the boy, in a voice mild as moss, "with a hurt horse."

"An *injured* horse. From the Latin *injuria*."

"Leg is big."

"It is *distended*."

"Small wagon, with bells."

"Frippery!" the old man said. "Frippery is sinful."

The boy nodded, and the old man palm-rubbed the boy's shaved scalp.

Horace turned to his wagon. Perhaps the bells were a bit much. Perhaps he had even indulged Newton, fed her too well, groomed her too often. He envied now how she stood at peace, somehow balanced despite the broken leg. She seemed to him the picture of patience, waiting without aspirations to any particular hope, without even an expectation. What she knew he needed to learn. Newton nickered toward the cooper's nag, who answered with bared teeth. Yes, the cooper said, he had a musket. He lowered himself from the bench to rummage, and flies moved from smear to smear of whatever the broken casks once carried. The sweet reek offended, and Horace pinched his nose. As the cooper pulled the rifle from a blanket roll, Horace noticed Bibles stacked in a corner of the wagon bed.

"I do, in fact, preach against the devil's works in the tradition of Mr. Edwards, late of Massachusetts colony," the cooper said. "There's a Hell, and it's by God's grace we're not swimming through its fires."

Horace had released Newton from the harness the night before, and now the cooper and the boy put their backs into moving Horace's wagon so the mare would have room to fall.

"I once thought to pursue ministry myself," Horace said. "My father had died. I saw his soul leave through his mouth. It scared me into studying God's ways."

The cooper said, "I've heard that about the soul at death."

Horace pet Newton's neck and wondered whether she could benefit from a breath of gas—how much for those immense lungs? Too late, though, wasn't it? If the mare had suffered, it was when she broke the leg and thereafter through this day. Soon the ball would cure any pain. Merciful. That's what the old farmers said. But how could they know? How could anyone know whether in that last moment pain fled the soul or joined it in eternity?

Horace's father—he knew.

Newton turned, nibbled at Horace's belt. The brown liquid of her eye, how she looked at him—so agreeable.

The cooper handed over the musket, and Horace took it, heavy but balanced, a pleasant weight. Alongside Newton's shoulder, he angled the barrel toward the fleshy part of her head behind the jaw. He thumbed the hammer so it clicked.

"Animals have no souls," said the cooper, as if to reassure. Then his thought carried him into theology. "Nor do Indians. I don't know about Negroes or Chinamen."

Newton, at the end of the barrel's length, tongued her own lips. Thirsty, Horace thought. I should let her drink. He felt too warm in his clothes, so he unbuttoned his shirt, rolled his cuffs. Once more he raised the musket. A sour taste surged from his throat, and he spit. To shoot Newton, he realized, he must want to shoot Newton. Such a simple truth. But how to want such a thing? He had not wanted to think Elizabeth would die from childbirth; *not*-Horace dug her grave. Nor had he wanted to work violence in mouths that already suffered. With his father—no, unimaginable wanting that. In none of those moments had the deepest, truest part of himself acted. He had no practice in such wanting. *Not*-Horace had spared him.

But now? Somehow, work with the gas had interrupted that mysterious transformation. In Warren's Boston hospital, in Horace's own dental office, no longer did *not*-Horace release him from intimacy with pain. Even now: his finger, none other, warmed the trigger.

The moment belonged to him and him alone.

When the musket roared, the cooper hopped back, and Newton's massive head lurched forward and down, her whole body following the spurt of blood, her knees buckling. But she caught and then righted herself. For a moment the mare stood long enough to convince Horace he would have to shoot her again. Then Newton shook her head as if to move flies, and she coughed a reddish spray. She staggered backward, but the broken leg couldn't support the weight, and Horace heard something in it rip and crunch. Her haunches sank, and she sat on her tail. Her head turned left and then right as if she searched for some answer, and Horace saw wild fear and confusion in her eyes. Then, because she could not balance that way forever, she folded sideways into a poison ivy patch beside the road.

"Catholics baptize Indians," Horace whispered, "so someone believes in their souls."

"Those fish-eaters will baptize anything! Even a peevish bear." The cooper's laugh sounded bitter.

Because the cooper's nag could not pull two wagons, and because the cooper refused to hitch his horse to frippery, Horace moved his few belongings (dentistry kit, shower-bath, a last bladder of gas) into the other, and the party drove south. Later, the cooper offered to share lunch, and Horace thanked him, but only took the biscuit in his fist, and sometimes forgot that he held it. The cooper gave language lessons to the boy, whom he called his apprentice, and ate so crumbs nestled in his beard. Wobbly-spined, Horace lurched with each bump and dip, recalling the resistance of the trigger under his finger, how it gave way, and he felt new, and he felt old.

Where they stopped that night the mosquitoes flew thick, so the cooper built a fire for the smoke. The Chinese boy sat on the crate that held the shower-bath, his legs splayed for balance, and he played melancholy tunes on a wooden flute. Now and then, Horace asked about wood-bending or scraping, but the cooper could not speak long about anything without finding his way back to wickedness and the devil, though his homilies sounded rote, a memory game or a stubborn tic more than a sincere effort to win Horace's salvation. Horace's fingers played around the faucet of the bladder in his lap.

"Is it a town?" asked Horace, "this New Covenant? Might they have a storekeeper?"

"Berry-pickers," the cooper said, his mouth full of biscuit, words even more garbled. "Sloth-mongers. No weeds ever grow in their gardens."

The cooper laughed for no reason Horace understood, then wiped his lips on his sleeve and spit into the fire. He began to hum what sounded like church music.

"Would they have an interest in hygiene? I have an invention."

The cooper looked at Horace quizzically. "Ah, Lord," he said, "I do love eating, but I weary of the time spent wiping my arse." The old man poked his way into the brush, and left Horace and the boy to stare at each other across the fire. Though he was about Charley's size in inches and girth, the boy's coordination and the bloodless cast to his eyes suggested he was nonetheless older. He wore a bird tattooed on the left side of his neck just below his ear. A raven or a crow—in all ways common—but with three legs. Horace offered a biscuit from the cooper's paper sack, but the boy ignored the gesture, now looking to the woods where the cooper had concealed himself.

"He frippery," the boy said.

By ferry they crossed the Delaware River, then arrived at New Covenant near dusk. The cooper set the wagon brake at the edge of what looked to be less a settlement than a camp. A bell rang, and suddenly smiling people surrounded the wagon as if welcoming loved ones. The cooper rose and in his graveyard voice bawled, "Fornicators!"—then babbled Bible verses so quickly Horace could not make them out. The people reached to shake hands and to hug. "Do you intend to join?" asked a grinning young fellow in a purple hat of some fashion Horace didn't recognize. "Have you heard the great voice sing?" queried another. Horace felt jostled by their good will, out of sorts, giddy despite himself. A ruddy complexion and spirit emanated, as if each person knew constant and happy exertion. Such infectious joy!

"What is this place?" Horace asked as he stepped to the ground.

"Look around," commanded a young woman, freckle-cheeked and in pants, her dairyman's high boots unlaced. Her arms swept the panorama—wall tents pitched amid moss and pine needles, a dusty bunch of Norfolk black turkeys (molting, Horace noted, outside their season), and countless dogs. "Look around," she said, her smile an invitation. "Our New Covenant is as close to Eden as mankind has achieved."

Eden? With rips and patches in the tent roofs and such unruly gardens? With people clothed as farmers or hunters, but with little sign of farming or hunting? Two fellows even dressed themselves as Indians, sporting feathers in their hair and necklaces of skulls such as from mice or voles, but there were no real Indians nor any Negroes.

People spoke to Horace of love and transcendence and planetary grace, and he could make no sense of it all. Eden, you say? He supposed it might be possible. Wouldn't Eden seem a weird refuge to the undeserving sinner? To himself?

Now the freckled woman in dairyman's boots had grasped the cooper's hands and, walking backward, she led him from his wagon. The apprentice followed.

"Tomorrow for broken casks," she said. "Come. Eat with us."

Horace fetched his notebook and chased after. Because dirt smudged every cheek and hand, he mentioned the shower-bath. "Interesting," said the man in the purple hat. His pronunciation suggested an expensive education.

"Is there a store?" Horace asked. "Where is the town?"

"Without government, there can be no town," said the man. "Without commerce, no store."

They came to a long framed house with walls made from tree bark, where inside people crowded around a communal table amid loud conversation. The cooper and his apprentice landed at the table's other end, beside the man in the purple hat. Horace found himself on a bench beside the freckle-faced woman. Her name, she told him, was Delia.

"This is how the Iroquois sheltered themselves," Delia said. "And it's how early Christians ate." She shared a bowl of boiled potatoes.

The potatoes needed salt, but he was glad for them, and for the turkey and squash. Bees hovered about the table, and a sweet rot of fermenting apple hung in the air.

Between bites, Horace wrote in his notebook the clumsy proper name of his hosts: The Association of the Lord's New Covenant for Edenic Return. Each day, Delia told him, they worked to liberate themselves from false doctrines and restore the freedoms of the first garden. They called each other Liberites.

"I once stole a silk dress," she said, "because I loved a slave man, and he had never touched silk. That's when everything changed." From a jar, she filled his cup with hard cider. "Have you read *Theory of the Four Movements and the General Destinies*?"

Inside a canvas tent reserved for New Covenant's guests, Delia had placed three mats woven of dried grasses over the hard-packed dirt. Now she and the purple-hatted man hauled a clay pot heavy with water through the tent's entry flap. Each crouched to bear the weight, water sloshing over the pot's rim. Once they eased their burden down aside a tent wall, Delia blew hair out of her eyes and slipped a ladle from her belt. "For drinking or washing," she said to the three guests, "or whatever use you see fit."

It was only now that the man introduced himself. Cuthbert, with a Dutch last name, a sound like a man blowing his nose. Bronk, perhaps. "From Manhattan," Delia said. "Descended from patroons." Cuthbert grinned, teeth white and right-sized, in perfect alignment. She snuggled closer. "And he's good with a rifle."

Cuthbert laughed and gathered her hair in a fist, tugged back her head to lift her chin. She received his kiss so Horace could see their tongues banging the insides of each other's cheeks. Their brazenness shocked him and gave him to ache for Elizabeth.

"Fornicators," muttered the cooper.

Delia answered that all pleasures are innocent. Then she and Cuthbert bade their guests sleep well.

Given the warm night, Horace bunched his blanket as another pillow. But he could not find a comfortable way to lie, and he could not shake that dream of nights past, of Elizabeth and Charley digging. It remained present and vivid as no nightmare ever had. Was nitrous oxide at fault? He had brought to the hut his last bladder, and now he cradled it, wanting to breathe but afraid to. When the cooper began to snore, Horace lifted the faucet to his lips as if it were open; his eager blood jumped. Lighting a candle, he wrote his concerns in his notebook. Had long absence from Elizabeth changed how nitrous oxide worked in that place deeper than his consciousness? Perhaps the gas somehow *sensed* their separation. Perhaps, he thought, it works in the same deep, unknowable place as does love. Or sin.

Across the hut, the cooper's arm enfolded the sleeping apprentice as if for warmth. Horace arranged himself upright, leaning against the heavy water pot. He made a note about his father and a last thought about Elizabeth, then put aside the unopened bladder and his bedding and stepped into the night.

When he found Delia's tent, he whispered her name until she answered, "A moment, please," then limped out as if one of her legs still slept, her whole body tilted to compensate. In nightcap and a long cotton gown, she refused his hand, but followed when he beckoned her to the woods' edge. The night exploded upward into a spray of stars, and the damp woods smelled of moss and sap.

Delia rubbed her nose with the back of her hand. "I'm no easy fuck, Dr. Wells," she said, "if that's your hope."

He could not deny that her presence comforted him as no man's could. But he raised his open hands as does a man to show his innocence. "I woke you because I had a dream. It terrified me. It won't wash from my mind."

Delia scrunched her brow. "In Eden," she said, "no one dreamed. Such perfect waking peace. There was no need. But now, angels speak to us in sleep."

She sat, tucking her legs underneath her, and he settled against the foot of an oak. Then she told him about the common passions, and about poverty and justice. Horace listened to her wide-ranging musings, and though he could not follow why the goodness called God favored laughter over obedience, or how a particular spiritual plane mimicked the design of a spider web, he heard a sturdy promise in her words. He heard kindness. The moon peeked above the tree tops and very soon showed its partial self, curved, a celestial hammock. Tree frogs sang, and Delia explained the roundness of the soul.

Yes, yes, exactly this, the truest reason for his exile: such a night, such words. He did not feel healed or absolved, no, but Delia's certainty about Creation and its openness, its possibilities, gave him hope for his own salvation and forgiveness. He shut his eyes against tears.

"The soul can break," she said, "like a cask. Also, it can be mended. The cooper understands this. He's silly, but . . ." She yawned. "Do you think you might sleep now?"

He did. So he walked her to her tent, and before she entered she turned and kissed the tip of his nose. "Stay in New Covenant as long as you like," she said. "But if you must go, go knowing that God is all of your potential, all of your promise."

Back in the guest tent, Horace found the cooper and apprentice as he had left them, the cooper's arms holding the apprentice tight. He settled under his own bedding, but later, when in search of a more comfortable pose Horace turned, he saw that the apprentice's eyes were open, that the boy was staring at the bladder. Then the boy's eyes moved and met Horace's, and it seemed to Horace that some understanding passed between them.

Outside: wind, just now rising.

⊷──⊶

The next morning, Horace assembled his shower-bath, mud from the night's rain squishing around his boots. He worked in open air with a canopy against the sun, and he hung a dressing curtain alongside. When people tried the bath, he sat on a broken rocking chair he'd carried from a nearby strawberry patch. He gave up that seat for those needing a tooth scraping or a nerve deadened. To preserve his remaining bladder of gas, he'd left it behind in the tent, calculating that no pain brought to his chair would require of him more stomach than had Newton's death. Some patients arrived already drunk, and to others he applied a swab of cocaine or clove oil and steeled himself. Raising his charges from Hartford prices, he hoped to earn enough to buy a horse, even one as poor as the cooper's nag.

Several patients had paid and left when Cuthbert arrived. "My teeth are fine," he said, using his purple hat to wave off Horace's question. He sat in the rocker and crossed his legs so one foot might bob. Expensive boots, Horace noted. Cuthbert lay the hat in his lap.

"I know," said Horace. "You have perfect teeth."

"You aren't the first dentist to say so." Cuthbert grinned as if sharing a secret. Then he blurted: "The Chinese boy told me about a magic sack."

Horace's smile in reply was false, an effort to convey calm as if this were no news at all. With a finger he cleaned mud from his own poor boot. "Observant boy," he said. Then he showed Cuthbert the tooth on the chain around his neck, and explained about painless surgery and nitrous oxide until Cuthbert's expression suggested Horace had said more than was necessary.

"Your nitrous oxide sounds like our ether," Cuthbert said.

"You have ether?" Horace's pulse jumped. He recalled the banks of the Hog River and Morton's question: "Nitrous oxide and what else?"

"Yes, for our frolics. Parties once a month." Cuthbert hopped from the chair and staggered as if he were a three-penny drunk clutching a whiskey jug. "We breathe ether out of balloons and act like fools. Or rather, we 'transcend our corporeal burdens.' One of our flock brought the practice home from England. Except there the men dress up like women and women like men, and . . . well, ours are different. We've planned one after dark. Come frolic with us. Bring your gas."

Then he slipped a calling card into Horace's apron pocket. "Should you ever wish to practice in Manhattan, look me up. I can introduce you to patients who will appreciate your science. If your gas performs as you proclaim, you'll have a fuller appointment calendar than President Polk's."

"You won't stay in New Covenant?"

Cuthbert topped his head with the purple hat and snorted. "The cooper would be disillusioned," he said, "to learn how rarely Liberites do fornicate."

At workday's end, Horace hadn't sold a single shower-bath. Though the day's dentistry had earned him enough money to buy a horse, probably, he'd ride that mount home with little to show for his journey's stated purpose: the sale of his invention. Keen and undeniable, his disappointment in that regard. He scrubbed his tools and hands in a bucket, rubbed blood from forceps, and used his fingernails to scrape what could not be rubbed. He tried to remember all he had read about ether. With a rag he dried tools, then wiped his hands on his trousers. Nearby, the cooper conversed with a Liberite. "He felt forsaken, yes," the cooper was saying, "but still he gave himself over to God's will."

Moments later, Horace arrived at the guest tent to find the apprentice huddled inside, giggling, knees against his chest, eyes lacking spark, Horace's remaining bladder beside him. So quick, so unexpected but honest, the bitter fury that hurried Horace to the sack, to finger its open valve. He twisted fists around the emptiness and nearly cried out his anguish. The last of his gas: gone.

24

Balloons wagged in clenched fists. An accordion player fingered a buoyant reel. Torch and bonfire flames stuttered and lit the glistening faces of Liberites swaying, whirling, their motions wild and impulsive. The night's ether frolic was underway.

Horace tried to count the balloons so he might record the number in his notebook, but they changed hands too quickly, Liberites lifting them as if to drink from inside but instead inhaling vapor, then pinching the ends and passing them on. Nor in the firelight could Horace tell the balloons' color: gray, perhaps brown.

Laughing dancers met dancing laughers. Jack-o'-lanterns flitted from the black wood to prettify the meadow. Or were those bonfire sparks and embers caught on breezes? Flickering, they orbited freckle-cheeked Delia, now in a silk skirt and blouse dyed lavender, who to and fro'd across a raised platform dandied up with cloth ribbons and illuminated by paper lights. Twice she swept near the edge, and twice Horace tensed to catch her should she fall. When she offered him her balloon, eagerness fairly choked him. He tucked its mouth between his lips. Breathed once. Twice. His fingers tingled; he felt himself rise. Not quite the experience of nitrous oxide, but . . .

With each inhalation, the night lengthened and its shape changed; his scribbled notes grew more haphazard.

He would need a workshop. In which his lungs could balloon with ether. *Ethereal. Etherealised.* He tried to write in his notebook. *The effect of ether on the person.* He didn't mind that the pencil fell from his fingers. To etherealise, he thought, means to infuse with heaven.

Breathe.

Then he clambered onto the platform and explained to Delia (winsome Delia, kindly Delia) how he had discovered painless surgery, the same tale he'd told Cuthbert—but his eloquence! Fine-spun. His etherealised tongue shaping words beaten to leafy gold. Every thought expressed in verse. Ovid's envy.

The bonfire's light colored her cheeks orange. A flame herself, Delia threw heat like liquid. Her breath singed his jaw whiskers, so he staggered to where the night's air cooled,

and wandered,

and wondered: had he left a sentence unfinished?

He stepped over a man curled on the ground like a cooked crayfish and who giggled. Gave room to another who dropped his trousers and sashayed cross-eyed in his undergarments. Paused as a ruddy woman with white hair straight as falling water reached hands to the sky and chanted predictions: the world would produce more poets than grocers; all plants would become hermaphroditic; every woman would choose from fifteen lovers each night; and people would learn to shit porcelain teacups!

A man's whisper in Horace's ear: "She read those somewhere. They aren't original."

The ruddy-faced sibyl cried out, "We'll breathe the air of a faithless heaven!"

It was Cuthbert who had whispered. He wore neither shirt nor shoes, but a fancy-buckled belt held up his trousers.

Horace observed, "Your second toe is longer than your big toe." He inhaled from the balloon once more before offering it to Cuthbert, who ignored the gesture and turned Horace by the shoulders so he faced the wood. "Look there," he said, pointing.

It was the cooper's apprentice. The boy watched from the edge of the meadow, making no effort to hide. In fact, he waved.

"What, the cooper lets him wander?" someone said.

"He'll be lashed," said another. "Probably missing tonight's sermon."

"Call him over." This was Cuthbert.

The boy ran to them, grinning. He spoke words Horace couldn't understand, though one sounded like "lullaby." The boy pointed to the balloon.

"This one breathed up all my nitrous oxide," Horace told Cuthbert. He turned his head toward a sound like someone retching, but saw nothing.

Cuthbert looked over the apprentice as if he were some sort of machine. "Do you suppose," he said, "that ether acts as does your nitrous oxide to destroy pain?"

"I am considering the possibility," said Horace, looking for his pencil. He'd brought a pencil, hadn't he?

Cuthbert wrapped his fist around the boy's upper arm and dragged him toward the bonfire, signaling to others for assistance. Horace gave his balloon to the sibyl, then chased after, ether joy making a goosedown cushion of his head. "Inquiry into the nature of things requires procedures," he said. "Procedures are the foundation of sound research!"

"Take notes, then," said Cuthbert. A small group, half a dozen, had gathered around him and the boy, who laughed and panted like a dog, stretching his neck toward a balloon in a Liberite's hand. A rag appeared bunched in Cuthbert's fist, and even from a few steps' distance Horace could smell the caustic scent of the ether in which it had been soaked. When Cuthbert smothered the boy's nose and mouth a panic brightened the boy's eyes, and he made a noise, muffled by the rag. Arms jerking, he pawed the dirt with his bare feet. Liberites grabbed his limbs, holding him upright, and Horace giggled at the resulting odd dance (science could be festive!), kicking his own legs in studied imitation, trying to create a memory of this behavior that would last until he found his pencil. Delia at his side watched, too, then offered Horace another balloon. "An angel's lung," he whispered before taking a long suck.

Soon, the boy ceased his struggles and appeared to sleep. "Doctor," Cuthbert called to Horace, "begin your research."

So many head-feathers now, but Horace concentrated and with fingers to the boy's wrist tried to count a pulse. He could find a beat, but not the space in his brain with which to count. "Weak pulse," he said.

"Maybe it needs to be weak," said Cuthbert. "Perhaps a weak pulse hasn't strength to carry pain 'round the body, much as a weak man can't carry a coal bin up stairs."

Cuthbert pressed his thumb against the boy's Adam's apple and held it until a gurgling noise crossed the boy's lips. Cuthbert asked, "Do you mark this, Dr. Wells?"

"Yes." He wanted to laugh at that gurgle, but his throat felt corkscrewed. He tried to swallow it clear. "The weakened pulse," he reminded. "Go easy."

Now Cuthbert grabbed the boy's wrist, and in the manner of a puppeteer motioned with the arm as if the boy were conducting a choir. In answer, the accordion player began to finger a tune. With hands under the boy's arms, Cuthbert bounced him about so his legs danced and his head flopped side to side.

Delia stepped in as the boy's partner. She clasped the small hands, and the trio stumbled through an appalling waltz. Now and then she let go one hand so as to lift her long skirt and kick. When the tune ended, Cuthbert dropped ass-first to the ground, puffing, and he cradled the cooper's apprentice in his lap, draping the ether rag once again over the boy's nose and mouth. "Too much," said Horace. "His lungs are young."

Delia leaned and kissed the foreheads of puppet dancer and puppeteer as a mother kisses her children. "Nothing wakes this one," she said, and she lifted her blouse to show Cuthbert and his puppet her naked breasts. Liberites whooped and cheered her revelation, but the cooper's apprentice showed no reaction.

"Mark this." Cuthbert stood, and Horace cried, "No!" even as Cuthbert stomped a booted heel hard on one of the boy's ankles. The boy's body jerked, but his eyes stayed closed, and afterward he lay as an overfed babe napping in its crib. Liberites hoo-hawed.

"A new day for science!" someone said.

"Maybe it's not the ether. Maybe Chinese don't feel pain."

"Make note of that hypothesis, Wells."

"What's that mark on the boy's neck?" someone asked. "Something a witch left?"

"Test his hand in the fire," said another.

Horace opened his mouth to object. But feathers inside his skull muffled his voice, and feathers felt good—a solace, those feathers. Vision blurred, he quick-breathed from the balloon in hand, and the skull-feathers became liquid, a syrup sloshing side to side. "Please," he said, or perhaps whispered. "Don't." But his body lowered itself to the warm ground near the bonfire, and the ether-syrup ran to his toes and comforted him. He heard the accordion's flirtatious groans, the Liberites' gay laughter, and he wondered where pain had fled in the midst of all this contentment? Where did it hide? Because it never disappeared, did it? He imagined pain as gargoyles flying dark-winged high above, or like black oil spilling to fill empty veins of earth, or dark hedges bunched at the far limits of New Covenant, waiting to spread limb and thorn . . .

"Let's try a knife," said Delia, now leaning over Cuthbert's shoulder. She pulled a wide, shiny blade from her boot. He reached; she yanked it back.

"No one touches my knife," she said.

Cuthbert made room, and she squatted, squinting and biting her upper lip. With faltering hand, she lowered the blade until its edge rested on the boy's pimpled brow.

. . . because all Edens fade, and then pain will wing or drip or grow back into waiting bodies, into hearts, into the souls of those who had breathed whatever vapor. Because pain never disappears.

Somewhere in the midst of these thoughts, which Horace did not write down and thus would forget, he fell asleep.

The cooper's voice strangled when he asked Horace, "Are you certain?"

The boy's body lay between them in the tent, the forehead sliced in a thin, precise line. Skin curled back from the cut and had stiffened, and flies hovered around the brow. Blood had spread thick and sticky across the boy's face and dried in the creases of his eyes. Delia crouched over him, a bucket at her side and damp rag in hand, and with careful, gentle motions, she washed him. She made no sound, though her mouth twisted in grotesque shapes.

The cooper would not look at the body. Instead, he looked at Horace. Horace held his own arms tight about him, a hand rubbing an elbow. He studied the boy, whose hair strayed like twigs and twine in strange, comic ways; whose face appeared blasted with the force of new knowledge.

The cooper asked, "That vapor, maybe it only chased his soul away. When it wears off, he could come back."

The cooper said, "He's dead now. I know."

He said, "Maybe another potion might open his eyes."

In the afternoon heat, the cooper walked about New Covenant speaking loud and beseeching prayers, his steps slow and loping. His arms reached high and wide as if to catch whatever mercy God might let fall from heaven. He recited Gospel verses, but grief mixed them in ways that might have been funny had one not known how his heart was broken.

"I'll not yet put dirt on his head," he told Delia, when she offered her own robe as a winding sheet. "Imagine if he wakes underground. It's best I keep him near."

That night, Horace sat on the packed dirt inside the shared tent and watched by candlelight as the cooper straightened the boy's limbs, covered him with blankets, tucked a pillow beneath his head. "If he stays dead," the cooper said, "I will cut my beard."

Horace rose then, and without a word carried his mat and blanket outside to a spot in the woods where exposed roots tangled and the moss was damp, a place utterly lacking in comfort. There he lay his mat and himself, so that roots poked his kidneys and the wet chilled through his shirt, and thus afflicted, he trembled before an inexplicable Heaven. A boy had died—and hadn't he died because of the gas? Horace begged to know why. And this, too: Since the revelation of the nitrous-oxide miracle, why had he, Horace, become an instrument of so much and such ruinous pain? He smeared wet, gritty dirt across his cheeks and asked and asked until language failed and asking became desolation and endless night, need and exhaustion.

When fat rain drops woke him, he sat and let himself be soaked through his blanket and clothes. At a distance stood the ragged tents of New Covenant, this contrary Eden, illumined by gray dawn. He clasped his hands as if to pray but instead covered his face. What must he do? He'd wanted during this exile to reclaim his better self, but he'd only come here, to this bitterness. Why? He recalled that morning when Riggs had pulled his tooth: all its potential, its promise. But then came Warren and humbug and failure, and Horace living as if his obligation to proclaim the miracle were ended. He thought of birds buried in a riverbank's muck, and of silly shower-baths, and of the chipped button on a woman's blouse—ways he'd turned from the gas or turned it to his own purposes. Perhaps that was his mistake. There could be no turning. Every miracle demanded its prophet. No matter how ill-suited that soul, no matter how unexpected the choice, it was Heaven's election and thus undeniable. With the gas, then, who else but Horace Wells? As with his broken-legged mare, his finger alone touched the trigger.

He wondered: could he make a new covenant?

It seemed that he must.

"Elizabeth," he said, her name coming from deep inside him like a cough, and again, "Elizabeth," to draw her near, to narrow the distance, with her to again begin.

V

HARTFORD
AND BOSTON

25

An early autumn wind bullied the cottage at Lord's Hill. Elizabeth sat on a braided rug in the bedroom she and Horace shared, her forehead pressed against the cool wood of his wardrobe, praying for relief from the awful strain in her chest. It felt as if she were on a rack, or—Lord forgive her presumption—crucified. She gulped air. Was this hysteria? Save me from a mad fascination with birds!

She laughed. Felt worse. When she blinked, her eyes watered, the recent grittiness in them somehow worse today.

Stand up, she thought, the curtains need beating. Stand up: tighten the bed ropes, and stir the potpourri in the guest room.

Charley complained from downstairs, his head itching with lice. Those filthy Wilcox boys. Her hands stank of the lard and sulfur she'd lathered into his scalp.

"Don't scratch!" she shouted to him. "I'll be there in a moment!"

A week before she herself had written to a friend: *Horace's brother to visit. We are not in a very inviting plight for visitors, but they must take what they can get.* Such a singsong tone. About now, she knew, Horace and his brother, Charles, a physician from New Hampshire, would start the walk from the train station up Lord's Hill. Would Charles ask: why not a wagon? She feared Horace would tell the truth, that he would talk of the dead mare, Newton, then admit that they hadn't the money to purchase a replacement for the wagon he'd abandoned. His tone would be serious, full of confession and virtue. "And the shower-bath?" Charles might ask. And Horace would say, "Thus far, a failure. I'm done with that foolishness." Such candor had been Horace's passion since he had arrived home, slumped on the sagging back of a near-dead nag, sorrow plain in his eyes. It seemed the road had stripped him of that second self we each and all present to our fellows, and what remained was the barest, truest Horace. "Keep my soul safe," he kept saying as he held her close, mumbling about a dead boy.

Their bank accounts remained thin; he practiced dentistry only on occasion and in limited ways. Instead he spent hours in his workshop experimenting with gases and making notes. But whereas once he had been furtive in this work, now he told her plainly of his day's plans. When friends and acquaintances asked, "How goes it with the Wells family?" he spoke frankly and in measured tones about their privations and his research.

One overcast morning as they walked to church, Charley ahead kicking stones in the road, she told Horace, "Not all Hartford must know how we struggle. Perhaps you could speak less openly of our lives."

He touched her shoulder and turned her to him. The way his eyes searched her face suggested that her words betrayed his new convictions, perhaps even jeopardized her own soul. "But I'm speaking truth," he said.

"Silence," she said, "can also be truth."

"Silence can also be a lie."

She returned a sad smile. She had come to understand more about deception than she thought possible, how a lie comes easily as truth when you are poor. When people asked *her* about the family, she'd say, "We have every confidence in Horace's shower-bath." When Aunt Dorothy asked why candlesticks she'd given as a wedding gift were no longer on the mantel, Elizabeth had said something about polish. She did not mention the shopkeeper off a South Green alley who told her, "I'll ship them to a buyer in Baltimore. Anything else? Knife sets are always in demand."

Now, in the bedroom, she pulled herself upright, her breath shallow, and waited until the spell in her chest had passed. She blinked, though that failed to clear her sight, then gathered items for the guest room—scissors, pillow cases, thread—and as she did, a gust rattled the panes. A draft cut in, and she thought ahead to the first snow. Would there be money for coal or wood?

She recalled the courier that morning at the front door, how he studied the ground, pawed it like a horse. Charley was crying then from the kitchen, and though her hands were greasy with lard and sulfur, she took the envelope. Twice she pressed the back of a wrist against her eyelids, snapped the paper open as if that might bring the words into focus. She called back the courier and asked that he read it to her.

"Not my place, Mrs. Wells."

"Read it to me, please."

Face reddening, he took the paper. Thus she learned from Col. Roberts's lawyer that Horace must immediately return the colonel's investment in the shower-bath. The lawyer assumed court would not be necessary.

The brothers arrived pink-eared and smiling from their long cold walk, pushing and prodding each other as if boys. Elizabeth kissed Charles's cheek, asked him please to sit. He rested on a bench near the door, boots muddy, legs spraddled, belly swelling with deep breaths, and told an ordinary story about his ordinary trip. Horace, meanwhile, had found Colonel Roberts's letter on the shelf where Elizabeth had known he would, in that same spot where he set his pocket purse each time he arrived home. He read, turning his attention now and then back to Charles's tale and laughing at the right moments. Then he folded and slipped the letter under the base of a table trivet. His eyes met hers, and she shook her head in a barely perceptible way meant only for him. When he scratched at his cheeks, she understood that he would keep silent—for her.

Horace asked, "Where is Charley? He must greet his namesake."

"Let him alone," said his brother, generally waving toward wherever in the house Charley might be. "He'll see me soon enough."

Though two years and six months separated Horace and Charles, a new acquaintance might have thought them to be twins. They shared long, thick-lobed ears, and their chins were creased with short, shallow clefts. Both stood roughly the same height, tended toward plumpness, and had lost hair at a young age, as if their medically inspired minds burned the follicles to ash. But their faces conveyed different—and deceptive—attitudes. Horace, older, always worrying some problem, nonetheless appeared light-hearted, the pinched corners of his mouth suggesting a never-ending smile. Charles—a calm, grateful optimist—showed the world a heavy brow and a frown. Voices revealed more accurately their personalities. Horace's was intense and beautiful. Love me, his voice had said to Elizabeth in their courting days, and what glows in our hearts will light the dark, a brighter star.

Which is why she had married him.

But when she imagined Charles courting (imagined him with other women, mostly, but with herself in surprising, compelling moments she would never admit) his voice would say, Love me, and I will eat every biscuit you bake, and afterward smoke a pipe on the porch, and with warm hands rub your feet at night.

Which is why now, distressed by couriers and lice and candlesticks sent to Baltimore, her skin tingled in Charles's presence, his flushed face quickening her breath. Worried, she began to rearrange the candles on their clay plates and worked not to look at him. Then, so as not to draw attention to how she ignored him, she did look.

"Charley is exiled," she said, explaining the lice. "I boiled the pillow cases," she added, hoping to ease Charles's concerns if he had any.

"Mother shaved our heads to the skin," Charles said. He had removed his muddy boots and pulled slippers from his traveling case. "Mary cried and cried."

"I don't recall that," said Horace.

"You were off studying at Hopkinton. The school closed, you know."

"Not a surprise," said Horace. "The headmaster knew his Plato but always hired someone else to teach bookkeeping."

Elizabeth clapped once to punctuate that sentence and suggested they move to the parlor for tea. Charles thanked her as he rose from the bench, his face having recovered its color. "Would coffee be possible?" he asked. "Tea fiddles with my stomach."

She did not want to say that there was no coffee. No lie came to mind, either, so she smiled close-lipped, blinked, and raised her hands to adjust her hair pins.

And somehow, Charles understood. His eyes searched her face, and the pity in them bruised her. She returned to him what she hoped was her proudest look. He said, "Tea, though, is better for the teeth. I've heard that somewhere. Coffee stains the enamel, doesn't it, Horace?"

"Everything stains the enamel. But stain has little to do with a tooth's health. That is more an aesthetic concern."

"Tea it is," said Charles, a kindness, and Elizabeth once again felt troubled by a satisfying momentary affection for her brother-in-law.

In the kitchen, she measured the loose leaves into a strainer, then filled a ceramic pot with steaming water. She could hear the men talk but couldn't make out the words. Something about a woman? For a moment she imagined Charles and a pretty wife, with a daughter who would never carry parasites in her scalp. Why a daughter? She knew why.

Elizabeth set the tea tray on a half-moon table in the parlor and apologized that there were no cakes. "Out of sugar," she said. "With the boy's troubles I hadn't time to fetch any." Rubbing her eyes as she poured, she missed a cup, and tea streamed to the rug. She yelped, and Horace turned in his seat nearby. "Are you all right?" He grasped a fold in her skirt.

"Tired. A few restless nights, and my hands get twitchy."

Charles waved Elizabeth to come near. She protested that the puddle needed sopping, but he insisted, and Horace fetched a mop, his mindfulness a balm. Charles lifted her arm at the wrist, felt for her pulse. No doubt her physician brother-in-law smelled the sulfur and lard stink, but he gave no sign. Then he stood, laid a thumb on either side of her eyes to spread them, and asked her to look up, look down. He touched cool fingertips to either side of her temples, palpated places about her neck. His breath smelled of nutty, sweet tobacco. She feared she might weep.

Damp cloth in hand and halting in step, Horace closed their bedroom door that night.

"Charles made a liniment," he said. "I'm to leave it over your eyes."

He had folded the cloth in a neat rectangle, she noticed. When he stepped to the bedside, leaned over where she lay, the concern on his face gave her sympathy for him.

"I can see the strain," he said. "Close those eyes, Elizabeth. Rest, is what the doctor says."

"It is what every doctor says. Rest is a luxury priced higher than we can pay."

But she let her lids slip shut, and in the darkness felt the cloth fall across her eyes. She heard the scrape of a chair pulled nearby. "Is it the rocker?" she asked.

The quilt shifted, and then his hands found her feet. His fingertips, warm and gentle and confident, kneaded along the arch, each toe in turn. His touch started a magic breeze that traveled up her legs, around her hips, even into her scalp.

She must ask. Though the question scared her.

"Will I go blind, Horace?" she said. "What does your brother say?"

"No word about blindness." He lifted the quilt away from her legs, touched cool lips to the skin over her shin. "He said I must take better care of you."

Hay dust swirled in the wind, and Elizabeth sneezed. This was the next day, in the North Meadows, a lowland that flooded most springs and proved generally useless except for this autumn gathering of cows and cow-buyers and cow-sellers, each beast and man loud with revelry or fractiousness. All around, farmers struck cows with switches or moved them with a shoulder shoved into a haunch. In a roped-off square, shirtless men wrestled while others gambled on the outcome and shared jugs and laughed too much—drunken, Elizabeth supposed. At her second sneeze, Charles and Horace each offered a *bless you*, then gave their attentions back to the pen and a trio of white-and-mahogany-colored cows wearing dramatic horns.

"I hear," said Charles, pointing, "that these Ayrshires will find grass where another cow might starve."

"A good beast to graze your New Hampshire rocks."

Charley stood on the fence rail between his uncle and his father, his hair still greased dark and matted from the lard, an arm stretched toward the cows and hand grasping, as if by invisible string he could draw one to him.

"What do you think, Charley?" Horace asked. "Shall we buy a cow, too?"

Elizabeth glanced from husband to son. But with the wind it seemed Charley hadn't heard his father's question.

"Charley?" said Horace, a bit louder.

"Look at the boy," Charles said. "The mirror of his grandfather. Those ears, that chin—handsome skips a generation, eh?"

He yanked his namesake off the rail and swung him in a circle by the arms—once, twice, three times. When Charley's giggling subsided, Charles said, "Let me take him 'round. I need a closer look if I plan to bring a few home."

Above, great clouds roiled, making space now and then for sun. Elizabeth blinked and shook her head. Despite Charles's liniment and Horace's ministering hands, her eyes still felt scraped with sand, worsened by this blowing dust. She squinted to mark Charles and Charley across the pen, and their motions suggested that uncle was showing nephew how best to approach a cow. She asked Horace.

"From the side," he said. "So it can see you. There's enough space at Lord's Hill for a cow. Maybe two."

"We can't afford that," she said.

"Dairy, not beef," he said, and she wondered whether he thought that made a difference. But no, he was just deep in his dreaming. Perhaps he hadn't even heard her. Then he laughed. "As a child, I shied away from slaughter days. Charles used to tease me. Can you imagine? These days I'd want to give the animal the gas."

"Charles teased?" The idea surprised her, her kind brother-in-law acting the bully.

"Mercilessly. The younger brother taking advantages where he could."

When he stepped from the rail, she followed, and they walked among stalls and pens. Elizabeth noticed a cow tonguing the side of her calf's head. Her family had not been farmers. She'd seen cattle near Hartford's slaughterhouses, and the neighbor Mr. Larkin kept a small herd, but her life had been as a woman in the city, among city women. The wives she saw here had knuckles red as clay, and nails cracked or black or missing altogether. She noticed one woman without fingers on a hand.

"It seems hard," she said, "to be a farmer's wife."

Horace searched the clouds. "They might think it hard to be a dentist's wife."

"What you said to Charley about a cow? I'm glad he didn't hear. He might have thought it possible."

"Sometimes my fancies run away with me. Can't seem to help it."

"Horace. That letter from Colonel Roberts—"

Another sneeze interrupted her. At the same moment, two sloppy-drunk farmers and a woman passed near, spewing vulgarities. The woman looked familiar to Elizabeth and put her in mind of birds. Geese? Turkeys? She glanced to Horace to see whether he recognized her, too, but he gave his attention to some spot on his jacket pocket. That didn't last, because one farmer shoved the other, who stumbled into Elizabeth. Horace caught her, kept her from tumbling.

"Watch yourself!" he called to the man.

"Watch your own damned self!" the drunkard said.

"I'll make a fist," Elizabeth shouted, and she meant it. "I'll bloody your nose."

The men laughed and tottered on—and Elizabeth remembered. Not turkeys. Chickens. She did not want to mention the bird panorama and raise cruel memories, but she wondered. Did her husband recall that this had been the same strange woman who'd attended his exhibition's first night, sitting in the front row? Even then Elizabeth had recognized her; Horace once pulled her lunatic daughter's tooth.

"A fist?" Horace said. "That's not so Christian."

"I'm not feeling as Christian as I ought."

He took her hand and led her along a path through willow brush to the river's edge, where they sat on a boulder. Water lapped against the rock; gulls cried overhead. Wind carried cattle calls, muffled at such a distance. "I have made life difficult," he said. "Though I hate the idea, I'll ask Charles for a loan. Perhaps enough to forestall Roberts and leave a bit for candlesticks." He laughed a short, joyless laugh.

A plop off the riverbank drew her attention, brown-blue ripples suggesting a frog. She folded her hands in her lap so he would not reach for them. Her hands, she noted, were fisted. She wondered about the exhilaration and regret that came with an honest bloodying of someone's nose.

"I don't want candlesticks," she said. "I'm not sure I want anything."

For a moment he seemed to be calculating. "Not even a daughter?"

She beat those fists against her lap. "It's all a numbness inside," she whispered. "None of it pleasing."

Wind gusts had messed his hair into a confusion. She felt an urge to comb, to bring order to his head. His lips moved a moment or two until he found words. "You call it loathsome, but something good will yet come of my work with the gas." He laughed. "Something must! I met a man from Manhattan. If I took my dentistry practice there he'd arrange for me to serve the wealthiest patients."

"Do not confuse what I'm saying with money."

"Since my return, I have worked to be a good Christian, to be an honest husband. Last night, you were happy that I fixed the sash cords. You complained of cold in the parlor, and I brought you a quilt."

He was right, of course. It had been years since he'd been as attentive as in these past weeks.

"And I remain your wife," she said, "for good or ill, in life and death, before the Almighty. That will never change. What I mean is that because of our circumstances, something vital in me has become like lead. I am all heavy inside, pressed by something dense. I can't explain more than that. But I wanted you to know."

She found herself squinting, unable to focus on him. She remembered that day in the shower-bath, how with water splashing in her eyes she asked God to let her see Horace clearly. She felt the pressure of tears, but none came.

"I admire your new candor," she said, "but of this matter, pray, speak only to me."

"I should never have gone away. Isn't that the problem?"

She shook her head that she had no answer for him.

They sat a while longer. He watched gulls circle over the water; she turned her face from the sun. Now and then, he clenched his jaw as if fighting some discomfort. When he reached into her lap, she let him, and he took her hands, peeled open the fists. Then he lifted her off the stone and into his arms, his hold firm, his lips near her ears. He whispered something she couldn't hear, but she nodded so he wouldn't speak again.

The family rode home in an open livery wagon, Charley napping across his uncle's lap. Horace used his hat to shoo flies off the boy, studied his son's face.

"Do you really think there's a resemblance to our father?" he asked. Though he meant the question for his brother, he glanced at Elizabeth, who sat beside the driver.

Since the water's edge, he'd looked to her often, measuring her mood. *All a numbness inside*, she had said. He—perhaps better than anyone— understood the consequences of an unfeeling state.

"You don't recall?" Charles brought his hands to the sides of his head, repositioned his ears so they pressed more tightly against his skull. "Like this? And father's chin? You could plow a furrow with it."

"I've a hard time remembering how he looked before he grew ill."

"That," said Charles, "is what I don't recall."

"You were younger. Mother thought it best that you not watch the nights."

"Still, I'd like to know, even now."

Horace turned toward the sun now tucking itself to sleep behind Talcott Mountain's long ridge. He saw veins burst in the skin gathered beneath his father's eyes. Lips flaked. Whiskers sharp, mean. Not like Charley's face, no.

"It was a death," he said. "Awful as any other, I suppose."

"All those hours together. He must have told you things." Charles's voice had changed; Horace heard a hint of entreaty.

But the wagon arrived now on Main Street, where lamplighters had started their work, and Horace asked to be let off at his office. "My apologies," he whispered to his brother. "My mood's turned sour. Work always heals."

When later he arrived home, that mood had changed. Charles and Charley were in the parlor building a stick house with glue, and Horace found Elizabeth in the kitchen ladling stew into bowls. He grinned and waved a sheet of paper at her.

"Yes," he said. "I have been experimenting with the gas. My head rings a bit, that's true. But also I have just received a letter. An offer of work."

He laughed, and she studied the smears of grease, clear and shiny, that she stirred across the broth's surface. He pinched a piece of floating meat, popped it into his mouth.

"It's from Morton," he said while chewing. "About a discovery. He stands to make a fortune, and he'd like to share."

Standing, he jerked a boot off one foot, then the other.

"Morton offered me a job," he said, then laughed again. "I'd sooner chew nails."

26

October 18, 1846
Boston
Friend Wells:
I write to inform you that I have discovered a *preparation* by inhaling which
a person is thrown into a sound sleep. The time required to produce sleep is
only a few moments, and the time in which the persons remain asleep can
be regulated at pleasure. While in this state the severest surgical or dental
operations may be performed, the patient not experiencing the slightest
pain. I have *patented* it, and am now about sending out agents to dispose of
the right to use it. I will dispose of a right to an individual to use in his own
practice alone, or for a town, county, or state. My object in writing you is to
know if you would not like to visit cities as my representative to dispose of
rights upon shares. I have used the compound in more than one hundred
and sixty cases in extracting teeth, and I have been invited to administer it to
patients in the Massachusetts General Hospital, and have succeeded in every
case. I have administered it in the hospital in the presence of the students
and physicians—the room for operations being full as possible.

Professor Warren has given me certificates to this effect. For further
particulars, I will refer you to extracts from the daily journals of this city,
which I forward to you.
Respectfully yours,
Wm. T. G. Morton

October 20, 1846
Dr. Morton—Dear Will:
Your letter is just received, and I hasten to answer it, for fear you will adopt a
method in disposing of your rights which will defeat your object. Before you

make any arrangements whatever, I wish to see you. I think I will be in Boston the first of next week, probably Monday night. If the operation of administering the gas is not attended with too much trouble, and will produce the effect you state, it will undoubtedly be a fortune to you, provided it is rightly managed.

Yours in haste,

H. Wells

27

At a small basin in a room with no mirror, Horace cupped icy water over his face, dried his hands on his robe, then sat on the only chair and waited. Nearby, in the room's best light (dim, through a smudged window), Elizabeth rummaged their traveling kit for his soap and razor. Horace shifted his weight this way, then that, and each time the chair's uneven legs nearly tipped him. He detested a cold-water shave, but Elizabeth had decided not to pay for a barber. Given Col. Roberts's threat, she had insisted on full control of their accounts, purses and wallets. Horace agreed.

"It's a poor blade," she said, testing the razor's edge with her thumb. "I don't want to hurt you."

"Six breaths of the gas, and I wouldn't feel a nick," he said. She didn't laugh, so he said, "The razor belonged to my father. Barber Coles says I should buy another."

Elizabeth felt uneasy, a leaden weight in her chest. The candles she had lit gave no comfort. Partly it was the unsettledness one feels in an unfamiliar city. Mostly it was having to rely on Horace to guide her through Boston, trusting herself to his care. Once, she would have done so without reservation. Once, she had confidence in him—and also in love, in God, and herself. Now she felt squeamish, vulnerable, her certainties shaken.

Mulling this, she fumbled the cake of shaving soap. Horace offered to fetch it from under the bed where it had tumbled, but she told him no. On her knees, she peered into that dark, concealing space, and saw amid the dust and dead insects a jumble of pink-and-white tissue—used candy wrappers. The soap sat, a clean and smooth white stone in a garden of cast-off blossoms. She reached, then hesitated. The discarded wrappers frightened her. She imagined grimy fingers, a mouth stuffed, breath choked. Candy sucked and chewed and swallowed until teeth felt coated with a residue of sin, of gluttony. Her stomach turned.

Elizabeth prayed a few words, then reached for the soap. When she stood with the prize, some wrappers clung to her sleeve, and she shook them loose. "No housemaid cleans under there," she said.

Her husband's jaw lathered, she scraped the razor along his chin, leaned near to see better. Scratched over and dry, her eyes still troubled her. She'd begun to wonder if what ailed them might be a great well of unwept tears. Of late she had not been one to cry at anything. Horace's brother had told her that women need to shed tears as naturally as they need to nurse after giving birth. Did it follow then that she had become unnatural? So she felt. The day before, on the train to Boston, she had noticed a shadow billowing across the sky outside her window. Carrier pigeons, a cloud of thousands, and they put her in mind of that bird-mad spring at Aunt Dorothy's house. Eyes burning, she had waited for memories to undam her sorrow. Nothing. The pigeons flew on; the sky cleared.

Horace fingered lather away from his lips. "Whatever Morton is up to, it could be dangerous if he doesn't take care. And he has never been a careful man. He must consider all reasonable precautions. I speak from experience."

"So this is why we've come to Boston? To save Will from his worst impulses?"

Horace smiled, and Elizabeth held her next stroke so as not to cut him.

"If I am honest," he said, "I must admit to other motives. He writes of painless surgery as though I'd not achieved it first. It fell to me to make this miracle widely known. That burden has proven costly—I don't need to tell you that—yet Morton hopes to earn a fortune from my—our—sacrifices." He grasped her skirt. "Your behavior at the cattle fair inspires me. If Morton has stolen my knowledge, maybe I'll bloody his nose."

"Be better than my poor example," she replied. "It ought not be difficult."

"What do you suppose is his preparation? Nitrous oxide with an added odor? Ether?"

With the fingers of one hand, she stretched his cheek; with the other she dragged the razor. But the chair tipped, his face followed, one of her fingers slipped, and the blade bit her fingertip. She watched the razor slip through skin and then come free. A moment passed as if nothing had happened, then blood welled.

Her yelp had to do with surprise. Of pain, she felt none.

In the same instant Horace had her by the hand, dipping her finger in the basin of icy water. When he lifted the hand and peered at the fingertip, blood pooled again. Once more, a dunk into the water. Then a clean rag over the cut. When next he examined the wound, he kissed it.

"These small cuts sometimes hurt the most," he said.

"You still have soap lather on your face."

He grinned, and something in his expression chipped at the lead she carried in her chest. He bandaged her finger, then let her guide him back to the treacherous chair, and she finished shaving his whiskers. With her apron, she wiped his cheeks clean.

Pretty, she thought, the soap's lavender smell.

Morton's new office. Spotless windowpanes. Light reflecting from beveled mirrors wide as angel wings. Polished brass trim on three chairs. Three chairs! Painted on the ceiling for patients to see as they leaned back: Orpheus playing his lyre in a meadow among sleepy lions and smiling bears. So many shiny tools, and on the shelves a dozen jars of gold foil for packing cavities. The air smelled of clove oil.

"So much of everything," said Horace. "There's hardly space for my envy."

Morton looked pleased with the comment, pleased, in fact, with all things. "Since my name appeared in the newspapers," he said, "I've enjoyed the attention of many investors. My Elizabeth now wears a corset made in Paris."

Morton himself wore a new red coat with beaver-fur lapels, and after he hung that coat on a wall peg, he donned an apron monogrammed with all four of his initials. He offered a duplicate to Horace, who declined but gave Morton his coat to hang. With his fingertips, Morton picked pills from the lapel and studied Horace, shoes to hat. "Gray and black. What, the shower-bath not paying off? Come work for me if you want to afford brighter colors."

"The shower-bath is with lawyers," Horace said. "I expect a settlement. How did you hear of it?"

Morton grinned. "My in-laws bought one."

Then Morton busied himself with the day's mail, and Horace drifted near a table set up as a miniature laboratory, on which a cat's tongue of flame heated a glass globe and the liquid inside. A long tube extended, and at its end he found a peculiar mouthpiece with its own valve knob. He fit it against his teeth, found it comfortable, then set it down and wiped it with a nearby rag.

"This is your preparation?" he asked.

"I call it Letheon. For the river Lethe, from which we drink and forget."

"The souls of the dead drank from that river."

"You'll see how well Letheon works. Confidence in the product will allow you to sell it honestly. You can make a great profit as my agent— enough to buy a new coat."

"Change the name if you want it to sell. What ingredients comprise this lethal potion? A disguised nitrous oxide? Your chemist friend Jackson did the mixing?"

Morton looked stern, as a teacher at an obstinate student. "Don't be an ass. Jackson is nobody. I've done this on my own."

No, Horace thought, you haven't.

The elegance of Morton's office offended him. Too sentimental, too ideal. He expected to hear harp or some such music in this dental heaven. And then, remarkably, he did. Morton hurried to the door, and Horace understood the celestial strains to be door chimes. Across the threshold came a woman, gliding, hair the shade of autumn oak leaves, waist small, bosom generous—more Nan, he thought, than Elizabeth (and chastised himself for thinking of Nan more often since that encounter at the cattle fair). With a childlike finger, Morton's patient tucked a curl of hair behind the easy curve of her ear, and Horace felt desire's pinprick. Morton kissed the woman's proffered and gloved hand, showed her to a chair, made proper introductions, smiled, cooed, assured, and when she was comfortable fit the mouthpiece between her teeth. "Now," said Morton, "watch."

But the longer Horace observed, the more agitated he became. The woman breathed through the mouthpiece. At first, she arched her back, lifted as if to rise from the chair, but with hands on her shoulders Morton held her in place. Her eyes darted, focus erratic. Her right knee bobbed.

"Exhilaration," Horace said. He rolled his sleeve cuffs to his elbows. "I've seen this before."

"You haven't. This is not nitrous oxide, Wells. If your exhibition proved anything it proved that nitrous oxide can't be trusted."

Then the patient calmed, also nothing new. Her eyelids fluttered, closed. Her breathing became regular, her limbs limp. Morton turned the faucet and removed the mouthpiece.

"*Voilà*," he said. He fingered open her mouth and reached blindly with the other hand. "Tooth key," he directed, as though Horace were already in his employ.

In her youth, Elizabeth had read of the time when people in Massachusetts believed in witches, and walking Boston's streets she understood why they might. A toothless woman leaning out a first-floor window did not so much laugh as cackle. Mangy cats shrieked and chased vermin; they hissed at Elizabeth's ankles as she passed. Unshaven men spit in the street, and she noticed one scarecrow of a fellow sprinkle a wall and shake himself before buttoning his trousers. "Boylston Street?" she asked a turnip seller, who shrugged. "Boylston Street?" she pleaded with a police officer, who pointed. She hurried that way for many blocks until her legs tired and her sense of direction turned about.

When a blind woman began to dog her heels, offering three times to wash Elizabeth's dirty laundry, she hired a passing livery driver.

"Where on Boylston?" he asked.

"I don't know," she said, relieved to note that the driver had teeth and working vision. "My husband says there are shops and theaters."

"Too early in the day for a show," the driver said as he snapped the reins. The horse's shoes clopped the stones. "You can probably buy a ticket for tonight, though."

"I don't go to plays," she said, which was mostly true. She had little opportunity. Hartford's elected council outlawed most theater as immoral and likewise prohibited display of many paintings and sculptures. Horace called such restrictions "old-fashioned prudery," but Elizabeth had been satisfied with what entertainments the law allowed. She'd attended historic and biblical exhibitions in which Hartford's school children portrayed George Washington, or Adam and Eve debating the serpent. But no, she'd never seen a play with paid actors and actresses. Truth to tell, she'd never seen much of anything. Born in Hartford, married there, and settled, too.

For their honeymoon, she and Horace did travel as far as the Connecticut shore. There she corked a vial of beach sand to bring home and thought herself clever until she learned that most visitors did the same.

"Oh, you've got to attend the theater," said the driver. The reins dangled from one of his hands, and with the fingers of the other he worried an angry pimple on his fat chin. "S'like spying on people's lives."

He reined his horse in the shadow of a great hall with wide stairs of polished granite. "The Boylston Theater House," he said. He studied the length of the building's columns, then tilted himself toward her and grinned. "You watch the play, waiting for everything usual to go topsy-turvy. And when it does—heavens! Sometimes it nearly stops your heart."

"My son once played Christian Charity in a panorama. Given his personality, he might have been better suited for Faith."

The driver grunted. "Nothing topsy-turvy in that."

"No," she agreed, and she was surprised to hear longing in her voice. Life offered enough of its own upset. Why would she want a play to provide more?

She paid the fare, and he motioned toward a shop she might like, said it was full of notions, first-rate stuff. Buttons shaped from ivory and the like. "I forbade my wife to go there," he said as she stepped to the street, and he shook the reins and drove on.

Elizabeth paced outside that shop for a while, glancing through the window at a needle kit and fine threads, and fought the tug to go inside. Odd how poverty made temptations more keen. She'd never been a spendthrift when she and Horace had money. But since the start of their privation, she had a peculiar urge to purchase beyond necessities, to buy all things, possess all things. Pretty baubles and bits of framed stained glass to dangle in the light of a window. Neat needle kits. A rainbow of spooled threads. Perfumes. She had never purchased a perfume. But now that she spent every hour of every day scheming how to get sugar and flour and beans, wanting had become her general condition—no matter the object.

So pace and glance and glance and pace, but best not to enter. Next door, however, was an art gallery. Perhaps she could pretend it was a museum where the exhibits weren't for sale. Before Charley was born, she and Horace had visited Hartford's atheneum and spent time with the historic scenes depicted by Mr. John Trumbull, paintings of an edifying or morally instructive nature and thus permitted for public display. The mortal sacrifices of generals. Gallant riders upon gallant steeds. She recalled her patriotic thrill to see Thomas Jefferson represented in his red waistcoat and red hair, looking most independent and craggy. Arm in arm, husband and wife whispered what details each noticed: the turn of a soldier's lapel, a flag's frayed edge. Serious business, their study, until Horace noted that everyone in the paintings was tight-lipped. Hiding their wooden teeth, he joked.

This Boston gallery welcomed sunlight through tall street-side windows to shine on its polished wood floor. A candle heated a bowl of scented oil so the room smelled of cinnamon, and an immense silence reached to the high ceilings, creating a space as for prayer. Behind a counter near the back, a man marked in a ledger book. He wore spectacles and a black frock coat; his shirt featured a chin collar piped with gold braid. His nose was elfin, his raven hair mussed in a way that looked as whipped and designed as frosting on a cake. With a manufactured smile, he raised his chin and offered to answer questions. Elizabeth nodded an acknowledgment, and then the room's silence expanded again, and the silence seemed unbreakable.

Nothing here resembled Mr. Trumbull's work, she saw that at a glance. Such color! On that canvas: linen white, gold, and darkening blue. The linen was the exotic dress of a woman, herself pale as death. She reclined on silk-cased pillows, staring toward Elizabeth and through her. Perhaps it was the painting's distant, ominous sky, or the woman's pallor, but Elizabeth sensed an unseen, looming destruction. What might it be? She searched the canvas, saw a loom and a brazier, and at the painting's edge an African woman—concealed in shadow, naked breast slipping from her blouse.

Elizabeth moved on.

Here, an Oriental setting—Istanbul, perhaps, or Palestine. In that one, a monkey painting a picture. There, a woman—astonishingly nude—carrying a rainbow-colored vase. And over there a man, at rest amid sculptures, contemplative, but all around him the paint pulsed, as though the sculptures enjoyed life's spark.

None of these paintings, she decided, could ever be exhibited in Hartford.

Nearer to the man in the frock coat, her attention was drawn to a canvas splashed with red and teal. A woman reclined on the red pillows of a sofa, her eyes heavy-lidded as if she were just waking from a nap. The teal was a wool blanket pulled high, but not so high as to conceal perfect shoulders and a perfect neck. Her blouse startled Elizabeth, how she wore it so low. Her small mouth almost matched the cushions red for red, and her nose was big and real, so the neck and shoulders seemed that much more angelic.

With her left hand she toyed with a twist of dark hair, which lay across her breast. The woman gazed past Elizabeth into the gallery, toward what or whom Elizabeth couldn't say. But she was struck by the woman's expression, satisfied yet expectant.

Then a jolt—not of body, but of soul—fixed her sight on a finger of the woman's left hand. She wore a wedding band.

Elizabeth raised fingers to her bottom lip. If she hadn't, she knew, she would have touched the canvas. She wished the oils ran wet again, so she could dip a fingertip in each color and thereby reclaim something familiar, something of her past.

Once, she had been this woman.

Once, it had been a honeymoon morning, overcast, the air tangy with saltwater spray. In the painting in her head, Elizabeth, just awake, enjoys the coziness of an unfamiliar bed, cool air on her bare shoulders, the *hush-hush* of waves easy against the beach. Her husband (the word thrills, its new meaning in her life), returns after a morning of bird-watching. Binoculars on a strap around his neck, silt and dune grass stuck to his boots, he prepares for her a plate of biscuits and sweet butter, speaks of sandpipers and curlews. With her left hand, she plays with her own hair.

In the presence of the painting, in the presence of the memory, Elizabeth lowered herself to her knees. The man in the frock coat spoke words that sounded French, sounded concerned, as if he could see the mix of joy and longing that had overcome her. He drew near, taking her elbow, and he helped her onto a small wooden stool. She placed the heel of her hand against her head, shut her eyes tight. She could cry now, she felt certain. But if she were to cry now . . .

She shook her hand at the walls. "I've never seen paintings like these."

"We specialize," the man said. "French artists only. You collect art?"

"No." She gasped, turning to another wall, where a woman in a white gown, black ribbon below her bosom, sat on the ground in a gray landscape. Legs stretched forward, head downcast. Her left arm was something she'd forgotten. It lay on the earth, palm upturned, a dead, beautiful thing.

Not now, not a tear . . .

"Where I live," she whispered, "we don't have paintings like these. They'd violate the laws."

The man laughed the smallest laugh she had ever heard, small and mean as a tick at the scalp, and the laugh rescued her; she knew she wouldn't cry. "Yes," he said, walking to his counter, shoe heels clicking on the hardwood. "*Les hommes d'etat* deny us all our consolations. These men of state—why do they want us to suffer?"

The last in a long line of patients had left. Morton rinsed the spittoon and set tools in order. Horace put up a jar of gold foil. Folded the blood-spotted aprons.

"You are certain your preparation will not damage the lungs or trachea?" he asked. "Have you consulted with patients weeks after? Monitored their breathing?"

"No one has complained." Morton waved to a woman passing on the sidewalk, visible through the window, and she smiled in turn. "Had I assistance, I would make those investigations you suggest. But I've been busy with other aspects of the discovery."

"It takes time to spend this much money."

"Yes," said Morton, and he laughed. "It does."

"Why don't you give me a taste of this Letheon? I'm still partial to nitrous oxide in my own work; my experience with ether—" He paused, seeing in his memory the body of the Chinese boy, how Delia washed the face. "—it ended badly. I've shied from it since. But if you want me to represent your gas, you'll need me to argue on its behalf over nitrous oxide. And who better?"

"I'm not saying this is ether." Morton stood and drained his mug. "But I knew you'd want a taste."

Soon Horace held the mouth-faucet between his incisors.

"Will you take notes?" Horace asked, and Morton nodded.

The vapor smelled and tasted aromatic, smoky and sweet, with neither the clarity of nitrous oxide nor the pungency of ether. But the immediate effect was similar.

Horace's fingers swelled and tingled. Morton's face, once gaunt, now stretched wide and high, his whaler's beard exaggerated to biblical lengths.

Morton in the Bible! Ha! Horace preached the verse: "Then Morton went out, and held a council against him, how Morton might destroy him." Morton the Pharisee. Fair to see. Nan's face is fair to see. . . . Genitals tingling, swelling like the fingers. Morton must make a note. Morton! The genitals tingle and swell! Morton's reply, breezing from one side of Horace's skull to the other . . .

Then, a darkness so deep he was not aware of the darkness.

A pinging noise brought him back.

What's that you say, Morton?

"You've had enough."

Horace gagged. He coughed twice.

"I made notes," Morton said. His face had become clear again. "Listen: 'Fair at spheres. Pharisees mask pain. Pray, pray pain, prain.' I spelled prain with an *i*, but I suppose it also could be spelled with a *y*."

"I said nothing that made sense?"

"Here's the most coherent: 'A clear argument for relief of pain must cause no pain by its clarity.'"

"The effects," said Horace, "resemble those of nitrous oxide."

"Enough with nitrous oxide. How are the legs?"

"Give me a moment. I spoke no Bible verse?"

Morton laughed, then said that while Horace recovered he'd bring the aprons to a laundry girl down the street. As he left, Heaven's doorchimes jingled.

Flimflam, Horace thought. An exhilarating gas is an exhilarating gas. Whatever Morton's preparation, he'd discovered nothing more valid than *discovering* that lake water could satisfy thirst as well as water from a rain barrel. Ether in disguise, that was Horace's best guess. A way to deceive and make money: the invention of a thief. French corsets and monogrammed aprons? Morton—I'll bloody your face.

His legs, though weak, carried him to his coat, and then to a shelf where he tucked a bottle of Morton's gold foil into his pocket. His due for a day's work.

Elizabeth sat cross-legged on the bed in their dark room, waiting for her husband. Outside in the alley below, a weeping man shouted a woman's name, and from the lodge next door Elizabeth heard a fiddle playing a waltz. The top buttons of her dress's collar lay open. She leaned close to the bed post and studied the swirl of its unpolished grain. In her lap, she held a box of saltwater taffy, each piece wrapped in blue and yellow tissue. Wait for Horace, she told herself. Unwrap them only when he comes to you.

At a pawn shop, he sold the gold foil, then found a chemist-apothecary who sold nitrous oxide in bladders under a sign that read For Lung Ailments.

"Tuberculosis?" asked the apothecary.

"Justice," said Horace.

The taffy turned to sweet silk on her tongue. She thought about the woman in the painting and the man who had painted her. Given the woman's expression, Elizabeth could imagine the painter, too. The focus with which he looked on her. All the lead inside her chest had liquefied, and she knew it had only been there as a bulwark against the sharp longing she felt for a better time with Horace, for their unencumbered love. That would never return, she knew. Even so, she wanted Horace to become again like that painter—to adjust her hair, to mark how light fell, and with a finger on her chin to turn her face into its brightness. She wanted to become the subject of his intensity.

But now he staggered through the door, no painter, but a man laughing without gaiety.

She swallowed the taffy, ran her tongue over her sticky teeth. She wanted to say *painting* and *husband* and *waves*, but the moment passed and instead she asked, "Has Morton discovered anything new?"

"No," he said. "No! It's my discovery dressed in a more expensive suit."

He fell to his knees at the bedside, gazed into her face, then smiled with closed lips. He kissed the tip of her bandaged finger. He said, "I bought something for you."

She had wanted to be that woman in the painting, the one who anticipated, the one who waited and then received. But she saw the eagerness in his eyes, and she understood that in his way, he, too, had waited. With a finger, she traced the lines of his muttonchops, then his jaw, then his lips. A curled strand of his hair sat caught in his collar. She left it there. So she became the painter.

He breathed the gas. Words rolled about the corridors of his brain, covered in fuzz and coming to rest in a room of pillows.

"If you despise it," he said, "you don't understand it."

He thumbed tears from her cheeks. She couldn't stop crying. "It hurt you," she said.

"Not the gas. People hurt me. The gas, the gas saves me. Will save me. You've never understood because you've never tried it."

She fed him a piece of candy. Salty and caramel, thick on his tongue. "It hurts me that you shun it," he said. "If I were a painter—"

She shook her head. "That's not why I told you about the woman."

"If you despised my oils . . ."

He held the bladder toward her, his offering, his plea. "You mustn't despise it."

A white moth in the room flitted between them, and she waved it away, then touched Horace's warm cheek. She wanted him not to hurt.

The faucet in her mouth clicked against her teeth. Her tongue touched it, a coppery taste. She counted her breaths. One. Two. Her feet warmed as though she rested them near a fire.

Three. Four.

Her breathing sounded loud—ocean waves inside her head. That fiddled tune still waltzed through the window. Her eyes closed, she could hear how the room groaned, how it talked. Listen to the room, she said to Horace. The wood, you can hear its age. I can hear the blood pulse in your throat.

Horace leaned her back into the bed. She heard the relief expressed by her buttons as they slipped from their buttonholes. Her skin singing to the air.

"You must understand," he whispered. "It's as if Morton has stolen my child."

With eyes closed, with perfect vision, she saw her husband in the dark. Familiar, strange. How long since he'd lowered his body toward hers. The moth returned to land on his shoulder and just as quickly lit into the air. His shoulders, their freckles visible in candlelight. She counted them, onetwothreefour.

When his fingertips touched her naked thigh, she flinched.

This way, that way, which way you will . . .

Their bodies pulsing, liquid and light.

A holy burn between them. When she scraped his chest with her fingernails so hard she drew blood, he lifted from the bed, and all their confusions crushed into pleasure.

The long silence broken.

Late the next morning, Dr. and Mrs. Wells arrived at La Tête Blanc gallery. While Mrs. Wells sat on a red stool, her husband promenaded the room. At the end of his tour, he pirouetted on his right foot and clapped. He claimed the paintings to be the most moving things he'd ever seen, asked their prices, and laughed in such a way she believed that together the two of them could build castles in the sky.

"Selling those," he said to her as they walked to the train station, "we could make a fortune."

28

NEW SALVO LAUNCHED
IN "ETHER WARS"
AS CHEMIST APPEALS
TO PARISIAN ACADEMY

The *Boston Post*'s regular readers may well find themselves *numbed* to see the word "ether" yet again in our newspaper. Nevertheless, we feel obliged to report that Dr. Charles T. Jackson, chemist and graduate of the Harvard Medical School, has posted letters to the French Academy of Science and Medicine in Paris detailing his claim to the title "discoverer of painless surgery." The letters are the latest development in a spat between Dr. Jackson and Dr. William T. G. Morton, the dentist who, in applying the gas he calls "Letheon" to surgical patients, has rid the scalpel of its horrors. Massachusetts General Hospital's finest surgeons have since used Morton's gas in several operations, successfully amputating limbs and removing tumors while patients sleep quietly through. Dr. Morton, however, has created a scandal in the medical community for refusing to disclose the nature of his Letheon. Dr. Jackson, in turn, claims Letheon is merely ether mixed with other elements to disguise its identity. He asserts that he provided Dr. Morton with the gas and instructions on how it might render a patient insensible to pain. To prove his case, he has sent letters and affidavits from some of Boston's leading medical men to Paris via steamship.

His is the second claim mounted against Dr. Morton's priority with regard to painless surgery. This newspaper has published letters from a Hartford dentist who asserts that he first applied the principles now credited to Dr. Morton.

Dr. Morton continues to argue his case in this and other newspapers and before the public's representatives to the federal government. Much is at stake. The United States Army has proposed a contract by which the discoverer of painless surgery will receive recompense for his procedures and gases as used by the military in the war with Mexico. We at the *Post* have learned that this contract, when awarded, will make the discoverer of painless surgery a latter-day Midas.

29

Elizabeth had decided that Horace needed a hat.

"That's the last thing we should buy," he said. "I have half a dozen."

The door to the hatter's shop proved stubborn on that December day, sticky snow clumping at the threshold, so she stood aside while Horace coughed clouds into the cold air, kicked the door at its low point, and shoved so the shop bell jangled. He allowed her to enter first, though she paused as she did to kiss his chin. Such public affection embarrassed him, she knew, but since Boston she could not help herself. She could not help much anymore, not when she felt the need for a good weeping, nor when she needed to laugh or sing, not when she pulled him to her in bed. Since Boston, all her best hopes had reawakened—and for reasons beyond the surprising settlement that gave Col. Roberts all rights to the shower-bath and put ten thousand dollars in the Wellses' household accounts. "Soon, we'll conceive a daughter," she had whispered one night, her lips grazing Horace's ear, "and by the time she is born you'll have discovered how to make childbirth painless." Then she closed her eyes as they touched and rolled and clenched and let go, until she cried out in that way, so like agony.

At the hat shop, Horace shouldered the stubborn door closed. "To buy a hat I don't need is a vanity," he said. "Don't you think vanity is the most appalling sin?"

"Every sin appalls equally." She shook the snow from her skirt and stamped her boots, then picked up a hat with a high crown and beaver fur for its shell and turned it over in her hands. "We are purchasing you a work uniform. How is it vain for a general to wear insignia? A man who intends to negotiate art sales in France must look the part. That you don't want the hat proves the purchase isn't vain." She winked.

"I'm uncomfortable in fancy clothes."

"Because we have never worn them."

She fitted the tall hat on his head as the hatmaker, Mr. Pounds, came from the back. Horace frowned, though Mr. Pounds agreed that Mrs. Wells had chosen a fine one.

"Fine enough for Paris?" she asked.

"My," said Mr. Pounds, "will Dr. Wells wear my hat in Paris?"

She turned Horace toward a mirror. He adjusted the brim forward, then to the side. The hat lengthened his face, dignified it. "Yes, Paris," Horace said. "Mrs. Wells and I plan a new business venture. We're to become importers of art. Can you imagine?" He chuckled as if the idea tickled him. "And while I'm abroad, I'll see about presenting my science before the French academies. Others seek credit for painless surgery. You might have read that in the papers."

Mr. Pounds nodded. "All Hartford recognizes the injustice," he said.

Elizabeth lay fingertips on a second hat, then a third, as if petting them. "My husband does not need ribbons and certificates," she said, "but we do care about truth."

"Did you know," Horace asked, "that the dentist to the French king is a Connecticut man? From Norwich." He handed the hat he'd tried to Mr. Pounds. "This one will do for all occasions, don't you think? Respectable, but not stuffy?"

"Scientists in Paris wear the most elegant hats," said Mr. Pounds. "I have seen them sketched in magazines. Mrs. Wells is right that you want Hartford's best."

"But only one," said Horace.

After they'd paid, Horace and Elizabeth stepped back into wind-swept winter, big splatters of snow smacking their cheeks. Twice he lifted her so she would not mess her boots in slush puddles.

On what was to be their last night together for nearly three months, Elizabeth latched the bedroom door. In the sheets, she kissed his neck five times, welcomed his hands. He said, "You should come with me," the words spoken as much out of love as concern. Since his return from New Covenant, he had practiced candor and worked to be a better husband, and to spread word of the nitrous oxide phenomenon as he was meant to do. His rewards were manifold: the money from Col. Roberts, yes, but especially this reawakened love. He wanted to stay home, yet he felt the necessity of Paris. He also wanted Paris—with good reason—yet felt the necessity of home. "Come with me," he whispered again, because in Elizabeth's grace he'd found a harbor where his soul could mend. Without her, he worried, it might break again. But Elizabeth had decided they could not afford the expense of two travelers, and someone needed to stay behind with Charley. "Take this with you in my place," she said. She bit his ear, an impulse, something she'd never done before. She bit hard, surprised to find a small anger lingering for the years he had neglected her, and along with it a nascent foreboding that he would again. She bit with all her desire to keep him home, to mark him as her own. He cried out, squeezed her wrist, and pressed her to the mattress. They were cruel with each other that night in a way they had never been and could not even recognize in themselves, and that cruelty heightened the pleasure so that Elizabeth turned her face into a pillow to keep her cries from waking their boy. Come morning, husband and wife tried not to look at each other, as if still trying to understand what two strangers had met in their bed the night before.

Two days after Christmas, Elizabeth finished writing her first letter to her husband, though she knew Horace still to be in transit aboard a steamship, bound for England and from there to a ferry across the channel to France. In the letter she wrote about the Christmas rejoicing and warned Horace to be wary when hiring an interpreter in Paris, because she had heard that interpreters especially cheat their American patrons. She mentioned newspaper articles about Morton and Jackson and what others were now calling the Ether Wars. She closed the letter with a mention that her eyes were tired or else she'd write more, then sealed the envelope and scribbled on the outside, "I wish I could get inside of this and come to you, don't you?"

VI

PARIS

30

Aboard the paddle-wheel ocean steamer *RMS Hibernia*, it fell to first mate Cyril Benson to fix any predicament involving passengers. The captain, whose aptitude for brutality had been honed over two decades in the Royal Navy, was accustomed to treating those aboard ship as cannon fodder, so while he directed the engineer and the helmsman and the shipwright, he left Mr. Benson to calm all storms involving what the captain called "the human freight." Mr. Benson was particularly suited for the work. A Nantucket Quaker born with a fancy for whaling but not the courage, he had nevertheless a mariner's talent with direction and orientation, including a sixth sense for circumnavigating the human heart. This talent explained how a Yank had worked his way to first mate on a Royal Mail ship. It also explained why women desired his company, though none would trust him; he understood them too well. Even those who slipped between the sheets in his berth stayed one night only. The ease with which they gave themselves to him—an ugly man, really, with a barnacle nose and a guppy's mouth—revealed weaknesses in themselves that they did not wish to confront.

He would have liked now and then to enjoy a stimulating conversation about the morals of Paris or the cuisine of England. But the well-mannered and educated passengers dined at the captain's table. Mr. Benson ate with those who might slurp from a soup bowl or sing too loudly. Or he might miss dinner altogether, instead working below deck to convince some lunatic with scissors not to cut his clothes into strips, or listening to a matron mourn her drowned son's unredeemed soul. Through years of such work, he believed, he had learned truths about human nature. Sympathy, for example, was to be avoided, because it too often smacked of condescension.

Better to listen as if disinterested, as the ship's engineer listened to the belching, groaning engine. All ailments could be discerned through sound. A whimper, a groan, a catch of breath. "Hold my hand," a passenger might say. Or: "Cramps nail me to the bed." Or: "Paddle yerself out my room and straight to Hell." Mr. Benson accommodated requests as best he could.

Moreover, he had learned that though all humanity suffer hardship and misfortune, there is no taxonomy of distress: no two people ever suffered in the same way, nor could much be gained from one person's complaint that would help resolve the next. On the most recent crossing, a thief had stolen wigs from two women, leading the brunette to hysterical calls for amputation of the villain's hands; the redhead just laughed. The captured thief tried to end his life with a plunge into the sea. To most people that seemed an overreaction, but not to Mr. Benson, who grasped that you could only call something an *overreaction* if you could predict a *reaction*. No one, he had decided, could ever foresee the behavior of God's children. The infinite variety of human wretchedness was best met with equanimity and a willingness to be surprised.

The captain of the *Hibernia* disliked surprises.

Thus Cyril Benson found himself one dark early morning outside the door of No. 32, a shared cabin assigned to a surgeon dentist—Dr. Horace Wells of Hartford, Connecticut—and to the mayor of a small town in New Jersey who had that day demanded a transfer to new quarters. "I know I have bad teeth," he told Mr. Benson, "but 'Let me cut here, pull there, I have a vapor that numbs.' The fanatic won't let up!" This was in the final week of 1846, the *Hibernia* churning for Liverpool across the chill, rough North Atlantic. The sun had yet to rise this day, and after it did the cloud cover—thick as whale fat—would choke the light. In one gloved hand, Mr. Benson held a hurricane lamp with wick burning bright. In his other were keys through which he fumbled to find the fit for No. 32. His task was twofold: to retrieve the mayor's belongings and to ascertain whether the dentist, as his cabinmate had claimed, was a danger to the ship. As Mr. Benson slid a key into the knob, a loose dog trotted toward him in the hall, a long-legged creature with draping cinnamon-colored fur and a narrow head, which swung to and fro. It paused to touch its nose to the seat of his trousers, then pranced on. He made a mental note to remind the Russian woman in No. 46 to leash her animal at all times.

About to turn the key, he paused to press his ear to the door. Nothing. Brushed his knuckles on the wood in a sort of knock. Then gave it a sharp rap, and then a pounding with the meaty side of his fist.

No answer.

When he opened the door, the escaping sigh of warm air with its fetid smell reminded him of a room he'd too often visited in Liverpool, and though he'd promised himself never again to go, a familiar quickening of blood now unnerved him. His eyes adjusted to the gloom, and he saw a man on the cabin's lower berth, asleep belly down, face in a pillow. The man's back rose and fell. Breathing. Thank heavens.

Mr. Benson hung his lamp from a hook above the washbasin, then pushed aside a half-filled bowl of gruel and a beaver-fur top hat to make a place to sit on the room's bench. The man, presumably the dentist, snored. The room was a scattered mess of beakers and bags and notebooks opened to indecipherable scribbles. Evidence that the dentist had been hard at some task, keeping odd hours, laboring to exhaustion. The sight made Mr. Benson uneasy. It put him again in mind of that Liverpool room: the back of an abandoned building, candlelight playing on the glass pipes, the stale sweat smell in the dusty pillow by the stove where he had laid his head. How he had dreamed opium dreams. How he woke empty of all things.

The infinite variety of human wretchedness.

But he did not smell opium here. He left the bench, drew near the sleeping dentist, palmed the man's shoulder, shook it roughly, and said the man's name.

The dentist yanked his knees toward his chest, thrust forth a hand as if to ward off a threat, and cried out, "I won't forget! I won't forget!"

"Forget what?" asked Mr. Benson. "Dr. Wells, you are aboard ship. What won't you forget?"

"I'll have justice," he said. His face was blotchy, pimples sprayed across the brow. His nose looked bloated, the hollows about his eyes darkened and shiny with sweat. The eyes themselves flitted, the eyelids ashudder. He waved at his indecipherable notes. "Others mustn't pervert my discovery to their selfish ends."

Mr. Benson picked up a record book, tried to read the page as he settled back on the folding chair. "We've missed you at meals," he said.

The dentist nodded, took the book from Mr. Benson, tucked it shut under the blankets of the upper berth. "Who are you?"

"Mr. Benson, first mate."

"What I just spoke," the dentist said, "pay no heed. Tell no one what you've seen here." He combed his hair with his fingers, but the strands stayed stubbornly scrambled. "I would not mind the passage," he said, "if the boat would stop its swaying. All the back and forth. It's unsettling."

"If it were steady," said Mr. Benson, "it wouldn't be ocean travel."

"Of course it wouldn't. I know that." The dentist looked about as if he'd lost something. He settled his head against a pillow, gathered a blanket over himself and bunched it at his neck. "Pain is my chief preoccupation," he said. "I am expert in pain. Justice is not a subject I've given much attention. Generally, I've trusted God and the judiciary to balance the scales. But lately I find the subject to be of interest. Pain and justice so often fraternize—and only now do I realize this. I am writing letters about my experiments." He scribbled in the air. "*Reasoning by analogy, I discovered*—it doesn't matter. You don't care. But you must care about pain. We all care about pain. Here," he said, handing Mr. Benson a glass globe from which two pipes arose like a devil's horns. "Breathe this."

"What is it?"

"Relief."

At the end of one horn was a cap, the other a mouthpiece. Inside: a liquid. After a moment, the dentist leapt from the bed and snatched back the globe.

"Don't, then."

"I didn't say no."

"You didn't say yes. You want to suffer, by heaven, then suffer."

"I am not suffering—"

"We all suffer." Slowly, with one hand, the dentist scratched his cheek. "The sea is a cold companion, isn't it? A desolation. Desolation puts those lines on your face, Mr. Benson, rubs raw that skin over your cheekbones, reddens your knuckles. You hurt, but you don't need to. No one needs to." He held forth the globe as if to say, *Watch me*, then wrapped his lips over the mouthpiece. He held the piece there with his teeth, pinched his swollen nose shut, and with his other hand turned the faucet's knob. He took a deep breath. Then a second. He sat himself on the bench, in the space Mr. Benson had cleared, then breathed again. His eyelids fluttered; his left foot in its stocking tapped the floor. With a languorous hand he turned the faucet shut, let the globe roll to his lap, the liquid inside sloshing. Mr. Benson waited and watched. What he'd known in Liverpool began to itch at the back of his throat. The captain did not like surprises. The captain had not liked it that endless night when he found Mr. Benson leaning over the ship's prow, stricken with melancholy and tempted by the dark, murderous waves—the struggle evident in his posture, in his pleading eyes. "Coward," spat the captain, pulling Mr. Benson by the collar away from the deck's rail. "Weakling."

Contentment eased across the dentist's face. The pimples and bruised eyes seemed a natural part of his landscape. He was awake; his eyes turned round in their sockets. But he seemed not to perceive what he saw. With a lazy finger, the dentist scratched his chin. A half smile lifted the left side of his face.

You know nothing about my desolation, Mr. Benson thought. But his anger stuck like a pill in his throat, and it told him that perhaps the dentist did know him, a little.

After the dentist fell asleep, Mr. Benson stepped into the corridor and shut the door. Lamp in hand, he paused, and though he was not a man to pray he spoke a prayer. At that moment, the ship's captain approached on his way to the galley for coffee. "First nursemaid!" he called. "There's a frightened woman in No. 10. Please go hold her hand." He laughed, and for the first time Mr. Benson understood that his position aboard ship was assured so long as the captain needed a human whetstone upon which to sharpen his cruelty.

That night, Mr. Benson lay in his cabin entangled with the Russian woman, her cheek tear-damp against his shoulder, her small white body squirming in his arms, her cinnamon dog curled on the floor at the bedside. "I'm so lonely," the woman said. "I do not deserve such loneliness. I should die." She kept crying. Mr. Benson said, "But you won't." That night at the railing, when he had considered the waves, he'd learned that when it comes to death, desire and misgiving often balance each other; he recognized that tension in the woman's eyes. "Steady as we go," he said.

When at last she slept, Mr. Benson listened to her breathe and could not himself stop thinking about the Nantucket whalers of his youth or of the dentist, a dead-alive sort of man, or of the way the captain looked on him—the easy sneer, his naked loathing.

The next morning, Mr. Benson brought a loaf of bread to No. 32, and he asked whether he might try the dentist's pipe.

"It's not a pipe," said the dentist, laughing.

"You should eat something," Mr. Benson said as he took the globe.

A few minutes later, full of the vapor, he felt brave, and he did not hate himself so much. Afterward, he said, "That's a better place you sent me. I expected to see God and His Angels."

The dentist used the side of his hand to brush breadcrumbs from the pages of his record book, where he had made notations. "It's not heaven," he said. "But for a time, it shortens the distance. Then you fall back."

31

No. 11 rue de la Paix. To welcome Horace was a bronze plaque, weathered green and bolted into the wall, on which he read the name he'd found in a newspaper article and carried all the way from home: Christopher Starr Brewster. An inch or so below were the royal crest and the likeness of a tooth. The French king's dentist—a Connecticut Yankee—signified in bronze.

Horace's long winter shadow crept up the door, painted red. To either side were broad, paned windows with curtains open. Peeking through, he glimpsed a waiting room twice the size of his whole Hartford office. Fashionably dressed women sat along the four walls in matching straight-back chairs, each gripping a toothbrush. In military-marching unison, they stuffed the brushes in their mouths, stroked forward and back, up and down, cheeks stretched. Then, as if governed by a single mind, they removed their toothbrushes and rested their hands in their laps.

A man in their midst pointed with a long, delicate finger to his own toothbrush, to his mouth, demonstrating brushing technique. He wore black—black coat, black shirt, black gloves—with a high collar and loose scarf, a pointed bit of beard, and his straight blond hair combed back as if he faced into a windstorm. A quick question appeared on his face when he glimpsed Horace, who at once let his gaze drift to the street, trying to appear as if he awaited a business associate or a lover.

Above, gossamer clouds tinted the blue. People hurried here and there, filling the air with carnations of white breath, and a towering red-faced man chased his top hat, wind-tumbled toward a puddle of snow melt. Horace believed he had left his own hat aboard the *Hibernia*; what happened to his gloves he couldn't say. Unsettling, how aboard ship he so immediately and completely gave himself to the gas. Like waking or falling into sleep, as if he had no say in the matter. And what dreams! Truer than they'd ever been—he had even kissed his father's cheek. Their felt presence still agitated him.

Toes stinging from cold, he stamped his booted feet on the cobblestones and wished even now for a breath of nitrous oxide. All around, people yelled—their words sounding to him like bubbles bursting. He flinched at the start of each new argument, not yet knowing how Parisians lived a never-ending quarrel: a cacophony of curses and insults, with trollops kicking beggars, soldiers berating shopkeepers, aristocrats exchanging evil looks with intellectuals, police clubbing everyone—even the nuns.

A nearby church bell tolled the hour, and a general bustle followed from inside the dentist's office: chair legs scraping the floor, a closet opened, women in conversation. Horace wiped his nose with a handkerchief, kicked snow from his boots, and stepped through the door.

The women—varied in age but uniformly tidy with cinched waists and ruffled dresses—were packing toothbrushes into handbags or purses, their French sounding again to Horace like bursting bubbles, though these blown from liquefied silk. The man kissed several women farewell, and accepted kisses, and when the last had left, he smiled at Horace and spoke something in French.

"Only English," Horace said, arms outstretched in apology.

The man's face opened with delight. "Fellow American!" Twice he slapped his chest. "Norwich, Connecticut! Come, sit down. Have you a problem with a tooth?"

"You are Dr. Brewster?"

"As it reads outside the door." Brewster gave Horace a long look, and Horace was glad to have shaved that morning, though he was aware that he'd lost weight since leaving home. His pants hung loose; his shoulders floated inside his coat. A feverish sweat broke over him, and his hands— why did they tremble as if still cold?

"I practice dentistry in Hartford. My name is Horace Wells."

"Dr. Wells?" Brewster whispered. Then, more loudly: "I've read about your experiments."

"What have you read?" Horace asked. He could not make sense of the new expression on Brewster's face. "What do you think?"

Brewster shook Horace's hand. "I think I'm embarrassed that I mistook you for a patient. Horace Wells!"

He laughed and led Horace out of the waiting room and into his office, which was warmed by a stove and well appointed with spittoons hammered from fine brass, drawerfuls of ready-made dentures, and a cabinet that held hundreds of dental tools. "It's a weakness," Brewster admitted. "I want them all." A life-size statue of Saint Apollonia seemed to bestow a blessing on the two patient chairs, each with headrests upholstered in black velvet. Horace recalled his little cottage in Hartford with its hand-size bust of the saint, a gift from a wealthy patient's husband, and felt himself poor, a feeling exacerbated when Brewster set out pastries, a half dozen cheeses, and a bottle of red wine.

The men sat in the patient chairs, which swiveled. Apollonia, over Brewster's shoulder, studied Horace with glass eyes. In legend, she was an old woman, a deaconess tortured by Romans who had yanked out her every tooth, blood and root. But here sainthood and a sculptor had rendered her as a woman of childbearing age—bosom full, eyelashes long, mouth expressing an ecstasy, head crowned with a shiny plate for a halo. Pincers in her right hand held a bright, golden molar. *It doesn't hurt*, he heard her say, but the voice belonged to the woman, Nan.

Horace unfolded the newspaper article from his pocket. In his mouth, the cheese crumbled, becoming thick and viscous as melted gold. "You are famous among Connecticut dentists," he said.

"As are you! Nitrous oxide. Painless surgery. The Ether Wars! Why didn't you send a letter to prepare your way? Why the surprise?"

Horace tried not to stare at Apollonia, the parted lips that suggested her bliss. Her eyes raised heavenward, her free hand stretched flat, palm almost caressing her cheek. Daylight dazzled in the office's mirrors, and how it fell on the statue gave Horace to think that Apollonia might actually be breathing, bosom rising and falling and rising.

"I fear tensions from America could have followed me. Might Morton have spies in Paris?"

Brewster groaned. "Spies? You make him sound like a government.

He has friends, perhaps even employees. All I can say for sure is that he and that boor Jackson have sent letter after letter warning me against you. 'Wells failed; his theories are humbug,' et cetera. Every day another envelope from Boston. Some days two! If they want us to take their arguments seriously, they should come here, as you have done."

Brewster poured again for each of them, a drop sliding down the bottle's neck to stain the label. "It's no guarantee our medical societies will give your discovery priority over the others, but your presence helps your case."

"There is no question," Horace said. "I discovered painless surgery."

"From the French perspective, that's not been settled. But I'm glad you're here nonetheless."

Not been settled? Horace wondered whether to show some indignation. But now Brewster asked questions about dates and details. Ought the dosage be less for children, and what about boys against girls? Had Dr. Wells noticed varied reactions in smokers or tuberculars? How often did patients laugh? Had he worked with ether? ("Just recently.") He asked how Horace had recorded his results, and who had witnessed the work. "Have you affidavits to support your claim?"

"Results have always been my chief concern. I am no lawyer. Never for a moment did I consider how best to argue the priority of my discovery. Now, apparently, it matters." Horace lifted his chin and emptied his glass. "You don't believe I was first?"

Brewster smiled and poured more wine. Glass-eyed Apollonia seemed to lean nearer, her blessing a tease.

"Not yet," Brewster said.

A few days later, Horace had been moved at government expense into an apartment with skylights and a featherbed, fancy with silk sheets. From a balcony he could see the Tuileries Palace and its flourishes: the French make a pastry of everything, he thought. A hatter had come by with samples, then returned that afternoon with a *chapeau* of such lightness and balance it seemed to Horace that he, like the saints, wore a halo.

Bathed, shaved, and fed, he could believe that even his most outrageous daydreams seemed likely. Parisian scientists (spectacles, white hair, waistcoats) would praise his work, then: Join us! Here in Paris! He pictured Elizabeth, ruddy with health, park-strolling in the company of a teenaged daughter, the two fluent in French and holding hands. He saw himself and a grown-up Charley dressed in fashionable suits, the wool so fine that not a thread itched. From his balcony, he picked out three houses he might buy.

He spent a week writing an account of his discovery, which Brewster had promised to have published in European journals. Morning and night, he scratched out recollections of Colton's exhibition, Cooley's leg, his own aching tooth, even his Boston failure. He considered but decided against calling the gas a miracle. The civilized world, Brewster had told him, did not want prophets and their heaven-sent wonders. It wanted scientists— scientists who also were heroes.

So he made no mention of unflattering particulars—no birds in the attic, nor a woman with a chipped button on her blouse, nor a Chinese boy. Silence, he recalled Elizabeth once saying, could also be truth.

An enclosed carriage arrived Tuesday, drawn by two white horses and accompanied by a driver and an attendant. Brewster was to introduce Horace to a noted landscape painter and also to show him the government's laboratories outside the city.

"We've started our own experiments using ether and nitrous oxide," Brewster said, pouring a glass of wine for Horace as the carriage got underway. "But it's with chloroform that France will make its mark."

Horace sipped. He had never tasted something that so enchanted his tongue, his mouth. "This is a royal carriage?" he asked. "Truly? Elizabeth will be flabbergasted."

Brewster smiled. The carriage drove them out of the city, and the men talked about art and dentistry, and it occurred to Horace that if this were always his life he might never again take a whiff of nitrous oxide or ether.

"What a lark," he said, "to put your fingers into the royal mouth!"

Brewster again lifted the bottle. He seemed always to be pouring wine.

They traveled through farmland, crusty snow in patches on north-facing slopes. The loamy smell of hot manure in cold air reminded Horace of his father, and he found he'd made fists of his hands. Flustered, he released the grip, studying his own knuckles, the now open palms.

Brewster corked the wine as the carriage slowed and stopped. Outside, he hurried Horace—stiff-legged and tipsy—toward a stone barn marked with the royal crest, triple the size of any barn Horace had ever seen.

Ivy climbed its walls, and the roof tiles, once orange, had browned from weather. "You work with the vapors in a barn?" Horace asked.

"This is where the horses are."

Brewster signaled an attendant, who rolled the barn doors in their runners to each side. A delicious warmth of straw and animals enveloped them.

"Horses? I don't understand."

"We experiment on horses. Not ideal, but we try to account for differences. If a horse is ten times a man's weight, for example, we expose it to ten times the gas."

"With due respect, Dr. Brewster, the horse can't relate to you the gas's effects."

"True. But we observe reactions." They'd arrived at the stalls and a dozen or more horses. A bay nearby made fluttering noises, lips working and skin shuddering away flies.

"Strange sensitivities in horses," Brewster said. "Have you noticed how they can ignore a rider's kick to the ribs, yet are aware of every fly?"

"That speaks to my point. A horse experiences sensation otherwise than us. We must study effects on people."

The barn's dormer windows made paths for clean sun, and in the light the bay's coat showed all its patches and grime. The horse reached to nibble at a button on Brewster's shirt cuff, and Brewster scratched its forehead. "Which people, Dr. Wells? The royalty? The bourgeoisie? Should we experiment on the workers? The criminals in our prisons? Horses have died in our tests. And you want us to work on people? Barbaric."

Brewster shouted French words toward a doorway, and shortly after a small man in a smock appeared, then pushed past them with hardly a nod. Thick-lensed spectacles warped the appearance of his eyes, and his front teeth gapped. He carried a bottle, a towel, and a hand-sized burner, unlit. "One of our concerns," Brewster said, "is ether's flammability. If Morton is using the vapor by another name, as you suspect, that's irresponsible. What if a patient's lungs ignite?"

Brewster gestured for Horace to make room. The man had tied a kerchief over his own nose and mouth and was now dousing the towel. Horace recognized ether's odor and felt a familiar pinch, a small but deep yearning. When the man pressed the towel against the horse's nostrils, the animal started, its eyes widening, then, after a few breaths, half closing. The horse staggered, confusion evident in its twitching ears. Its unbalance—its struggle against awkwardness—struck Horace as its own barbarism. He recalled staggering about his workshop, his headaches, the confusions, and his now shaky hands. True, he had never experimented on horses. He'd worked that abuse on himself.

A few more breaths for the horse, and the small man lifted the lit burner near the horse's muzzle, all the while leaning away as if the animal itself were a threat.

Then it exhaled across the burner's flame.

Blue fire flickered from its nose.

"Congratulate us," said Brewster. "We've invented dragons."

The carriage wheels found so many ruts and bumps on the road to the painter's farm that Horace suspected the driver deliberately steered toward them. At each jolt and jostle, bottles of French chloroform in Horace's satchel rolled, clinked. "For experimentation," Brewster had said. "Tell us what you learn. This time, arrange for witnesses."

The painter's farm looked nothing like the government's. Unkempt hedges lined the drive. The farmhouse and barn had weathered gray, some roof shingles blown away. Chickens roamed, whispering to each other, and a goat eyed the dentists with mistrust as they stepped from the carriage. Leafless silver maples sheltered the walk, and the men ducked as they passed under so as not to bump the myriad thingamabobs strung with catgut line from the bare limbs. These bird houses Horace might have expected, but not their rainbow colors, and not artificial birds fashioned from twigs and rag scraps, snow dusting their wings. Bits of shattered mirror glass dangled, too, dancing in the day's last light. Overseeing it all stood a headless scarecrow wearing an expensive brocade dress.

"Marie Antoinette," said Brewster.

From somewhere a dog's thunderous bark. Through a squeaky-hinged door, they entered a kitchen where an odor of oil paints—strong, noxious—almost turned Horace around. But he followed Brewster, deeper into the odor and then to a barn of a room with tall windows and several oil lamps burning in sconces. The walls had been white, but now were speckled with colors; the floor stones the same. Lilac and flax and blue sky and tan the color of a fawn's coat. Here the air was most pungent, and the caustic smells mixed with such vivid colors made Horace's head go floating. If not for a growing nausea, he might have thought he'd been breathing nitrous oxide.

On the room's far side, a woman in a farmwife's gown stood on the seat of a wicker chair, dabbing with a brush at a high, wide canvas. Her straw hat's brim ran nearly as wide as her shoulders, and her white hair struck out in all directions. Her bare feet were spattered with violent hues.

"Madame DeNoie," called Brewster, his tone deferential.

She replied in French, her attitude nonchalant, her attention on her dabbing.

Brewster kept his peace. She dabbed more. Then, cat-quick, she pounced from the chair to snatch a rag—they seemed to breed on the floor—and with it smeared paint around the canvas. Somehow (magic to Horace), those oils became a river. Then, her grunt suggesting she was done if not satisfied, she plunged her hands into a water bucket, and as she scrubbed spoke to Brewster, who turned to ask Horace how he liked his coffee.

"Cream and a spoonful," Horace said.

Still studying the canvas, she ambled out of the room. Brewster waved at a stool and a barrel to indicate they should sit.

"You didn't translate," he said. "She speaks English?"

Brewster nodded. "And Italian. Very educated. These landscapes? *Premier coup.* You'll want to buy."

Though Horace's understanding of art was limited, to him some quality seemed new in the freshly made canvas. Dark trees menaced the left, and how she'd applied the oils suggested leaves ruffling, branches asway. In the distance, clouds churned thin and gray to threaten not only the forest but the towers of an old abbey, itself only a suggestion of sandy brown oils. The paint itself made a commotion. Elizabeth would say, "Buy it."

"I had expected a man."

"We all do. She signs her paintings P. H. DeNoie. That way misogynists will buy, and the Salon at least consider them."

They heard her voice down the hall, louder as she drew near, until she burst into the room, her words hurrying past Horace. Brewster shouted, "Eh, eh! Speak only English to him."

She smiled and held a bottle forward. "Absinthe?"

"What does *absinthe* mean?" His words sounded more clipped than he'd intended. An irritation nicked at him. Was she playing a game, still speaking French?

Brewster and Madame DeNoie began another loud exchange, this one longer than the first, and she laughed, and Brewster sipped his coffee, and for nearly half an hour Horace tried to understand from their faces what was being communicated, until the effort and the fumes left him drowsy. Put me to bed, he thought. At last the painter turned to him.

"Brewster says you know nothing about paintings."

"I didn't say that!"

"But you invented an important something that takes away pain, and so you are a genius." She winked at Horace. "Also, you have money."

"He did discover something important. I did say that."

"Why would you make such a thing to take away all pain?"

Why take away pain? Wasn't the answer obvious? Taken off-guard by the question, Horace set his cup on the floor, as though he couldn't answer and balance a cup at the same time.

"I don't want people to suffer."

She frowned. She had been dripping water over sugar and into her absinthe drink, and now she sipped. "It is good to hurt," she said. "My husband died, and his farmwife, me, he deserved that I hurt for him. He is a great loss. So I left for Paris to study great art and to be sad. Because I am lost. Now. Look." She spread her arms and turned a circle, stately, as if the room were an achievement. She waved an invitation or maybe a challenge for him to answer. "Your gases?"

"Yes."

"Someday everyone will breathe them?" She hummed, then, not a tune, but a noise to fill space until she found the English word. Brewster helped. He was holding the bottle of absinthe, sniffing its mouth. "Manufacture," he said.

"Yes! *Manufacture*! Everyone will breathe gas and be happy, and art dies."

"That's an overreaction," Horace said.

"Monsieur Genius," she said, "does it hurt you that people suffer?" Her eyes widened; she expected an answer. But what to say? A bat flew across the ceiling of Horace's mind, lit on his father's gray brow. Horace cradled his son in the cold dirt of a fresh grave. *Hurt?* Madame DeNoie spoke the word as if it had no power.

"Look!" she said, stabbing a finger his way. "Pain plus genius, and you, *le dentiste*, make an important thing. A great thing. That is the life secret. Everything is made from pain! But the thing you make?" She shook her head as if dismissing it. "Too much. No one makes anything ever again."

"I'm here to buy paintings."

"There are no paintings without pain." She straightened her back, seemed proud of her wordplay in a foreign tongue. Then she clasped her hands over her heart and grinned in a pantomime of agony. "No progress," she croaked, "without pain."

Brewster laughed, but in Horace a cold thing rose from his belly to his throat, choking him. He, of all people, needed no lecture on pain. His lips worked for a moment before he spoke. "Respectfully, Madame DeNoie, that is a stupid thing to say. And cruel."

She stopped smiling. After a moment, she spoke furious bubble-words at Brewster; they burst like fireworks. She kicked at the air. Brewster shouted, and then Madame DeNoie spun and splashed her coffee across Horace's face.

She said in a loud voice, "I am with the workers. We make things from pain. The bourgeoisie want comfort. They will perish in their feather beds. The workers will live."

She stomped from the room, leaving Horace to wipe coffee from his cheeks with a paint rag, and Brewster coughing so as not to laugh. "You provoke an argument like a true Parisian," he said. "But give her the last word, or we'll sleep with the goats."

They ate supper at a farmhouse table, gouged and stained as if she had used the surface to slaughter chickens. She served cheese soup with radishes, along with a hard-crusted bread, and the food settled Horace's stomach. "Do not apologize," Brewster had warned. "Pretend as if the argument never happened." So Horace kept quiet, let Brewster and Madame DeNoie talk, and now and then she opened her mouth to point at a tooth high toward the back on her left side. After dinner she showed Horace several paintings, all in the same tumultuous style. Brewster translated prices, which Horace recorded with pencil in a notepad, though he did not agree to any purchases. He sensed how this annoyed her. But later, after she showed the dentists where to find fresh water and where to empty their chamber pots and then to their separate rooms, she kissed Horace's cheek good-night in a way that made him feel like a son.

In his room: a feather bed, which surprised him given her earlier speech. If he spoke French, he would have explained that his gas might never rid the world of pain. No one had breathed more nitrous oxide than he, and still he suffered, still heard *humbug* and the Chinese boy's flute, and when he thought of Elizabeth and Charley so far away, an animal trap snapped shut on his heart. The gas destroyed some pains, true, but he had begun to hypothesize that it exaggerated others. Before the gas, a scraped knuckle or tweaked knee had never been anything to him but a short-lived distraction. After? The slightest affliction pressed to the forefront of every moment. Stubbed toe. Mosquito bite. Even a disappointment. The distraction of small hurts grew beyond the hurts themselves, unbalanced his hours, gave him reason to consider the gas and then test it. Oftimes he'd inhale as a relief from routine, as if routine itself were a sort of upset.

You do not learn such things, Brewster, when only horses breathe the gas.

A breeze had come up, and he heard the mirror shards in the trees tinkling against each other. The sound first put him in mind of Charley and his toys, and he wished he could show the boy how horses breathe fire, and those thoughts led him to Elizabeth. But then the breeze grew to a wind, the mirror shards clashed, and he recalled the chloroform bottles in his satchel in the carriage.

Out of bed and in his boots, he stepped into the hallway, from which vantage he could see the length of a long hall and into Madame DeNoie's studio. Lantern light shined out that open door, and she in silhouette sat on her wicker chair, a giant white dog lying beside her. She'd pulled her knees up against her chest, and one arm hung low. The fingers of that hand played in the dog's deep fur, though she seemed not to know the animal was there, her attention on something Horace couldn't see, perhaps a hope or a memory. Nowhere in the house had he seen a painting that might portray her husband, and he wondered why not. He wondered what consolation he might require were Elizabeth to die.

As if sensing his thoughts, the dog turned its massive head toward him, its soulful eyes dark and unconcerned, and the sight pricked in Horace a recollection of that other white dog, of mangled leg and blood-stained snow, of barking at the edge of blackness.

Were he fluent in French, he might dare say more over the next morning's eggs and jam, about pain and about respect and honesty, about giving shape to what hurts. But he was not that fluent, not even in English. Shivering, he retreated from the long hall, deciding—in a determined way—to leave the chloroform in the carriage, that for tonight at least the comfort of a feather bed ought to be enough.

32

As the carriage turned, Horace leaned a shoulder into the door, glimpsed Paris's spires over a distant hill, and with his tongue worked a bit of smoked fish out of his teeth. He tucked the satchel holding chloroform bottles more securely under his arm.

"Last night," he said, "you told Madame DeNoie that I'd made a great discovery. You said it without qualification, as if you believe my claim."

Brewster nodded, and with a ribbon bookmarked the novel he'd been reading, then set it on a cushion on his lap. "I've read your accounts now, listened to you talk. Yes. I'm convinced."

He offered his hand to shake, and Horace felt a deep welling cry wanting to escape his chest, but he gripped it as tightly as he did Brewster's hand.

The road rose, the sun flashed into the carriage, and Brewster drew a curtain. "On Saturday," he said, "we present before the Medical Society of Paris."

"What?" Horace raised his open hand as if signaling Brewster to halt. "That's three days."

"And after that, the French Academy of Sciences, then the Society for Medical Observation. Don't look so frantic."

The city gates opened, and the driver lashed the horses forward. A few blocks in, the carriage slowed on a turn, and then, just as Horace began to ask whether any dentists sat on the Medical Society, the window behind his head shattered. Cold bits of glass stung his cheek, and Brewster shoved him by the shoulders hard to the carriage floor. For a strange moment Horace thought he'd been hit by a snowball. But against his leg lay a brick, what had smashed the glass. Outside: angry shouts and a whip's snap. The carriage jerked forward in a rush. Someone shrieked, and horse hooves clattered over boulevard stones. Pistol fire echoed.

"Stay down!" Brewster yelled.

A gallop—several blocks? a mile?—and they arrived at Horace's apartment. Brewster, hair damp with sweat, lifted Horace off the carriage floor. "My god, my god," Horace repeated, and when the door opened his feet couldn't find the steps. The attendant, off his perch beside the driver and now awaiting Horace's descent, offered a white-gloved hand, helped him down.

"Politics here have been violent for too long," said Brewster, disembarking just after. "They called it a revolution, but it was more a civil war. And civil wars, it seems, never ever end. Perhaps there's a vapor to fix that." He smiled sadly.

The attendant, older, with gray in his neatly trimmed eyebrows, brushed glass shards off Horace's coat with his hand, then peered to pick at smaller flecks. The man's cheeks had gone white, too, and sweat beaded above his lip.

"Are you all right?" Horace asked.

The attendant pursed his lips. Nodded. But his eyes sparkled with too much life.

"Brewster!" Horace said, stepping out of the attendant's reach. "Your man!"

The attendant stared at his fingertip and thumb, as if still trying to find a fleck of glass. A dark wet stain had spread across his coat, midwaist. Now Brewster was at his side, French words like bubbles at a boil. Queasy, Horace swallowed to keep the fish down. Brewster was helping the man out of his coat, the fellow complying in an awkward, hesitant way as if meaning no disrespect by undressing.

"Let him breathe this," Horace said, groping for a bottle in his satchel.

"He needs a surgeon," Brewster said.

"For the surgery. That's what I mean. Look at his pain!"

The attendant lurched as if some sharpness shifted inside his midsection, and he bumped Horace, who fumbled the bottle into the man's chest. "Take it," Horace said, and with his good arm the attendant did. "Breathe its fumes before the surgery."

"Wells, we don't know enough."

"It's only breathing," Horace told the attendant. With his hand, he pantomimed air sweeping up into his nostrils.

"You're not being helpful."

Brewster was leading his attendant into the carriage compartment, shouting to the driver. The wounded man clutched the bottle, turned from Brewster to Horace. He mouthed *Merci*, then stepped into the carriage.

Later that night, Horace instructed a valet to draw a bath and to leave a bottle of chloroform on the edge. "Make the water steam," he said. He himself felt on an edge. At Madame DeNoie's he'd gone without chloroform or any such gas, despite the urge to partake, and in doing so felt virtuous. The same eagerness tugged now, consorting with the need for chloroform experiments. But he did not like to think of scientific inquiry as a temptation, akin to the glutton's next bite or the gambler's dice throw. He did not want to think that at all.

In the bath chamber, he noted the date in his record book, and also the time, his mood (on edge), his pulse rate, what he'd eaten and drunk. Then he eased himself into the steam, imagined Madame DeNoie's voice accusing him: "Bourgeois." Submerged to his shoulders, his flesh pinkened, he watched the hairs on his belly float toward the surface, and he reached for the chloroform bottle on its silver tray. He scratched behind his scrotum, where air bubbles itched, then dunked a towel until it was soaked through. This he put over his head as a hood, hiding his face and the bottle at his nose.

Pungent, this chloroform, sweet smelling, like sugared mint. He breathed, nose membranes tingling, then stopped the bottle. Counted ten. Rubbed his nose with the back of his hand. Exhaled. In his ears a rushing sound echoed. He uncorked the bottle, breathed, and his heart sped. The room narrowed and expanded so he could count each fiber of the towel draped before his eyes, see strands loop back on themselves as if describing an orbit. Through the nose, into the lungs, belly swelling, and he imagined himself to be the sun, and a planet in his orbit flew past, leaving in its wake a long, tremulous note as if from a violin, and there was no want for anything, and he, Horace Wells, destroyer of pain, generated a radiance greater than brilliant.

Perhaps he would have drowned, but his valet returned with hot water and discovered Horace hard asleep and slipped low, wet towel draped over his face, the waterline just below his nose, the chloroform liquid swirling, the empty bottle afloat.

The wretched began to gather the next morning outside Horace's apartment building long before he woke. First came a syphilitic, the oldest son of a wealthy exporter of soaps, who could not bear to be touched for the burning sensation that erupted over his skin. Soon, a young woman arrived who felt her skull cleave whenever she ventured into bright sun, like this day's. Next, a mother brought her child, whose skin around his eyes had gone purple, and she pushed him in a potato cart because the grinding in his hips kept him from walking or sleeping. Discomfort, twinge, torment—more joined the miserable company, and last came a scrawny, bent man whose arms crisscrossed his abdomen because without warning his viscera cramped as though cinched by the tightest belt.

Shut off from them all, indoors and warmed by a hearth, Horace sat at the breakfast table while his valet stood near, watching him not eat. The valet held up both hands, showed all his fingers. "This many," he said. "More, also."

With great care, Horace folded his napkin. "Aren't they cold? Can we invite them in?"

The valet shook his head. He had served the royal court for a dozen years, and he understood his responsibilities.

Horace lay down his fork and lifted the knife, then put down the knife and asked for coffee. Brewster had given him three chloroform bottles. One had gone to the wounded attendant, another's liquid had sloshed down the tub drain. Of course he could get more. But how soon could Brewster produce another? Horace had meant to study effects again that coming afternoon.

Some clammy need wormed its way up the back of his neck. The chloroform was his; he did not need to share. And yet.

"I am not a physician," he said, talking more to himself than to the valet. "I can't cure what afflicts them. Unless they require dental surgery—"

He glanced away from the table as if he could see out to the street and to the ruddy, agonized faces of those who waited. "Even then, I'd rather not."

Some minutes later, dressed in overcoat and boots, he shook the last drops from the bottle into the pot he'd filled with chloroform, then soaked kitchen rags in the liquid. When he stepped out into the sparkling cold morning, Horace could smell sour ruin come off the gathered unfortunates, those wrapped in blankets and bandages, propped up by a crutch here or a shaky arm there, this one coughing, that one moaning. One and all turned his way, faces contorted with hope, lurid with pain.

The scrawny man doubled over, snarling, his hands fisted.

"What's wrong with that man?" Horace asked. "Who speaks English?"

The mother to the boy who could not walk or sleep smiled a pleasant, helpless smile but like the rest kept silent. The syphilitic pressed forward.

Horace reached into the pot and squeezed a rag to rid the excess. Then he waved it near his nose, a demonstration. The scrawny man stumbled up the stairs, his hands seizing Horace by the forearm. He thrust his dirty face into the rag, as if wanting to be smothered, and Horace—alarmed— almost pulled away. The man's eyelids fluttered. Tears wet his cheeks, and his knees weakened. When he sighed, Horace eased him down, taking care as he lay the man's head on the polished marble step.

The remaining rags, soaked in relief, he handed to the others, who accepted them as if receiving holy relics or alms from God. And he helped each breathe until those who had cried and those who had ground their teeth and those who had prayed for death now leaned against the iron rods of a garden fence, or slumped into the street gutter, or lay flat on the sidewalk, facing up into the blue. Smothered, yes. But a temporary murder. A kindness.

Sunlight glimmered off the crystal snow. The boy's mother crouched near her son, touching his cheeks, cooing, and she made a pillow of her coat for his head.

Horace alone stood upright, ears red from the cold, a wet rag clenched in each fist. All these sleeping faces. Such innocence. Such serenity as children know. Astonishing. His eyes misted with a father's tenderness.

33

The man with the Scottish brogue and the gavel had asked a question. Horace rolled his tongue into the hole Riggs had left in his mouth, probing the smooth absence as if the correct reply could be found in the empty socket.

"Answer him," hissed Brewster.

The Scotsman leaned away from the table where he sat with his medical society fellows, whispered to an aide. Why couldn't Horace remember the man's question? Why couldn't he concentrate to answer? Behind his eyes, he felt a pecking thing, a scavenging bird working its beak.

Gray daylight through the chamber's high windows. Table lamps lit, the oils scented with balsam. The crowd. So many! The medical society itself numbered a dozen or so, and each dignitary had two or three aides—holding themselves in world-weary poses until summoned with a whisper or a finger. Elbow to elbow at the journalists' bench, too, and in the gallery—the audience conspiring like spies. Horace heard *humbug* as though from a distance, searched faces for Morton's or Jackson's.

"Wells." It was Brewster again. "Say something."

"What I know," Horace said, "is that I *needed* to find a way to stop pain during surgery. Need drove me. Out of necessity, I was first."

"But what proof do you have for us, Dr. Wells?"

"Morton recognized an opportunity when I failed in Boston. For all I know, he sabotaged my effort. What he needed, what he has always needed, is money. The only thing he has discovered is how to increase his wealth by disguising my work as his own."

"Affidavits? Appointment books? Dr. Morton sent us notes in an envelope sealed the day he made his discovery—"

"Replicated, please. He replicated my discovery."

"We have yet to decide that, Dr. Wells."

"Then until you decide, you mustn't say Morton made a discovery as if it were fact."

The Scot's eyebrows lifted, and he took a breath so deep Horace could see his chest expand. Before the man could retort, Horace interrupted.

"I do not have affidavits, because I foresaw no need. I had made the discovery, and it was not important that I get whatever fortune or fame Morton hopes to gain. It was—it *is*—essential that humanity benefit. Perhaps I rushed things." Rushing now, he knew. Saying too much, too fast. Head muddled, no stopping. "I'm not good with pain, my mother will tell you. I cried loudest even when it was my brother she caned. Time and again the pain I inflicted on patients compelled me to shutter my practice. Don't know why I chose dentistry to begin with. Small, quick fingers, I suppose. And I've always liked working with tools."

"Thus," said the Scot, "lack of proof proves your case? As would a child, you stumbled into a new land and were so excited to proclaim your discovery you forgot to bring back a native species, and now no one believes you."

"Dr. Brewster believes me. There are others. And witnesses. I will send sworn testimonies."

"Until then, we have your story and nothing else?"

"You have the truth. Straight as a loon's leg."

Over a late breakfast at Horace's apartment, Brewster translated the journalists' columns, read aloud as he dropped flakes of croissant to his Bichon Frise mewling at their feet. "It's your honesty they adore," he said, "how you admit to your Boston humiliation. The newspaper editors love a story of frustrated genius."

Clean sunlight shined like a blessing on the table, gracing the porcelain of the cups, the tines of silver forks, the reflective shallows of each spoon. An egg yolk on Horace's plate was as pure a yellow as he'd ever seen. He shook open a newspaper, dusty in the light, and pointed to a word.

"What does this mean?"

"Snip. Cut. Something like that."

He pointed to another.

Brewster put a hand across the newspaper, lowered it to the table. "What happened yesterday, Wells? You never answered questions as asked. You told a good story, yes, but in such a confused jumble. You sounded deranged at times—Morton sabotaged you?—and irritable."

Horace kept his finger on the page. "Can't you tell me this word?"

Brewster glanced. "Wink."

Horace pronounced the French silently, then poured more coffee. His hand trembled, so he steadied it with the other, giving Brewster a look to say, it's all of a piece.

"Quick-tempered," Horace said. "Bedeviled by headaches. Distracted. Morbidly suspicious? It's possible. My memories don't stick. Something happens, but a moment later I can't grasp it. I reach, but it's like a sweetmeat canned and locked up for winter."

"Chloroform?"

Horace shrugged. "This began before. Back home. Though it's worsened since."

"You should refrain. From chloroform, ether, any exhilarating gas."

Brewster spoke French to the dog, and the dog sat on its hind legs. Horace wanted to know the words for things in French. Why wouldn't Brewster help him with the words? What was he hiding? Horace clawed at his cheeks. When he yanked back the newspaper, his elbow sent a bowl of egg shells crashing to the floor.

"Your dog knows more French than I do!" he cried.

Brewster lifted his pet, cradled the dog against his bosom. His eyes searched Horace's face with such sincere good will that Horace turned away. "Please," Brewster said. "Refrain. We don't know all the consequences."

"When will we know? In this lifetime? In a thousand years? It doesn't matter."

Brewster pointed toward a phrase on the page, showed it to Horace. "'The famous American dentist.' This is what the newspapers call you. There are other ways to occupy yourself in Paris than experimenting with gases. Especially when you are famous. Your life is about to become hectic. You'll need to keep your wits about you. You'll also need a new wardrobe."

That very afternoon a tailor arrived to fit Horace for coats and shirts and ruffled collars, all of which the government purchased. He wore his new clothes the following Tuesday to lunch with a *comte* and *comtesse*, and on Wednesday to a gallery where he purchased a bawdy scene (the painting recalled Dutch Point, except with finery—crudeness *and* elegant fashion), and then to a piano concert that same evening. Brewster brought him invitation after invitation, so Horace asked for a secretary, who then wrote in a leather-covered appointment book the addresses and names of those who would host the six-course dinners on *mardi, mercredi, jeudi, vendredi*. By the end of one week Horace had lunched or dined, it seemed, with every important Parisian except King Louis-Philippe. Over and again he amused hosts with the tale of his discovery ("*This way, that way*"), and when they showed him the bladder of nitrous oxide they had just obtained "for this occasion," he'd illustrate its use, then enjoy the results (this lady reveals her corset, that gentleman licks her décolletage). The king's portraitist asked him to sit, which he did over several mornings, and when he saw the finished painting—his face glowing with health, his grin contented, his hair thick and lustrous (all falsehoods)—he lied to the artist in turn, saying, "You have painted me as I see myself."

"Of course," cried the painter. "I do not paint the man. I paint the genius!"

L'Académie des Sciences Parisien. La Société des Philosophes de la Médecine. Hearing after hearing after hearing, and Horace began to wonder whether every Parisian belonged to a separate medical association. Then, at last, what Brewster deemed the most prestigious: *La Société Médicale de Paris.* Brewster made his argument to the learned men, and though Horace hadn't understood a word, he nodded at the applause that followed, his jaw set to convey gravity, significance.

Then another man stood. Ancient and fat, he placed his hands on the lectern, and the fingers spread like melted cheese. He wore a dark cloak and a crimson waistcoat. A wart protruded from the corner of his left eye, and his short white hair was uncombed. He fit a monocle over an eye, then read from a sheaf of papers in a voice that a senator would envy. Brewster whispered to Horace, "His name is Courbet, a physician of good reputation. He's here, he says, to represent Morton."

"Should we be concerned?"

Brewster didn't answer. When Courbet finished with his pages, much mumbling and discourse followed. Members of the academy asked questions and allowed Brewster a query or two as well. Then Courbet raised his hand to request a last word. He pointed a sausage of a finger at Horace and Brewster, saying slowly in French a phrase that sounded to Horace like *Eel moan comb* something something.

People laughed, even those with the academy, even Brewster.

"What did he say?" asked Horace, feeling heat in his cheeks.

"It's a French proverb. *Il ment comme un arracheur des dents.* It means, 'He lies like a tooth puller.'"

Then he answered the question apparent on Horace's face.

"Don't worry," he said, sighing his pleasure at the fat man's joke. "This won't hurt a bit."

Morton! Adder!

Horace yanked off his fancy clothes—turning sleeves inside out, popping buttons—and left them heaped on the bed in his apartment, discarded as his hopes. Bitter and caustic, his gorge rose, and as if summoned by that hateful name, here came again the papery fluttering in his chest: Boston's parchment bird, nesting in his lungs. The fat man's arrival seemed the final jewel to crown Morton's elegant lie, the French legitimacy that Horace's champion could never offer ("I'm an American," Brewster had admitted. "*Un étranger.* It does make a difference."). So why dress Horace in French clothes? Why the charade? He imagined Morton installed in this very apartment, saw the tailor run a measuring tape across Morton's shoulders, envisioned the king's portraitist with a fingertip on Morton's chin, turning his face to the light. And what of Horace? Likely a life spent hunched over a chair in an office without even a rug, scraping the yellowed incisors of some Hartford insurance peddler. Such images ballooned in his mind's eye, interrupted only when the valet knocked. He had brought an envelope on a silver tray.

Horace walked to his reading desk, but hesitated to open the letter, addressed in Elizabeth's handwriting, the too-tight *H* and the too-small *e*. Was this five she'd sent, or six? And despite several starts, he'd not finished one reply. None to Charley, either. Chagrined, he turned the desk lamp brighter, read:

> How do you do this evening! I wish you would answer me; I imagine I
> could hear you. To day old Mr. Whitman has been buried—the old gentleman

who has been so long with Mr. Robins in the retreat. He was buried in the back yard of the Center Church.

Her charity work with the insane. But who were Whitman and Robins? She mentioned them as if he'd know. He searched his memory and recalled that disrobed fellow from the long-ago day when he pulled the tooth of Maggie, Nan's daughter. "You ring like a bell," the madman had said. Unredeemed in Connecticut. Had that man died?

> I wish you would be punctual and write as often as possible. Don't think me foolish. I have as much courage as possible during your absence. Your letters will do me more good than you are aware. Even writing this has done me good. Our folks say I have acted today as if I had a load off my heart. If you are sick let me know. It will be better than suspense.
>
> Charley lies here fast asleep on the sofa; he has been brimful of mischief today.
>
> Your aff wife. Elizabeth W.

As always when he read her letters, he felt part of himself returning home to Lord's Hill: Charley pushing a model tallship across the floor, and Elizabeth sewing nearby in a straight-back chair. Horace folded the pages of her letter into the envelope, but Hartford was not so easily put away, and his family lingered until the valet knocked to ask his needs.

In Hartford, he would never have the services of a valet.

Perhaps that's why he'd not finished any letter home. To write Elizabeth was akin to sending himself back, to becoming again a provincial tooth-digger rather than a celebrated scientist. Once again, a humbug.

"Monsieur?" the valet asked.

No. Not a humbug. Never again.

He pushed himself away from the desk. When he asked for wine, he received it in a crystal goblet. In the parlor, he struck a few keys on the piano, each note a symphony. "Can you play?" he asked. The valet shook his head, so Horace excused him.

At his bedside, Horace shook out his Parisian clothes. He slipped into the shirt, buttoned the collar, snapped the jacket straight, buckled the shoes. Thus arrayed, he stepped through the balcony doors. The city and its lights opened, vast and twinkling. He lifted his face to the sky, so the night might wash over him. Raising his crystal goblet of wine, he toasted himself, who had given painless surgery to humanity.

You see? he told himself. Nothing is preordained. Not failure. Not even pain.

On the eve of his last day in Paris, coal fires burned furiously against the cold, and their smoke choked the stars. Horace and Brewster staggered from a carriage parked before a monument of a building—some offspring of a Roman temple and a Gothic palazzo. In Horace's breast pocket he carried a flask filled with chloroform. Brewster wielded a half-empty bottle of red that he had uncorked in the carriage and shared.

"Promise me you'll take what this night gives," he said. "You deserve what this city can offer. Let it leave its imprint on you. Paris wants to be remembered."

"Tonight," Horace shouted. "I will leave my imprint on Paris!" Then he felt silly.

"But no vapors, yes? Can we agree?" Brewster waved his wine bottle at Horace's face. "Let the time-tested vices suffice."

Horace received the bottle, drank from its mouth, then gave it back. Now valets took their coats and hats, and Brewster said something about women, and Horace meant to reply, but the two had reached the ballroom, and the vision struck him dumb.

Never had he seen such a vast indoors—a canyon of a room possessed of its own geography. The ceilings high as sky, each wall a distant and hardly visible horizon. The room even had shifting weather, a pocket of warmth here and a coolness there, wind currents carrying an air of perfume and cigar smoke. The crowd—surely it equaled Hartford's whole population. Everywhere Horace looked he saw splendor: sashes and canes with ornate, often grotesque pommels; plumed hats; military pins; brocade gowns and silk gloves; hair twisted into impossible architectures. So many red mouths. Did everything in Paris exceed proportion? Conversation in the hall echoed into a muddled curtain of sound through which he could just discern distant music, like no tunes he'd ever heard except, perhaps, in vaporous dreams.

Brewster? How had he lost Brewster?

Without his guide, he wandered, drifting where the crowd allowed. He imagined himself in a boat at sea, bedazzled by sunlight sharp off the water—except the flashes came from that brooch, or that ribboned medal, and all those gems around all those French necks. Seeking better vantage, he climbed stairs to a less crowded concourse and spied over a rail into the swarming heads below. When he still could not spot his companion, he stayed above, near where servers attended to a group of buffet tables, each bountiful with game sausages, small baked hens, sauces, dried figs, pickled cucumbers, sugared nuts. At the center were a half dozen roasted hogs, skin crackly. It seemed enough to feed Paris twice over, yet only a few people partook, including a smartly dressed woman—plump, he noticed, even sumptuous, perhaps his age, and with an ideal neck—who picked at small somethings.

At one table, near a platter of odorous cheeses, Horace brushed away a fly, though it returned. The woman, noticing, smiled his way. A moment later, when he glanced up from a tray of crackers, she, across the table, raised her head. Horace and the woman each explored in polite bites (a fork of cake, a dried apricot, a finger of cheese). After a while only Horace and the woman sampled from the table, and he wondered whether they were violating some custom, eating ahead of a dinner bell or a blessing. He decided to ask as she drew close enough to speak, but she questioned him first, in English, accented by French.

"Are you the American dentist?"

He admitted it. Her face was wide, clean as polished marble, features small except for her dark eyes, which were large and delicate as a newborn fawn's. Her brown hair was gathered in a chignon, held by a jade comb. She introduced herself as the Comtesse d'Haussonville, and she accepted his kiss on her proffered hand, the red silk of her gloves a luxury to his lips. In a small voice, she asked about his discovery, and listened with one arm across her waist, the other raised so a red-silked knuckle touched her lips. He thought, She's flirting with me, and felt a warm expansion in his chest. When he asked how she came to speak English, she leaned near, and because good manners gave him an excuse, he leaned nearer, too. So close to his ear he could feel the tickle of her lips, she whispered, "I am the Paris that wants to be remembered."

He smiled. "You know my friend, Brewster?"

Her breath again, warm in his ear. Her perfume, vanilla and bergamot.

Had she spoken again? He couldn't tell. She finger-waved *au revoir*, then slipped, easy as mist floats, down a nearby staircase to vanish into the crowd.

Then a waiter with a tray handed him a glass. Champagne was new to Horace, and he liked it. An enchanted drink for an enchanted kingdom. A fine example, this one, a sip of sweet air. A good argument for the time-tested vices.

On the main floor he gave his empty glass to a passing waiter and took another, but his right hand, holding the flute, started to tremble. Shoving that hand in his pocket, he drank with his less adept left, so dribbled on his chin. Bumping along, ignorant of conversations, he could not decipher whether a smile directed his way meant good will or something else: even, perhaps (as on that man's face there), a plea. So many visages to read, so much noise to interpret. He marked how with a tilt of his head a grin could be a grimace, and for the first time the festivity struck him as vaguely sinister. He sensed an ancient despondency, unacknowledged but permeating the crowd, as if this ball were not a celebration but instead an elaborate machine meant to conceal some dissatisfaction.

Still no sign of Brewster or the comtesse. But someone shouted, applause followed, and Horace turned to see at some distance a raised platform, and atop that two golden statues: gymnasts, classical in their depiction. One statue stood as if a pillar; the other struck a one-armed handstand atop his partner's shaved head. Shouldering his way amidst the onlookers, Horace saw that each nearly nude figure was muscled in ideal proportions, and had he the language, he would have commented to the man beside him regarding the sculptor's skill. Then the smaller figure in his handstand began—almost imperceptibly—to bend at the waist. Jot by jot, he lowered himself in a slow ballet. Legs rigid. Bare toes pointed. Horace tried not to blink. Long seconds passed, and somehow, without disengaging, the statues shaped themselves into a new pose: a fusion of one's spread-eagle and the other's push-up. Neither seemed to have breathed. They showed no sign of exertion. In their new pose, they once more stiffened into statues.

Horace pressed closer. He studied knees, faces, spines, fingers. At last he noticed the slightest tremor in the larger one's wrist.

They were men, after all. Inspired—but not magic, not a trick. How marvelous.

Then, the golden men leaped upright, fully animate, chests rising and falling with their heaving breaths, arms raised to welcome applause, and Horace clapped loudest. He could not himself bend stiff-kneed to buckle his shoe, yet he warmed with an affinity for these two acrobats, felt a vague fraternity, some secret shared. Horace clapped and found that when he did his right hand no longer trembled.

Then cymbals crashed, and Moors paraded past playing bells and strings and reeds. A white horse followed their clamor, its headgear decorated with peacock feathers, a bare-breasted, brown-skinned woman astride its back. Horace's pulse quickened, his skin tingling pleasantly. He imagined trying to explain this vision of steed and woman to Elizabeth and Charley. Beyond comprehension!

Ball-goers swirled 'round the musicians, followed in their wake, and Horace with them. By golly, he was almost dancing. As he'd almost danced in London, a few days after the *Hibernia* docked. Quite the crowd then, too, for the queen's procession to parliament, an event he'd stumbled upon, his head foggy with ether. He recalled beggars and their jigs, how he shuffled his feet at their invitation to "Dance, you Yankee! Dance!" how their women tugged his sleeves, coughing croupy breath his way, their missing limbs and toothless grins, the tumors they displayed. The coins he gave away.

"Perhaps it was just the neighborhood . . ." He was relating the account to the comtesse, curious as to how she'd found him again in the vast hall, how he'd come to hold a fresh champagne glass. " . . . but London seemed to be the poorest city on earth."

Now, by hand, she was leading him away from the *beau monde*, up a narrow corkscrew of a staircase. Dizzy, he was glad for any quiet someplace.

"This was a standee spot, near the palace," he was saying. He told her about the queen and her equipage leaving the gates, Prince Albert seated beside her, and how he'd thought the queen pretty, especially given what he'd always heard. The comtesse turned her head, fawn eyes focused on his, and she smiled in such a way he felt unnerved. They'd arrived at a pocket door, for which she had a key. "The horses," he said, "I couldn't count them. I swear, the carriage was forged of gold. The queen's crown? Half as high again as her own head."

Behind the pocket door was a four-poster bed with a high mattress and diaphanous fabrics swathing the posts. Squat candles burned from every ledge, and a gilt-framed mirror hung in such a position as to reflect whoever lay upon the bed. He noticed the flask of chloroform in his coat pocket gaining weight, a curious thing, and he cradled it with his free hand. The comtesse had placed a glass of wine in his other.

The day after the queen's procession, he told her, he'd gone to see the crown itself displayed at the Tower of London. "They told me it cost five million dollars," he said. "Five million! And I had given money to beggars. Where is the queen while her people struggle? I ask you."

"Sleeping comfortably," said the comtesse, "in a bed much richer than this one." She touched the draped fabric, let it caress her cheek.

He liked the wine's taste, rough, with the sweet smoke of a berry, if a berry could be burned. Drowsiness pressed his brow from within, tipped him toward the bed.

"Those starving people." He spoke into the bowl of his glass. "Sick. Suffering."

She undid his neck tie, lifted his shaking hand to kiss the palm, though the hand felt separate from him as if her lips had grazed another man's skin. "But here you are," she said, "a guest of France's king, living off his abundance. Our poor starve, too, you know." Her eyes opened rounder in false, teasing surprise. "We reconcile ourselves to these realities. What's this?" She tapped a fingernail against the flask in his breast pocket. "Your discovery?"

Her hand insinuated itself inside his coat, then she set the flask on a bedside taboret. Reflected candlelight flickered in the metal.

"Brewster says I shouldn't."

"Shouldn't what?"

She pushed one glove down her arm, rubbed herself against him.

There. He sensed it again. The despondency.

"I can't seem to stand straight. My head keeps floating off without me."

"You don't need to stand."

She tugged the cork from his flask, waved it under her nose, shivered at what she smelled, her lips shaping an o, red and petite.

He said, "Don't you want the poor to be happier?" But he knew he'd not paid those beggars to make them happy. He'd only wanted them to take their pain elsewhere.

"I want me to be happier," she said. "And right now, I want you to be happier."

She stepped behind him, grazing his belt with the edge of her hand. He heard the pocket door slide shut. Her fingers played in the hair curled at his shirt collar.

He had not told it right, about the beggars. If he had told it correctly, she would understand. He had left something out. The beggars were only part of the story. He knew this because it was a story he'd been trying to tell for so long—since he was a boy. About his father's death and later about Charley's birth. About a girl shackled to a chair, a tooth's root dug from its socket, a mutilated dog. About need. About pain. He had wanted to tell the story to Nan that shameful day in his office, he knew that. But everything had become confused.

"You Americans," the comtesse said. "You work so hard to save us all. But you never consider the consequences." She sniffed again at the chloroform, tilted her head back with the pleasure of it and showed her powdered neck. "Or the inevitable corruptions."

The room shrank and darkened, the edges of his vision blurred. Though he couldn't see it, he sensed pain nearby, perched, patient, called by that word *corruptions*, and how she'd said it, as if it were a cream pastry on her tongue, something to swallow. Pain, that slippery thing. So clever, so quick.

She handed him the flask. The sweet odor filled his nose and mouth, and he wanted it and understood that he would always want it, desire so keen it hurt. Pain and need—that story would never end. He'd never be able to tell it, not even to Elizabeth, with whom he had lived it. This time, though, he wanted no confusion, no lingering stab of guilt. He replaced the stopper, slipped the flask into his coat pocket.

From below he heard muffled laughter, a horn and a cello, the clinking din of plates and glasses. The comtesse nestled among the bed's pillows. She yawned, gloved hand over mouth, then, as though surprised at herself, whispered an apology.

He rested his hand over the flask, over his heart, and he felt warmth there. "Here's to *happier*," he said. As he opened the pocket door, he read in her modest smile that she understood, their evening was ended—roles performed aptly, no ill will. Then she asked him, please, before leaving, to snuff the candles.

34

More than a month earlier, in Liverpool, Mr. Cyril Benson, first mate on the *Hibernia*, found a buyer for the dentist's top hat. With that money, added to a bit saved on his own, he visited a gunsmith with hope of purchasing a pistol.

The gunsmith had lost a leg to grapeshot and amputation while fighting with Pakenham at New Orleans, and though the surgeon had told him he'd feel a ghost ache where the flesh and bone had gone missing, he'd decided he wouldn't. He hadn't, and would go into the earth at St. James having never. With formidable will and a great pride, he'd taught himself never to use crutches in public. On the overcast day Mr. Benson visited, he hopped from cabinet to cabinet gathering pistols, impressing Mr. Benson because from waist up he appeared to be walking, albeit with a limp. He showed Mr. Benson a range of bargains: an ugly percussion-cap derringer that looked as if it had been assembled out of parts made in a prison; a finer Birmingham model with a varnished handle and a pleasing Damascus pattern on the barrel; and a set of German dueling pistols with ebony stocks. Mr. Benson pretended to aim each as if his were an expert eye. In the end he chose the Damascus-pattern derringer. "Can't do better than a pistol from Birmingham," he bluffed.

"Fifty caliber," explained the gunsmith, who took the ignorance of amateurs as an offense against himself and all true-blooded men. "Black powder. One shot's all it's got, one shot's all you need. Nice little gun for the wife."

Mr. Benson smiled. The captain's abuse had taught him that insults to one's manhood were never subtle. He spent some moments moving the pistol hand to hand, learning its balance, feeling the clean barrel oil on his fingers, wondering whether he'd have the courage to blow out the captain's brain.

This is how Mr. Benson came to possess the dentist's top hat:

In port, after the passengers—including the dentist—had disembarked, Mr. Benson instructed the deck hand cleaning No. 32 to bring him anything unusual found there. He'd hoped for that liquid and its vapors, but instead the deck hand returned with the top hat. Two weeks passed in dock while the company refitted the *Hibernia*, during which time Mr. Benson read the newspapers and learned that the dentist was famous, caught up in this controversy about vapors and gases and who'd discovered what. Journalists placed him in Paris, so Mr. Benson took the hat to the Liverpool market and returned with the derringer tucked into his boot.

An ocean chill frosted his soul when he imagined the captain dead. He worried that the iciness meant cowardice. His great fear was that an elaborate plan to kill the captain would lead to a final moment of weakness when he could not pull the trigger. So he held the derringer in reserve and trusted that his temper teetered on the edge of rage, and at some moment an action or insult would spark violence. In his fantasies the captain slandered him in the galley, in the engine room, at dinner, and dozens of times a pistol shot exploded the captain's bone and blood. Mr. Benson understood there would be consequences, but those had no relevance for him; he needed the captain dead. This way, he prepared himself. Murder began to feel inevitable.

He was in the midst of such a fantasy one March day, even as he checked the *Hibernia's* manifest against those passengers coming aboard for the trip to New York. When the dentist appeared at the front of the queue, Mr. Benson startled.

He wore a replacement top hat. To Mr. Benson's untrained eye, it looked twice the value of the old one. Maybe even more.

"Hello, Mr. Benson," the dentist said. "Number thirty-two again?"

Relying on his professional training, Mr. Benson forced himself to look the dentist in the eyes and to smile. He hoped his initial expression had betrayed neither his hope for more of the dentist's potion nor Mr. Benson's fear of being fingered as a hat thief. He paged through the manifest. "Not this time, Dr. Wells. We've got you in seventeen. You'll like it. It's farther astern. A smoother ride when we hit rough seas. You paid for a single this time?"

Dr. Wells laughed in a sad way, and Mr. Benson sensed he did not want to acknowledge their shared history. "You're busy now," the dentist said. "Later, I have a question about a hat."

Dr. Wells was no recluse as he had been on the first crossing, but his appearances were rare. Now and then, when the sun reached its high point, he'd show for a stroll above deck. Nightly, he joined other passengers in the galley for dinner but never lingered for dessert. He even sat for an impromptu whist tournament, though he seemed pleased to be eliminated in the first round. Still, Mr. Benson found it impossible to catch him alone when either he or Dr. Wells might be more comfortable suggesting a go at the vapors.

At the end of the first week, on a day when warm southern sun cut the wind's chill, Mr. Benson recognized Dr. Wells and his new top hat near the ship's stern. The dentist stood alone, gazing into the blue cold. Only an hour earlier, with mock concern, the captain had made Mr. Benson unlace his shirt to show whether cowardice had tainted his skin yellow. The insult had not provoked rage and murder as in his fantasies, so now, abashed and glum, Mr. Benson hungered for consolation of the type Dr. Wells had once provided.

The men greeted each other. Mr. Benson noticed that the dentist's intensity, so evident on the first crossing, had been displaced by sobriety, as if he had seen a part of himself into the grave and now sat at his own wake. The men stood a while in silence, as do those who sense in each other a separate sorrow, offering comfort without words. Mr. Benson let the ocean spray his beard, and he licked the salt from his lips. Dr. Wells kept his coat buttoned to the collar.

"The cook's planning beef steaks for tonight," Mr. Benson said at last, "to celebrate the end of the first week. It's his custom."

Dr. Wells nodded. "Good news." A gust prompted him to steady his hat.

"Watch that or you'll lose it overboard."

"It's from Paris."

"Yes, I've read about you in the newspapers."

The dentist's smile struck Mr. Benson as one tinged with regret. "It will be a year before the societies make any decisions. So I'm told."

"I don't read the medical journals, but the papers favor Morton."

Dr. Wells turned to take the sun full in his face, and he closed his eyes. "That's the common talk, based on the assumption that nitrous oxide doesn't work. Even some of the medical men say so."

"But that's not true, is it?" Mr. Benson asked, though he knew nothing of the science. It was his empathy demanding he try to cheer the dentist. "A few more experiments, and you'll prove that."

A seagull rounded close in front of them, then careened starboard out of sight.

"I'd try a whiff again," said Benson, "if you need a subject for testing. It sure worked on me." He laughed.

"That wasn't nitrous oxide. You inhaled ether. It's likely to be dangerous. I shouldn't have encouraged you, and I apologize."

"If I may say so, you're a more sober man, Dr. Wells."

"I'm trying." He took off his hat to scratch the top of his head, which shined in the sun, then put the hat snugly back in place. "I'm reminded," he said. "Did I leave a top hat aboard ship? I've missed it since London, but I thought I might have lost it earlier."

"Not that I've heard," Mr. Benson said. It was not the first lie he'd ever told, but for Mr. Benson it broke a trust he believed they'd just fashioned. Another craven act added to his history.

"Is there a lost and found?"

Mr. Benson gave the clerk's name.

"I'd like to see the engines sometime," Dr. Wells said. "Could you arrange that with the ship's engineer? I'm interested in how machines work."

Mr. Benson nodded, said, "Watch that hat. The wind has yet to blow its hardest."

The next day, after he'd left Dr. Wells with the ship's engineer, Mr. Benson slipped a key into the lock of No. 17. Given the sea's pitch, the lamp swung in his hands, throwing a net of shadows here, then there. He latched the door open so that passersby might see him clearly snooping about Dr. Wells's cabin. Legitimate business here. A complaint, he'd say. Too much whistling from the porthole.

Dr. Wells's quarters looked pin-perfect, the berth made up, sheets snapped straight, razor kit hanging from a hook near the wash basin. He'd arranged his shoes in the corner side by side. The tidiness made it easier for Mr. Benson to find the dentist's satchel and inside that a collection of bottles labeled Chloroform. He'd read enough in the newspapers to know that some—like Dr. Wells—favored nitrous oxide, while others preferred ether or chloroform. Ether, Dr. Wells had said, might be dangerous. He'd given no such warning about this chloroform.

He could not steal it. Dr. Wells would notice, and given the hat question, Mr. Benson did not want to raise suspicion. A quick sniff was all he wanted. He uncorked a bottle. A little sweetness, yes, and a hint of something happening. Mr. Benson sat on the berth, breathed in until his nose tingled and lungs—

When Horace noticed the familiar odor of chloroform in the hallway outside No. 17, he wanted to rush toward the bottle and feared to. He'd been searching for Mr. Benson to thank him for arranging the engine tour, but he hadn't expected to find him here or sprawled this way, the man's coat soaked and an empty bottle of chloroform rolling across the cabin floor.

Lord, don't let him be dead.

He checked Mr. Benson's neck for a pulse. Weak, but there. Spilled the whole bottle, Horace noticed. Emptied all over himself. His clothes exuded vapors.

If he shut the door the vapors would concentrate in the tight space, but he needed privacy. Horace opened the porthole, felt the cold air like a brick to the face, then locked the cabin door.

He had refrained from any vapor since Paris, but now, as he pulled Benson out of his coat, he could feel an itch in his lungs. The man's shirt was wet, so he unlaced that, too. As he pulled it over Benson's head, the first mate flopped, arms bent at the elbows, fingers curled back on the palms as though wanting to hold something. Even as Horace thought *dead fish*, the space between this and the chloroform world began to shrink. His head filled with silken bubbles, each carrying away a burden or a grief or an insight. As if he had no choice, he lifted the shirt to his face, breathed deeply. The ship rose, and the window swung shut, and Horace tumbled onto his berth.

He saw Benson's head loll with the ship's pitch. His small head. A bubble burst, let escape its grief. "You stole my hat," Horace said.

Mr. Benson didn't answer. Horace closed his eyes and felt himself fly with the *Hibernia's* rise and fall, seagulls careening toward him and away, teaching him how to make the most of the bubbles in his brain. The birds wore top hats.

He sat on the floor.

"You stole my hat!" he yelled at Benson.

The first mate woke. He looked at Horace with heavy-lidded eyes. "I came to fix your porthole," he said. "It whistled."

Mr. Benson couldn't make sense of things. His stomach crunched and expanded, and he smelled something pungent. Not the chloroform, no. He shivered and missed his coat. He fingered his crotch, the warm wetness there, wiped the tips of his fingers on his naked chest. What would the captain do with all this? He remembered, vaguely (as he sometimes remembered the outline of shore after weeks at sea), the pleasure of the dentist's bottle. But now that was gone, and in its place a grayness wide as all dead water.

"Benson! You stole my hat!"

Yes, but I pissed myself. And where is my coat? Where, for that matter, is my shirt? So sad. Opium had been too much like this. Thoughts turned to mush, as if two paddle wheels churned his brain. "One more chance," the captain had said after the last opium den. Now Mr. Benson would be fired at best, chained in the hold at worst. He imagined humiliations the captain would devise before turning him over to the authorities. The slanders he'd tell. And if Benson outlived those, he knew another captain waited for him. And another. The earth was lousy with captains, each wanting his own Mr. Benson to abuse. There wasn't enough opium or chloroform to erase them all.

He retrieved the pistol from his boot, waved it near his head, the barrel's end tracing a path around his face, an erratic insect looking for a spot to land. The cheek. The jawbone. He'd begun to sob. There was nothing quiet about how he felt. A violence shook his chest, churned in his stomach. He kept drawing his legs up, one after the other, then stretching them again, trying to slow-kick his shame away from him.

"One shot's all you need," said Mr. Benson. The pistol barrel settled at his temple. "Here?" he asked.

Horace could not think where to stand. Where would Benson fire? At himself? At Horace? Was this the chloroform again? He laughed.

"Here?" Benson moved the barrel into his mouth.

"No," Horace said, trying not to grin.

"If I blow my brains on your walls, they'll give you another cabin." Mr. Benson laughed. "Probably they'll refund your fare."

"I'll take the gun."

"They'll give you whatever you want."

"I'd like the gun. In trade for the hat."

"Which is the braver thing to do, do you think?"

Ear. Chin. Point of his nose.

"You give me the gun. We don't speak of this again. You never return to my cabin. You never ask about the vapors." Stop smiling, Horace!

Jawbone. Roof of the mouth.

"I've never believed that men could be just."

Bridge of the nose.

"Death is not like the . . ." Horace stopped. Stared into a fog of words. ". . . the gas. The allure is . . . similar. But death? You can enjoy it only the once. Be prudent."

Left eye. Right eye.

Mr. Benson leaned and set the pistol on the floor before him. Straight up again, he sniffed the barrel oil on his fingertips, wiped it on his trousers.

When Mr. Benson left he forgot to take his shirt and coat, so the chloroform fumes lingered, and silken bubbles still floated in Horace's head, though fewer now. Horace wrapped Benson's shirt inside the coat, unlatched the porthole, and stuffed the bundle through, not watching as it caught wind and opened and fluttered to the waves. Then he locked the door, returned to his berth, and huddled on the mattress.

In his hands, Benson's derringer. His now, with all its possibilities.

The next time Mr. Benson saw Dr. Wells, the *Hibernia* was two days from New York City, with a hard wind off port making the going slow. The sea was in a petulant mood, and Mr. Benson's job was to clear the deck of passengers. Most had gone below; he found only one. Near the prow, he wore his fine French top hat and a good coat, and he had a bucket from which he threw fistfuls of kitchen scraps at the gulls—an entertainment.

Mostly, the birds chased the bits to the water, but now and then a skilled one snatched a morsel from the air. Wind swirled about the deck, so hard the black smoke from the stacks twisted with it. One moment you thought you'd hid from it, and the next your eyes would smart from a face full. It was an attacking thing, the wind, smarter than you.

"Come below, Dr. Wells!" Mr. Benson shouted. "Captain's orders!"

The dentist threw another fistful of fish guts into the air. Mr. Benson thought the wind's roar and the crash of waves against the prow might make it hard for the dentist to hear, so he started to approach.

As he did, a gust pushed so hard he had to quick spread his legs or fall. He saw the dentist lose his footing and reach for the rail, and his hat lifted from his head, this time somersaulting into the air, up where the gulls rose and dived. The dentist didn't reach for it as a man is wont to do when the wind takes his hat—no snatching at the empty air, no chasing. He turned a little and watched it snapped by wind, off far to starboard, and then to the deck, skidding against a far wall.

Gripping the rail, his feathery hair whipping around his head, Dr. Wells worked his way to the side where the hat had flown. When at last he turned, hat snugged down to his ears, his shoulders fell as if he'd exhaled a deep breath or sighed. He came near on his way below, and Mr. Benson saw that the dentist's eyes were damp, stung perhaps by the icy wind and exhaust. The dentist smiled what seemed a true smile, as if the hat had been something he'd wanted dearly to keep.

VII

HARTFORD

35

The woman whimpered, grief rocking her left and right on the sofa where she sat, Elizabeth beside her and rubbing a hand across the woman's broad back. This was a bitter cold morning in late November 1847, one of those days each week when Elizabeth visited at the Hartford Retreat, in an office cheerful with yellow-and-blue wallpaper. A sunbeam through a frosted window lit upon a loose thread in the woman's dress collar, and because there was so little comfort to offer, Elizabeth tucked the thread into its hem.

"Maggie loved this life, but she could hurt herself so badly," said the woman, the retreat's matron. Her name was Mrs. Cornish. This office belonged to her. On the walls, framed, hung inspirational scriptures she herself had embroidered.

Rejoice evermore.

Pray without ceasing.

In every thing give thanks.

"My husband pulled that girl's tooth, once," said Elizabeth, "but I haven't seen her since." In Elizabeth's memory it had been November, then as now, but a warmer day, the roads not hard-packed to biting ice. Then, the girl wore leg shackles and worried a ribbon tied 'round her finger. Now, the girl was dead.

"You wouldn't have," said Mrs. Cornish. "We keep you Samaritans away from the frenzied patients. Never know when they might bite." Her fingers, blunt and warm, kneaded Elizabeth's. The women had known each other several years; they had shared baking recipes. Earlier, when Mrs. Cornish had waved an invitation to her office, Elizabeth thought there might be a new crumb cake to taste, but then she saw the matron's face, her twisted mouth.

For six years, Mrs. Cornish said, they'd kept the girl safe, alert for scissors and sewing needles and bricks. But then, as if they'd saved the moth from flame only for the toad to snatch it, death came not from Maggie's own hand but from a malady no doctor could explain. Attendants come to fetch her for breakfast had found her shivering with fever, the flesh of her right hip hardening, red and hot to the touch. Lay a finger on the spot and Maggie screamed as if tortured. Anything she ate or drank she vomited right back. The doctors iced her leg, then sliced the skin to relieve the pressure, and she bled long enough that she grew calm, sleepy. But that fever never broke, the affliction inflamed her groin, then her abdomen.

I am the vine, ye are the branches.

Elizabeth knew Mrs. Cornish to be a pleasant woman who seldom remembered names so called most everyone "good heart," as in "Dry your eyes, good heart. If you cry for one, you'll cry for them all." Now, eyelashes damp, she said, "Maggie's mother visits, but so infrequently. We've no idea where she lives. I don't judge. It's not easy, a daughter this way. The woman's got no money, in any event. So Maggie will go down to a pauper's grave once the ground thaws. There's no shame in that, but I don't like her to go without an escort to the churchyard. There'll be the chaplain and Mr. Cornish and myself. Would you join us?"

She remembered the mother, too, Elizabeth did, the woman who huddled against a wall rather than beside her ailing daughter. Not worth Elizabeth's attention then, nor later at the cattle fair where she had cavorted with rude, drunken men.

"We'll try," Elizabeth said. "Dr. Wells keeps a busy schedule."

"Him, too?" said Mrs. Cornish, her voice pinched with surprise.

"No one need doubt my husband's compassion," Elizabeth told Mrs. Cornish, then hoped she did not sound too prickly. She took no insult. Most in Hartford still knew Horace's disposition to be all eggshells and tempests. But Horace had come home from Paris a better man—his best boyish qualities mixed suitably with those acquired in maturity. "My nature improves in your company," he told her, then gave her reasons to believe. He now slept through most nights and spent more time with Charley, helping the boy learn to balance one-legged on a fence rail or to nurture a foxglove seedling into bloom as a gift for Aunt Dorothy.

Even when they sold their imported French paintings to a gallery at deep financial loss, Horace didn't, as he said, "go to the birds." In fact, it was Elizabeth who wept. "It isn't the money," she told him. "It's the injustice to the paintings and their artists." The two stood before Elizabeth's favorite among the canvases, a landscape by Madame DeNoie, out of its crate and propped against a wall in the cottage. "So much life," she said, "and no private collector wanted it." Horace squeezed her hand, kissed her damp eyes. "That inspired work goes unappreciated," he said, "makes the work no less vital."

That was the man he'd become. He still argued his priority in newspapers and journals, and waited too eagerly each day for a decision from Paris societies. Debt yet shackled the household. But he sought income by plying exhilarating gases to patients of Hartford's better medical surgeons, proving himself able to annul the agonies of amputation and tumor excision. Because he experimented less frequently on himself, life on Lord's Hill seemed less fragile and had even acquired, perhaps, a whit of grace.

Later that morning, Elizabeth played word games with the retreat's residents and helped them fold laundry. Only now and then did she consider the girl who had died, a hesitation as she combed a knot from Cecilia's hair or with Edie scattered stale bread across the snow for pigeons and squirrels. That hesitation never lasted more than a moment, as if she'd heard a plop on a pond's surface, saw the ripple dissipate, then wondered how to feel.

On her way home, she stopped at a dry goods market for flour and sugar. There she chatted with a clerk about the healing properties of certain comfits, then bought half a pound, because it seemed a good day to spend money on hope.

At last, during her solitary trudge up Asylum Avenue to Lord's Hill, she opened herself to the dead girl's company, let the girl catch up and walk alongside. As in Elizabeth's memory, the girl wore a ribbon on her finger. But now she carried a wedge of watermelon, though it was winter, and she took slurpy bites and spit black seeds.

The road roughened here, on Hartford's outskirts, all frozen hoofprints and wagon ruts. Snow of at least a foot would need to fall before the sleighs could run again. Elizabeth staggered up the hill, listing with the weight of her sacks. The girl, a nimble spirit, kept pace, seeming at ease, giggling.

You're happy now, Elizabeth thought. That's good.

The girl skipped ahead, back and forth across the width of the road. She sang some children's song, though her voice sounded so distant Elizabeth couldn't be sure of any sound but the crunch of snow and ice underfoot. She wanted to undo the girl's braids and brush her hair, to wipe the watermelon smear from her chin, to cut a piece and share.

Thirteen years old, and gone, just so; such an ailment could strike Charley. Elizabeth told herself not to think that. But it could.

Squinting against the low, tenacious sun, she again considered the girl's mother. Propriety called for Christian sympathy, but Elizabeth had none to offer a woman who had abandoned her little girl. Not when some had no daughters. And others never would.

About halfway to the cottage, the burdens became too much. Though Elizabeth had climbed this hill hundreds of times—and with heavier loads—her legs refused to take another step. Her lungs ached with cold fire. The flour and sugar sacks slipped from her hands. She lay an open palm over her belly. Since Boston, she had been hopeful, and Horace, too. For months, they had shared disappointment.

If you cry for one, good heart—

Elizabeth retied the scarf over her hat, tucked her mittened hands under her arms against the wind. The girl skipped around to face her, those saucer eyes and feverish cheeks familiar as Elizabeth's own. Then the girl laughed, tossed the watermelon rind into the air. She launched herself headlong toward the city, rushing downhill and with each stride catching the slope before she might tumble, and by not tumbling seeming to glide, past Elizabeth and onward, arms spread wide as wings, hat come loose, bright hair trailing, then farther still, and then out of sight.

The girls that live, the girls that die, the girls that never will be.

Outside the house, Elizabeth set herself on the threshold to rest. She could hear Charley somewhere inside counting in a loud voice. A chill wind stung the back of her neck, and she huddled into her shoulders. Back from where she'd come, back where the girl had vanished, a dull sky spread over the fields and road, all ugly-wet with winter.

I will walk with you again, she told the girl. You'll not go motherless to the grave.

She found Charley on a sofa, on his back with legs lifted straight to the ceiling, balancing a collapsed umbrella across the soles of his socked feet.

"I'm counting how long I can keep an umbrella in the air. I'm at eighty-four."

"Has your father returned from surgery with Dr. Ellsworth?"

"Eighty-five. Eighty-six."

"Has he?"

"He's in his workshop."

"Then we'll not disturb him."

She lifted away the umbrella, sat beside her boy, and pulled him into her lap. "I'd like you to sit here and pray with me," she said, her tone meant to comfort him—and her, too. "A girl died today. Let's ask God and Heaven to welcome her."

He cozied into her, so she felt filled by a warm liquid weakness. "What girl?"

"A girl at the retreat."

"Can it be a silent prayer?"

"It's better so."

Charley swung his legs, kicking at nothing, until she touched his knee. He breathed hard out his nose as if that would help him to pray for a girl he didn't know, and Elizabeth felt hopeful about her son's place in Heaven, about the goodness of his soul.

"She was sad," said Elizabeth. "Now, pray that she's happy."

They sat that way a moment, and then Elizabeth heard a door unlatch, and as if he had sensed her disquiet and come to console, Horace stepped into the room. "What goes on?" he said. "I heard only silence. It concerned me."

"A girl died," said Charley, with perhaps too much thrill in his voice.

"One we know?" Horace kneeled beside them, his fingertips smoothing her hair.

"A lunatic girl from the retreat," Elizabeth said. "A difficult child. You pulled her tooth a long time ago. Her name was Maggie."

"I remember Maggie," he said quickly, the name coming off his tongue as though he were accustomed to it, and this surprised her. He noticed, too, and when their eyes met, he felt a bee's sting of chagrin, and he wondered how to deny the familiarity. But before either could speak, Charley fidgeted out of his mother's lap and asked whether Father would take him to feed apples to neighbor Larkin's horse.

Even on a bone-chilling winter's morning, Dutch Point smelled of a sweet sawdust reek Horace associated with loud flies and broken windows. A cow ambled along Ellery Street, pausing for a long steaming piss before heading toward the river. Horace, teeth chattering despite his heaviest coat and mittens, circled a spilled garbage bin and curled his lip at the sound of a man retching from a room above. He would rather not see or be seen in Dutch Point ever again, which is why he'd come at dawn when the rats—human and rodent—still slept in their holes.

Turn and go home, he told himself. You owe Nan nothing. But since Elizabeth had told him about Maggie, he had three times thrown drafts of a note into the stove. Now he carried the last in his pocket, a few simple words. What compelled him he couldn't name, but its weight and momentum were familiar. Turn and go home, he told himself, right up to the moment he punched the note over a rusted nail fixed in the door of Levi Knowles's tavern. There. Done.

Tell Nan her Maggie is dead—HW.

He hurried away, nearly at a jog, choosing a speedier though perhaps less safe route. He must have a story for Elizabeth, a place he'd gone. For years he'd kept the secret of his father's death, mere silence enough to cover the old scar, long faded into flesh. This younger secret—Nan, Maggie—could show itself as a fresh wound, visible. Concealing it required invention.

Rounding a hard corner, Horace's boot sole caught ice, and he nearly crashed into a man asleep in a chair beside a handcart. By the dawn's bluing light, Horace read words painted on the cart: Teeth pulled—no pain.

The fellow needed a shave; his stubbled jowls hung in loose layers to his collarbones. His nightcap had been fancy once, and he wore it snug. A blanket, sewn to repair a dozen tears, wrapped him like a winding-sheet and smelled like wet sheep. In his lap, a clay bowl, empty except for a greasy spoon and translucent bits of cooked onion stuck to its sides. Horace pulled off the man's hat and let it fall into the bowl.

"What's this about?" he said, shoving the fellow's shoulder.

The man startled. He coughed once, pinched the end of his nose, and took a deep mouth-breath. "Christ, it's cold," he said.

"What's this? Painless tooth-pulling?"

"Do you need one out?" The man kept his eyes shut. "If you aren't sure, better to do it. Easier to live without the tooth than to live with the pain."

Horace could see the man's cheeks stretch as his tongue explored inside his mouth, then over his incisors to pooch his lips.

"How much?"

"A quarter dollar."

"What's your training?"

"The finest." The man bent slowly over his handcart, rummaged about, and came up with a green-glass bottle and a rag. "You breathe, I pull."

"Chloroform?" Horace asked. "Ether?"

The man shrugged, struggled up out of his chair. His breath smelled fetid, and when he smiled he showed two black incisors.

"Where did you learn dentistry?"

"Around here."

Horace laughed, a sharp, bitter syllable. "What does that mean?"

"It means, 'around here,'" the man said. "Which tooth?"

Horace's head rattled. He wanted to laugh more; it seemed the only answer, one Morton would give. But his chuckle got stuck somewhere in his throat. He coughed, but couldn't shake it loose.

"Which tooth?" The man's voice rose with annoyance.

"Not a one," said Horace, palms outturned while he backed away, as if to ward off this farce. The other made an obscene gesture as a send-off.

36

In the windowless cell that had been Maggie's, Mrs. Cornish's husband laid the girl's earthly remains into a pine-box coffin he'd built. Mrs. Cornish then placed a small pillow she had embroidered with Revelation 21:4 to cushion Maggie's head, and tucked a shroud around her body as she would a quilt over a sleeping child. When her husband fit the lid, she winced, and did so again each time he hammered a nail into the splintery wood. As the man lifted the coffin at the head, Horace obliged at the feet, and together they carried the box outside to a cart with a gray-white mare in harness. The retreat's chaplain awaited, his arms enfolding a Bible against his chest, wet snow collecting on his black-robed shoulders, as it fell also upon Elizabeth's hat and coat.

The chaplain set a slow pace onto Hartford's streets. The cart followed, axles and springs creaking, Mr. Cornish with the reins, his wife sitting at his left. Horace and Elizabeth walked on either side. The company brought Maggie east, toward the river, funeral bells of the Episcopal church already tolling her home. Low clouds choked light, ingraining the day with a hard, shadowless gray. With no wind, chimney ash spilled from the air to stain the snow. Such a day enervates the soul, and few men doffed their hats as the small cortège passed. Only a driver or two noticed the chaplain and out of respect reined a horse to walk or to stop altogether. No one wondered about the departed. The pine box, its smallness, and so few mourners—all these told enough.

So as not to outpace the cart, Elizabeth swayed with a to-and-fro creep that stitched up the low muscles of her back and made every step a Christian mortification. She prayed as she walked, asking grace and mercy for the souls of motherless daughters and then, in a way she hoped was not selfish, the same benefaction for daughterless women. She rested a gloved hand against the cart's sideboard, a way to guide her feet as her eyes shut tight and head fell forward. There is sufficient love on this earth, she told the girl, Maggie. Had you lived, love would have found you. I believe that. I'm sorry about your mother. Sometimes God mismatches us. He has His reasons.

Opposite her, Horace gripped the cart's rail with such strength his forearm trembled. He would not be weak, not as on that long-ago day when he met Maggie. He should then have fixed her tooth, not pulled it. Out of cowardice, he had chosen the easy way, the least painful for them both. Later, with the gas, he'd have made a different choice, though he would not have been braver. The gas, after all, was not courage. Sometimes, it seemed the opposite. He glanced at his wife, her head bowed, eyes closed, and he thought, She's praying, and loved her for her selfless example, decided he should pray, too. *For courage and strength. Amen.*

A horse's gallop sounded from behind, and he turned to make sure the animal wasn't loose, wasn't a danger, and yes, a rider spurred it on and around them. But then another movement caught his eye—a sight more chilling than the air.

Nan followed.

Except in memory and imagination, he hadn't seen her since his brother's visit and the cattle fair—that brief glimpse he acknowledged to no one, hardly to himself. She had changed since then, of course, though at such a remove Horace could not see the scar that now creased her upper lip, or how her skin had mottled from the dyes in the textile factory where she sometimes worked. What he did notice was an unfamiliar weariness rounding her shoulders, her dark hair crowding her face. She didn't conceal herself as she came after them, only lagged behind as if unsure of her station. One certainty was her grief. Faint though it was, Horace could hear her keening.

He thought to ask Mr. Cornish, please, stop the cart. But he kept quiet. If Nan wanted to remain distant, only to watch, that was between her and God and had nothing to do with him.

At the graveyard, Mr. Cornish halted the mare near where Maggie would be buried when the ground thawed, and from there, coffin still in the cart, the chaplain began the necessary prayers. Horace stood beside Elizabeth, her arms hooked through his as if they might stroll afterward. When the mare nickered, Horace lifted his head toward the sound, then looked about the church grounds to see whether Nan remained nearby. Yes. There, outside the tall iron bars of the graveyard fence. None of the party seemed to have noticed her, all attention on the chaplain, who had fumbled his Bible into the snow and was now brushing it clean. Horace looked back to Nan, who maintained her separate place but had come close enough that he could see her hands fisted at her mouth, how she bit her own knuckles. She no longer keened, but in her silence Horace heard her pain, louder than before. It was a hymn, a tolling bell, a wind's low whistle. It clarified, abided, a song from God's caged bird. He concentrated, listened with such fervor that the whole of him dissolved into the sound. Nan pressed against the fence, and Horace stared and tried not to stare. When he noticed Elizabeth's glance go Nan's way, he worried that he'd drawn attention. But then Elizabeth turned back to the coffin, whispered, "Amen," and the moment passed.

Prayers finished, Mr. Cornish and Horace slid the coffin from the back of the cart, its bottom rasping over the planks, and carried it to a nearby shed, where it would remain until the thaw. Then, men who had never known Maggie would dig her grave and with squeaking ropes lower the box into the ground. They'd cover it with straw, then shovel the hole full.

When Mr. Cornish and Horace returned from the shed, their wives and the chaplain sat in the back of the cart, wrapped in wool blankets and talking in quiet voices about quiet things. Mr. Cornish took the driver's spot, but Horace turned once more to the fence, hoping to glimpse Nan, but also hoping she'd be gone.

She was not. She pushed herself against the bars, arms stretching through, hands clasped as though beseeching the company to leave. Her knees buckled, and her mouth opened and closed, shaping strange, noiseless words, but what Horace heard—her resounding pain—deafened him. Elizabeth's voice, scarcely audible, called his name from an impossible distance. Out of a darker sky the snow came heavier now, settling on limbs of the graveyard trees so a branch cracked under the wet weight, but didn't fall.

Horace felt leaden, beaten toward earth. *Strength*, he prayed. *Courage*. He faced Elizabeth, who waved him toward the cart. But Nan's pain insisted—that hymn, that tolling bell. It astonished him how no one else seemed to hear. Perhaps God meant the sound for his ears alone, divine instruction for one practiced at answering the need. *Please,* he said, *no,* but Heaven gave no reply; God's will was plain. Horace stepped away from the cart, between headstones, toward the fence. When he neared, Nan's body began to convulse. Her shoulders rose and fell and fell. She grasped at the air, cried, "My girl." When he took her hands, she pulled him into the bars. Her arms encircled him, his coat bunched in her fists, and he squeezed himself against her as best he could, touched her back, her head. His fingers worked deep in her hair. "I know," he said. "Her name was Maggie. I know." Nan's animal moans broke the brittle air. "I know," he said.

Then she was running from the graveyard, scrambling past a vendor selling half cabbages, under an awning sign for a candle maker, turning into an alley and away. His arms, he realized, remained through the bars. His gloved hands clutched cold iron.

On the cart bench, he sat next to Mr. Cornish, careful as he did not to look into anyone's face. Mr. Cornish released the brake, snapped the reins. The horse lifted its tail, and the cart jolted forward. It was Elizabeth's voice that came first, just as they were about to leave the graveyard ground and enter the street. In all their years, he had never heard her so clearly.

"Horace. Will you tell us who was that woman you seemed to know so well?"

He did.

That hand, his son's. Those fingers tapping against his leg, too. "You turned two pages at once," Charley complained. "You missed the part about the canoe."

That woman at the table writing a letter—his wife, now unfamiliar. Quill scratching against paper. Snow, gray as ash, falling past the window. These weak sofa cushions, insufficiently stuffed. Charley seated beside, turning pages back and back and pointing: an accusation. "Here. When he looks through the bullet hole in the side."

"Perhaps you should read to me."

"It takes me too long." And Charley pointed again. "Here," he commanded.

So Horace read, the words tongued to life but empty of meaning. What he wanted was to seize Charley, clasp his son to his chest, turn flesh-of-his-flesh into a bulwark against whatever might come. He glanced across the room to Elizabeth. who wrote words she would not share, to whom he didn't know. If he had brought shame to her years ago on Mr. Colton's stage, then this fresh transgression—a public embrace of a woman not his wife—would be far worse. All that day he had shadowed her, shoveling the walk while Elizabeth beat the hearth rug, fixing a shelf in the pantry as she organized spice jars, reading now with Charley in the parlor as she penned that letter. His conscience plagued him with visions of Nan in his dentist chair, his fingers slipping loose the buttons on her blouse. That those memories might not show on his face, he imagined Elizabeth, angry and asking questions—How did you recognize her? Why such an intimacy?—and he rehearsed some lies, some shadings of truth. Though he wanted her to raise the business, to show by her expression what their future held, her eyes avoided his, and throughout the day she remained inscrutable. Around dusk, in the kitchen, she wiped sticky dough off her fingers with a towel, touched his shoulder and said, "We'll talk later. Help me roll out this crust." And Horace dared hope that his actions at the graveyard had, after all, made less trouble than that business with Colton.

But aside from a remark about firewood or water to be fetched, Elizabeth said little for days. Though he lived by her side, joined her in bed at night, hour by hour he felt himself becoming like a vapor—unseen, unheard, less substantial than dust stirred in an attic's drafts. Sleeplessness drove him to his workshop, where he fidgeted with bladders and bottles. Breathing ether and chloroform, he felt confused and angry, because while the vapors granted relief, they never gave him hope. He'd expected otherwise though could not say why. Hand shaking from fury, he marked in his notebook. "Hope & relief: NOT the same—"

One night, when he came to their bedroom, Elizabeth had crawled under the quilts ahead of him and left a candle burning. He smelled a potpourri, something piney and warm, and when she propped herself up on the pillows, he saw that her neck and shoulders were bare, her face intent.

"Latch the door," she said, her tone cold.

Perplexed, he shed his clothes, and beside her warm body he lay facing the ceiling.

She pressed one leg over his, grazed her lips over his chin. "Kiss me," she said.

Because he did not dare anything else, he pecked her cheek. Tasting wetness and salt, he opened his eyes to see whether she cried. "Are you unwell?" he asked. But she turned her face from the light.

She reached low, gently, then lifted herself above him, the candlelight glistening along the edges of her skin, her face shadowed. He closed his eyes as she guided him. He did not mean for it to happen, but it did: even as Elizabeth moaned and shifted, Nan's face appeared to him. Panic seized his heart, and he bit hard on the soft flesh inside his cheek. Elizabeth rocked against him, encouraging, inviting, and though his heart thumped with apprehension, he followed her. His whole self became taut, and at the moment of his greatest pleasure he groaned with the sense that some bygone sin was expelled out of himself and into her, a clemency—but a horror, too, because it was now an evil she carried.

They lay together a while, neither speaking, and maybe he dozed. When at last he opened his eyes, she had moved the candle. In the light, she brought her face near to his, except it was not her same face. Now it was unnatural. Lips contorted, jaw slack as if unhinged, her eyes swollen and pink. Her righteous glare. Studying him. Seeing every truth. Her fingertips flitted over his cheek, unable to touch, or strike, or withdraw.

He could not stop staring at what she'd become, at what he'd made.

She said, "Have you betrayed me?"

The pain in her eyes. Pain deciding, as always, how things end. *The inevitable corruptions.*

"Yes," he said.

37

The night's impure blackness, stars sprayed across a moonless eternity, the cattle lowing, pasture stubble breaking under hoof falls, a melody on the cold air—that hymn played on the pianoforte, there, inside the farmhouse. Two men: one swinging on a hanging bench in the garden, his belly full of goose meat and buttered potatoes, the tip of his cigar aglow like a January firefly; the other on a folding cane chair, scratching at his cheeks, too casual with the loaded derringer he keeps switching hand to hand.

"How are your teeth?" asked Morton.

"To hell with my teeth."

Blame the scene on Riggs. He had noticed Morton lathered up at Coles Barber Shop and informed Horace. His friend had been so unpredictable of late (domestic troubles, an evident coldness between him and his wife) that Riggs hoped to spare him the ugliness of a chance meeting with Morton, the ether feud and such still unresolved. "On a visit with his Elizabeth to her family," he had said, trying hard to meet Horace's eyes. "A day or so, and he'll be gone."

Later that night, Horace had visited Riggs, muttered something about a patient in Wethersfield, and Riggs, though worried, loaned his horse. He suspected, but couldn't know, that a hard ride later, at the farmhouse belonging to Morton's in-laws, Horace would knock at the back door, say that he had heard about a dentist on the premises, and with a hooked finger stretch his cheek as if to show an inflamed gum.

Now Horace and Morton sat in the dark garden, a trellis of last summer's morning glory vines tangled and dry behind Horace's head.

"Aren't you cold without a coat?" said Morton. "I am."

"Is it cold?"

"It's January, Wells."

Horace nodded, adding the present month to other facts rushing around in his head, none willing to settle down and be considered. In this part of the garden there was washed gravel underfoot, decorative, and Morton dragged his boot soles over the small stones, a musical clatter. He shivered and brought his cigar to his lips.

Horace hoo-hawed. "Look how well my student has done."

"The cigar? A good Connecticut leaf wrapper. My father-in-law's. He can afford these. I'm broke. Don't let anyone tell you the government's word is any good. No one honors my Letheon patent. Surgeons from New York to Georgia have learned that it's mostly ether, which they use and no one pays me a penny. Manufactured fifteen hundred of my inhalers but only sold fifty. It happens that a sponge works well enough."

Horace stared into the derringer's barrel, a darkness truer than the night's. In silence, Elizabeth had packed his clothes in a trunk while he sat at the kitchen table, unable to stop his knees from bouncing. Earlier she had said, "Any city but Hartford." He asked for how long. She never answered.

Morton turned the cigar in his fingers, fashioned a V in the gravel with his feet. "Which one of us do you hope to kill, Wells?"

Horace slapped at his ear as if there were a fly there, but Morton knew it to be too cold for flies.

"I took the pistol from a man who had stolen my hat."

"Maybe you'd best go home to your Elizabeth."

Horace smiled as if holding back a secret, but there was no happiness in it. "Why did you marry a woman with the same name as my wife?"

"That was a coincidence."

That fact swirled inside Horace's head a moment, then rocketed out of his ear into the sky, and he watched it until it became lost among the stars.

"I don't think so," he said. "God preordains."

"Then you'll have to ask God. A single-shot, that pistol?"

"What's your philosophy, Morton?"

"Your questions scare me a little."

"A man should have a philosophy. I don't, not really, and I think I've suffered because of it. There were these gymnasts in Paris—"

He stopped at the sound of footsteps nearby, coming closer. The shape of a heavy man, big in the hips, wearing work gloves and a coat. He smelled of straw. Horace folded his arms, tucked the pistol away. Morton stuck the cigar in his mouth.

"That you, William?" the man asked. "Is there still bread pudding?"

"There should be," said Morton. He waved toward Horace. "Ben, this is my old friend, Horace Wells. Horace, this is Elizabeth's cousin, Ben."

"*The* Doctor Wells? I hear you knocked out Nancy Hasket from New Britain when the surgeon cut out her tumor. Nancy's my wife's sister."

"I hope she's doing well."

"Very well. Sings your praises to the Almighty every night, from what I hear."

"Give her my best."

"I will."

Ben stuffed his hands in his pockets. He bounced a time or three on his toes. "Shall we go inside?" he said.

Morton tapped ash from the end of his cigar, studied Horace, who kept his arms folded and his gaze cast down.

"You should look up," said Morton. "Tonight's an impressive heaven."

Ben, correctly appraising nothing casual or festive in the moment, tipped his hat to both men. "You two should get yourselves some coats," he said, his back to them as he walked the path to the house. "It's icy out here."

Then Horace shivered, feeling the cold for the first time this night. "Two old friends," he said, "having a chat." A big dog barked somewhere, and Horace's borrowed horse whinnied in a way that sounded like a woman's scream. Horace glanced to where he'd tied the animal—to a post just off the Hartford Road. Morton blew smoke, spit a shred of tobacco onto the gravel.

"You knocked out Mrs. Hasket with the nitrous oxide?"

"I did."

Morton nodded. "So between the nitrous oxide and the ether, we really have done something, you and I."

Horace pointed the pistol at Morton's face, and Morton felt a hot something jump up his throat. "I did it, Morton. You replicated my work and called it new."

Morton's eyelid began to twitch. "You quit the job unfinished," he said. "I stepped into the space you left."

"You keep telling people that I gave up because nitrous oxide didn't work."

"Would you rather I publish in the journals that you lost your mind to birds?"

"I have a pistol, Morton."

"All the more reason for me to speak truth. Cleanse my soul."

"Neither of us has time enough for that." Horace laughed, then tumbled from his seat to the gravel near Morton's feet. Morton startled—dropped his cigar—but the gun did not fire. "You see?" Horace said. "I've lost my equilibrium." He began to sweep his hand across the gravel, making that musical clatter, and he mumbled. *"This way, that way, which way you will. I'm sure I sing nothing that you can take ill."*

Morton leaned as far back as he could into the swing, retrieved his cigar from where it had fallen, said low-voiced, "I told you once, Horace, that you need to wear brighter clothes. A red necktie. A purple handkerchief."

"Vanity and greed," said Horace. "Your chief sins."

"It doesn't feel that way to me."

"In the land of pain, everything is in excess. Too much or too little. Money, love, hunger, pride, need, blood, warmth, cold. It's all the same. Too much or too little of a thing, and you hurt. That's why in the land of pain everyone is either a martyr or a villain. The rivers are all rapids. The sky always throws hail."

"You were a good teacher to me, Horace. You will not believe me, but I've never meant you ill."

"I've become a student of pain." Horace gathered a deep breath. "For naught."

From inside the house, a new hymn began, this one with voice accompaniment. Morton checked his pocket watch.

"It hurts me to see you this way," he said. "I wanted you on my side. I'm sorry for the scandal, the bankruptcies, the slanders, but I can't stop now. What's begun, I need to win. For my wife's sake and my own."

The derringer, Morton noticed, lay near in the gravel. With his boot, he drew the pistol closer, then stepped to cover it. Horace was by turns rubbing his temples and scratching his cheeks.

"I thought I saw it once," Horace said, "something that could be my philosophy. These gymnasts with golden skin. Human sculptures. I was about to tell you before. In Paris. They worked with unnatural effort to contort themselves into perfectly balanced positions." He lifted himself to stand, raised one leg bent at the knee, stretched arms to grasp at the sky. Fixed and trembling, he counted aloud until at last he tipped. "You see?" he said. "You'd hope God would make it easy for us to steady ourselves. I mean, in spirit or body or mind. But it's not so. Up close, I saw how those golden men struggled. It's too much work, I think."

Morton stood, brushed his hands on his trousers, then helped Horace to his feet.

"You are overly dramatic," he said, "as bad a poet as I am a banker. You've always been so." He offered a hand, and the men shook. "Good night, Horace," he said. "God keep you. It's a long ride back."

"Back to where?" Horace asked, as he retreated into the night.

VIII
MANHATTAN

38

Water ran brown from the tap, so Horace set the empty cup on the basin's wide ledge, opting not to drink.

"*Mud*hattan water," said Cuthbert Bronk. "If you want to drink something clear, I know where you can find a stiff horn of liquor."

"No, thank you," Horace said, voice scraping. He'd spoken little the last several days.

"How about a roasted chestnut?" Cuthbert tossed one from a paper bagful into his mouth. His boot heels and his voice echoed in the bleak, unadorned apartment. The glass chimney of the room's one lamp was soot black, dimming its light. Wallpaper fell in ragged, shadowy peels. The floor, unfinished boards, lay rough with slivers. The rest was rodent smells and a straw mattress for one, frayed quilt scrunched at the foot, with a coverless pillow, bone-yellow in the depression where heads had rested.

A place where love comes after it is broken, Horace thought.

"So, will it suit you?"

With the side of his gloved hand, Horace brushed turds from the table top. "Mice?"

Cuthbert nodded. He picked up a palm-sized insect from the dusty floor, its body a twig, its wings gossamer. Dead. "All sorts of things find their way in here," he said. "In the woods, we call it nature. Here, it's filth. How does that make sense?"

The wallpaper's pattern repeated the same scene: a leaping stag, a unicorn, a maiden. Over the basin, someone had penned a huge penis onto one of the unicorns. Beside it parts of a maiden had been peeled away, her bodice shredded. Horace found it discomfiting to look at the woman.

"I'll need a good chair."

"Spend the loan however you want. I'll expect you to start paying your share of the rent after the first month. Nights when I need the bed, I recommend you be on the street or in that room." He pointed to a door off the east wall.

"The bed might confuse my patients. Can we move it to that other room?"

"No, I prefer this spot. It has the window."

Here in the city, Cuthbert no longer wore the buckskin and farmer's boots of a New Covenant Liberite. He dressed in a suit and coat of current fashion, with fitted leather gloves. His hair was trimmed at the temples.

"What happened to your purple hat?" Horace asked.

"What? Oh. I don't know. That Delia woman took it, I think. Or I gave it to her."

Horace twisted his wedding ring round his finger. He sat on the bed's edge and cupped his face with his hands. "I thought you might have married Delia," he said.

Cuthbert barked. "Her family had no money, and my father won't approve of women without. But women with money won't have me. If it weren't for whores, I don't know how I'd cope. Murder my father, I suppose."

Horace looked at the pillow, the yellow spot.

"I smothered mine," he said, then wondered whether he should take the words back. He'd never spoken them before, not to anyone. Not even to God. He picked up the pillow, crushed it against his belly and bent forward so his head nearly touched the floor. "I thought it was the worst thing I would ever do."

Cuthbert laughed. "Killing my father," he said, "would be the best thing I could do." He was still smiling when he again offered Horace a chestnut. Horace declined, and then Cuthbert didn't smile anymore. "You're not serious?" he said, "about your father?"

So long unsaid, those words to describe a deed. Horace wondered himself whether to believe them, to believe the memory they evoked.

"You become pain," he said, smiling sadly. "Pain has no limits. It's infinite. Like God."

39

TEETH EXTRACTED WITHOUT PAIN—H. Wells, Surgeon-Dentist, who is known as the discoverer of the wonderful effect of various stimulating gases in annulling pain, would inform the citizens of New York, that he has removed to this city, and will for the present attend personally to those who may require his professional services. It is now over three years since he first made this valuable discovery, and from that time to the present, not one of his numerous patients has experienced the slightest ill effects from it; the sensation is highly pleasurable. Residence, 120 Chambers Street, West of Broadway.

40

On that third Monday in January, the day his notices appeared in the morning papers, Horace swept the apartment floor. He hung a mirror shard over the basin to hide that shredded-wallpaper maiden, then shaved with gritty water from the sink. Buttoned his sleeve cuffs. Turned his chair to face the window. The chair was a high-back he'd bought from a dining room set at a pawn shop; he hadn't noticed the off-kilter legs until he'd carried it up the stairs, but it would have to do. The daylight, however, worried him. What came through the curtainless window was dingy, unlikely to illuminate the deep recesses of patients' mouths. At least he had the gases, purchased from a chemist on Broadway along with other components: acids and bases and alcohols he might mix for testing. More complicated concoctions were yet to arrive.

As the ten o'clock bells tolled, he opened his door to an empty hallway. No one waited with broken tooth or infected gum. They'll come, he told himself. But a half hour passed, and only one man had glanced into his office—another tenant, he guessed, skulking, hollow-cheeked, unshaven. Downstairs, Horace checked the street-level door to make sure it was unlocked. Perhaps he needed to hang his name and profession outside. He decided to visit a sign painter the next day.

The return up three flights left him wooly in the head. Crumpled onto Cuthbert's straw mattress, he tried to remember when he'd last eaten. His tongue recalled a vague taste—creamed potatoes? a chowder?—but his attention drifted. On the walls, stags leapt and unicorns stood vigilant. The maidens—their dissolving colors, their peeling gowns—lounged repeatedly. Dark lights burst behind Horace's eyes, and the maidens rolled off the walls to crowd his bed. They spoke to him all the chastisements he deserved and had wanted Elizabeth to say, and they did so in her voice. A chorus of Elizabeths. With faces that belonged to Nan.

He startled awake. Someone knocked at the door.

The chemist's delivery boy padded into the room. Horace rolled off Cuthbert's mattress onto all fours. Picked himself up. He signed for the package, then staggered toward his worktable, gave the boy a new list.

"Morton's inhaler? Pricey instrument. You know a sponge works as well."

The boy was not much taller than Charley. Perhaps the same age. A delivery job might do Charley good. "I know," Horace said. "But if it's in your stock . . ."

The boy said he'd ask the chemist. "I'll deliver tomorrow at the earliest."

After the boy left, Horace returned the broom and dust pan to the closet. On the shelf where he set the pan, he discovered other abandoned tools: a plumb line, a plane, a chisel sticky with cobwebs, a wall scraper spattered with whitewash, its handle dark from some worker's oily grip. He brought them into the room's dim light, washed the lot in the basin. The scraper fit his palm nicely. Its blade, though rusted, had kept an edge. At a spot where the wallpaper hung loose, its paste decayed, he scraped at a stag, peeled its head from its torso. Then, the maiden beside it. She let go the wall at one stroke.

Sorry shape, that paper. Horace could peel every last scrap, clean the walls and paint them white. The idea of the work felt right, necessary. It would be no atonement. God alone could decide the state of his soul. But perhaps some defiled part of him could be cleansed. He envisioned the walls empty except for one last maiden, the blade behind her as she fell away, a fresh whiteness in her place. Cuthbert would thank him. Elizabeth, when again they met, would see his brighter self.

The next day when he heard boots clomping up the stairs, he set aside the scraper, patted his brow with a rag. Flecks of wallpaper littered the floor, but not so many as he'd hoped. A glance told him it would be weeks before he finished.

The chemist's boy appeared at the door, presenting Morton's inhaler.

"My employer wants you to have this sponge, too," he said. "At no cost. He told me to laugh when I gave it to you, but I don't think it's a funny joke."

"I don't either," said Horace.

The boy took his money, and Horace returned to his chore, sometimes using a fingernail where the scraper had failed. He worked for hours until every muscle and bone felt too much a burden. Even his shadow weighed more than he could bear. At his work table, he cradled Morton's globe, so airy and elegant, his oily fingers smudging the glass, and he thought he also needed to be airy and elegant. He needed less of himself. So, having filled the bowl, he sat in his chair and rocked on its uneven legs, and inhaled, and heard his own voice—singsong, as if calling to faraway children: *El-iii-zabeth, Char-leeeey, Char-leeeey, El-iii-zabeth.*

In that empty, windowless room attached to the office, Horace sat propped against the wall, on his pillow, listening for Cuthbert's arrival. The night's chill seeped through the wall's many cracks, enough draft to turn a wisp of dust and animal fur about the space. To shelter the lit wick, he had set his candle in a corner, and he didn't care that its drippings clotted on the floorboards. He held Morton's orb toward the light and watched the chloroform inside catch and refract the flame, watched the flickering liquid dance.

A beautiful thing, what Morton had made. He could grant that to the man. The advantage, Horace found, was that Morton's inhaler preserved the liquid longer, concentrated the vapors. Though designed for ether, it functioned with chloroform as well. A clear glass globe, brass fittings on the two extensions, one fashioned to fit gently between the lips. He opened the inhaler's faucet and breathed the fumes. His toes tingled, his heart lightened. With his other hand, he squeezed the sponge the chemist had sent.

"I don't think it's a funny joke, either," he said, and then smiled. "*Ether.* I don't ether. I chloro-form. I breathe and form a chloro-world."

He tried to form Elizabeth. Focus, he told himself. What is the hour? Might she be in bed? Outside feeding the horse? What horse? Newton is dead. He worked to envision Elizabeth's hand over Charley's to correct his penmanship in a school paragraph. But Charley wrote: Newton is dead. So Horace tried to seat Elizabeth in a chair in her aunt's parlor, or lay her in bed shrugging aside a too-warm quilt, but his imagination was imprecise, weak; he failed to form her. Another breath, and some raw thing inside him contracted his rib cage; sharp gravel raked the bone. Elizabeth slipped from him, as did a sob, and he slid to his side, knees curled to his chest like an infant's. *My god,* he cried, *how can the vapor make it worse?*

Over his own low moan, his hearing grew precise as that of some blind night animal; perhaps it was the chloroform, or his own grief—he could not say. But he heard the crackle of the guttering wick. A man on the street calling, "Stewed oysters!" The key turning the bolt in the office door. The wheezing breath of a woman accompanying Cuthbert. The creak of lathing, the rustle when gray-white plaster dust fell through the spaces inside the walls. Her skirt's whisper as she lifted it above her knees, the clicking of Cuthbert's teeth, her pulse traveling the length of her neck.

He had tried to form Elizabeth, but it was not her lying on the floor beside him. It was dead Maggie, shredded, like paper.

"Horace! Horace! Damn you, wake up!"

So dark. Candle burned out. The door crashing open, but still no light.

"Horace! For God's sake!"

Pulling himself up, on all fours, a blanket tangled in his legs. That taste in his mouth. Blood?

"The bitch! This is not how it's supposed to work."

The flare of a hurricane lamp. The room returning in swatches of brown and charcoal. Cuthbert standing by the work table, lamp in hand. His voice rumbling in Horace's head, as if Cuthbert shouted through water. "Vitriol? Do you have vitriol?"

"Sulfuric acid, you mean?" Horace grunted—that ache in his neck. Rubbed an eye that didn't want to open. "Yes," he said. "In a vial. Somewhere."

"Would you look at this cloak?" Cuthbert beat the air with it. "She vomited all over it, all over me. And I mean to give her back worse. I want that acid."

Horace floated to the table, lifting vials and bottles, peering at labels. He handed one to Cuthbert. "What will you do with it?" he asked. He stumbled against the table, his legs unsure of their duties.

Cuthbert uncorked the vial, pried a skinny nail from the wall and pushed the nail through the cork, lengthwise. Then he removed the nail and replaced the cork in the vial.

"I'll burn holes in her pretty things," he said.

He banged down the stairwell, and Horace looked out the window after him but through the murky glass saw only a puddled light here and there.

If he were not so dizzy, not so fogged by the vapors, he might have followed Cuthbert to the street. He did not like Cuthbert, no, but he liked less being alone. Already he missed how Cuthbert's rage had filled the soundless spaces in his head.

Stripped to his shirt and in a fever-sweat, he soaked the chemist's sponge in dirty water from the basin, squeezed it over his head. Shivering. Coughing. He tried the window, but it had been nailed shut. With the broom handle, he broke a pane, the tinkling fall of the shattered glass a comfort. Air and daylight rushed in carrying the smell of new snow and a coffee roastery, and a man's shout: "Hard drops of white horehound candy! An aid for the consumptive!" Bells tolled; Horace counted but lost interest at three. Coughed and spit on the floor. Hours, days, nights. Why had time ever mattered?

He opened a bottle, let chloroform pour into Morton's magic globe.

On his work table. The vial with a nail hole in its cork. When had Cuthbert returned it? Will it still be there, he wondered, when I'm awake?

His room became the smallest of infinite spaces, time the briefest of eternities. When he dreamed he imagined himself awake. When he was awake, he believed himself to be in a dream. With his scraper, he clawed at the wallpaper, at pretty women in pretty gowns.

A noise woke him, so he gathered himself and traded the darkness of the small room for the darkness of the office.

The woman in bed with Cuthbert snickered. Not her from before. Another. So then, another night? Moonlight came through the window's broken pane and touched the nakedness at the small of this woman's back.

"Wells, get to the other room or get out of the building! But get out."

A smell reminded him of bergamot, but over-sweet as if spoiled, an orchard of rotting fruit. Black flies eating and laying eggs. He rubbed his nose with the back of his hand and recalled the bed behind the pocket door in Paris.

"Wells!"

"They're no lasting solace, Cuthbert. They comfort you, and then they ruin your cloak." At the worktable, he lifted the vial of acid.

But Cuthbert had him by the shoulders, rousting him into the hallway so that Horace banged his knee against a stair post, a bright jolt of pain. He shouted and gripped the railing to catch himself, but the momentum was too great. An ungainly descent, this scramble step to step, with Cuthbert's profanity and the woman's mocking howls trailing him as he careened down and down.

"What's the day?" Horace asked a woman on moonlit Broadway.

"Friday," she said, "for an hour more." She had been strolling arm in arm with another woman, a friend. Their skirts and jackets fit loosely, revealed skin and shadows at their necks. Neither wore gloves or hats despite the cold. One with dark eyebrows and yellow hair. The other with freckles and a scabbed-over cut on her lip. The same height. In a tidy way, the women balanced each other. And he, Horace, without his counterweight, his Elizabeth, to steady him, reeled along a crumbling ledge.

He had not yet finished scraping maidens from his office walls.

"Which Friday?" he asked, blowing hot air on his raw fist. "What is the date?"

She told him. This was the one with the cut lip. He would bite Elizabeth's lip, draw her blood, because he loved her and she had sent him away. He needed to go back, to bite her lip and never let go. He said, "Today is my birthday."

"It's my birthday, too!" said the other. She wore rabbit pelts sewn into the shoulders of her coat, frost dusting the fur. She placed a finger to the side of Horace's head, traced a line down his cheek to his chin and to his smile. She touched his lip. The white puff of her breath was sweet with decay, her gums red. "We should celebrate!"

"Conceived in springtime," he said. "Born into winter."

"What do gypsies say about that?" asked the one with the cut lip.

The other kissed his cheek.

He snapped his head away. Her face showed surprise. Her pretty face. They all had pretty faces, didn't they? Prettiness worsened the pain. He said, "Did you ruin Cuthbert's cloak?"

"Who?"

A policeman walked through the yellow light of a streetlamp and drew near. The woman with the cut lip pointed at Horace's head and shouted, "It's his birthday!"

"Happy birthday!" cried the officer.

The ledge gave way, and Horace felt himself slip. Elizabeth?

"It's all ruin and decay," he said.

He flung acid, liquid fire to burn their cheeks. The women screamed. The one with yellow hair grabbed her neck and fell, her head making a cracking noise as it struck the paving stones. The other crouched and covered her face with her hands. He stood over them, and he flung his vial, fiery rain spattering one's cloak, the other's hair. They gave back panicked cries, curled at his feet.

The officer shouted—he was right there in Horace's ear—and Horace felt himself rise. The blow skidded from one side of his head to the other. His neck jerked. His ears deafened. He slammed through rage into a fixed darkness.

41

His crooked teeth had always been a pride and a shame to Erasmus Dwyer. Like gravestones settling in wet earth, tilted to and fro. Like the pilings of a sea-smashed pier, barnacles and seaweed and the like affixed to them. He'd never known another person with such awful teeth as his own, and he'd seen some frightful mouths in his years as a jailer at the Tombs. By necessity, he owned a tooth pick carved from whale bone, and he kept it looped on a string around his neck. Not long ago, he'd taken the offspring down Broadway to Mr. Barnum's museum. Among the many curiosities, they'd seen the jaws of a shark, and the oldest girl started them all to calling it "Daddy." Nobody crueler than your own kids. You'd eat them if you didn't love them so.

"Any youngsters?" he'd asked the new prisoner, whom he'd heard was a famous dentist. The dentist mentioned a son, then the conversation stalled, and Erasmus Dwyer understood there'd be no more talk about family. Instead, the dentist asked whether he might retrieve his Bible from his apartment. Comfort for the dark hour. A judge said yes, the dentist being famous and such, so long as a jailer accompanied.

On the drive, Erasmus kept his mouth shut as was his habit. An advantage to prison work—no need to smile at his clientele. With straight teeth he might have been a banker. As it was, he gave prisoners a frown, not because he disliked them (though many he did), but because he didn't want miscreants to mock his teeth. A jumble they might be, but no one else had the like—Erasmus Dwyer only. Which is why, as they climbed stairs to the dentist's office, Erasmus began to wonder whether this fellow might take a professional interest. Even if the dentist had spent his career perfecting the teeth of Astors and Vanderbilts, wouldn't he want to glimpse a mouth such as Dwyer's?

But having crossed the threshold, Dwyer understood his prisoner as not so high and mighty. Sordid, that apartment. Frigid as the snowy outdoors, mattress with soiled sheets, stink like a pigeon corpse in a chimney. The dentist shuffled about his cluttered work table. "My Bible's somewhere," he said. "Would you check that room?" Erasmus discovered only a spent candle, and when he returned to say so found the dentist staring out the broken window, face pale and screwed up as if with some distress, his whole self ashiver. Erasmus understood it was no time for a smile, and thus held to his frowning habit. By the end of his shift that Saturday he'd still not shown the dentist his teeth.

His youngsters expressed no interest in news of their dad's famous dentist. "Some potion," he told them. "You never hurt." It was the Sabbath, his day off the job, and he'd interrupted Bible study. But his children hadn't yet known the suffering that makes a soul long for death, so the dentist's potion only puzzled them. After dinner, he said to Mrs. Dwyer, "I think I'll ask him to look at my chompers. He might want to make a casting, display them in his office. Do you suppose he'd pay me for the privilege?"

Monday, Erasmus Dwyer woke feeling pleasant and hopeful, sensing Providence at work, God's finger nudging the dentist toward Erasmus's crooked mouth. At the Tombs, he picked his teeth in a looking glass, then lugged a bucket of fast-cooling gruel down the halls. The bars clanged as he knocked a wooden bowl against them.

"Up and to the day, Dr. Wells. Come on."

The dentist lay on his cot, on his left side, facing the wall. His fists tucked under his head as a pillow. The blanket, though, bunched at his feet, told the tale. Because it was cold in January in the cell. A living man would want the warmth.

In years to come, Erasmus Dwyer would recount again and again how he'd been the one to find the famous dentist, first to enter the cell, what prayer he offered, how blood had gone tacky. He'd present the key, which he'd kept. It was not bragging, what he'd say, though he worried it might sound so. Rather, he repeated the particulars as if picking at a scab. How he'd gathered the dentist's Bible, his razor. The bottle with its potion. The small notebook in which the dentist had put his last words. What Erasmus read therein.

42

Puddles form in the low spots on the floor of my cell. Water, after all, from a stone. A lime trail down the wall. My lungs ache.

The jailers say "the dentist" and "Blackwell's Island." Thusly, they mark me as mad.

The women told authorities that I had approached them previously on the street. Had I? If true, I fear what I wanted from them.

It is not so quiet here. Footsteps heavy on metal grates. Water rushing through pipes overhead. And in the distance what I take to be guards beating a prisoner: a man grunts and others yell and then, in a quiet moment, the thud of a stick against flesh.

Warren and those other academic mandarins of Boston? They make their reputations finding fault with others. They maintain their positions by scheming against the weak. But the weak understand better than anyone how the world must improve. The Warrens look down their beaks from lofty, comfortable aeries, but the distance is too great: their dull eyes can't discern how the rest of us struggle.

Let me ask you this, Dr. Warren. Were you strapped to the table, a tumor swelling your testicles, and I held the surgeon's blade, would you turn down my *humbug?*

Dwyer, my jailer. A kind fellow. I asked permission to retrieve my Bible from my rooms on Chamber Street, and he appealed to the presiding judge. We leave in an hour.

In my prison cell I find, stuck by dampness to the wall, a downy feather—a seagull's, I think. How did it get here? Dragged by a rat, perhaps. There's a truth there.

The secret Charley whispered as I sat at his bed's edge that last night at Lord's Hill, after I'd cocooned him snugly in his quilts:

"I knew a long time ago. Even when you sleep here, you are always going away. But I didn't tell."

When we left the Tombs, Dwyer did not shackle me. He let me ride the wagon bench as we drove. From the dark dankness of my cell into the bright day of New York City! Coal fire smoke and steaming hog manure, the stink of fish bones. Every breath chokes me.

An inhalation expands the lungs. An exhalation contracts. Inhale, open. Exhale, close. An argument with oneself.

My Bible, yes, of course, why we took the trip. But I lied like a tooth puller. I planned the razor all along.

Cuthbert Bronk. Cyril Benson. Christopher S. Brewster. Curious.

When you have given mankind such a gift as I have, you have the right to judge your time on earth a success and to depart by whatever means. So let no one judge me. Let no one condemn me or speak ill.

A memory I've had several times since coming here, and each time it is recalled as a tremor through my whole body: the blue tint to my father's lips; the softness of the pillow I pressed to his face. God's inevitable work done, just a little sooner. We all felt better.

The torn tag on my mattress. The wood button moldering in that puddle. The echo of a drip. Rats' claws tick-ticking. Smells of mushrooms and mold. Strange how my senses remain hyperalert, as if the proximity of death is itself an exhilarant.

I could say I am not in my right mind—but I no longer recognize my right mind. To contemplate as I do—throat or wrists? or femoral artery?—shows that my mind is in a morbid state. Not right.

The inevitable corruptions. That phrase dogs me. I've shown how to destroy pain, but what shall come of it?

Elizabeth

Wasps high in the corner of this cell, chewing paper, building a place to rest.

43

In the way things sometimes happen—and they do happen this way—at the moment Elizabeth Wells arrived for services at First Congregational that fourth Sunday of January 1848 (the day before Erasmus Dwyer discovered her husband's body), Horace himself shambled with a line of prisoners into the Tombs chapel. It was less coincidence than likelihood that each Sunday service would be held at the ten o'clock bell. In hamlets and cities from Bangor to Charleston, believers by the hundreds of thousands greeted a minister, prayed for a quick sermon and well-behaved children, feared divine retribution and anticipated grace—all in this same ten-o'clock-in-the-morning blink of God's eye.

In the Tombs, the chapel's white-washed walls flaked with mildew, and the only light glowed from an oil lamp on the dusty tavern table that served as an altar. Against each wall stood a jailer armed with a pistol, and the prisoners—about two dozen—crowded shoulder to shoulder. The young chaplain was a presbyter, seven months out of seminary, and fearful. Time and again his voice broke, and twice he lost his place when reading. Horace, unshaven, his eyes sunken to dark, purplish caves, sat at the end of a pew with his Bible under his arm. His lower back ached from lying too long on the cot. To his left sat a fellow about his age, dark-haired and pointy-nosed, sour with liquor sweat, his fingernails long and yellow. Horace coughed several times, especially when he tried to sing hymns. Some prisoners, like the man with long fingernails, sang as if their zeal might make their innocence plain. Others kept silent. Horace sang because he sensed the chaplain's weakness and wanted him not to be afraid. He sang because it was important now that he, Horace, be rigid and correct. Firm in all his actions.

At First Congregational in Hartford, Elizabeth sat between Charley and Aunt Dorothy, reminding herself to hold her back straight. Even so, the emptiness at her center sometimes curled her forward. When Reverend Hawes began a prayer of thanks, Elizabeth reached for Aunt Dorothy's hand, grateful for the money her aunt had spent on Charley's school tuition and their tithes, for her glance that silenced gossips, for the fingertip brushed under Elizabeth's chin to remind her of her own dignity. True, Elizabeth's soul had fractured, but she knew Dorothy would help gather the shards.

Then Reverend Hawes began his sermon. A tall man with a melon belly, he spoke of the eternal's rapid approach, of the need for thorough preparation. "We are the creatures of a day," he told the congregation, "passing through life as an arrow through the air—spirits come from God and going to God."

At the Tombs, the frightened chaplain tried to lift the avenging sword, his homily meant to terrify with details of that fiery place worse than any jail. But he knew nothing about the Tombs, nor about any Hell into which his congregants had already fallen. Horace pressed knuckles into his brow, crushed his eyes shut. Chloroform had become such a Hell. This chapel, too. Wherever Charley and Elizabeth were not, that also was a Hell. He prayed for his family all the things a dying man must, though he no longer had faith that his pleas meant anything to God. To rely on the Almighty was also a Hell.

At the precise instant Horace began a silent confession, Elizabeth clasped her hands to pray. She asked for strength to persevere without her husband, and also for strength to persevere should he return. Who could say which would be the greater trial? That morning, she had found Charley, in his church clothes, cross-legged on the floor and facing his father's workshop door. Elizabeth hadn't unlocked the room after Horace left, but here Charley sat. She wondered whether he expected his father to open it from the other side and step through. As if hearing her thoughts, he turned to her, and in his eyes she saw her own power, that sorcerous gaze that demanded truth. Without Father we are better off, those eyes told her, and I wish it weren't so.

When Elizabeth in the church pew reached for Charley's hand, brought it to her lips for a kiss, at that exact moment Horace held a shaking fist to his mouth and bit his thumb until he tasted blood.

He recalled Charley's first tooth. The musical pitch of his infant squalling. The just-born's perfect bruises, and Horace's immediate love. But he could never forget how that small creature had nearly killed his own mother. Memory: Horace's first vice. And Elizabeth, he loved her, though his love had proved too weak to endure her most violent pains. If the Lord granted him a chance to tell Charley anything, to give the boy a final wisdom, he would say that there is no greater love than to bear another's suffering. He would confess that because he had not borne Elizabeth's, in the end, he had multiplied it.

Elizabeth yet loved her husband, and this no longer surprised her. She knew that love to be different than what she felt for Charley, different than the love she felt for God. That evening when she had turned her eyes against him and asked if he'd betrayed her, she did so believing that she loved God's truth more than she did her husband, and in that way she would survive his answer. But she did not love truth more than she loved Horace. She'd never known until that night how she could suffer grief even in the smallest part of her smallest finger.

After the service, Reverend Hawes greeted his flock one by one on the church steps, his face kind and doleful when he took Elizabeth's hand, vague sympathies offered as though her husband had died. And at the Tombs, the chaplain stood at the door telling each prisoner, one at a time, to "fear the Lord's wrath and mend thy ways."

Horace interrupted to ask, "Have you ever seen the soul leave the body? At death, does it depart through the mouth?"

The chaplain looked startled. "No, I've never," he said.

"They didn't instruct about this at seminary?"

The chaplain shook his head. "God keeps some secrets," he said.

"Perhaps He'd reveal them," said Horace, "if we paid better attention."

Returned to his cell, he sat on his cot—under which he'd concealed his razor and the bottle of chloroform. His Bible rested closed upon his thigh, his hand on its frayed leather cover. Of all the Elizabeths he could imagine, he brought forth the most tranquil to sit beside him. She hummed a tune so cheerful it made him sad, so she stopped, and he listened to her breathe, and kept her with him in that damp dark. Meanwhile, at Lord's Hill, the true Elizabeth prepared barley soup for Charley's lunch, and she felt the knife edge of her husband's absence cut through her softest self. His workshop door stayed closed. Charley brushed his teeth without his father's instruction. And never did anyone come from outside to get warm by the stove while whistling the song of the *Sylvia coronata*.

POSTSCRIPT

PARIS, January 12, 1848.

MY DEAR WELLS :

I have just returned from a meeting of the Paris Medical Society, where they have voted that to Horace Wells of Hartford, Conn., U.S.A., is due all the honor of having first discovered and successfully applied the use of vapors or gases whereby surgical operations could be performed without pain. They have done more, for they have elected you an honorary member of their society. This was the third meeting that the society had deliberated upon the subject. On the two previous occasions M. Courbet, the agent of Dr. Morton, was present, and endeavored to show that to his client was due the honor, but he completely failed. Though chloroform has supplanted nitrous oxide, the first person who discovered and performed surgical operations without pain was Horace Wells, and to the last day of time must suffering humanity bless his name.

Your diploma and the vote of the Paris Medical Society shall be forwarded to you. In the interim you may use this letter as you please. Believe me ever truly yours,

BREWSTER

ACKNOWLEDGMENTS

This novel is fiction, not history, but I am indebted to historians whose detailed research sparked my imagination and helped shape this story. Readers interested in learning more about the historic Horace Wells and his world can consult *The Life and Letters of Horace Wells: Discoverer of Anesthesia*, edited by W. Harry Archer; *Mad Yankees: The Hartford Retreat for the Insane and Nineteenth-Century Psychiatry*, by Lawrence B. Goodheart; and *The Reshaping of Everyday Life, 1790–1840*, by Jack Larkin. *In the Land of Pain* by Alphone Daudet, translated by Julian Barnes, helped me understand nineteenth-century attitudes about suffering. Richard Holmes's *The Age of Wonder: How the Romantic Generation Discovered the Beauty and Terror of Science* was especially helpful.

Several institutions provided funding or time and space in support of this novel, including Towson University's Academy of Scholars, the Maryland State Arts Council, the Mid Atlantic Arts Foundation, Virginia Center for the Creative Arts, and The Anderson Center for Interdisciplinary Studies.

For historical advice and research assistance, many thanks to Dr. Scott Swank, DDS, of the Dr. Samuel Harris National Museum of Dentistry in Baltimore; to the staff of the Connecticut Historical Society; and to Jennifer Miglus of the Hartford Medical Society Historical Library.

For their advice through early drafts, I'm grateful to Geoffrey Becker, Jessica Anya Blau, Ron Tanner, and John Reimringer. Thanks also to Esmond Harmsworth of Aevitas Creative for his insight, good humor, and faith.

Nicola Mason and Acre Books: Thank you for making my debut novel your own.